Maybe Tomorrow

A Novel of the Vietnam War

Jim O'Donnell

Wylisc Press
Silver Spring, MD

Author's Note

This is a work of fiction. I am grateful to the men, women, and children who inspired the narrative, but no actual people, except public figures, appear here.

I have followed a practice in American journalism of not indicating diacritical marks for Vietnamese proper nouns. Other Vietnamese words and expressions, where used, appear with such marks.

Published 2019 by Wylisc Press

Maybe Tomorrow
A Novel of the Vietnam War
Jim O'Donnell
ISBN 9781733572545 Trade Paperback
ISBN 9781733572552 E-Book
6 x 9
283 pages
Publication Date: October 2019

Cover design by Molly A. Wallace
Cover photo *The Dalat Pass, Vietnam* courtesy of Ryan Waring

Wylisc Press
Inthewallacemanner.com

For Mary

So we must be ready to fight in Viet-Nam, but the ultimate victory will depend upon the hearts and minds of the people who actually live out there.

President Lyndon Johnson, 1965

Stories are for eternity, when memory is erased, when there is nothing to remember except the story.

Tim O'Brien, *The Things They Carried*

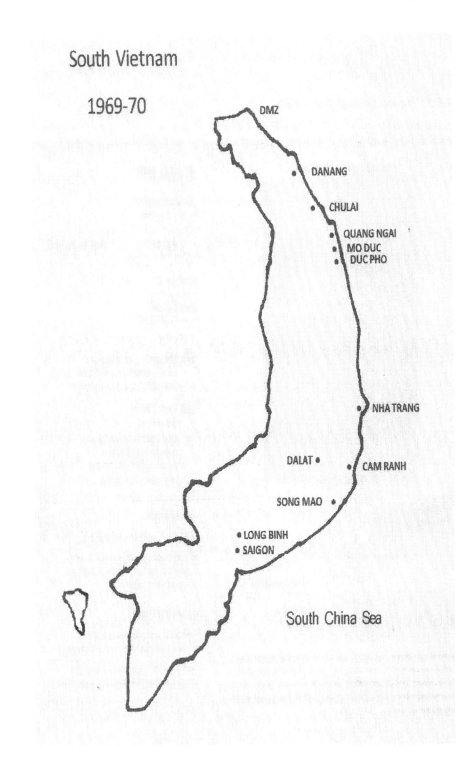

South Vietnam

1969-70

DMZ

DANANG

CHULAI

QUANG NGAI
MO DUC
DUC PHO

NHA TRANG

DALAT • • CAM RANH

SONG MAO •

• LONG BINH
• SAIGON

South China Sea

Chapter 1: Soldier of Fortune

Specialist 4th Class Patrick Nolan stood looking at a wasteland, a flat desert of scrub and rock bordering a landing strip of perforated steel pallets laid end to end. He had imagined Song Mao to be lush and beautiful, cleared from thick, green rain forests where limpid streams fed a river that meandered through the town. "Sông" in Vietnamese meant "river," and he thought the town's name to be evocative of the Perfume River that flowed through Hue. His language teachers at Fort Bliss had described the beauties of Hue and Da Lat, all the more memorable because his female teachers wore colorful silk aó dài, buttoned at the neck, close-fitting at the bust, and then draping elegantly down to dainty feet. Newly arrived in country, he wondered if he had been too naïve in his assumptions about this land. He had to tell himself that this was just the airfield, and he could better judge the place later. But he wondered also about being a "lucky" draftee singled out in basic training because of his education to go to a Vietnamese language school instead of the infantry. How lucky was that?

Standing a safe distance off the strip, he gazed back at the wings of the plane that had just deposited him here for his new assignment, noting again the ungainly albatross-like body. The twin-propped Caribou plane, nicknamed "Wallaby" for its Australian pilots, stood ready to re-ascend, seemingly impatient at the delay. Before flying in, he had heard that the pot-bellied plane adapted well to short landing strips, and that appeared true enough. But he felt some relief being on firm ground again, now mercifully past the nausea he had experienced from the aircraft's endless sharp banking and circling.

Heat waves danced along the horizon, the late morning sun leaving nothing unexposed. He shielded its brightness with an upraised hand. On the ground only two minutes, he felt sweat beads form on the back of his neck. He leaned down, placing his M-14 rifle against the larger of the duffel bags containing his gear. Close behind him stood the only building on the field, a wooden shack not much bigger than a ticket booth, now empty. A jeep alongside the shack bore the insignia of an artillery unit on its front bumper, the driver in the process of reseating himself after apparently having arrived to pick up the other two passengers from the plane, who clambered aboard with their baggage only a second or two before the jeep lurched forward, leaving behind lazy swirls of dust.

Nolan hadn't had a chance to ask the driver anything. He realized now that the driver could have doubled as the terminal clerk, loading mail and maybe light refreshments for the pilots, but there had been no embarking passengers. He had been told in Nha Trang that someone from the Civil Affairs team would meet him. Now he was alone for the first time in weeks. That was fine with him. For the time being, it felt better to be merely a quiet observer of the world instead of chattel being moved about within it. The propellers of the plane churned more loudly as the plane pivoted to take off, wheels scraping on the pallets, its ineffectual green camouflage passing by. Within seconds it was airborne, with many yards of pallet lying untouched. Nolan watched it rise, slowly at first, but then suddenly with a sharp upturn. Gradually, the grating engine noise diminished to a faint whine. The plane climbed steadily into the pale blue sky before banking and finally disappearing. At last, the air fell completely silent.

An acrid odor remained. A column of cinders rose from an embankment beyond the shack, signs of a rubbish dump and not effluents from the plane as he first thought. He looked about, following the upper line of the earthworks stretched around the field until he caught sight of a small, sand-bagged bunker about two hundred and fifty yards away. He was reminded of the long-distance shots that European film directors would hold for ten seconds or more, a heightening of the viewer's attention as if to be one with the camera. Perhaps, this bunker offered the only defense for the field. Still, he felt

2

detached, seeing nothing of real interest. After a few more seconds, he saw a flash of movement. Though possessing keen eyesight, he barely made out the silhouette of a figure inside the bunker. Someone appeared to be filling sandbags. So, he realized with an odd indifference, he was not completely alone.

The heat rising, Nolan hoped his ride would appear soon, but he wasn't worried. It was peaceful, and there was no telling if the plane kept a regular schedule. Civil Affairs would show up before long.

In contrast, his fears the first few days in-country had been childlike. The deepest was his anticipation of combat, the physical threat. He felt it more palpable now than it had been in the months back in language school when his fellow students could distract him with their attempts to find humor in the day-to-day grind of Army life. Yet, he knew that a survival instinct drove that fear. Only a crazy man didn't fear death. He found more annoying his ceaseless anxiety prompted by the unknown. Where was he headed? Was he actually going to be working as an interpreter? He had learned that irony was endemic to the Army's ways, and he possessed no confidence that his assignment would match his training. Even though he had spent his weekdays over nine months learning Vietnamese, he could just as easily end up in the infantry because a battalion commander simply demanded replacements. For that matter, a company clerk could exercise a whim: Where does this next guy end up? Does the clerk like his name? Nolan knew that he needed some luck.

Thirty draftees sorted into sections of ten constituted his class at Fort Bliss, the first such assigned to a language school during the war. More so than the Army planned, the class was strikingly homogenous. All had graduated from college and had taken some foreign language courses. However, the selection process proved to be biased in that the model language used for the test bore strong similarities to Latin. Not surprisingly, ten of the thirty students had attended Jesuit

3

schools that required Latin as core courses for a Bachelor of Arts.

Determining aptitude for Vietnamese, as for many Asian languages, required measuring an ability to distinguish differences in tone as indicated by diacritical marks that accented syllables. Words of a single syllable could have several distinct meanings depending on the accent used. No Asian-Americans had ended up in the class, or, for that matter, any young men of color. All were white, lower or middle class, and conscripts, young men who saw two years of military service as more acceptable than the three or four required in enlistment, all the sooner to return to civilian life. Standing at the head of a morning formation of his charges, the first sergeant for the school company had referred to them as "young and fluent." Nolan and the others smirked at the malapropism. The NCO had seen privilege in their backgrounds, but privilege, Nolan knew, was a relative term. Most of the men in his class had worked through college, and many owed big debts on student loans. Nolan questioned how fortunate he and the others were, only a step away from Vietnam.

He had found virtually all his fellow students questioned the war, some more openly than others. He himself had signed a petition protesting the war that *The New York Times* had published as a full-page ad just as he was being drafted. He assumed that Army investigators had not known that when they determined that he merited a "secret" security clearance. Joining a non-combat unit meant that he and the others could still feel less compromised by the questionable morality of the war. Only a few days in country, they could hold onto principles for now, but time was running short.

Their playfulness had helped them bear up against monotony in the classroom back at Fort Bliss. Nolan and the others had found humor essential whenever an instructor was unwilling to digress from the curriculum of the day even when all ten students demonstrated they had mastered that day's

4

lesson. On one occasion, they had been asked to recite, over and over again, a memorized dialogue about a forward observer requesting additional air support in a combat mission.

By coincidence, a key Vietnamese phrase fit perfectly the rhythms of "Guantanamera," the traditional Cuban song popularized in America during the 60s by Pete Seeger, the Sandpipers, and other recording artists. One student, tired of reciting the lines everyone already knew, impetuously decided to accentuate a rhythmic similarity by singing the phrase một phi cơ nữa ("one more fighter plane") to the refrain "Guan-ta-na-mera." The others instantly recognized the connection, and soon everyone was singing the refrain in Vietnamese, except for the puzzled teacher.

"Why did everyone start singing?" her puzzled look mimed. In Vietnam she had never heard "Guan-ta-na –mera" sung lustily aloud. She got the message, though. It was time to move onto new material, no matter what the Department of Defense dictated would be the sole content of that hour.

Repetition threatens sanity, as some of Nolan's older married friends reported, having to read *Goodnight Moon* aloud to their toddlers for what seemed the millionth time. Nolan and his classmates didn't set out to frustrate their teachers. With each change in the teaching rotation, they greeted their new instructor with smiles and enthusiasm. They knew that the teachers feared losing their jobs and, thus, their visas if the brass found out they weren't following the curriculum to the letter. It was only as a week dragged on with repeated recitation of a new "lesson" hour after hour that the young men acted out in these verbal gambits. Boredom reached a breaking point. Occasionally, they were fortunate enough to have a more perceptive and bolder teacher such as Tran, a slender 30ish man, who quickly moved the class to an open question hour when he could hear that all ten students had sufficiently memorized the lesson.

The students felt comfortable asking him for additional information, anticipating trouble spots. "Tran, how do you say 'Could you repeat that? I didn't understand you.'" He would point out colloquial shortcuts as well—how people more likely talked outside of formal situations. The students rewarded him with rapt attention and sincere thanks. Soon after, the last vestiges of formality in student-teacher interaction wore off. Tran, along with a few of the female teachers, invited the most eager students to share a Vietnamese meal one weekend, and later other get-togethers followed at the dog track in El Paso and a bullfight in Juarez.

Nolan and the others looked forward to these social occasions off base to ward off the tedium of Army life as well as to learn more both first and second-hand about Vietnamese culture. He realized that without these extracurricular events he would have known so much less than he did, even if he had doubts now about the sufficiency of what he did know. He at least knew something about the delicate flavors in Vietnamese cuisine and the sentimentality of their songs. He also recognized that his teachers had grown up more privileged than many Vietnamese. French colonization had shaped much of their backgrounds. Many had relatives living as exiles in France to escape the war. Well educated and curious about other cultures, the instructors appreciated the boldness of American music and film, though El Paso would not have been their American home by choice. Like Nolan and his classmates, they lived a transient lifestyle dictated by a war for which they had no enthusiasm.

So, while his teachers remained in American exile, Nolan had begun his tour in Vietnam. Naturally, upon arrival, he appreciated having his classmates with him. Their shared concern about their unknown assignments encouraged them to hang together at the large reception center in Long Binh. Other transients told them that it would likely be two days or more before they heard their names called. Once one man heard his flight destination, the others could expect to hear theirs soon after.

Time lay heavily on them. They pulled stand-by duty doing KP and litter details, bags only partially unpacked, sleeping mostly fitfully on sheet-less mattresses in dimly lit barracks, unglamorous oases in the sand of Long Binh. A network of crisscrossing boardwalks connected the barracks, latrines, and mess halls. Nolan construed, he thought, an appropriate metaphor from the boardwalks: Narrow paths had been laid out for all to follow, and stepping off to the side was out of the question. In his case, orientation back in basic training about the venomous snakes of Vietnam still resonated.

Over the PA system outside the mess hall, twice a day clerks read out manifests listing passengers scheduled on flights to different parts of South Vietnam. Anticipation high, the would-be interpreters stood in the crowd of fellow GIs, ears straining at each reading. Time passed slowly between readings, yet never free of anxiety. Maybe the Army thought that the waiting would make acceptance of any destination more welcome.

When they finally heard their names called, the class members took heart in discovering that they had been equally sorted into four groups that matched the four tactical Corps in the country, a sign that personnel officers had an actual plan for assignments. So far, their placements as interpreters seemed in order. That didn't assuage Nolan completely. Instead, he considered that the authority to assign jobs might now rest with the commanders of smaller units. The real danger could be at the next stop where the immediate needs of the combat mission would carry more weight.

The very next day Nolan and several other class members boarded a plane to Nha Trang, a coastal city northeast of Saigon. There they bunked again in temporary quarters, these barracks being somewhat more comfortable, less crowded for one thing. To while away time, they read paperbacks and wrote letters home. Since they didn't know their ultimate destinations, they couldn't provide a useful return address. That meant a longer wait for any incoming mail. Nolan felt ties slipping away, not just to his fellow students, but to the outside world, as well. In Vietnam less than a week, he heard and felt already the pain in the expression "back in the world." Being a transient affected identity, weakening confidence, breaking off the connection to community.

Now, standing on the airfield in Song Mao, Nolan found solace in having arrived *someplace* at last. Soon, he thought, he would have a place to re-center himself. He took a large breath and straightened up a bit, gazing again to the bunker where the movements continued silhouetted against an otherwise passive landscape. The sun had climbed higher, and he felt thirst. But he had emptied his canteen on the flight to avoid dehydration. He imagined a lake, a placid one, maybe Cobbosseecontee near his home in Maine, where birds swooped and soared, seemingly aimless and purposeful at the same time. His eyes lost some focus as he daydreamed. Realizing his mind was drifting, he shook himself alert, looking back in the direction the jeep had gone, not wanting to be caught off guard. Within another minute, though, he was gazing absentmindedly once more at the bunker.

He remembered his optimism while climbing into the back of the truck at Nha Trang to go to the airport. He and several others received confirmation that their jobs in the 41st Civil Affairs Company were language related and didn't directly involve combat. Song Mao in Binh Thuan province would be his new home.

"Not a bad place, Nolan, not a bad place at all," a company clerk in Nha Trang reassured him. "In fact, when things get tedious here at company headquarters, we make up a story about needing to check out things in Song Mao. In-country R&R, you know?"

Ten minutes, more or less, in Song Mao, Nolan couldn't say that he was impressed so far.

He had been in a good mood when he boarded the Wallaby. He strapped himself to the floor of the plane, using one of the duffels bags to support his back at the base of the wall and laying the other alongside the M-14 at his flank. The cargo bay of the plane was windowless, so for a while he contented himself by watching the ventilation flaps open and close above him. The props appeared to whine irregularly to his ears, which eventually prompted him to worry about mechanical failure. The other two passengers sat some distance away, so he couldn't distract himself in conversation. He tried to focus on Song Mao, hoping that his luck would turn out as good as he had been told.

To be sure, he possessed some doubts about his untested language proficiency, but he knew that experience would allow him gradually to meet his new team's needs. Languages came easily to him, even if Vietnamese tones could be tricky. He remembered some female teachers blushing at careless things class members said and refusing to explain the mistakes, some of them unwitting obscenities no doubt. Most likely the teachers laughed later when they reported these gaffes to each other. If he weren't in combat, he didn't think his own mistakes would be lethal. The company briefing in Nha Trang had been explicit about the "constructive" mission of the district teams. Binh Thuan province was not a hotbed of Viet Cong activity, he had been told, so they could accomplish tasks in relative safety. Other Americans might be dropping napalm on the countryside, "wasting" the suspected enemy and displacing villagers from their homes. He would be overseeing the distribution of foodstuff to refugees from free fire zones and accompanying advisers and doctors in their rounds. He could imagine for himself a separate peace, some distance from the war. If he could help these distressed villagers and not think about their political standing, he would accept a compromise that outweighed in immediate effects merely signing an anti-war petition in a newspaper. He might be able to live with that for a year.

Even the weapon at his side took on new meaning. When the company armorer issued the last M-16, the standard issue featherweight rifle with the plastic stock, he gave Nolan an M-14 instead, the training weapon back in basic training. Holding the cumbersome stock again, he remembered the absurd games from basic and how unlikely a hero he felt holding it despite surprising himself by earning a sharpshooter's rating with the weapon. Yet, he saw something honest about the feel of the rifle, so different from the toy-like M-16 with parts reportedly made by Mattel. He could see defending himself with the M-14, while he found repulsive the myriad images from TV news clips and training films of GIs shooting the 16 from the hip and discharging shells that tumbled end over end when hitting a body, chewing away as they penetrated. He didn't want the role of a combat cowboy, and somehow the M-14 allowed him to think he could be an honorable soldier. About a half hour into the flight, the nausea began, and he wondered how much longer he could hold his breakfast down. He drank plenty of water from his canteen to avoid getting dehydrated, but now each time a ventilation flap opened and closed, he felt queasier. He stopped looking at the flaps. The plane banked several times without apparently descending much at all. He tried willing it to land. But without windows, he couldn't get a sense of the earth's proximity. He felt boxed in. His anticipation for reaching Song Mao turned to near desperation. He didn't want to embarrass himself puking in front of his fellow soldiers. Most of all, he wanted to be assured that Song Mao existed as he wanted it to be, a refuge from an undesired war.

Now a full fifteen minutes in Song Mao, on firm ground, he was gradually regaining his optimism. The surroundings were so peaceful. The figure in the bunker had stopped moving and appeared to be resting. From the sun's position, Nolan looked at his wristwatch to confirm that it was nearing noon. Once again, he glanced in the direction from which he assumed his ride would be coming, but nothing disturbed the serenity of the land.

He turned back toward the bunker and, to his surprise, saw someone standing out front. A person had apparently emerged from the bunker and was slowly moving toward him. The same guy he had seen earlier? Nolan couldn't be sure. He was too far away for any clear identification. The silhouette suggested a stocky man, most likely another GI. No rifle and no hat. Nolan wasn't disturbed that the figure was coming in his direction, considering the barrenness of the terrain. The stranger appeared to shuffle his feet as if not quite balanced. He was in no great hurry. Did the shack have a toilet crammed into it?

He strained to see more clearly this fellow moving nearer. Without much concern, he had watched him working in the bunker, but now he realized the guy was headed straight toward him. Nolan could see that he was not wearing a fatigue jacket or an armored vest, probably a concession while working in the heat. He would most likely be glad to take a break. Nolan looked down at his own uniform, creaseless and untailored, but obviously brand new fatigues. A few traces of perspiration marked the surface, cheaply earned he acknowledged.

Close enough now, he could see the guy was wearing the green Vietnam issue T-shirt and baggy trousers bloused over the top of his boots, one with an untied lace. As befit his labor, the guy was a grunt, not an officer. No care shown in his appearance, and likely no deep love felt for the U.S. Army. Probably young, maybe the same age as himself. Nolan watched as the fellow closed the distance, an almost comic figure embarked on an unknown mission.

He certainly wasn't imposing. The sun gave a reddish glow to his hair, and Nolan now saw that he was more pudgy than stocky. Slowly his face came into focus. He was younger, barely eighteen, Nolan guessed. Working in the sun without a hat had reddened his face, but his tanned arms apparently received more frequent exposure. His was the kind of skin that freckled, not unlike Nolan's own.

Nolan thought he recognized something in the young soldier's face. Did he know him from somewhere? He strained to remember as the boy's eyes turned directly on him. Clearly, he had sought Nolan out. Just a few yards away now, he came into clear focus. Nolan *had* seen him before but not face to face. He looked several years older and no longer skinny, but Nolan would swear that he had seen this boy on the cover of *Saturday Evening Post,* a drawing by Norman Rockwell most likely. Then, he had been a wide-eyed, freckle-faced kid running away in undressed haste from a pond or lake posted "NO SWIMMING." Nolan had seen both guilt and innocence in that face as he saw in the one before him now.

That boy a soldier here in Vietnam? He would more likely be still living in some small town finishing high school, not too distant from the days of putting worms down his sister's back. This wasn't the place for a kid. Nolan waited for him to speak, but for a few seconds he just stood and looked Nolan over as if he could settle a question without asking. His eyes were not hard. What did he want? Finally, the kid broke the silence.

"Are you my replacement?"

Nolan's answer was instantaneous, louder than intended, "No."

Really, how could he be? This couldn't be part of the Civil Affairs team's duties, could it? Defense of this airfield? He thought that was extremely unlikely, but then what did he know for sure? No sign of his ride.

Nolan said nothing to explain his presence. The kid waited a few seconds, hands loose at his sides. Without saying anything more, he turned around and started his trudge back to the bunker.

Nolan shifted his stance. High noon. He longed for some shade to sit in. He thought of the many days to come, the vital work he would supposedly be doing, and how it would vary from a sandbag detail. He wondered if the boy had many days left in his tour. Nolan was just beginning his, but here they both were.

The whine of a nearing vehicle shook Nolan out of his reverie. He tugged at his duffel bags and hooked the M-14 over his shoulder. The kid had almost reached the bunker now, once again a small figure against a barren landscape, too far away and too late, Nolan realized, to say anything more. The kid didn't seem to need any other words. Nolan turned away to face the approaching jeep.

Chapter 2: Roll of the Dice

Dom picked up the black plastic cup from the table with his right hand, twisted his wrist back and forth a few times, and then emptied the contents with a deft downward turn. The dice clattered as they bounced off each other and finally settled to reveal an array of black letters on the pale, upturned faces. The best strategy lay in going for four-letter words first to get easy points. The young, dark-haired man quickly arranged the dice into "W-A-R-N" as a few grains of salt fell through the throat of the egg-timer. Nolan, sitting across the table, recorded the word in a column on the left side of a lined pad and glanced at the dice to see what he could have made of the possibilities had he gotten the same roll.

Dressed in green Army fatigues, the two young men sat in a sparsely furnished kitchen—a wooden table, a refrigerator, a stove, and a bit of functional shelving. It struck Nolan that the room could serve as the set for Jackie Gleason's *The Honeymooners.* A lone ceiling fan slowly revolved above them, lazily pushing some warm evening air about, even though it was December. The sun would be setting any moment now. Neither man seemed to have a care other than the game at hand. They could easily forget that they were members of a US Army Civil Affairs company in a war zone, though it would be the briefest of respites. Nolan had seen in the news that the draft lottery back in the States had spun out his birth date, February 26, at 365, the next-to-last day selected out of 366, leap year accounted for. He second-guessed himself about not having taken a high school teaching job in Maine instead of submitting to the draft a year ago. With such a high draft number, his name would never have been called. Just his luck.

The pressure of having only two minutes on the timer kept Dom intent on his task. Only the captain's bars sewn onto the shoulders of his uniform indicated his authority as the team leader. His slight physique and boyish bearing seemed at odds with the military. An olive complexion and unlined face mirrored his Italian lineage. His facial expressions, while typically serious, relaxed easily into wry smiles. He appeared glad to have Nolan as a competitor since no one else on the Song Mao Civil Affairs team would indulge him any longer in this word game. His education included both a bachelor of arts and a law degree from Fordham, providing too strong an advantage in the minds of the other teammates. Nolan had turned out to be a welcome addition to the Song Mao team, a bright and likable guy who was Dom's match much of the time in the word game and whose demeanor didn't change whether he won or lost.

Dom quickly saw two words, arranging the dice one way and then another as he spoke. "D-R-A-W, W-A-R-D."

Anagrams were likely payoffs but needed to be quickly evident. He moved the cubes about with agile hands. A few tiny drops of perspiration appeared on his brow.

Having another interpreter on the team the past few weeks pleased Dom, as well. The Song Mao area offered plenty of work to do, and while some advisers could get by somewhat with Pidgin English and a few simple Vietnamese phrases, Nolan's arrival essentially doubled the opportunities for better communication. Dom, who delegated authority liberally, had not heard Nolan in action, so he asked the team members who had worked with him about his fluency.

"Pretty good" was the consensus, though they couldn't really assess Nolan's accuracy yet. He didn't fumble for words that often. Nolan had conversed on several occasions with Bui, the local middle-aged man who had served as the sole interpreter for two of the last four months during which Dom had overseen the team. When the three men met in the hallway one morning, Dom asked Bui, "What do you think of Nolan's Vietnamese? Can you understand him?"

Nolan didn't feel any discomfort with the questions. Everyone was friendly here, using first names instead of rank and last names, but he told them calling him by his last name was fine. He was used to that, especially since being inducted into the Army.

"He OK," Bui replied with a shrug. "He a good man, Đại úy," he added, noting Dom's rank.

Nolan smiled knowing that Bui was graciously overlooking some of the American's rough handling of the native language. Bui understood the challenges, Nolan thought. While Americans had trouble with tones, Vietnamese deemed English articles and verb forms confounding. And Bui learned his English outside of school, teaching himself, and asking questions.

The positive evaluation of Nolan's skills appeared to satisfy Dom, who knew Bui could reasonably resent an interloper at this point in the war. If the number of trained American interpreters sent over continued to increase, he would be losing the good money he made from the Americans, supplemented only by a few dollars from the household tasks his wife occasionally did around the compound. Bui didn't show much worry. He appeared happy enough to share responsibilities with this new American, especially since Nolan readily smiled and consistently treated him with the respect due an elder.

Most likely, too, he trusted Dom, who appeared to everyone as a kind man with a gentle smile, someone not interested in assuming the bravado of a tough military officer. Dom allowed a camaraderie that the men could easily appreciate, no one bothering with saluting or rank-pulling, though ultimately Dom called the shots. Yet Bui always addressed him as Đại úy, befitting a captain. Everyone else might use his nickname. Bui would show respect.

The last grains of sand had passed through the neck of the timer. Nolan tallied Dom's score and then tossed the dice back into the cup. He vigorously shook the cup a few seconds with his right hand and rolled. The dice settled quickly into place.

"D-A-M-N" was an easy picking. He paused. "M-A-N-D," he more tentatively offered.

"That's not a word," Dom said.

"Are you sure? There's 'remand,' so there has to be 'mand,' I would think."

Dom smiled. "Nope. Nice try, though."

"Damn, I sure would like to use 'mand.'"

Dom laughed at the witticism. Humor transformed the routine of the men's days into something much more enjoyable. It also pervaded the storytelling that whiled away the long evenings, providing much needed distraction. He and the others didn't talk much about the dangers they faced outside the compound, but the fear never completely disappeared, ever present in the back of their minds. They didn't take big risks, making sure the roads they rode on were well-traveled, but if they weren't, that at least the minesweeping units had passed that way earlier in the day.

The men knew that they had so far been very lucky. While mines and small skirmishes outside of town presented constant dangers, for the most part the war followed a more languid pace here. Since Dom had arrived in Song Mao, no fatalities had occurred among those on the small compound, a former Buddhist training center. In fact, no team member or military adviser in the other buildings had suffered a combat wound. The Civil Affairs team's building, which the men referred to only a bit ironically as a villa, stood set off to one side, a white-washed cement structure in a modified pagoda style, no interior doors, just arched openings. Fortified before Dom had arrived, the villa boasted a concrete bunker a few feet behind the rear entrance to the kitchen, blocking for anyone seated inside a clear view of the rearward perimeter, but also any incoming shots. Another bunker, sand-bagged and smaller, squatted about twenty yards away from a side entrance. Both bunkers contained M-60 machine guns mounted and ready for use. Thankfully, the men had fired them only at a makeshift firing range near the airstrip.

The word game concluded with a narrow victory for Dom. Sometimes they played a second game, but both seemed content this time to sit back, relax and talk a while. The other members of the team had gone over to the main building some fifty yards away to watch a film that a helicopter had dropped off the day before, along with the usual weekly rations. Nolan had seen the film in El Paso some months ago—a western— and had no interest in seeing it again. He enjoyed talking with Dom, and having been in Song Mao only a few weeks, he still had plenty of personal history to share. So did Dom, who had joined ROTC in college only for the financial help, and like Nolan would not be making the Army a career.

Somewhat smugly, perhaps, they considered themselves well read in the Western tradition, having decent knowledge of classical Latin and Greek, and the Great Books. In high school both had translated Caesar's accounts of his wars against the Gauls as well as *The Aeneid*, and in college, Livy's accounts of myriad wars and some of *The Anabasis* by Xenophon. They had read Norman Mailer's *The Naked and the Dead,* as well as Stephen Crane's *The Red Badge of Courage* and Erich Remarque's *All Quiet on the Western Front.* They also had watched countless war movies in theaters or on TV, so they thought they knew quite a bit about the nature of war and its horrors. How much that second-hand experience had steeled them remained to be seen.

Just a few years apart in age, they shared many commonalities of college life, the lengthy bull sessions that ate into study time, the late-night diner runs, the films of Ingmar Bergman and the French cine', and perspectives on such pressing issues as civil rights, social justice, and nuclear disarmament. With twilight ushering in a warm, pleasant night, Nolan felt they could talk for hours. On previous nights they had barely touched on their various misadventures in high school and college. The evening opened invitingly before them, no sense of urgency in their conversation now that the timer was put aside.

18

The Song Mao Civil Affairs team presented a mix quite different from the homogenous group Nolan had been part of in language school. The nine men, including Nolan, stood out as distinct representations of the American male, at least the young adult male.

Woody was the oldest, in his mid-30s, and the only lifer, an E-6 from New Hampshire. With a dark brush cut and lean build, he was talkative, unusual for a northern New Englander in Nolan's experience. He seemed at times conflicted by the free rein Dom allowed in the household, not that he ever said anything directly about it. He had a nervous energy as if he expected things at any minute to snap back to regular Army discipline.

Tony, a mustachioed lieutenant of small stature from New Jersey, was also ROTC and of Italian heritage like Dom. He stood second in charge, though it seldom came down to any demonstration. He shared Dom's casual collegiate approach totally and displayed a knack for needling his teammates, though always in good fun.

The two other officers remained more distant from the team as a whole, but they were not unfriendly. Hal, the lanky, blond engineering officer, missed his wife terribly. He didn't have to say much to show that. Forever in motion, even during down time, he dug trenches around the building, took runs both inside and outside the compound, and kept more to himself than the rest of the team did. He didn't seem to need Nolan's or Bui's help on the job as much as the others did, preferring to go it alone in many cases. All the men looked forward to getting mail from home, but for Hal, a newly married man, mail meant a lifeline.

The remaining lieutenant, nicknamed "Perk," was a wiry, rural Californian with a passion for surfing. He didn't interact much with the team except for his sidekick, Walker, a young, sturdily built corporal who shared Perk's small-town roots and a penchant for playing with explosives. To the others on the team they were Batman and Robin, inseparable most days.

The two took responsibility for keeping the defensive positions in order, maintaining the machine guns, and of course, testing grenades and sundry explosives. They also cared for the loris, a nocturnal animal with long arms and legs, kept in a hanging cage in the hallway. The loris crept ever so slowly and silently about its cage when darkness fell, though somnolent otherwise. Perk and Walker would find spiders and other insects to feed the unnamed creature each night. Nolan was glad the cage didn't hang in the kitchen.

Wes and Matt completed the team, both enlisted men with occupational specialties well suited to Civil Affairs. Wes, from Houston and the only man of color, had trained as a medic to assist in hygiene and minor medical situations in the local refugee camps and rural villages. A large man with a bigger smile and soft laugh, he committed himself to helping people. Nolan, who had had only one black friend previously and no friends from Texas, enjoyed working with him on daily rounds. He also liked Matt, the agricultural specialist from rural Tennessee, who had been working on a project to teach villagers, including the Montagnards, how to breed rabbits. Much to Matt's dismay, the selected pairs seldom had time to breed, as the temptation to enjoy a rabbit dinner proved too strong for the villagers. Every few weeks Matt would have to start all over again and ask headquarters for more rabbits. Nolan, who accompanied Matt frequently, would try to translate Matt's imploring words to the impatient and hungry residents as diplomatically as he could.

"Sorry, Matt, but it doesn't appear that your pleading is having much effect. It's the bird in hand story, so to speak."

"Yeah, maybe the uncertainty day to day in war time is too much for them. I bet many don't have a chance to eat meat that often. Gosh darn [his strongest expletive], I sure wish they had a bit more patience, though, so they could see the results."

One additional and unofficial team member bore the name Texas—a yellow mongrel, very corpulent on account of his neutering and GI pampering. Given the lore that the

Vietnamese would consume dog if other meat were scarce, Nolan and the others often referred to him as Tasty instead of Texas. Nolan secretly worried about Tasty, though. Team members would come and go, but who would vouch for Tasty's well-being over the long term? What would happen when the war, at last, ended and the Civil Affairs team and other Americans left? Nolan's family had included an Irish setter while Nolan was growing up, and he loved dogs, generally. Sometimes he would gently hold Tasty's head still with both hands, look deep into his eyes, and say to him, "Con chó gí mà con chó!"—"What a dog you are!"—employing a construction that had amused him in language school. In reality, though, Tasty chose to accompany Bui on most occasions, and in that way his fate was determined. More precisely, Bui would eventually decide Tasty's future.

With darkness setting in, Nolan stretched his long legs under the kitchen table. Nothing plush about the surroundings, but he could not be any more comfortable, he mused. Across from him, the animated Dom was relating a story about a professor in law school who, for all his sober pronouncements, possessed a weakness for puns. Something about "tort" and "torte." Corny stuff indeed, Nolan thought, but he laughed at the incredulity in Dom's voice.

"I have to confess, Dom, that I like puns, too."

"Thanks for the warning."

With the words barely out of Dom's mouth, a tremendous clatter filled the air. B-B-R-R-R-P, B-B-R-R-R-P, B-B-R-R-R-R-R-R-R-P. Automatic gunfire had erupted, so loud that Nolan thought intruders must only be feet away. How did they get so close to the damn building? Dom and Nolan locked eyes for barely a second, and without another full second passing, they had jumped to their feet. "We're under attack," Dom yelled superfluously while darting toward the rear bunker, a scant six feet outside the kitchen entry.

Nolan reckoned instantly that he had to make it to the side bunker. Without stopping to get the M-14 stowed in his room, he made a beeline out of the kitchen through the central hallway and toward the side entry. He sensed that going through the opening might be the last moments of his life, but it could also be his only chance to defend himself. Without hesitation, he jumped through the opening into the dusk, bounding toward the bunker and leaping in, rolling onto his side as he landed. He had made it. And yet he had no memory of his feet actually touching the ground. Adrenaline raced through him.

He could hear Dom's M-60 to his left firing out into the darkening distance, tracers lighting the line of fire. He rose to his knees and leveled his own machine gun in the same direction, pressing both thumb triggers tentatively at first to get his line. The gun emitted a steady line of bullets into the frontier. He saw no movement, no sign of attackers. Suddenly, on his left he saw a flash, and then a body rolling into the bunker. To his great relief, he recognized Walker, unhurt, jumping to his feet, though crouched. If the Viet Cong had attacked from the side, Nolan never would have known what hit him. The automatic fire and his own heartbeat dominated his hearing. He immediately made room for Walker, letting him, because of his greater experience with weaponry, man the machine gun.

"Have you seen any?" Walker demanded.

"No." Down on his knees, Nolan found the grenade launcher on the bunker floor. He remembered that he needed to clear his thumb if he was going to fire it, that warning in basic training still fresh even after so many months of language school that included no additional combat preparation. Too late now for regret.

The tracers gave Walker his bearings, but he fired off only a few dozen rounds. When he stopped, everyone stopped. Nothing coming in, nothing going out. Walker glanced at Nolan. "Wait a few seconds." No one fired. An eerie silence took hold.

A sulfurous odor hung in the air, but not as strong as Nolan thought it should have been after so many spent rounds. After a few seconds, they could hear a few American shouts. They stood up gingerly, still peering out toward the horizon, puzzled by its emptiness. Neither spoke, trying hard to hide his fear. It took a few more seconds for their heartbeats to return to normal.

"Are they gone?" Nolan asked.

"Damned if I know. I can't see anybody moving."

The shouts continued, but no one fired a round. Nolan put the grenade launcher down and stepped away from the bunker. When they went back into the villa through the side door, the rest of the team was already assembling in the hall, nerves still raw, chattering away.

"What was that?" Matt implored. "Sappers? Why weren't there some mortar rounds first?"

"Those weren't sappers," Woody said. "That was an M-50, and the VC don't have M-50s."

"Hell, friendly fire?!!"

Nolan wasn't sure who shouted. Big Wes, standing beside him, muttered "friendly" in disbelief several times.

All GI's knew that M-50s, with their large armor-piercing shells, clearly violated the Geneva Convention regarding use against personnel. It was an awesome machine gun, and the GIs were glad to have them on their side even if NVA tanks seldom showed up in the coastal areas of central Vietnam.

"Who would be firing on us? What the hey?" Tony wondered aloud, his usual flippancy absent.

"It must have come from the artillery base," Dom said. "And that's a mile away. We just happen to be directly down range."

Perk ambled in, covered in dust but, per his usual affect, nonchalant. "No serious casualties. An ARVN looey had his lip split with a pebble from a ricochet."

The men all looked at Dom, who made one of his wry faces and shook his head. "We were lucky, my friends."

Nolan unconsciously repeated the head gesture but said nothing. He had experienced his first brush with death. He wanted this all explained, of course, but for now he just felt relief. Reports trickled in from residents of the building where the movie had been playing on the main floor. Bullets had riddled the frontier-facing walls of the soldiers' rooms that lay around a balcony above. Had anyone been in those rooms instead of watching the movie downstairs, they might very well have been killed or at least seriously wounded.

The next morning Dom rode along with the senior military adviser, a major, to the artillery base to get answers. They heard an all-too-familiar story in the war zone. A guard on night watch thinks he sees or hears something out in the concertina wire and panics, opening fire with a machine gun, heedless of errant rounds. But why did this guy fire so many rounds? Did he think a battalion of NVA was attacking? Could he have been doped up?

"Possibly high," Dom acknowledged in his oral report to the team later. "And if it's any consolation, we've been told it won't happen again."

The men laughed sardonically.

Upon rising that very next morning, Nolan had been amazed that he had slept so soundly after the strafing gunfire. Maybe the sudden drop in adrenaline figured in. Everyone seemed in decent spirits despite not knowing what had really transpired the previous evening. The daily rhythms of compound life had changed not at all. While Dom was investigating the shooting, Nolan had gone off with Hal and Matt for two hours after breakfast to look at a site for a chicken coop at a nearby village. Hal had measured the area while Matt and Nolan talked to a farmer and his wife. It was a simple job, but Hal had some concerns about drainage. Riding alone in the back of the canvas-covered truck, Nolan let his mind go back to the previous night's event, and he was eager to hear Dom's report.

24

Hearing Dom's account left him in a quiet mood. He didn't care to talk with the other men about what he had felt during the shooting. He kept it all inside.

Later that night, he stepped outside the Civil Affairs villa and looked up at a sky full of stars. The panoply of moon and constellations should have reassured him, presenting a familiar winter covering in the northern hemisphere. He could make out both bears, Ursa Major and Minor, as well as Virgo and Cassopeia. Some things never changed. He was consciously reprising a childhood habit of stargazing. He didn't smoke like some of the others, but this certainly would be the time to do so. Even so long after sunset, it was still warm. Nolan thought it odd to be out in this kind of weather with Christmas nearing. Not anything like this in frost-laden Maine where his family soon would be gathering. This year marked his first Christmas without family. Last December the Christmas season interrupted basic training, sending the trainees home for two weeks, meaning that they could get soft again, only to endure the rigors of getting back in shape for the final few weeks. While nothing about his surroundings now reminded him specifically of Christmas, he felt a pang of loneliness. On the plus side, he knew that he was in good company.

After a few minutes Dom joined him outside.

"Light 'em if you've got 'em," the Captain cracked.

Nolan chuckled at the reminder from basic training. He hesitated before replying, "We lit 'em up last night, didn't we? The tracers were almost beautiful."

"Yeah, from a weird, disembodied perspective. You could almost forget how deadly a machine gun can be. We definitely all used up at least one of our nine lives."

Nolan nodded. He didn't think he could explain his feelings about his own part in the action. His teammates had depended upon him, and he had reacted instinctively. He surprised himself. Before his Army induction, he had wondered if he could declare he was a conscientious objector, that he couldn't kill another human being, not even in defense of himself or others. He didn't know then what he could do. War had never tested him.

Now, a little more than twenty-four hours after his initiation into combat, or at least into an equally dangerous confusion of war, he felt like a veteran. He couldn't joke about it with Dom, despite their growing friendship. He sensed something was different. He had passed through a door into another world, a place much more dangerous than the one he had known since birth.

Chapter 3: Legends

"Hand me a wrench, will ya, Nol?" The voice rising from underneath the truck's hood was Woody's, a familiar rasp to the Civil Affairs team and the other American advisers on the compound.

"What size?" asked Nolan, peering into the metal box atop the front fender of the 3/4-ton.

"Shoot, doesn't matter. The adjustable one's fine."

Nolan placed the adjustable wrench in the palm of the grease-stained hand Woody blindly held out. Woody finished tightening the nut on the new belt with two final grunts before stepping aside and unfolding from his jackknifed position. He stretched his back a bit, rolling his shoulders, and grinned, a few gray flecks visible in his stubble. He didn't see any need to shave on Saturday.

"That should hold 'er, Newt. Not a bad job if I say so myself. You wanna start up the motor and we'll see if I'm right?"

Nolan at once complied, climbing up into the cab. The engine came to life with just a second of hesitation and then a steady whirr. He stepped out of the truck as Woody dropped the hood, letting it slam while feigning that his arm was not fully out of the way.

"Whoa! That's how my brother Lefty got his name, Nol. What a sorry cuss, he is."

Nolan doubted that Woody had a brother named Lefty, but he laughed anyway. Woody loved to talk, no matter if he were happy or worried about something. Most of the time he was happy. This was his second tour in Nam, the first just a year or so ago that had included the Tet Offensive. He had told Nolan how he had survived an enemy ambush while driving a truck at the rear of a small convoy along the highway somewhere north of Nha Trang. He had managed to get his truck turned around because the NVA or VC—he wasn't sure which--hadn't waited long enough to spring the trap with perfect timing. He had driven like a madman, executing a sharp u-turn, and then hurtling back down the road to a checkpoint where he was able to call in a gunship. Several ARVN were killed in the attack, along with an American adviser who had been in a jeep at the front of the convoy.

"Just dumb luck on my part. I knew how to drive a truck. That's why I wasn't in that jeep."

Woody had told Nolan this story a day or two after the friendly fire incident. Nolan had said something about close calls, leading Woody to tell him his story, to which he added his thoughts about how much chance played a role in a soldier's survival.

"It sounds to me, Woody, that it was skill on your part, too. You got out of there and found help as fast as anyone could without a radio."

"Yeah, maybe, but it doesn't matter how savvy you are. Sometimes it's just plain ol' luck. Take the other night. A little lower aim on that M-50, and there would have been some guys killed. Probably me. After all, how much luck can one guy have? This is my last tour here, I know that. Too many whacked out GIs with weapons to spray around. You hear about the MACV adviser that nearly killed the guy you replaced?"

"No. What happened?"

"It wasn't too long before I got here. This sergeant, a military adviser who never said much to anybody, got drunk one night on his side of the compound and then wandered over to our villa. When the CA interpreter went to the door to check out the noise, the drunk aimed a weapon at him. He might have killed him if the interpreter hadn't pushed the barrel away and knocked the guy down. It wasn't anything personal. The guy was drunk and apparently had all these paranoid thoughts inside him that just had to come out sometime. War does that to people. Same with the pothead guard the other night."

28

Nolan chewed on the story for a moment.

"With some people, I suspect it doesn't take much at all for them to go off like this."

"Roger that. I think you and I are OK, Nol. We're not hiding anything. At least, I'm not."

He looked at Nolan with a sly tilt of his head.

"You're probably safe, Woody, but to quell your fears I'll keep my M-14 unloaded whenever we have a beer together."

They both chuckled at that.

Now on this December Saturday morning, with Christmas in sight, they decided to drive the short distance to the main street with the repaired truck, a test drive but also a chance to have some Vietnamese coffee, Woody's favorite pick-me-up. The drive took place entirely on dirt roads, but fortunately dry and smooth ones. Nolan had been surprised to find out how dusty this part of Vietnam could be. The Catholic Church in town featured a temporary crèche beneath its modest tower, but they didn't see any other Christmas displays in town. The most prominent feature on the main street was a memorial to Vietnamese resistance against past invaders, a stylized figure mounted on a steed, probably a war god, one presenting a bellicose look and holding forth a spear, suggesting the expulsion of the invaders. The statue in peeling paint stood high on a stone plinth in the middle of a broad, dusty intersection, a reminder of past glory. The town was far from thriving now, though the GI presence at the steam bath and the tiny cafés boosted the economy a few ticks.

At a worn table in the front of a café bordering the street, they drank the sweet coffee from small cups. It was drip style, the coffee slowly dropping from an odd metal contraption the size of a toy bank onto a layer of condensed milk before being ready for stirring. Woody said the taste reminded him of how his grandfather had made coffee, a chicory flavor and always with condensed milk. A few dozen locals passed by on foot and bicycle in the interval, but the morning was passing quietly with little motorized traffic. Woody glanced up the street toward the intersection.

"Nol, who's that supposed to be, standing on the memorial out there? Some famous leader?"

Nolan peered over his shoulder at the large warrior and horse on their pedestal.

"It could be a symbolic figure and not anyone in particular, a figure representing heroic resistance among the people. Back at Fort Bliss, a teacher mentioned there being four immortals in Vietnamese folklore and I'm wondering now if this warrior might be Thanh Giong, who is usually depicted in battle on a horse. I think that's his name."

"Really, a horse, huh? I haven't seen one here in either tour. Plenty of water buffalo, though."

"Yeah, so I've noticed. The story goes that Thanh Giong and his horse ascended to heaven after repelling invaders from the Chinese mainland many centuries ago."

"A winged horse like for Mobil gas?"

"Well, something like that. Just as amazing is how this three-year-old boy suddenly transformed to a superhero. Supposedly, the boy neither walked nor talked at age three, but when the invasion began, he immediately began talking like an adult and insisted on being fed prodigious amounts by the villagers. In no time at all he grew to be a giant warrior ready to drive out the invaders. Great underdog story, I would say."

"This guy Young sounds like Popeye and his spinach."

"Suppose so. I haven't seen any photos of statues depicting Thanh Giong, but I think there's one somewhere up near Hanoi, which makes sense, seeing that the boy's village was located near there."

"Ah, so this hero may be more popular in the North these days. You know, "let's drive the Yankee dogs out. We drove out so many others, including the French just a decade ago.'"

Nolan nodded. "This peninsula has been invaded many times, that's for sure."

"So, who are the other immortals? Maybe I'm related." Woody ran his fingers through his brush cut, one of his comic mannerisms that he used to entertain his fellow team members. Nolan smirked at the gesture.

"I don't remember all the names. One was a goddess, I think. Another was the god of mountains. The last was a poor young fisherman—you'll like this—whom a beautiful princess chooses to marry after they see each other naked, by chance, in a marsh. Each one thought they would have privacy in the marsh."

"Wow, racy stuff. In fairy tales, there's almost always a beautiful princess around. Notice that? I don't know about naked, though."

"Well, Woody, I know you always have an eye out for a princess. Even now when we're just having coffee."

"Guilty as charged. Why in the last two minutes, I've seen at least three walking down the street."

"You bet, even a quiet ville like Song Mao has its beauties."

Nolan could have come right out and admitted that he liked watching the girls, too. He definitely missed that part of campus life. He remained silent, instead.

"Holding hands in their white aó dài, too," Woody mused aloud. "Does that mean they're off limits?

"Too young for you, yes. The brighter colors are usually worn by women of marriageable age, but that's not a hard-and-fast rule. It may have more to do with what a family can afford. Some of the unmarried teachers in our El Paso classes wore pastel colors in the classroom and appeared to have extensive wardrobes. From wealthier families, and with passports to stay in the States for extended periods, they wore regular Western attire outside of class. I don't think they would necessarily be typical Vietnamese now that I've seen how people act and dress here. I'm still learning like you are."

"Funny customs, huh? I've seen ARVNs walking hand in hand on the street, too."

"Yep, usually just a sign of friendship. It seems, though, that it's only the young who do this. And you don't see a man and a woman walking hand in hand, let alone a hug or a kiss in public. I suppose that makes it easier on us invaders, what do you think? We don't see a lot of romancing going on to remind us of what we're missing."

"Speak for yourself, pal. I know what I'm missing."

"There's hope for you yet, Woody, with your dashing good looks and sparkling wit. Maybe Bui's wife can find you someone suitable. Not likely a goddess or princess, though."

"I'm not looking to get married while I'm here, Nol. So, I guess that limits my chances."

"Most likely. Even the girls who learn English and work for the Americans probably have long-term prospects in mind. I suspect some would like a free ticket out of here, though nothing's free, right?"

"That's for damn sure. I guess I'll have to stick with bars or the steam baths, relying on some hard-earned cash to have a good time. What about you and your Vietnamese? You can chat up these gals."

"It's not that simple, Woody. How would I know any relationship was for real? There's still a huge cultural gap. You need some common interests. I don't think finding a girlfriend in Song Mao is very likely. I'll take my chances in the States."

Not quite true, Nolan knew. Somehow, he couldn't admit that he longed for the company of women.

Woody took another sip from his cup.

"You got a girl back there? Don't hold out on me now."

"Again, it's not that simple. We don't have an exclusive arrangement. Let's just say there's mutual interest."

"Sounds like you're a free man, my friend. I bet that you've been eyeing the young lovelies all this while, too. Am I right?"

"Yeah, you got me, Woody. Just admiring the passing scene, of course."

"Of course," Woody snickered. He casually glanced at his wristwatch. "We can't chew the fat all day, though. Guess we should head back to the compound if you're finished with your java. It sure hit the spot."

Nolan drained his cup and rose slowly from his chair, making a mental note to ask Bui some time what he knew about the immortals of Vietnamese folklore, particularly about the goddess whose name he couldn't remember. All the other immortals were male.

By Monday morning, though, he had almost completely forgotten about that line of inquiry until he caught sight of Bui arriving on foot at the compound wearing his outsized bush hat, accompanied by a young member of the Rural Forces, the RF. Bui greeted him cheerfully, so Nolan figured that this was a good time to ask about the goddess. To his surprise, Bui shook him off quickly.

"I do not know her. Must be goddess from the North. I do not remember any from school. But my nephew Truong, he probably know. He went to university."

Bui turned to the young soldier by his side, whose glasses provided him a somewhat scholarly mien, and repeated Nolan's question in rapid-fire Vietnamese.

Nolan listened carefully, but he couldn't catch everything Truong said. Bui translated. "Yes, there is Princess Lieu Thanh. Beaucoup stories about her from long ago."

"Is she divine or human?"

Nolan was not surprised to hear "Both." He asked if she was good or evil. And again, "both" was the answer. Apparently, it depended upon the storyteller. To some, Lieu Thanh took the human form of a good woman faithful to her husband, only to return to heaven after a few years. In other stories, she was more demonic, and men who tried to possess her went insane. She sounded like a sorceress to Nolan.

"Truong say that she can be like geisha," Bui added.

Nolan was surprised by the comparison. He knew that Woody would want to hear more about Lieu Thanh, so he asked a few more questions before Truong made it clear he had to go. For the time being, this would have to do.

Woody was indeed fascinated when Nolan reported.

"What happened to this geisha? She didn't go to heaven on a horse, like the kid, did she?"

"No. One version has her being thrown into a river to drown, a punishment for her seductive behavior."

"But isn't she immortal?"

"Apparently, she changes form. She eventually appears on earth again, yes, but as a different person."

"Wow, that's some story. A little hard to swallow, Nol."

"Skeptical, huh? You probably read *The Iliad* in high school, right? It's not that much different from what those gods, goddesses, and heroes did."

"Including the hanky-panky, you mean?"

"Yeah, that too. Basically, we could see them as larger-than-life figures with overwhelming passions and desires, but not necessarily role models for mortals. The humans almost always pay for their faults. The gods, of course, just continue on their merry way."

"Sounds about right. Trouble ahead and trouble behind for our kind. Got any more of these stories?"

"That's all I know for now, but I'll let you know what I hear."

"You do that. Heck, I might as well learn something while I'm here."

Nolan enjoyed being the "ears" of the team, but he knew his limits, too. He relied upon his dictionary very heavily, or as in the case of Truong's information, or Bui's, on someone else's translation. Communication was getting easier in situations where there was a clear context, such as checking with village officials about their material needs. The vocabulary didn't vary all that much. He always carried a small black notebook that could fit in his pocket, along with a pen, too. The book offered a repository not only for his own notes, but also for the Vietnamese officials he worked with to write out an unfamiliar

34

phrase or term. No one seemed particularly concerned that he still had so much more to learn. The Vietnamese, for their part, weren't used to hearing Americans fluent in their language, but they invariably seemed to find Nolan's attempts a sign of respect. As for his team members, they acted impressed he knew as much as he did, Woody especially.

"Nol, you're a handy guy to have around. Maybe you can teach me a few terms that would be helpful with the sweet young gals of Song Mao."

"Woody, I don't want to create a public menace. How about trying the strong, silent approach instead?"

"Not my style, Nol."

Joking aside, companionship in the vehicles made less tedious the short trips the team members made around the district—somebody to chat with, to share observations and long-term plans. He knew, of course, that once stateside again Dom would continue in law, Tony most likely would go for an MBA or become a CPA, Hal would work as an engineer, and Wes would apply to medical school. Woody, he might continue to add stripes and retire after thirty years, but the more Nolan got to know him, that didn't seem as much of a given.

Woody had a restless spirit. He was handy at fixing things and appeared happiest when he had minor mechanical tasks to do. While he loved conversation, he wasn't content just sitting around and talking as the others did in the evening. In that way, he resembled Hal, more independent and capable of whiling away time with a one-man project or two. Nolan could see him as having his own small business back in New Hampshire, something with machinery, maybe auto repair, heating and cooling, or even a woodshop. He didn't appear to be driven by ambition. He merely wanted things to work when he needed them.

Woody liked a good time, though, and when he heard that a rock 'n roll band was stopping at the compound the week before Christmas, he was excited.

"It's not exactly Bob Hope and Joey Heatherton, but it should be a blast. Real, live girls, for one thing."

"I should hope so," said Tony. "The alternative sounds like a bummer."

The plan called for an early afternoon arrival of the troupe at the airstrip courtesy of a Wallaby, and then jeep and truck rides to the compound. There would be a chance for the visitors to mingle with the residents for a bit, followed by a shared meal and the band performance. The visitors' departure would follow the next morning. No one in Civil Affairs had a part in any of the planning, but given the paucity of entertainment options on the compound, this was a big deal, and everyone likely would attend. Otherwise, it turned out to be a typical day for Civil Affairs, with village visits in the morning and later Nolan spending much of the afternoon at a local school helping a teacher with an English class. After work, he sauntered over to the mess hall with Dom, but not until Hal had returned from a hastily eaten meal.

"I wasn't in the mood for Christmas carols," Hal said when Dom asked him why he had come back so soon. It was probably better to have someone looking after things in the villa anyhow. Nolan could tell Dom felt more comfortable with that arrangement.

The band members, four young guys from the Philippines, according to Woody, were already setting up their equipment when Dom and Nolan walked in. The Christmas music, familiar carols, blared from a boom box on a table, but most apparent was the presence of two young Caucasian women, one blonde and the other brunette, chatting with some of the advisers and team members. The women wore powder-blue, short-sleeved dresses, closer to nurses' uniforms than casual stateside attire, with red stocking caps over their tresses to mark the festive occasion. While some Vietnamese women worked regularly in the kitchen and laundry area, the energy in the room was running uncommonly high that evening. All eyes zeroed in on the two smiling, light-skinned Red Cross volunteers, the

36

Doughnut Dollies, who made it a point to circulate around the room and chat with as many men as possible.

By the time the two young women had reached Dom and Nolan's table, the band was nearly done warming up. Someone had turned off the boom box. The four young people had just enough time to exchange names and hometowns, a few family details, the usual pleasantries for a first meeting. Nikki was from the Chicago area and had a brother who was now safely stateside after a tour in Nam; Helen was from rural Indiana and talked about doing her part for her country. They seemed sincere, two bubbly women a few years out of high school, enjoying a little male attention while doing something they deemed useful. Nolan noted the simplicity of their hairdos and makeup, nothing flashy, more the girl-next-door look, adding just a hint of silliness with the Santa caps.

The band started out with "Jumpin' Jack Flash," the Rolling Stones song. The lead singer and the musicians nailed the Stones' sound from the get-go. Within a few seconds, all the smiles and bobbing heads showed that the band had won over their audience completely. Dom and Nolan exchanged knowing glances, but the volume of the music precluded any prolonged conversation. The place rocked.

By the second song, Nikki and Helen were on their feet swaying to the music with eager partners. Nolan, though never a big fan of loud music, found himself tapping his feet to the beat. The mood was contagious. Woody stood just to the side of the band, chatting away with a MACV adviser, who in the din most likely couldn't follow all that Woody was saying, but smiled nonetheless. The women had found new partners for the third song, having dragooned two guys from the table at the front. Getting full participation appeared to be their strategy.

Dom leaned his head over toward Nolan as the band belted out the tune. "I don't dance," he said, with a slight emphasis on the negative.

That didn't surprise Nolan, who was not much of a dancer himself. "Have you had enough, then? I guess I have, too."

"You don't have to escort me home, Nolan."

Nolan laughed. "It's fine. I suspect we will be able to hear the music from our place."

They got up and departed without anyone seeming to notice.

The next day the Civil Affairs schedule went back to normal. At breakfast, Woody reported the various goings on after Dom and Nolan had left the gathering. Nolan had been right about being able to hear the music from the team villa, but he found pleasure in encouraging Woody's enthusiasm.

"I have to say, Woody, that "We Gotta Get out of This Place" hit home with me. That was a great song to wrap things up."

"Written about an English slum I heard, but the younger guys last night sure took to it. They were hootin' and hollerin'. I wonder what the mama-sans in the kitchen thought?"

Nolan turned his thoughts to the two American girls. "Nikki and Helen must have been worn out from all the dancing."

"If not from dancing, surely soon after."

"What do you mean?"

"There are different ways to boost morale, Nol, and dancing is just one way. Do I have to spell it out for you?"

"You're not serious."

"Yes, I am. Word got around the room that Nikki or Helen would consider $100 a pop agreeable if there was anyone interested."

Nolan could sense his jaw dropping.

"Were there any takers?

"I don't know. I didn't stick around. I wasn't sure how happy Dom would be if I had an overnight guest."

"Well, I'm pretty sure there were no guests in this building last night. I was up early. And you don't know if the rumor was accurate anyhow, right?"

"No, but I'lll probably hear something about it later on today. Each girl probably had her own room. There are plenty of rooms in that building."

"I have my doubts about this, Woody."

"So, you don't think these gals would try to make some extra money on the side? Just innocent young things?"

Nolan wasn't sure why he was annoyed. He didn't think himself as being particularly naïve. "Woody, I really can't say what their motives might be. It could be that boosting morale among the troops leads to sex in some cases. That wouldn't shock me."

"In many cases, Nol. Let me tell ya, folks back home would be surprised to know all that goes on here."

"As in any war, yes, shit happens. Still, stories tend to get exaggerated, I would think. And rumors can be just rumors. You can't believe all you hear."

"And you can't ignore what you don't want to hear either," Woody said. He raised his eyebrows as he tilted his head toward Nolan. "Sure, bullshit has no end, Nol. Who doesn't like telling or hearing a good story? But I bet that the craziest ones we hear in Nam are mostly true. You just have to consider who's telling you the story."

Chapter 4: The Weir

"Do you fish, Nolan?"

While still a newcomer on the Civil Affairs team, Nolan knew that Matt wasn't pulling his leg, pretending to invite him to take a leisurely fishing trip on the river. Not in a war zone. This was small talk about life back in the world. Matt presented himself as a friendly enough guy, with a wide, easy grin to accompany his Appalachian drawl. "Not a lot, but I did as a kid now and then. During summers I fished with my brother and friends off a small bridge on a lake a few miles from our house. I enjoyed it as a change of pace. But I can't say I got hooked, so to speak."

Matt ignored the word play. "Never caught a big one, huh?"

"No, just a few perch and sunfish, with worms for bait."

"I thought that, being from Maine, you might have fished in the ocean."

"Nah, that's not for me. Guess I'm a landlubber. Or maybe I just don't seek out adventure."

Matt looked like he was ready to chat some more, leaning back against the truck in the morning sun, soaking up the rays. They were killing time outside the Civil Affairs villa in the warm morning air, waiting for Hal, the engineering officer, to finish a quick shower after his first run of the day.

Nolan figured it might be a few minutes more, so he broke the silence. "I do remember my first fish, however, which didn't come out of a Maine lake. I recall it happened on the same Cape Cod vacation when I learned how to swim. Well, I suspended myself in water for a few seconds. My father took a couple of us kids one afternoon to fish off a tall bridge over the Bass River. I didn't catch any bass and felt nary a nibble on my line all afternoon. I was about to consider the whole enterprise a bust as the sun was setting, but then when I reeled my line in, I discovered a small flounder on the hook. It may have been there a pretty long time. Even though it wasn't much of a trophy, my dad took a photo of me holding it."

"Did your ma cook it for you?"

"She did."

"Those are the ones that taste the best."

"I know what you mean. She didn't mind cleaning the flounder either, but there wasn't enough there to feed us all, just me. To be honest, Matt, I can't say I have ever cleaned a fish."

"Like most city folks, I suspect. Well, at least you know how to use a reel, Nolan, and won't starve out in the wild."

That almost passed for praise, Nolan thought, coming from this rural Tennessean. Matt stood up straight, put on his bush hat, and stretched. He already sported a deep tan on his arms from the field work in contrast to Nolan, who burned easily with his rosy skin.

"Well," Matt said, "the reason we need your help today is that there's a hamlet over by the river that appears to be a good fishing spot. However, unless someone is well off enough to have their own sampan, the fishing is done from the shore with very basic traps—woven baskets, mostly. I was telling Hal about it, wondering if a weir might work better. You could help us get info from the locals to start a simple project."

"Glad to help. I have to say I should know more about weirs, but I don't. My grandparents in Massachusetts lived in the section of their city known as the Weir. All the times I visited them, I think I saw the actual weir once. It's kind of like a dam, isn't it?"

"Kinda. It doesn't create a reservoir as the water continues to flow, but it can make control of the flow easier. And you can set up nets or baskets to trap fish."

"Yeah, okay. I remember hearing that the local Indians had fished there long before the settlers thought about constructing any weir. They probably used baskets much like the locals do here, right?"

"Or maybe if the fish were large and plentiful enough, they used spears. Like with salmon out in the far western states. But, yeah, you're right. Basket-like traps work much better with smaller, quick-moving fish. That was more likely the case, I imagine, but I don't know much about New England fish."

"You ready, guys?" Hal called as he stepped out into the sun from the villa, invigorated by the run and shower. Though blond, he was also, like his two teammates, tall, lanky, and in his early 20s, not long out of college. He took in the morning air with a deep breath. "I think I have enough stuff here to take some soundings."

Hal placed his gear in the back of the ¾-ton and swung behind the wheel. While the front cab could accommodate three guys in a pinch, Nolan quickly volunteered to sit in the canvas-covered back. He hoisted himself nimbly over the high rear bumper, having first laid his M-14 down next to Hal's gear. He knew Hal wasn't much of a conversationalist, and Matt and Hal had worked together before, Hal advising Matt on materials for some agricultural projects. Nolan could hear a few words and laughs from the cab. Hal was in a good mood. Maybe he had heard from his wife yesterday. Christmas had been a tough occasion for all of them, but with the New Year approaching, time at least seemed to be passing more quickly now. No doubt Hal was already planning a rendezvous in Hawaii with his wife, the site married GIs almost unanimously chose for an R&R.

Pleasantly warm, with just a bit of breeze, the morning offered great promise for outdoor work. If all went as planned, an hour or so of surveying could remove any need for standing very long in the afternoon sun. The tides of the South China Sea did not have much effect on the river this far from its mouth. The water level did vary, though, depending on seasonal rains. Upon arrival at the hamlet, the three young men were led down to the river bank by two older men in flip-flops. Three or four barefoot children followed at a short distance, shy but curious about these tall, mostly fair-skinned foreigners, probably the first they had ever seen up close. The water lay in a shallow channel close to the bank, a narrow island, not much more than a sandbar with some low vegetation, separating that channel from the main currents of the river.

"The herring season just ended a few weeks ago, so there's probably not a lot of fish right now," Matt observed quietly. He looked out over the slow-moving water as if he was ready for a swim.

"Isn't that a catfish?" Nolan asked, pointing to a stationary, shadowy blob not far off the bank.

"Yep, so it is, Nolan. I guess you're a bit of a country boy, after all. Do you recognize it, Hal?"

Hal had grown up in a western suburb of Chicago, close to O'Hare airport where his father had piloted jets for United Airlines. He may have gone camping a few times in northern Illinois or southern Wisconsin, but he just grunted at the question.

"Let's see how deep it is here" he said, unfolding his measuring rod. One of the old men, in his shorts and flip-flops, immediately jumped down off the bank into the water and reached back for the rod. The water came up to his waist. It didn't look much deeper at any point clear over to the island.

"I really should do this myself," Hal muttered, beckoning with his hand for the old man to come back to the bank. He reached down to extend his hand for the man to grab, lifting him easily up to dry ground. Then, he sat down on the bank and removed his boots and pants. Matt decided to do the same.

Stepping off the bank in his shorts, Hal said, "What we need you to do, Nolan, is to ask the men how deep the water is at different times of the year. I'll measure the current depths."

Nolan knew his months and seasons in Vietnamese, so he set about with his questions, knowing full well that the answers would not be as precise as Hal's soundings. The old men eagerly indicated approximate depth by placing hands in relation to their bodies. They enjoyed the game, disagreeing with each other only a couple of times about the years when there had been particularly rainy or dry periods, each saying the other was too old to remember anything clearly. Nolan enjoyed listening to their banter and joined them in the laughter. It didn't appear that the water ever got much higher than seven feet, but it could get down to just two or three feet sometimes at the end of the dry season. The occasional flood years happened, though, even in a drier province like Binh Thuan. Just the natural cycle, Nolan thought. People here had to adjust, like people anywhere, to the elements. Nolan saw a difference, though. These locals had impacted nature less than most humans, maintaining their traditional ways over centuries without use of gas-driven or electric machinery.

"We'll probably have to check with district officials about their records," Hal said. "Right now, I'll see if the depth is relatively uniform across to the island. You hold this end of the line, Matt."

Matt was already recording numbers in a small notebook, which he held in one hand while taking the line from Hal with the other. The channel stretched only thirty yards or so over to the island's shore, and with no hesitation, Hal began wading across. Nolan stood to the side, curious how long the island actually was, a bend in the near bank preventing any clear view of the end point. He didn't have that much to contribute after getting the rough measurements from the old men.

"If you don't need me for a while, I'll walk along the bank here to the bend and see what we've got for other features. I'll be back in a few minutes."

"No hurry," Matt called over his shoulder. "We got it under control here."

Nolan saw no need to go back to the truck for his rifle. It may have been the soft air that morning, but he didn't feel any danger standing on the riverbank. He was not planning to walk very far anyhow, just around the bend a few minutes to get a better view of the island. He should be fine. Probably mosquitoes presented a greater danger here than the VC,

44

though Nolan and the others took quinine pills to reduce the chances of contracting malaria from the bites.

The worn path, never more than a few yards from the edge of the riverbank, wove between tall grass and low trees, palms and others unfamiliar to Nolan. Once around the bend, he couldn't see Hal and Matt any longer. Downriver the lower tip of the island emerged. He guessed the island was a quarter mile long or so, and no more than fifty yards wide at any point. At total peace, he stood and gazed out onto the river. He didn't see any sampans or anything else moving. He could tell from his perspiration that the temperature was rising, still slowly enough to encourage his walk on a beautiful morning. He decided to walk a little further, but before he left the trees to step out into a clearing, he caught a flash of movement in the shallow water below him.

There stood a striking-looking young woman, with long, black hair and bare to the waist. She was standing in a few feet of water opposite a small beach, obviously bathing. She was astonishingly beautiful, he thought, skin lightly bronzed, and though her back was mostly turned toward him, the curvature of one breast was clearly outlined. She was unaware of his presence, and he stood as still as he could, barely breathing. He knew he was invading her privacy. She wouldn't be bathing here if she thought any males were around, and there were probably few younger men in the hamlet with the war going on.

Her natural pose and apparent lack of self-consciousness added to her sexual attraction. He stood watching her from behind a tree as she rubbed with quick swipes a small cloth under her breasts and across her shoulders. She was an apparition, and he couldn't avert his eyes. She shifted her stance to bend down and rinse her upper body in the water. Then she threw back her hair, its luster splendid in the sun. As she did, both breasts came into full view, startling him. It couldn't have been more than a minute or two that he watched, but he grew conscious of time passing and the chance that she might turn her head up in his direction and see him. Hunched over to avoid being seen, he slowly backpedaled a few yards, reluctant to remove his gaze completely. When he felt he was completely out of view, he stood up straight and quickly headed back along the path to his comrades. He saw no particular reason to keep secret what he had seen from Matt and Hal, but he decided to tell them first about the extent of the island. Pointing downriver, he matter-of-factly called out as he approached.

"The island ends a few hundred yards downstream. There's a small beach just around the bend, probably a place for bathing and washing clothes, but I didn't see a better place to connect to the island. This is definitely the shortest point across." He paused. "Not the prettiest, though."

Matt was quick to note the last part and the passing smile on Nolan's face. "How so, Nolan? What else did you see?"

"Well, there was a beautiful young woman bathing in the river. I got quite an eyeful. She was like a water nymph, really."

"You lucky dog, you! Did she see you?" Matt grinned.

"No, I made sure she didn't. I'm sure seeing any grown male would have spooked her, but an American—that would have totally embarrassed her."

"So, you just stood there and played Peeping Tom?"

Hal's tone was not light and envious like Matt's. He didn't show even a hint of a smile.

Nolan glanced at Matt for a second. Was Hal really offended?

"Yeah, I did. It wasn't like I did something sleazy, though. I was walking along a path minding my own business. And there she was."

Hal said nothing, but his face and neck had reddened. A few seconds passed. He turned away and looked out to the island, his hands going to his hips.

Nolan was annoyed that Hal was shaming him, but he willed himself to stay calm. "To change the subject, does it look like a weir will work here?"

"We think so—yes," Matt replied, checking to see if Hal wanted to add anything. He shrugged his shoulders in Nolan's direction when it was apparent that Hal's attention had shifted elsewhere.

"We're thinking of extending a steel wire, the thickness yet to be determined, across to a pole we would position on the island. If we can set up a simple winch on this side, the locals can lower or raise the wire as the water level dictates. We can attach some netting to the wire and we then figure out some way to empty and position the nets, maybe with clips. If the locals check every day, the nets should provide a lot of fish most of the year, more than the hamlet needs for its own meals. They should have plenty for market, too."

"Sounds great," Nolan said. "Clever, but not very complicated. I suppose you'll need permission from district officials, though."

"That shouldn't be too hard to get, though I bet they'll come up with some unofficial fees. Can't expect to get much done without those."

"Baksheesh, eh? I don't know if I can ever get used to that, but you do get the sense everything would stop without it. Everyone wants his cut."

Matt nodded. Hal sat down on the bank again to put his pants and boots back on, ignoring the others. Nolan decided to stay quiet, too. No sense in starting a quarrel about watching the woman, something so petty. He would talk with Matt later when they were alone to get his take. While Matt got back into uniform, Nolan looked out at the river, avoiding further conversation.

On the ride back to the compound, Nolan sat again in the rear of the truck. Matt and Hal weren't saying very much in the cab, Matt letting Hal's mood lie undisturbed. Nolan's thoughts slipped back to the bathing woman, the pleasing image still sharp. Would Hal really not have watched her? She might as well have been a statue in a museum. He knew Woody would love hearing about what he saw. He expected some crack from Woody about needing to do some fishing himself.

Back at the villa, Woody didn't disappoint him. He was all ears.

"Damn, Nol, you do have the luck of the Irish. All I got to see today was a bunch of GI grease monkeys over at C Company's motor pool. No mama-sans, let alone a water nymph, like you called her."

Later, though, when he found Matt alone writing down more project notes for Dom, Nolan found that he really wasn't all that interested any more in talking about seeing the young woman or about Hal's judgmental reaction. His mind ruminated on a parallel to their present situation. He had been thinking about the weir and the fishing nets, along with what had brought guys like them to Vietnam, ones who had little interest in fighting foreign wars. They stood out among tens of millions of young men in America whose lives had been caught up in the military draft, just like fish being netted in a river. Did Matt see the analogy?

"Yeah, but," Matt replied, "in America a lot of the biggest fish seem to evade the net. How does that happen? You would think it would be the smallest ones that would slip through. It may not be baksheesh exactly, but money talks in America, too. Now, technically, I wasn't drafted, but I wouldn't have enlisted except for the draft. I wanted to avoid the infantry. Something my family wanted, too. So, I dodged one net by allowing myself to get caught up by another one."

"I came real close to going to mortar school at Fort Polk myself," Nolan said. "I guess the language test I took turned out to be another net, right?"

Matt flashed his wide grin. "I'd be tempted to call these 'safety nets,' but that doesn't sound exactly right considering where we are, right?"

Nolan laughed. He felt lucky to be in the company of men who could share these ironies. Usually they all got along. He knew, too, that Hal was basically a good guy, and that he should just let the earlier words with him go. Some subjects, like sexual attraction, were better avoided around him. Later tonight the quiet, sometimes tightly-wound engineer could easily be laughing along with the others at something, too— maybe one of Tony's witticisms or Woody's humorous complaints—able to put aside if only briefly his longing for his wife. Nolan had been part of the team long enough now to recognize the tendencies. The men possessed different personalities and just as many approaches to a given day's happenings, yes, but they shared the same purpose—to get through another day, to be one day closer to going home.

Later, after their evening meal, he drank a couple of beers hanging around with the guys in the villa. No film showing that night in the main building. The conversation sparkled here and there, but largely proved inconsequential. Wes and Nolan did talk a bit about a trip to the Montagnard camp the next day. Perk was cutting up some fruit, while Walker was peering into the jar of insects he had collected for their eerie pet's diet. The loris had awakened now that it was dark, and the two friends enjoyed watching it feed. Dom and Tony were good naturedly disputing the actors supposedly featured in a movie they both had seen many years ago. Nolan felt pleasantly tired. It couldn't really be exhaustion since he hadn't done much physical work all day. He was still getting used to the climate he guessed. He decided to go off to his room and read.

The air hung humid around him as he undressed for bed. He slept in only his boxer shorts, usually with just a cover sheet, but some nights even the sheet was too much. Before he had a chance to read even a few pages, his eyes started to close and soon the paperback slipped from his hands. Half asleep, he reached over to hit the light, and within seconds, he dozed off, oblivious to any sounds from the other rooms. He slid quickly into a dream.

The moon shone on water. He found himself in a small boat, not a sampan, though. More like a row boat. He appeared to be alone, sitting in the middle of the boat. He was steering the boat toward a shore with a single paddle. The current moved lazily. He could have easily drifted to shore, but his mind seemed intent on reaching land. Just yards now from the bow, a small beach appeared, only a few yards of sand across. He may have been on a river or even a lake—he wasn't sure. Was it Song Mao? When he stepped out of the boat, he found he was wearing only a loin cloth like some Indian brave in a movie. He stood in the water facing away from shore, and suddenly there she was. The water nymph stood before him in her undeniably svelte form, her supple breasts bare as they had been this morning in the river, the face small featured, sweet and demure. Her dark hair, reflecting sheen from the moonlight, hung to her shoulders. She didn't seem to be a temptress. She said nothing. She remained completely still in waist-high water as if just waiting for him to draw nearer. She looked expectant and unafraid.

In the moonlight, he could make out her dark brown eyes and a slight tilt downward of her chin. She may have been a little taller than he had remembered, but even without recognizing her face, he was sure it was the same woman. She was not embarrassed to be seen by him and made no attempt to leave. He stood watching her, saying nothing. Though he had never worn a loin cloth before, except for a towel perhaps, it all seemed natural to be standing that way together in the water. In the darkness, he could make out netting to one side, seemingly floating freely on the moon-dappled water. Nothing appeared strange to him, though he had never dreamed anything like this before.

He waded slowly toward her, but still they didn't speak. She reached out an arm as if to pull him closer, and he felt her other hand gently touch his chest, a caress. It was more than pleasant—it was electric, and he felt an erection forming. Yet, something wasn't right. He felt a flickering brush of hair across his chest.

Startled, he awoke and shook something off his chest. What was it? Certainly too heavy for a mosquito. A spider?

In the dark, he couldn't make out anything, but there had been something on his chest, he was sure of it. He reached over to turn on the light. The harsh glare immediately hit his eyes. He could hear low voices in the adjoining room, male voices. He thought one was Walker's. Maybe the other one was Perk's.

"He's gone."

"You must have left the cage unlatched. No telling where he is now. Get a flashlight."

Nolan's senses had sprung to alert by now. He got out of bed in his shorts, tugging the cloth to make sure all was back to normal, and went to the doorway.

"In here, guys. I think it's in my room."

A few seconds later, Perk and Walker appeared in the doorway with some netting and a flashlight in hand. Nolan pointed to the corner of the room where his bed sat.

"It's over there, I think."

He knew he wasn't going to sleep all that well now. The spell had vanished. He watched silently as the two others cornered the loris and threw a net over it. After they left with the escapee, Nolan returned to his cot and lay on his back for what seemed an eternity. Though he tried, he couldn't re-create the scene in the water. Some dreams, he realized, would have to wait.

Chapter 5: Playing One's Hand

The Montagnard camp in Song Mao sat bleakly on a low incline by the river only a mile west of the Civil Affairs/MACV compound, but whenever Nolan accompanied Wes for a medical visit in a team jeep, the cultural distance seemed immense. Never before had he seen poverty like that, though growing up in Maine he had frequently passed tarpaper-covered houses that did little to keep out the frigid cold in the winter. He thought then that he knew what poverty looked like. Here he was stepping back centuries to walk among crude huts constructed of dried mud and bamboo poles, crowded together on this narrow rise from the river, the sulfurous fire-pits for cooking spaced here and there within the small quadrangle outlined by the huts, with the long, pungent sanitation trenches stretched along the perimeter.

The GIs in the boonies tended to like the Montagnards more than the Chinese-descended Vietnamese because of what they perceived to be the former's stronger loyalty and fighting spirit. Darker than other Vietnamese, the Montagnards were easier to identify as allies. They lived independently of the Saigon government in the Central Highlands, where they hunted and practiced slash and burn agriculture and tended to move their encampments frequently. The tribes spoke their own languages, but leaders needed to learn Vietnamese for trade and political logistics, protecting their livelihood from the bureaucracy of provincial officials. They were called mói (savages) by other Vietnamese, but Americans used the French coinage for "mountain people."

In Song Mao, they existed as refugees only, driven from the highlands by fierce fighting and the US/ARVN policy of developing free-fire zones for artillery. Now without forested land or hunting grounds, they possessed only the bare essentials. They herded a few goats but depended on the

Americans for handouts of food and clothing in addition to materials for strengthening their humble shelters. In these circumstances, happiness appeared an impossible luxury, yet none of the tribe members seemed depressed.

On each arrival the stench of creosote and human waste assaulted the two Americans. "Have you ever smelled anything like it?" Wes asked Nolan the first time the interpreter accompanied him for a visit.

"No, I haven't. Or seen anything like it either. This is worse than a prison camp, I would think. Where do we even start? To begin with, these people could use a full village of their own, with some arable land."

"That isn't going to happen, Nolan. They're lucky they have this small plot of land on loan. The slope presented problems for the local farmers. That's why it's available. When the river is running high, the lower part is underwater. These are people unaccustomed to planting crops anyhow. No question that they will hightail it back to the highlands as soon as that area gets secured. If it ever does."

Nolan knew that the tribe had been here in Song Mao for many months already. They could be here for years. Assimilation into the local community looked impossible. Nolan looked out over the camp, dismayed.

"For the time being, though, couldn't they at least get some tin sheets for the roofs? They need fresh water, too."

"We're supplying some water now for drinking. They definitely could use more materials, especially for roofing. We can look into that. Maybe Hal will have some ideas about what to requisition. I think we can improve the situation quite a bit."

Nolan appreciated that even under these adverse circumstances Wes remained upbeat and optimistic, always showing enthusiasm to get started on days marked for a visit. On the morning of Nolan's second visit, Wes conferred first with Dom about the team schedule and then tracked down Nolan in the kitchen.

"C'mon, Nolan, my man, I will need your silver tongue today. You might take along a clove of garlic, too."

"It's tempting, but I wouldn't do that to Nap," Nolan replied, referring to the tribal chief. "He wouldn't have anything to do with us if he saw that."

"Maybe you could tell Nap that it's a good luck charm to ward off evil spirits. That wouldn't be too far from the truth."

Upon arrival at the camp, Wes always checked first with Nap to find out about anyone sick or injured. Nap and Wes had a friendship that Nolan admired, the husky American winning over Nap with his gentle care-giving and easygoing manner. The small, wiry Nap reciprocated with a jaunty directness and welcoming smile. Wes was a compassionate man, by nature, Nolan thought; he couldn't be otherwise. But the fact that the Montagnards were an ostracized minority within the larger culture certainly provided him an added incentive to help. Wes had grown up black and strapped for cash in east Texas.

"My grandmother always told me to do good by others. I never questioned that. And here I am," he chuckled.

"Admirable, Wes. But didn't she say anything about staying out of a war zone?"

"She probably did. She had opinions about everything and left none unspoken."

"Sounds like my mother."

"We are definitely products of our environment, my friend. I think I was lucky in that I had folks around me who set me straight, and I suspect you did, too. You went directly from high school to college, didn't you?"

"And then straight to graduate school, Wes. I don't think I really understood the concept of a tough childhood until I got to basic training. The stories I heard then. Wow. I've been lucky, I guess."

"Let's hope we have some luck left. We used up some of it with that friendly fire."

Nolan and Wes didn't talk about race as Nolan had done with his black friend, Carl, in grad school. They did talk about

54

family, each having come from a family of five kids, with religion playing a major role in shaping values. Wes appreciated Nolan's language skills, which Nolan acknowledged to himself were less strained in communication with Nap because they were both second-language speakers in Vietnamese and spoke slowly and simply with each other. The vocabulary stayed basic with no need for abstraction. On visits to villages outside Song Mao, Nolan would sometimes switch to French when he encountered officials essentially left over from the French colonial system. They could skirt an occasional impasse in Vietnamese that way. That amused Wes, who knew a few French phrases himself.

"I can parlez-vous if you need some help, Nolan."

"I do need help, Wes, that's for sure. All the military terms I learned in Texas don't help very much. Civil Affairs calls for a different vocabulary."

In the Vietnamese villages, the situations stood less dire than the poverty they saw in the camp. The villagers, though, had livelihoods. The Montagnards missed their freedom to roam and find what they needed. They weren't inclined to stay put. Nolan saw why Wes considered the camp his top priority.

"Too bad, Nap doesn't know French, Wes. You seem to do pretty well getting your points across, but I'm glad to help with the trickier phrases. I could teach you some basic Vietnamese, but I suspect you're going to be busy enough with the health challenges we've been seeing. What did you pick up from talking with Hal and Dom?"

"They agreed that we need additional resources. Dom thought that maybe CORDS can increase its aid."

Civil Operations and Revolutionary Development Support, the major US pacification program underway in the country, had been established in Song Mao over a year earlier. Progress in the camp looked minimal.

Fortunately, more immediate help came from an unexpected source. Not long after Nolan's first visit to the Montagnard camp, an American Army doctor assigned to a local artillery unit volunteered to conduct a medical clinic at the camp on his day off. Nolan recognized the doctor immediately when they met. He had been a dorm prefect, a senior, when Nolan was in a freshman dorm at Holy Cross. They had never conversed, other than to nod hello, having lived on different floors. Still, Nolan felt some pride in this shared value of "service to others."

Together with Wes, the doctor and Nolan patiently administered to a long line of camp dwellers, just under a hundred, for the clinic. Each patient received only a few minutes of attention, though the doctor could, if needed, refer more serious cases to a hospital. It was Nolan's role to ask if the person had any pain, and if so, where. Everyone in line reported some pain either in the head or stomach, often pantomimed by the patient just to make sure Nolan understood the location. Many of the camp dwellers seemed perfectly healthy, but the chance to get some aspirin, an analgesic, a salve, or just some bars of soap was too good to pass up. Everything was free, of course. Nolan might have to explain dosage, and he sometimes used his fingers for numbers. But soon a rote pattern emerged in the overall process, the medical problems falling into clear categories.

American soldiers typically carried water purification tablets to protect them from tainted water, and they had given the Montagnards tablets when fresh water wasn't available in bulk. The doctor said the Montagnards may have developed sufficient antibodies over their lifespan to prevent serious problems. The fact remained, however, that the Americans couldn't be sure how serious the water problem was. Nolan and his teammates took daily or every other day showers, though they did try to keep them brief in order to conserve water. The Montagnards bathed in the river, but hygiene remained well below Western standards because of the polluted water.

"Nearly everyone would test positive for TB, I'm sure," the doctor noted. "But I doubt we'll see many heart problems or indications of cancer."

In the end, soap emerged as the best medicine he could offer. The patients smiled and nodded thanks for their new treasure. Nolan tried to stay alert to the possibility that there might be some camp dwellers who connived to get back in line for seconds. That wouldn't be so terrible as long as there was enough for everyone. Fortunately, distribution worked out perfectly, with no one being left out. The three-man team ended the long day with a general agreement to schedule another clinic in a month or so. A few older Montagnards resided in the camp, but life expectancy was quite a bit lower than in other parts of Vietnamese culture.

Nap appeared pleased about the clinic, and the Americans were, too. Wes said good-bye to Nap with the Vietnamese form for friend or brother, "Chào anh." As it had turned out, no one in line appeared to be in danger of death any time soon, at least not from natural causes.

Once night fell, though, the camp presented an easy target for the Viet Cong. The residents relied for defense on only some flimsy fencing and no real fortifications to speak of. Nap and most of the other men had been provided with M-16s and ammunition. With luck, they could count on some backup from US and ARVN forces stationed a mile or two away, but the nights loomed dangerously. One moonlit night, the local CORDS man, Thayer, was visiting at the team villa when reports of an attack on the camp came through over the field radio. Visibly alarmed, Wes paced at the doorway, looking in the direction of the camp, hearing small arms fire in the distance. Thayer, slight of stature, and the epitome of a WASP, with blond hair and blue eyes visible through his trendy frameless glasses, surprised Nolan and the others by being the first to voice concern.

"Those are my people. I want to be there."

Wes and Nolan looked at him and then at each other. It was hard to see a family connection. As the CORDS man, Thayer received training to gather information as expeditiously as possible and assess local needs, not to lead the US Cavalry to save the day. Certainly, they all wanted Nap and his tribe to be safe, but really only the firepower from trained military forces could answer this need, not one guy waving a .38 pistol. Big help he would be, Nolan thought. Glancing at Wes, Nolan saw him shake his head in disbelief. Neither said anything. It made no sense to assert who had the closer connection to the tribe. The frustration of not being of real help to the Montagnards hit all of them hard. Thayer had, no doubt, met with Nap on numerous occasions and did care about him. Nolan wondered, though, if guilt figured into Thayer's reaction. Did he now recognize that he not done enough to help keep the tribe safe? The guy had possessed the clout to get aid fast if he had so wanted.

The firefight didn't last long. An American gunship came to the rescue, which made for quite a show at night as seen from the safe confines of the MACV compound. The machine gun fire, tracers and all, in addition to the loud, fluttering noises made by the chopper's rotors, told the tale. But the intervening hours until Dom deemed it safe to drive over to the camp passed so slowly. Early the next day Wes and Nolan jumped into a jeep and drove out to see what medical help was needed, hoping for the best.

The camp did not look or smell any different. Amazingly, no huts had burned down during the attack. Nap, jaunty as a bantam rooster, stood erect by the entrance to his hut in mismatched clothes and flip-flops, with several half-naked, small children playing around him. Other such raids might take place soon, yet he appeared resolute and ready for whatever trouble came his way.

Spotting the Civil Affairs team, he greeted them with hearty handshakes.

"Are you OK, Nap?" Wes asked.

Nolan translated Nap's words for Wes.

Nap responded, "Don't worry, my brother. We can fight better than the VC."

"Tell him, I know that. He just doesn't have to win the war all by himself."

Nap appreciated the joke after Nolan struggled to translate. Maybe unintentionally, his version was funnier, Nolan thought.

The wounded, only a few, had already been taken to a nearby hospital. The Montagnards fortunately had suffered no fatalities.

Almost two weeks went by without another visit to the camp. Then Wes got word that Nap was seriously ill, and though it was Sunday and not a usual work day, he asked Nolan if he would go along with him to see if there was something they could do. Apparently, Nap was experiencing severe stomach pain. As far as they knew, Nap hadn't been wounded in the firefight. Wes took his medical kit along, and the two drove in a jeep over to the camp in late morning. As they approached Nap's hut on foot, Wes called out his name. They could hear a voice inside. Taking that as a welcome, Wes parted the ragged cloth that hung over the entrance. The odor of burning incense assailed their nostrils. Peering into the darkness, they could make out Nap lying face up on a cot, and above him a dark figure standing and chanting. The shaman, they realized. Wes was alarmed, but before he could speak or step closer, Nolan tugged his arm.

"Wes, we gotta go. We can come back later."

Wes let himself be guided back outside. However, he wasn't ready to leave.

"That guy isn't going to help. Nap needs medical attention."

Nolan's mind raced. "We have to wait, Wes. If Nap sends the guy away and accepts your help, he'll lose face in the village. He can't turn away from his tribe."

Reluctantly, Wes agreed to leave, looking back at the camp as Nolan drove. The big Texan stewed about the incident the rest of the day.

"Maybe I could have helped. I could have at least examined him."

Back at the villa, Dom reassured him that he could go back the next morning. For now, they could only hope Nap would be OK. A half day proved to be another long wait for both Wes and Nolan. When they returned to the camp the next day, they were relieved to see Nap up on his feet, seemingly weak, but not in great pain. He agreed to let Wes look at his stomach, which was tender and somewhat distended. He didn't want to go to a hospital, insisting he was feeling better. Wes and Nolan left, feeling only a little better themselves. Wes was not convinced that all was OK.

"It could be an ulcer, diverticulitis, or a parasite. Any number of things. I can't rule out appendicitis."

There wasn't much Nolan could say. Wes knew his stuff.

"We'll find an excuse to go back in a day or so, Wes. Whenever you want. Your call."

As luck would have it—or tribal magic, Nolan thought,— Nap improved. In the weeks that followed he continued to lead the tribe without any apparent serious concerns about his fitness. Nolan wondered what had gone through Nap's mind in deciding his course of action during the illness. Was he at all a believer in Western medicine? Had his friendship with Wes or the medical clinics themselves influenced his thinking? Nolan saw the challenge Nap faced. He may have been just trying to please the Americans, to let them think he was moving toward accepting the so-called modern advances of the West. Nap had to be extra careful making decisions to avoid anything that might offend either the Americans or his people. He was walking a tightrope.

Nolan sensed that it was more than just a matter of sharing a second language that would reveal what Nap really thought and if he actually welcomed more change. Someone would have to earn his trust. Wes had made inroads there, for sure. Nolan didn't say much to Wes about his doubts. Wes was totally invested in helping the Montagnards with his Western expertise. Maybe if Nolan had more time around Nap, he could get him to open up about his beliefs and wishes for his tribe.

Another complication had arisen, though. Word had reached the team that the 41st Civil Affairs Company would likely be part of a drawdown of American forces in country. The policy of Vietnamization of the war—a term whose irony was not lost on Nolan—would mean fewer American troops across the board, gradual though a withdrawal might be. Soon, the Montagnards would be on their own, the local Vietnamese officials being less inclined to help them out with the Civil Affairs team gone. They might have to risk an early return to the highlands, perilous though that would be.

"There's so much left to do," Nolan complained to Dom and Wes one evening, "and not just for the Montagnards, though they need us the most."

"We've got some good possibilities for more medical clinics here, Dom. Any chance of delaying our departure?" Wes asked.

"Zero, I suspect. This decision is made much higher up than Nha Trang. The numbers have to be right to meet the withdrawal target."

Only a few months in Song Mao, and comfortable with much of his work and his teammates, Nolan faced being reassigned to a new unit in Vietnam since he had insufficient time in country to be sent home. He thought he was beginning to make small inroads into the local community, to get closer to the residents. Recently, he had been visiting a local high school one afternoon a week and assisting a young male teacher there with English classes. The teacher didn't seem to care that Nolan had a master's degree, that he was on a career track to be a giào sư ("teacher" or "professor"). What he wanted Nolan to do was simply correct pronunciation of English words by the students in their drills. Nolan went along, deciding that he shouldn't let this opportunity be about his ego. He lacked any practical experience in the classroom, after all. The teacher had much more training than Nolan did and probably set specific goals that he needed to meet. Nolan acknowledged to himself that he should see this as an opportunity to create goodwill. The teacher's plan seemed to be working, too. The kids acted happy to see Nolan, smiling broadly and chattering upon his arrival even though he didn't offer any candy or gum as many grunts did when they came across kids in hamlets. He had, however, learned how much a smile and a slight bow could do.

Leaving Song Mao would be hard. He was doing his part and he had purpose. And it wasn't all about helping others, good though that felt. He sensed he was growing. He saw his assistant teacher role as valuable experience since he was not naturally outgoing or used to speaking before a group. He thought about his father, of how he had joined the Toastmasters to improve his public speaking, sometimes reciting at home a standard opening: "Unaccustomed though I am to public speaking . . . ." His father always stopped there in this family levity. Like many other breadwinners of the day, he had read Dale Carnegie's *How to Win Friends and Influence People*. His example wasn't lost on his children. Nolan and a brother had joined the high school debate club. Neither had stuck with it for very long as underclassmen seldom got to debate, but they had enjoyed the visits to local colleges that hosted debates. Higher education and self-improvement rated high on the family scale.

On the other hand, Nolan didn't think that speaking Vietnamese itself would become a significant factor in his long-range plans. In fact, it crossed his mind that some high-ranking American officer in Saigon or Nha Trang might get wind of a promising young interpreter and want him for his own use, like a personal pet, removing him from Civil Affairs altogether. Nolan decided he had better not, then, show too much linguistic skill outside of the camp and village visits. He didn't want to end up as some colonel's or general's prize because he was an American who spoke fluent Vietnamese. Let the Army think he was just an ordinary Joe who did simple support work adequately. Basic training taught soldiers a very important survival skill: You don't want to make yourself conspicuous. You certainly don't want to be seen as a fuck-up, but sometimes extra effort could make you a target as well. No, staying in the middle of the pack, just being a good teammate, was better.

For the near term, he remained apprehensive, too, about reassignment, recognizing that so much in a new location could be out of his control. In Song Mao, Dom trusted him to do good work not only in ways prescribed by the company brass, but also of his own devising. To a large degree, this satisfied Nolan. He couldn't say that it justified his presence in Vietnam—the validity of the war was still the core issue—and yet he could put aside for the time being any strong feelings of guilt, chipping in as best he could to make the lives of those he encountered more hopeful and possibly materially better, even if only for few months.

The other men seemed equally ill at ease with the impending change. All the joking around and playing of cards ceased almost entirely. Dom, sensing the disappointment, tried to pick up spirits.

"A withdrawal of the team, guys, doesn't mean we haven't done some good here," the captain said one morning at the kitchen table. "It's a matter of troop numbers. We'll just keep working until we get the order to stop."

Several of the team members were sitting around the table, the fan gently stirring the warm air overhead. The spartan conditions in the building always seemed so luxurious after a visit to the Montagnard camp. Nolan realized that the team members were fortunate in so many ways regardless of the danger they faced.

"I sure would like to be here long enough to see another generation of rabbits," Matt drawled.

"As long as it isn't for another generation of humans," Tony rejoined.

Nolan laughed with the others. He knew that despite their college-dorm demeanors, his teammates felt much the same way he did. A definite idealistic streak ran through all the pragmatism and prevailing levity. Nothing wrong with the mix.

No one spoke for a few seconds. Expectation hung in the air. It was up to the captain to break the spell. Only once in a while did he pull rank.

"Whatever else we can do, let's do," said Dom. He looked around at the downcast faces of his comrades and assumed the most serious expression he could muster.

"Off you go. No sense moping around. We can't control what the higher ups might do."

Or any greater powers, Nolan thought.

Chapter 6: A Long Good-Bye

Through the netting, Nolan saw a dark-skinned young man, approximately his age and height, quite handsome in a bright white shirt and long, loosely fitting pants. The Chams were worthy adversaries in volleyball, taller than several players on the Song Mao Civil Affairs team except for Nolan, Hal, and a new guy, Ron, a former football player from New Jersey. Nolan was pleased to have opponents as tall as he was, an inch over six feet, as the Chinese-descended Vietnamese were often a half-foot or more shorter. Playing the latter at the net made for unfair and unsatisfying competition.

A full-bird American colonel, an intelligence officer who had brought the Chams to the compound, played on the Cham team, too. Nolan exercised care not to spike too much in his direction, not that he feared some off-the-court retaliation— the gray-haired colonel was a good sport—but because he wanted his primary competition to be an equal physically. The young Cham men were that and definitely had played before. The volleyball had begun intramurally not long after Nolan had arrived, the team members then numerous enough to field two sides, though court coverage remained a problem. Outside competition came later, and the men welcomed it.

While Nolan had visited the Cham village nearby, he knew little about their culture. Invariably, the officials welcomed Nolan and his partners with smiles and offers of tea. Speaking their own language at home and Vietnamese with visitors or among business contacts, the Chams lived peacefully among the Vietnamese now. Dom told Nolan that hostilities more or less subsided after the Chams were driven from their kingdom in the Central Highlands. Many Muslim Chams had migrated to Cambodia over the years, beginning with the Chinese invasion centuries before. This particular group, Dom said, was Hindu and had lived in Binh Thuan for generations.

Nolan had never had conversations with any of the young women, a cultural taboo, but he had noted their colorful long-sleeve dresses, modest as the aó dàis in coverage and yet alluring in the way the garments required graceful posture when women walked. He imagined that his sudden attentiveness to their movements in the village resembled a bird dog spotting a pheasant. His hosts didn't appear to notice this, for which he was grateful.

The physical interaction with the young men proved to be good-natured and athletic, a pleasing way to spend the early evening hours. Nolan's prowess at the net often surprised opponents. He was slender, and by no means a physical specimen. But his sense for timing a jump and especially his long arms gave him an advantage at reaching a ball well above the net before others could. He played strategically, too, being clever enough to vary the type and direction of his hand contact, as well as whether to attempt or feint a block. He never acted too eager or aggressive as he prepared to jump. He rose quickly, reaching up to the sky, sometimes with his left arm at his side, other times with both hands upraised in the best position to block. These moments made him feel intensely alive, at his full physical prime. Danger seemed far away. Here reigned the joy of unadulterated athletic competition.

Much of the time no one was available to referee, so calling touches of the net constituted a matter of honor. Yet for the most part, the two sides reached agreement without serious disagreement. Line calls presented thornier cases and sometimes cried out for the least aggressive solution: replay the point. If only political disagreements could be solved so simply. What need would exist for war?

Nolan realized that outside of conversation with Bui and the limited contact he had with camp and village officials, he had not really immersed himself in Vietnamese life. He had lived and worked with Americans since his arrival, happily sharing the easier friendships with his compatriots. The downside was that both his Vietnamese fluency and cultural knowledge grew only incrementally, more slowly than he had anticipated. Social interaction with Vietnamese speakers remained too limited, restricted mostly to the work at hand. At times he felt more like an observer than a participant in the larger culture outside the compound gate. He saw a parallel to the British in India, which displeased him because of the assumption of cultural superiority by the colonists. Limited though the occasions were, the volleyball activity with the Chams had appealed to him as an egalitarian experience and a bridge over a cultural chasm. He hoped that the play could be just a beginning, an opening to greater interaction.

The Army, however, had made other plans.

The pleasant evenings marked by enthusiastic and amiable play gradually gave way to the reality of a team departure. The Song Mao team had received official word that the 41st Civil Affairs Company was being sent home as part of President Nixon's ordered troop reduction in Vietnam, the current number standing at over a half million soldiers. In the larger picture of a prolonged, fruitless war, a troop reduction looked promising. Nolan and the others had been getting news all along about the growing disapproval of the war's conduct among Americans. Polls were showing that a majority wanted US withdrawal, though a sizable number, they realized, wanted a still more aggressive military strategy. Few on the team, though, favored this latter option. If anything, they eagerly wanted to go home, the sooner the better.

Only Perk and Walker, the Dynamic Duo, had completed enough months in their tours to see that benefit anytime soon. Everyone else would disperse to other in-country locales, some to places that would be considerably more dangerous, north toward the DMZ, for example. Nolan felt some relief at reading that his new orders were to join the 29th Civil Affairs Company in Quang Ngai province, up in I Corps, what the GIs pronounced "eye" Corps. Most likely, he would be doing the same kind of work, but still well south of the DMZ, and for that matter, Da Nang. So, it was not quite the state of fear of the unknown that he had harbored a few months earlier. This time he thought he had a better idea of what to expect. But, of course, doubts remained.

"Quang Ngai?" Tony, the second-in-charge, mused. "Isn't that where Ho Chi Minh was from?"

"Really? You're not kidding me, are you?"

"I seem to remember hearing that. How getting control of Quang Ngai was a personal thing with him."

"Great. That's just what I need."

"Yeah, I bet there's some kind of bounty for bagging an interpreter."

"Even ones who are not that good? Yes, we know the VC are not happy with American attempts to win over 'hearts and minds.' If captured, I suppose I can always just tell them, 'I'm from Jersey and don't know beans.'"

Nolan liked Tony. Their needling each other never went too far. All the men understood the pressure generated by the war and the powerful role luck played in what happened in Vietnam.   Unless it was a desk job in division headquarters, such as Dom's new assignment, members of the Civil Affairs team would likely be facing greater risk wherever they ended up. Binh Thuan, the driest province in the country and one of the quietest during the war, would be a tough act to follow. Add to that the team cohesiveness that Dom had fostered. How common was it? Nolan sensed that not all Army officers hungered for the experience of war. Enlistments had slowed to a crawl with the rising resistance to a conflict that was beginning to look like a stalemate. The new officers, many of them ROTC, knew how the political tide was changing back home. Wouldn't they see that the best plan was to lose the fewest men possible? Risks could be limited to just what was needed for defense. Yet, Nolan knew some career officers would be looking for something distinctive, even heroic, for their advancement. He had heard that's how a military career was built. Once again, he saw that he was a pawn.

On the interpersonal level, too, the change unsettled him. Nolan liked these guys. He would miss them all. It had been tough enough parting with his language school buddies back in November, and after forging new friendships quickly in Song Mao, the time had come to say good-bye again. Dom, Wes, and Woody, as well as the others, appealed to different chords within him, all somehow harmonic. Sure, they would exchange addresses with the best of intentions to stay in touch, but already the time for writing letters home seemed too limited, as were the quiet places in which to write. Nolan wondered if the likelihood of mixed fortunes would be a disincentive, as well. Could he write in full candor to a buddy who, for all he knew, could be in a dicey situation and tell him about the wonderful patch of clover in which he had landed? He feared weighing down a buddy's spirit because he knew how much morale could fluctuate from day to day. Probably just focusing on their new jobs and not looking back on shared time made more sense. They shouldn't get sentimental. Better to contact each other after getting home and exchange stories in retrospect like veterans of other wars did.

On the plus side, maybe his new living quarters would put him in closer contact with Vietnamese civilians. The enclave might give way to a more immersive arrangement. He could benefit from getting to know the natives better. Why should he waste the language skills he had, speaking Vietnamese only a few minutes a day? There remained so much to learn about Vietnam.

He returned one last time to the local school to say good-bye to the children, not as emotional as it could have been since he hadn't even learned names. The teacher had kept things quite formal. He wondered if the group greetings and smiles of the pupils had been orchestrated from the start, reminiscent of how nuns in a parochial school schooled their charges about how to greet or answer a priest who stopped by a classroom.

In the villages, matters tended to be more casual. Like other GIs, he often rolled up the shirtsleeves in the heat as he walked through a village or camp, and small kids in packs ran alongside to feel the soft down on his arms. To them, arm hair was exotic. He sometimes chatted a bit with the children, surprising them with his array of Vietnamese phrases they probably never had heard from a foreigner. Of course, these encounters tended to be brief. The children usually scurried away like squirrels when village officials came into view, the elders intent on keeping matters orderly when visitors appeared.

One hazy morning Nolan rode with Wes over to the Montagnard camp one last time to say good-bye to Nap. After greetings, Wes didn't say too much to his friend about what help might be coming from other sources. He didn't really know, for one thing, but he also didn't want to make hollow promises to a person he respected so much. Nolan could tell Wes was holding back his emotions.

Nap, for his part, was stoic. He clearly liked Wes. Even dwarfed by the bulk of the GI medic, he appeared at ease and smiled during their exchanges. He had gotten along fine, too, with Nolan, who was careful to yield to Wes in any discussion with Nap. Nolan realized that the Montagnard chief was used to seeing Americans come and go, promises or not. He would build new relationships for the sake of his people. Maybe, Nolan began to see, Nap had good reason not to give his trust totally to the Americans. For now, he shook hands firmly with the two Americans, just the latest to leave after offers to help.

Wes quickly picked up on the note of abandonment. "Damn, that was hard, man," he confided to Nolan as they walked back to the jeep. "What's down the line for those folks? Somehow I don't think Thayer and CORDS will do as much as we did for them."

Nolan had no answer for Wes or for the Vietnamese village officials who sounded him out when they heard the team was leaving. He saw them look for hints in his eyes. As for Bui, while he was used to turnover on the team, he wasn't ready for this development of losing simultaneously the whole team and his job. On the last day he mournfully shook hands with everyone. They all wished him luck, passing some small gifts to him, mostly things that would lighten their load a little on the journey north to Cam Ranh Bay to turn in the team's vehicles at the huge depot there. Bui could expect to get some work with other Americans, though maybe guys not so congenial.

Nolan petted Tasty a few last times before Bui took him home. He hoped the bond between man and dog would not be broken. Perk was passing on the loris and its cage to a MACV adviser on the compound. Nolan would not miss that creature.

Moving day had arrived more quickly than they expected. The Civil Affairs team pulled out of the compound on a bright, sunny morning, a small convoy of jeeps and ¾-ton trucks, Nolan driving the truck at the rear. It struck him as odd not to be headed to a local village or camp, the routine of the last few months. After one last glance back at the main street, he focused his eyes on the vehicle ahead as the convoy drove up gradually into some higher ground on the way north.

The trip might take over an hour, he had been told, but he wasn't worried about being alone in the truck. The road was as secure as any in Vietnam because of the strategic importance of the supply depot at Cam Ranh Bay. Nonetheless, when Nolan saw a ¾-ton truck ahead parked alongside the road, he slowed instinctively. The hood was up and a lanky, sandy-haired GI was standing nearby. It was Murphy, one of his classmates from language school, who had been assigned to another team in the 41st. Up to now, they hadn't a chance to meet up. Nolan pulled over, hopped out of the cab, and called out to his fellow student.

"Murph, what's the problem? Overheating?"

Murphy squinted through his wire rims. "Oh, hey, Nolan. Yeah, it looks that way."

They shook hands. Murphy always seemed to be listening to some music in his head, never quite in the moment with others around. In class, he frequently seemed startled when it was his turn to recite the day's lesson, his eyes widening as he realized he was "on." But he was smart enough and had a dry sense of humor worth waiting for. They chatted a bit, letting the radiator cool off, the steam rising in a narrow plume. It seemed strange to Nolan for the two of them to be standing there in the middle of nowhere, yet still in a war zone, taking respite from it all. For a few minutes they could, through reminiscing, replace in their minds these forbiddingly foreign hills, full of mystery and potential danger, with the wide, empty, expanse of sand at Fort Bliss. Ignorance was indeed Bliss. When they loped to and from class, the horizon remained so distant across the flat desert. Vietnam had been so far away then.

Nolan thought back to the slow, low-key class days, but he suspected even that halcyon interval of almost nine months had created more than a bit of stress for Murphy. They caught up somewhat on Nam experiences, Nolan finding out that Murphy's team in a neighboring district had been more given to traditional Army ways. When Murphy asked about his experience, Nolan didn't want to rub his luck in, saying simply, "It's been OK, man." After a few minutes of small talk, Murphy appeared to remember at last his task and straightened up from his leaning position against the door. Unfastening the large canister of water attached to the rear of the truck, he began slowly filling the radiator again. Nolan knew it was time to say good-bye.

"Well, it looks like you've got things under control, Murph. I'd better get moving to catch up with my team. They may think I went AWOL."

"Yeah, how far is it to Canada, anyway?"

Nolan laughed. "Would you settle for Da Lat? We've heard so much about it. We could detour to the west instead of going to Cam Ranh."

Murphy paused a few seconds as if he were seriously considering the suggestion. In language school, one of most entertaining dialogues to be memorized had been a paean to the beauty of Da Lat, the famous resort city in the highlands. Ruefully, he glanced at Nolan.

"See you in Cam Ranh, man."

It didn't take Nolan long to catch up with the team. The other vehicles in the convoy had pulled over a half mile up the road for an impromptu bladder break and a nibble on provisions. His buddies had assumed Nolan had stopped earlier for a similar reason. Still, they seemed glad to see him as he didn't have a radio to stay in contact. They drove on to the depot without another stop, finding the appropriate hangar after a brief search among the avenues of similar structures arranged in orderly rows. The waiting time reduced the enlisted men to idleness and chit-chat, Dom and the other officers taking care of the paperwork. After what seemed an hour or two, the officers appeared and everyone boarded a bus that took an indirect route to a helipad, which would have been a much shorter distance as the crow flies. Once there they climbed aboard helicopters for the up-the-coast hop to Nha Trang, Murphy and his team joining with them for the ride. Gone were their vehicles, along with their weapons and combat gear. Everything seemed more final now as the choppers rose noisily in the afternoon heat.

The helicopters flew just over the treetops to avoid giving an easy target to snipers, an open door allowing the machine gunners a clear view below. In his chopper, Nolan sat directly behind the gunner. The ride proved to be exhilarating, unlike the one in the Wallaby that had brought Nolan to Song Mao. It helped to see the ground this time. He felt himself letting go of his fear, despite the knowledge that a whirlybird presented a sitting duck for ground fire. Probably adrenaline was kicking in again. When his bird touched down, he gave a hand wave to the gunner and jumped down into a crouch, scuttling forward

73

until well clear of the pad and the rotor. The team gathered inside a small terminal for a hasty planning session. In Nha Trang, the officers and enlisted men would billet in separate quarters for the first time in months. But for another day or so they could hang out together and determine the best use of their remaining hours as a team.

Dom, his dark hair ruffled from the ride, offered an option: "I don't know about you guys, but a little distance from the base suits me. How about spending most of tomorrow at the beach?"

Everyone thought that was a great idea.

"Think you could find a surfboard, Perk?" Tony asked.

"Probably just some minor body surfing tomorrow, but I'll take that. It's hard to imagine it's the same ocean, though."

This first night in the barracks reminded Nolan of his brief stay in Nha Trang just a few months earlier. Time seemed to be retreating. He obviously felt some of the same misgivings about his future as he had felt then. Yet, he had lost the edge off his worry. Now he was mostly sad.

The beach in Nha Trang turned out to be an easy walk the next day. The men stripped to their green boxer shorts and splashed in the warm waters of the South China Sea. Conversations, though, lacked the ease and wit of so many that had taken place in Song Mao. They tried to relax the best they could, the weather being perfect for that, warm and breezy. But the next day all would be heading out in different directions. That would be it for the team. Nolan wasn't sure whose idea it was but talk arose of having one last meal together that evening. Woody said he was out as he was meeting some old friends at the NCO club, and Matt, Wes, and Walker opted out, too. Ron, who had been only a few weeks in Song Mao, and Nolan looked at each other. They were the only two enlisted men free.

"The Officers' Club it is then. You have civvies, right?" Dom asked.

At Song Mao, the casual attitude toward rank and military discipline in the Civil Affairs villa was one thing. Here in Nha Trang that attitude wouldn't fly. Nolan and Ron essentially would be performing a masquerade, and detection could bring punishment. Nolan didn't bother to ask what that would be. If they were to avoid discovery, the Last Supper was going to require some serious *sang froid* from the two enlisted men. So, Nolan felt very conscious of the way he was walking when he entered the Officers' Club with the others that evening. Ron's football build likely conformed more closely to an officer's expected carriage. Nolan tried to stand a little straighter and not fall into that slouch so endemic in the lower ranks.

Once seated at a table enjoying a beer, he felt more comfortable. This might be easier than he thought. They all looked much the same, like college kids except for the short haircuts. The conversation was lively and crisp unlike the starts and stops of their exchanges earlier in the day. Nolan was feeling better. He flinched just a bit when he felt the tap on his shoulder. "Patrick," he heard, surprised someone was speaking his given name. Behind him stood a second lieutenant, well built in a freshly pressed uniform. It took him a second, but then he saw it was Glenn, a guy he had worked with on the grounds crew at a golf course a few summers earlier in Maine.

"Glenn, how are you? Funny place to see you."

"That's for sure. Where are you stationed?"

"I'm in transit, on my way to Da Nang tomorrow, and then Quang Ngai. This is part of our Civil Affairs team. The company is being disbanded, so we're all moving on. How about you?"

"I'm here in Nha Trang. Just arrived as an engineer. You've been here for some months, I take it."

"Yeah, a few months. Just a few more to go, and then I hope to be back in the States in the fall."

"When did you enlist?"

Nolan realized he had to be evasive. "I've been in a total of fifteen months. Time's gone fast."

Glenn's forehead furrowed. Nolan could tell he was calculating the months. Officers didn't do just two years.

"It's a little complicated, Glenn. I'll fill you in later. Let me have your address, and I'll write down mine, at least the Da Nang HQ."

"OK, Patrick, let's do that."

Glenn was a good guy, Nolan thought. He wouldn't blow his cover, but still it was better not to explain everything here. They might be overheard. Dom and the others were grinning at Nolan's predicament. Glenn went back to his table, probably suspecting something. Dinner resumed, with the food and beer tasting especially good after all the water and sun.

An hour or so later, the Song Mao contingent was standing in the darkness outside the club. Stars filled the sky, but the moon was not full. A sole light bulb at the exit cast shadows on the sidewalk. The time had finally come to part ways. Nolan's flight north to Da Nang would leave early the next day. He had mixed feelings about what to say or do now the end had finally come—how serious to be. He might never see any of these guys again. It would have been great to have extended the night, to spend just a little more time together, but a few hours of sound sleep would do all of them some good. The others seemed to feel the same way. He said his good-byes one by one, shaking hands, and exchanging good luck wishes. He shook Dom's hand last. Ron was already waiting for him on the path back to the enlisted men's barracks.

As Nolan slowly released Dom's hand, he softly said, "Good luck, Dominic." He had always used the nickname before.

He turned and started walking away. Then, he heard Dom's voice.

"Take care of yourself, Nolan—hear?"

Nolan smiled as he called out over his shoulder, "Is that a mand, Dom?"

Chapter 7: Adjustments

Up in the air again, this time in a single-engine Cessna on a cloudless day, Nolan peered down at the curving coastline of Vietnam below him. No one would ever know that it was a land ravaged by war: dark green canopy, azure blue water, and occasional white sand beaches, all of it inviting to the eye. Nolan knew that offshore made for the safest route, out of range for enemy sniper fire, even if engine trouble arose, necessitating proximity to a landing strip. He had never flown in a plane as small as the Cessna, but the day appeared perfect for flying, and he did not intend to make room for dark thoughts. Keeping positive was his goal. He would be ready for the new challenges ahead. He had to be.

He also possessed another reason to be optimistic. The Army offered an attractive option in this time of troop reduction, an "early out." If a soldier requested an early separation within ninety days of the scheduled separation, he could have his service time reduced provided he was enrolling immediately in a school of higher education. Nolan had not thought a great deal about returning to graduate school once he left the Army. He wasn't sure what he would do. His first impulse naturally would be to relax and recover from his stint not only in Vietnam, but also in the Army overall. It might take some time to get his head back to normal. He would be his own man, reveling in his regained freedom and wary of giving over control so soon again to a large institution. Getting back to the States early, though, presented an opportunity too good to pass up, and he would have the G.I. Bill available for financial support. Yes, going back to school would mean stepping out of one discipline into another discipline with hardly time to catch a breath, but leaving the war zone early—that was a wondrous thing. He would start the paperwork as soon as he could.

A smooth approach and landing in Da Nang pushed the earlier Wallaby flight to Song Mao out of Nolan's mind. Flying was definitely OK. He grabbed his gear, a single duffel bag and a carryall now after turning in his M-14, helmet, and flak jacket in Cam Ranh. Exiting the small plane, he strolled into the low, rectangular building that served as the terminal looking for someone bearing a "29th Civil Affairs "sign. Just inside the entrance stood a short, dark-haired fellow flashing a wry, crooked smile.

"Nolan? I'm D'Amico, company clerk, occasional chauffeur, and oh so short."

The cheerful greeter wasn't referring to his height, Nolan was sure, so he played along. "How short are you?" Those with only a few weeks or days left in their tour expected as much.

"I'm so short that you could slide me under Hugh Hefner's bearskin rug."

"I didn't know toupees were made of bearskin these days."

"You're thinking of Howard Cosell, Nolan. Three weeks and three days is the exact count."

"Congrats. You're a lucky dog."

"And so are you, Nolan. You're going to love Mo Duc. That's your assignment. Most of the paperwork is done. I did it myself. No thanks necessary."

They had walked out the opposite exit to the street while talking and approached a lone jeep parked haphazardly a few yards away. "Hop in," D'Amico said with that same mysterious smile, "and I'll tell you more."

A minute later they were swerving in a jumble of pedicabs, bicycles, and Lambrettas, the tiny three-wheeled buses that always seemed dangerously overloaded. Somehow the jeep managed to avoid hitting anything, though that seemed more luck than skill. After several narrow misses and a few muttered imprecations, D'Amico suddenly turned the steering wheel off the road to the right and stopped abruptly in front of a row of roadside huts. A young Vietnamese man in shorts and flip flops emerged from one and approached the jeep on the

78

run. The exchange was quick and wordless, a small package for some greenbacks.

"I hope you don't mind, Nolan. I'll share some with you tonight. Some pretty good stuff. I bet you had great weed down in Binh Thuan."

D'Amico twisted the steering wheel back toward the road and hit the gas pedal hard. Nolan held firmly onto the seat brace, glancing instinctively over his shoulder to make sure the coast was clear. He wasn't sure D'Amico had even looked. Once again on the road, he turned his attention to the question.

"I couldn't tell you about the dope. We had enlisted men and officers living together. I never asked, but I assumed smoking dope wouldn't be condoned in our digs. So, tell me more about Mo Duc."

"Charlie is active in Mo Duc. You will need to keep your head down. The prime minister of the North, some guy named Dong, is from Mo Duc, so he has a special interest in it."

"I heard it was Ho Chi Minh who was from Quang Ngai."

"Don't think so. And anyhow Uncle Ho is dead. You need to worry about Dong."

No problem doing that, Nolan thought. Delivered in one piece to company headquarters and only mildly shaken, he got an afternoon briefing from a captain about the mission in Quang Ngai province, finding out he was to be the assistant to a lieutenant. Just two-man team teams in the 29th. Their job was to assess the material needs of the refugees in the area, who had been forced to leave their paddies at the foot of the mountains to live in camps alongside Highway One, the north-south paved road. Supplies would be sent upon a documentation of needs, and Nolan and his boss would oversee distribution. He heard no mention of medical clinics or opportunities to teach English. The scope of the mission was clearly much narrower in Quang Ngai than in Binh Thuan.

Still a bit apprehensive about the change, he didn't mind at all sharing a joint with D'Amico later that evening in the barracks. Everyone else had cleared out. He had smoked marijuana only once before, but he didn't mention that to his affable host. D'Amico had picked up a boom box somewhere, maybe from a source similar to the one for his dope, and it was playing some Jefferson Airplane.

Nolan wondered about the extent of the black market in Da Nang. When he purchased something in the civilian community, he always used Vietnamese currency, not Military Payment Certificates, or MPC, the scrip with which soldiers were paid in Vietnam, and certainly not greenbacks. To thwart traffickers in currency, the US military periodically reissued the MPC in a new series, making previous MPC worthless. Nolan heard rumors about guys getting greenbacks sent from home that would go further in civilian transactions, but he hadn't seen anyone involved in that until today.

"We're pretty much left alone after work is done," D'Amico said over the din and passing a thick joint to Nolan. "Down in the town some guys drink, and some rent a girl for an hour, maybe both. Me, I just smoke. I'm too short to mess with a lot of night life."

"Well, D'Amico. I'm content to be here tonight. And, thanks to your dope, I don't think I could go anywhere anyhow."

"We're someplace else even while we're going nowhere, man."

"Now, you're being positively philosophical."

That sounded funny to Nolan at the time.

"That's me, the philosopher-king. By the way, did I tell you I'm short?"

"I believe you did."

Not much left to this evening, Nolan realized through his mental fog—a good time to just let go. D'Amico continued to chatter, and Nolan mostly nodded.

Later he managed to climb into an empty bunk, where he fell into a heavy sleep and rose the next morning none too worse for wear. A shower and breakfast did their part, as well, and he was ready to head for Quang Ngai province.

As it turned out, Lt. Collins, his new boss, had driven up from Mo Duc the previous afternoon, so D'Amico didn't need to find Nolan a ride. Once Nolan was issued an M-16 and other combat gear, Collins put their jeep on the road. It wasn't even ten yet. Lean and weathered like the Marlboro man, the lieutenant filled Nolan in on the situation in Mo Duc.

"We're getting more refugees every week. Our artillery is shelling the foothills every evening, and the villagers have no viable option but to vacate. Not a good time for these people."

Collins seemed a good guy, not as expansive in his world view as Dom and Tony but committed to his work. A straight shooter, he had just two months left in his tour. He didn't reveal any misgivings.

Collins decided to stop at an Army compound in Quang Ngai for a few supplies and afterward said they had time for quick refreshment, the place in mind being the windowless compound bar. Amazingly, inside it was wood paneled, air conditioned, and equipped with a color TV showing a basketball game from the States. Collins read Nolan's face.

"Yeah, all the comforts of home. There's a helipad just a few yards away, and a combat platoon can be here drinking cold beer, watching a game, and a few minutes later be dropped into a jungle firefight that's sure to cause casualties. It's surreal."

"I suppose it's a morale thing to have all this, but I would think it would make you schizoid," Nolan offered. He saw two warrant officers, most likely helicopter pilots, get up from their seats and go toward the door. He had read that their job was the most dangerous in Nam. Though versatile, helicopters were not stealth aircraft. He didn't envy the pilots. They risked death every mission. True heroes.

Collins looked around appraisingly at the surroundings. "We have just constructed a bar of sorts in Mo Duc, too, minus the color TV and with limited air conditioning. Funny what you get done during quiet evenings. There isn't much to do in Mo Duc."

Back on the road once more, Collins noted aloud that MoDuc remained some fifteen klicks away, military slang for kilometers. The rice paddies stretched out along either side of the highway, seemingly all the way to the western foothills on Nolan's right. On the shoulder of the road, he saw his first dead VC body, a young man in black pajamas left in a heap like roadkill. Most likely left for family members to collect, the corpse also served as an object lesson for those tempted to join the VC. Collins read Nolan's expression again.

"I'm still not used to seeing that, and yet it's common enough. This area can be dangerous, I'm sure you've heard. The village of My Lai that is being talked about so much in the states these days is less than ten klicks from here. It's best to keep that M-16 ready to fire. You'll hear gunfire now and then and wonder if it's just bored ARVNs shooting in the air or VC snipers aiming at the jeep."

Nolan silently nodded and increased his vigilance scanning the paddies to his right. Back in Song Mao, the team members had talked about My Lai, speculating on how far the Army investigation would go. This area was obviously dangerous, but everything looked normal within the verdant landscape. He saw an occasional farmer, sometimes with a ponderous water buffalo, in the near distance. More mysteriously, the low mountains beyond the paddies stood dark against the horizon. They had seen a corpse, so they knew that violence could erupt without any notice. The paved road lay smoothly before them, and Collins stomped harder on the gas once there were no other vehicles in sight.

"We definitely want to scoot through these paddies," he hollered over the engine noise. "Slowing down or stopping for the next mile or two is not wise."

Nolan instinctively gripped the side bar of the jeep as it accelerated. Conversation became useless. At least, the breeze felt good. No congested areas popped up, just an occasional small bridge with a few ARVNs as guards, and a hut or two sprinkled here and there in the paddies. The jeep reached top speed, and the miles disappeared behind them. After ten klicks or so, without saying anything, Collins suddenly slowed down and made a sharp right onto a rutted dirt road. A few yards further through a makeshift iron gate sat a single-storey building, heavily bunkered and topped by concertina wire, with machine guns protruding from the nests.

"Here we are. This is home," Collins said. Nolan didn't see a smile.

Bleak though the compound was, he resolved not to betray any wary thoughts, focusing solely on the business at hand. He shouldered his gear and followed Collins through the door of the low building. Obviously constructed by the US Army and not local builders, the structure featured drywall on the inside, concrete mostly outside, with much lower ceilings than his Song Mao digs. Collins introduced him to several members of the MACV team including the short and stocky major, Weems, who commanded this small outpost. Counting the major, there were fewer than ten men, and most were career NCOs. He found out later that even Major Weems had served as an NCO initially before seeking a commission. Nolan realized that this was not going to be a group who would welcome him as one of theirs. He was a college kid and an interpreter, an egghead in their eyes. That made him different. No one was outwardly unfriendly, though. He would adjust. If it wasn't the close team at Song Mao, it was probably not much different from most advisory teams in I Corps. Now he could, at least, more fully appreciate D'Amico's irony. He'd "love" Mo Duc. Right.

After eating supper that night, he used the down time to write letters home. He told himself he wasn't homesick, but he knew that he was fortunate to have experienced stability in his life, moving only once in his childhood, from Connecticut to Maine, when he was still young enough to appreciate the adventure of it all. Four years at the same high school, four more at the one college, a year in graduate school, basic training at Fort Dix, and more recently nine months of language school in west Texas—these were big chunks of time without much disruption. Really, he hadn't faced much turbulence in his life, but he feared Quang Ngai province would change all that. His surroundings suggested as much.

First and foremost, he wanted to assure his loved ones back home that things were OK. He wouldn't mention all that he had seen and done, certainly not the corpse. He would give them just the basic facts about where he was and what his job entailed, presenting himself as feeling and doing fine. He had already enlisted family members in sending him some addresses of former teachers he could ask to be references along with grad school application materials for the University of Wisconsin in Madison. A good friend he knew from language school had started his studies there before he himself was drafted, and he told Nolan the English program was good. Maybe more importantly to Nolan, his on-and-off girlfriend currently took classes in another department there, the girl he had mentioned to Woody, someone he still cared about and had visited for a few days after language school finished in Texas. They were not yet a serious item, but they both looked forward to his return and picking up where they left off. He found writing her was a little easier in a way. He could open up a little, but even then he censored himself. He wasn't looking for pity, and he didn't want people to worry any more than they already were. He also found that just writing words to reassure them about his safety made him feel that he could better cope with his new situation. He wasn't telling lies, just omitting what was necessary for him to feel hopeful. So he reasoned.

Collins and Nolan did not conduct their work at a feverish pitch. Even more than team members in Song Mao, they exercised caution in where and when they traveled. Usually, they didn't make appointments with village or camp leaders. It was better, certainly safer, not to announce a schedule. They made exceptions, of course, if an aid shipment was imminent. They needed to monitor the distribution of tin sheets for roofing, bags of cement for building wells, and foodstuff like bulgur, which the Americans substituted for rice. Camp officials compiled names of refugee recipients to justify the amounts distributed, but Collins and Nolan had no certainty that all the names were accurate. Nolan suspected some of the named may not have been residents of the camp and some could even have been deceased. The team chose to content themselves with a more immediate concern that the Vietnamese truck drivers delivered exactly what was on the shipping list and didn't siphon off materials for the black market. Maybe the drivers suspected or even knew that the camp officials padded the number of residents, but they didn't point fingers. They just looked disappointed to hear these idealistic Americans insist that a few bags of cement could not be left in the truck as these materials belonged to the camp dwellers, who obviously needed them badly.

Neither Collins nor Nolan came with an engineering background, so they of necessity took many matters on trust in regard to the work getting done. The wells needed to be free of any contamination from the latrines. Many of the huts depended on bamboo poles for their structure, a plan the displaced farmers accepted out of familiarity. Sheets of tin provided the roofing, which probably represented an upgrade in regard to keeping interiors dry, but runoff presented a problem. Nolan realized that someone with Hal's engineering expertise on the team would have helped considerably. Still, Collins reassured him, their work represented progress. At least, people weren't starving, and the shelter was adequate, though that didn't make up for the deprivation of familiar land and surroundings, let alone one's livelihood.

Accordingly, Collins and Nolan felt justified in disrupting the informal but prevalent system of petty graft that the drivers and other workers practiced. They also saw that the camps' problems would grow with time. While a greater degree of permanence and order reigned there than in the Montagnard camp back in Song Mao, the number of refugees kept growing. Either such camps needed to expand or officials needed to find new locations to handle the influx. All the camps for safety reasons stood close to the highway, so Collins and Nolan could get to them easily enough. Life in these camps must have been boring, Nolan thought. These people, used to working in rice paddies most daylight hours, here had little to do with their time. Camps provided a solution for the short term. The long term was another matter.

A few weeks went by, and the only real change occurred within the team. Collins was being reassigned for his remaining month to Da Nang to help with administrative work at headquarters. A new lieutenant would take his place, but headquarters in Da Nang decided that the new man and Nolan would relocate to the larger MACV compound in Duc Pho about ten miles to the south. The sole Civil Affairs person there was ending his tour. Duc Pho hosted a larger population—there was actually a town—though Mo Duc would remain in the territory for the new team.

Both Nolan and Collins stayed on a while longer as lame ducks. Nolan felt no regret at the prospect of leaving Mo Duc. He sensed that Duc Pho could be an improvement. With Lt. Collins, a man he respected, moving up to Da Nang, he would feel more isolated in Mo Duc. It crossed his mind that Collins may have even suggested to HQ moving the team to Duc Pho. The lieutenant never said anything directly to him about problems at the Mo Duc compound, but he didn't seem particularly happy there either.

Major Weems took great pride in the new bar built into the common room, which was still in a natural state when Nolan arrived. To while away some time, Nolan had been sandpapering to prep it. It wasn't something anyone ordered him to do. He just didn't want to appear idle while off duty in the compound, and the others, not the least the major, would have seen his reading as slacking off or even showing off. He never saw anyone else with a book, and he certainly didn't want to appear antisocial by staying in his room. The others were almost to the man career soldiers. Nolan kept his thoughts to himself, even with Collins. He just marked the time.

Sandpapering the bar's top provided him with a project he could appreciate, as well. It required him to pay attention to detail, though it didn't demand any sophisticated thinking. He liked that the work relaxed his mind. Several steps marked his progress. First, he applied the rough sandpaper, then the fine paper, making sure he moved in the same direction along the grain. He loved the sense of the wood growing smoother, along with the rich, resinous smell of the oak as he worked. The major openly expressed pride in obtaining such a fine piece of lumber. He forbade anyone to place a container of liquid on the surface while the work took place. Surprisingly, this didn't cause Nolan to feel any more pressure. Over two weeks, he spent an hour or so each evening at the task, glad to be free of conversation on other topics. The work made it less likely for him to blunder into speaking his mind about the war, a sentiment he knew he had to keep to himself. The task reached its conclusion. Finally, he realized he couldn't avoid any longer applying the finish. He checked first with Major Weems for a go-ahead. After two coats, applied on successive nights, he stopped. On one hand, he felt satisfied. The bar looked good, and the surface was smooth. But now he lacked diversion.

One afternoon he encountered an AWOL GI outside who wandered into the compound on foot. No weapon, no hat, the fellow acted disoriented, but not completely incapacitated. Nolan brought him inside where Weems and the senior NCO met them at the entrance, curious about the new arrival. Weems immediately began questioning the fellow, who appeared befuddled and could only mutter brief replies, leaving out "sir." The NCO reached out and slapped him on the side of his head.

"You're addressing an officer. Shake out of it, soldier."

Weems smiled briefly at the intervention, and the soldier did start making more sense, claiming he was left behind when the truck carrying him and his buddies stopped for a bathroom break. That might have been case. There was virtually no chance of blending into the surroundings if he had actually intended to escape the war. Nolan recognized the signs of someone stoned, having had his own recent experience in the Da Nang barracks. He suspected the others in the truck had been stoned, too, but he didn't say anything. The major ordered his radio operator to call the soldier's unit, and less than an hour later two burly MPs arrived in a jeep to take the befuddled fellow away.

Afterward, the incident left Nolan wondering how common this was, soldiers getting stoned during daytime hours, losing their bearings, and obviously not doing their jobs. By being on a MACV compound was he shielded from a larger phenomenon of declining military morale? He suspected that it wasn't just fear of death or maiming that would be causing the malaise. More likely, a lack of purpose prevailed, of not seeing positive reasons in what one was doing there amid such alien and dangerous surroundings. He realized that each GI possessed his own perceptions and experiences shaping his perspective, but the influence of his peers on that perspective would matter, too. Working in Civil Affairs gave team members a sense of purpose. Maybe Nolan was lucky, after all.

Occasionally, Collins and Nolan would encounter a convoy of American armored cavalry along Highway One. Collins would pull the jeep over to the side as the huge tanks and armored carriers passed by ever so slowly, like floats in the Rose Bowl parade. Young soldiers, many of them Black, would ride atop these vehicles, usually hatless, sometimes with chains or beads around their necks, and flash a V sign, less for "victory" than for "peace," Nolan thought. Stenciled on the vehicles' sides would be slogans like "Born to raise hell" or names reflecting hometowns—"Newark Reapers" and "Detroit Wheels." These guys put on a brave face, but it had to be a tough grind. The encounters reminded Nolan of his own good fortune as a fellow draftee, as well as how isolated from real Vietnamese culture the American combat GIs really were.

"Somehow our Mo Duc lifestyle doesn't seem so bad, sir." Nolan had never ventured anything remotely like this observation before to Lt. Collins.

"Maybe. I'm not going to miss it too much."

Time passed quickly. Collins was winding up his work. A single incident of note occurred before they left Mo Duc. Joseph Alsop, the renowned columnist and an early "hawk" on the war, was stopping for a visit, fact finding as it were. Seymour Hersh's reporting on the civilian massacre at My Lai may have been the reason why Alsop chose this area, but that went unremarked on the compound. Collins and Nolan went about their business as usual that morning, after Major Weems was satisfied that the small compound looked tidy. They might not have even been aware that Alsop had visited as promised had not their jeep later that day been pressed to move off the road quickly as the one bearing Alsop came barreling the other way on a slapdash run to the helipad. Nolan wondered, was it Alsop's busy schedule that had necessitated the rush, or was this just his way of saying "Let me out of this hellhole"? He never found out, but it was easy to imagine that it was the latter.

Chapter 8: Maybe Tomorrow

Unlike Mo Duc, Duc Pho presented itself as an actual town as well as a district, boasting the main road and a few short cross streets. Along these streets squatted a mix of substantial buildings and much flimsier huts. The MACV advisory team, which consisted of only a single Civil Affairs official before Nolan arrived, occupied a sprawling, two-storey, plaster building just thirty yards or so directly across from the district military headquarters. Both buildings, along with some smaller ones in the rear, stood inside a walled compound in the middle of the town. At first glance, Nolan thought of Fort Apache from American film westerns. The tall gate serving the compound resembled one for a wooden fort, though the surrounding walls appeared to be mainly plaster. Nolan could only hope that those walls could withstand mortar attacks. He didn't see any bunkers at first. Maybe they occupied the roofs. With only a few strands of rusty barbed wire visible atop the exterior walls, the place failed to inspire confidence about defending against an organized attack. In contrast, the Mo Duc compound could rely on a mostly barren frontier as a buffer, rolls of concertina wire impeding enemy infiltration. Here the close proximity of civilian neighbors suggested both support and danger. Nolan welcomed the idea of seeing more people during the day, but at night he preferred a perimeter that looked less permeable. In a war zone having fewer civilians surrounding one's "home" made sleeping easier.

Nolan told himself to suck it up and suppress any apprehension as he did upon first seeing the compound at Mo Duc. He was happy to find that the higher ceilings in the MACV building reduced his sense of claustrophobia. At least here, some natural light actually pervaded the outer rooms. He shared a larger inner room with three other enlisted men, bunks not needed. The others, good-naturedly, made room for him and his gear. He liked the fact that a half dozen Vietnamese regularly came and went between the buildings, not only those who cooked or did laundry, but others, too, some who seemed to have some unofficial capacity on the compound. For all he knew, they might have been the Vietnamese major's spies, but he saw no harm in chatting with them in simple Vietnamese.

He learned that a nickname for Americans, appropriately enough, was mũi dài, which meant "long noses." And while the Vietnamese he met had a sense of wonder about America itself, they considered its people to be mostly lucky rather than industrious, fortunate to have a land so rich in resources, and not particularly good models of behavior. He didn't sense that American soldiers, generally, had impressed people with their intelligence or dignity. However, when he identified himself as a giào sư, stretching the meaning from a full-fledged teacher to his own standing as a prospective teacher with a master's degree, he began to experience deference much greater than a low-ranked American soldier could reasonably expect.

The specter of the Ugly American had established itself some years earlier. Townspeople who met soldiers in their community probably saw almost exclusively the randy and boorish behavior that young men too long in a war zone shamelessly exhibit. Few could speak Vietnamese, and then only a few phrases, so making loud requests in Pidgin English became common currency. "Mama-san" and "Papa-san" were the terms of address, long in use by GIs in Korea and other parts of the Far East. For his part, Nolan asked questions, inquiring about people's family and health. He carefully chose the form most appropriate for address, distinguishing between the levels of acquaintance, marital status, and so on. He spoke softly and smiled, with a slight nod of his head. People felt comfortable around him, despite his foreign height—and long nose.

One visitor that first day, a wiry, weasel-faced man, stood out as more furtive and less interested in making small talk.

When introduced to Nolan, he briefly smiled in a lopsided grin, more a tic than anything genuine. His name was Long, and he barely made eye contact with Nolan, his mind clearly elsewhere. Instead, without a good-bye, he hastened off to a distant corner to confer with Lt. O'Hare, the young baby-faced officer who was a liaison for something called the Phoenix program, which was still to Nolan a mystery. Nolan was learning gradually, though, that not all Vietnamese counterparts were openly friendly. One had to earn their trust.

He didn't receive an especially warm welcome from all the Americans either. Nolan had arrived in Duc Pho before Collins' replacement, so he had hoped to get a chance to talk with Lt. Hobson, the departing team member, for advice about specific challenges facing the new team. Hobson exhibited a red-eyed, drawn appearance, suggesting that he hadn't been sleeping well recently. He hadn't said much to Nolan when they were introduced. A few hours later, when Nolan approached him with questions about the mission in Duc Pho, he didn't seem any more interested in talking.

"Look, Nolan, time's short, and the new officer will have been briefed in Da Nang about the mission. He'll fill you in on the messy details. We can skip those for now. That's your vehicle over there. It's dependable enough, I suppose. You'll need to maintain it. We don't have a motor pool here."

Hobson pointed across the courtyard to a standard Army jeep, nothing distinctive save for the lettering stenciled in white paint beneath the windshield: "Maybe Tomorrow." When Nolan worked with the larger team in Song Mao, Woody took charge of maintaining all the vehicles. No such specialization here apparently. Nolan faced a daunting task.

"Maybe Tomorrow," Nolan muttered aloud. He thought initially that the name referred to a hope of the war ending soon, but it turned out to be much more cynical than that.

"You'll find out for yourself soon enough," Hobson said with a weary frown. "Things don't get done quickly here. Good luck with that."

92

Nolan already knew about the difficulty finding village officials on the visits Lt. Collins and he had made around Mo Duc. In response to their inquiries about the expected return of an official, they, too, had heard the Vietnamese phrase that translated to "Maybe tomorrow." Sometimes he wondered if any officials actually lived in the villages they administered. There would certainly be safer places to stay at night. They knew that the Viet Cong would treat them harshly for having cooperated with the Americans. Death would be likely. Those who survived longest were most likely clever enough to know how to appease both sides with occasional exchanges of information--not necessarily accurate information, but with enough truth to put off suspicion.

Major Stewart, the animated MACV team commanding officer, didn't waste any time in asserting his wishes. "Nolan, I want you to stand watch tonight on the roof. We have a full moon, and that's when Charley likes to be active. He doesn't need any artificial light to move around that would give his presence away. Someone will wake you around two. You'll be on duty until dawn. Think you can handle it?"

"Yes, sir." Nolan thought he could hear a paternal note in the major's voice. Maybe Duc Pho would be a more congenial assignment than Mo Duc.

He probably did sleep an hour or two, but it seemed like only minutes after his head hit the pillow that one of his roommates woke him up for his turn on watch. He was so groggy that he wasn't sure who woke him. Nolan had a flashlight, but he found he didn't need it once he had a few seconds to adjust. The moon shone brightly, so he could easily see his way up the stairs to the roof without other lighting.

Nolan took guard duty very seriously, a first for him in Nam. No way would he doze off. His senses blazed on high alert. The night gave off odors of tropical flowers and petroleum, too late to be cooking oil, he thought, but nevertheless a potent mix. This first watch started very quietly, only occasional artillery fire from the nearby base and that at what he presumed to be distant targets. If any VC were on the prowl, they would move stealthily in a small cadre among the buildings, probably no more than two together, just enough to set up and fire mortars before quickly moving to avoid detection.

He knew better than to stand in the open, which would make him an easy target on the roof. He alternately crouched and sat, comfortable enough to do in the warm air. In villages and camps, he often rested on his haunches like the Vietnamese did, their bums a few inches off the ground to avoid any wetness. You needed to be slim and loose limbed to do that. He was reminded how he and his middle brother, with whom he shared a bedroom growing up, would sometimes on warmer summer nights remove the screen from a window and climb out onto the adjoining sunroom roof. They sat and star gazed, looking for the Big Dipper and constellations they seldom agreed on. For an hour or so they listened to owls that perched in the bordering woods, the darkness here and there lit by fireflies. No question that all kinds of nocturnal animals were roaming around the large yard, separated from the woods by only a low stone wall. Raccoons, deer, and even an occasional moose wandered the nearly three-acre yard, some drawn to the large vegetable garden. Such an adolescent adventure he never thought he would be repeating a half world away. If he could have just put aside the danger this time, it might have been equally as enjoyable.

As dawn neared, he heard rattling noises and a hand pump being worked nearby. In the growing light he detected a few solitary figures scattered about the town. He knew that privacy was a relative matter in Vietnam. He had not forgotten how he had spied on the young woman at the river. Here anyone might bathe in the open air next to a well and stand only partially clothed. But any offense to modesty would be on the part of a person watching, by not granting the bather privacy for what was necessary. From now on, he thought, he would behave more respectfully. So, when he noticed these

94

few solitary figures moving about in different areas below, he checked once to assure himself that no threat was imminent, that these were but morning rituals of the townspeople. Then, he turned his attention elsewhere.

As his sentinel duty drew to a close in the early morning, he thought some more about the months remaining. He hoped to hear about acceptance to graduate school at the University of Wisconsin, his ticket for an early departure from the war zone. As far as he knew, all the paperwork was in, including letters of reference from former professors. With luck, he would soon be at the midpoint of his tour, over the hump, as it were, and able to welcome each remaining morning as one less day to be in peril.

He checked his watch frequently as the light grew, not wanting to appear too eager to relinquish his post. He had hoped he would have an opportunity for a few hours sleep before presenting himself for breakfast, but when he left his post, it was only to lie in bed peacefully for what seemed minutes, not hours. He knew better than to sleep in on his first full day. When he arrived in the dining area after a quick wash up, talk was hushed at the tables, with Major Stewart the first to raise his voice:

"Nolan, ask the cook if she has any mustard."

This was the first test of his language skills, he realized. The question form in Vietnamese did not challenge him. Nolan would address the older woman as Bà. But what was the word for "mustard"? He suspected it was cognate with a French word, though the word wouldn't end in a "d" sound. Had the question been if the woman had seen any tanks or airplanes, he could have asked instantly. The instructors at the language school had drilled such military vocabulary into their students' memory. Now he hesitated. Pho, the major's young interpreter, a slim and taller than average Viet, walked into the room just at that moment.

"Mù tạc," he cued.

"Càm ơn, Pho," Nolan replied with a grateful nod to his rescuer. He made the request, with Major Stewart getting his mustard and a hearty chuckle, as well. Nolan realized he was going to have to build up his vocabulary for these domestic moments, or he would be constantly relying on and thanking the accommodating Pho. And since Pho spent his nights in the Vietnamese barracks some yards away, sometimes Nolan would need to fend for himself.

Besides Major Stewart and Pho, the breakfast group included two lieutenants, O'Hare and the departing Hobson; three older sergeants, all E-7s; a younger E-5; and the radio operator. Another enlisted man, PFC Elston, had apparently finished breakfast and was out in the courtyard working on a carpentry project before the air heated up. The officers all sat at the same table, the senior NCOs at a second, with Nolan sitting at a third with Grabowski, the radio operator, and Pho. This seating arrangement came nowhere near the egalitarian approach back in Song Mao, but neither had the domestic arrangements at Mo Duc, and Nolan had adjusted to those. He didn't know who might become his friends, but he had already established some rapport with Pho the previous afternoon talking in both Vietnamese and English. Pho's gentle and thoughtful demeanor appealed to Nolan. He also saw in the fine-featured young man with the floppy dark hair a resemblance to a good friend from graduate school. They could have been cousins, he thought, though his Bloomington friend was Chinese, not Vietnamese.

As for the compound's leadership, Nolan felt a more benign presence here in Duc Pho. Major Stewart's garrulity suggested a sense of approachability, Nolan thought, the peremptory tone in the dining room notwithstanding. Maybe the Major would not be concerned about spit and polish all that much—that is, as long as he got his mustard.

With their Civil Affairs mission, Hobson and Nolan belonged to USARV (United States Army, Vietnam), a separate chain of command from MACV (Military Advisory Command,

Vietnam). While the Civil Affairs team received orders from company headquarters in Nha Trang, Major Stewart as the ranking officer oversaw all the US personnel and called the shots about various duties and responsibilities for the upkeep and defense of the American part of the compound. His counterpart, Major Thieu, ran the operations on the Vietnamese side of the compound.

As in Mo Duc, gasoline-powered generators supplied the electricity for the compound.   From what Nolan knew of these generators, outages occurred rather frequently, not only because fuel ran out, but also because some part failed. Someone who had good mechanical sense needed to maintain them, a requirement that ruled him out, Nolan thought.

Major Stewart had already told him that everyone including the junior officers took turns manning the compound's radio at night to spell Grabowski. In the evening, calls came from local artillery units requesting political clearance to fire shells at suspected Viet Cong movement. Major Thieu provided the locations of friendly Vietnamese units each night to Major Stewart, and radio operators would plot these on a map with grids. For the artillery units to receive permission to fire at a target, five hundred meters distance from these friendly units constituted the minimum. Plotting the coordinates demanded accuracy, as did calibration of the big guns by US artillery.

Major Stewart considered guard duty at night on the roof necessary only when the moon was full. Still, Nolan recognized that he would be losing some sleep every few nights because of radio duty. Grabowski told him that later that afternoon he would give him the lowdown on procedures, but for the short term he remained at loose ends. He heard that the new lieutenant would be arriving that afternoon. He had time to reconnoiter on the second floor that housed a large lounge, with a refrigerator and a make-shift projection booth. Grabowski, a friendly, bespectacled guy, said that films about a year out of distribution in the States apparently arrived weekly along with pallets of American beer by helicopter every once in a while. When he was a boy, Nolan had watched his grandfather run a projector in a movie theater on two occasions, so he would be able to help out in that capacity if needed. The pecking order expected, even without anything said, that he make himself useful during down time, as he had when sanding and varnishing the bar top in Mo Duc. He accepted the role without resentment.

For diversion, boxes of paperback books in new condition occasionally arrived at compounds courtesy of the USO. He picked up a copy of M. Scott Momaday's *House Made of Dawn* from the top of an open box on the floor. It didn't look like he would have any problem getting first choice for his reading material since the box was still full. He wondered if books were stored elsewhere around the room, but he didn't see any reading material on the other tables except for a copy of the military newspaper *Stars and Stripes*. Being alone for the time being, he sat down to read a few pages of Momaday's novel, allotting himself no more than fifteen minutes. He treasured these times in Vietnam when he could escape into a faraway place, someone else's imaginative world. Otherwise, the military's customs and protocol controlled so much of his day. He knew, of course, that Momaday wrote from his experience about the harsh reality of many Native Americans, the short, tragic lives on a Southwest reservation. Nolan had learned in school that the European settlers of the United States and their descendants had caused great pain for the natives, similar to the pain the Vietnamese had incurred from invasions. The circumstances described in the novel did not make for light reading. Still, it pleased him immensely to steal just a few minutes for himself. He had felt uncomfortable being seemingly the sole reader on the Mo Duc compound.

He remembered some writer's quip about the pleasure one could find reading in an unshared bed. For a few minutes anyhow, he had the entire second floor to himself. He appreciated the quiet and sense of security, so much more relaxing than guard duty no matter how pleasant the night air had been. He read quickly, hungry for a far-off experience.

    With the job-weary Hobson on his way north to Da Nang, Nolan's new boss, Lieutenant Hardy, arrived that afternoon by helicopter. He appeared not much older than Nolan, though stockier, with a high forehead and a capable air about him. When they shook hands, Hardy, in a modulated Southern accent, expressed his desire to get the lay of the land the next morning— "if that would somehow accommodate" Nolan. Both the polite circumlocution and the plan sat well with Nolan. While he had seen some of the villages between Mo Duc and Duc Pho, he still felt like a newcomer here.

    Late in the afternoon, they both got to meet Mr. Nguyen, the district welfare officer, a thirtyish man of slight stature with a wispy moustache. He wore a white long-sleeve shirt open at the neck, dark pants, and flip-flop sandals, what would prove over time to be his basic uniform. He was friendly and seemingly dedicated to his work. Nolan liked him right away, and he realized he liked Lt. Hardy, too, who was patient with him when he fumbled now and then interpreting the conversation. The thought of spending so much time together riding in the jeep, visiting camps and villages to oversee projects and distribution of supplies didn't daunt him as much as it did a few hours earlier. They would make a good team, he decided.

    In bed that night, he fell off to sleep within a minute, it seemed, as he was likely making up for the early rise that morning for guard duty. He was hopeful that he could sleep straight through. He dreamed about Song Mao, the first time that had happened since the 41st CA had disbanded. In the dream he interacted with his former comrades in the old kitchen, laughing about some unidentified event that had happened, a happy one, a comic misadventure he had experienced with Woody, apparently. Something in town? He could hear Dom's laugh, not loud—more like a cackle. With his distinctive self-deprecatory gestures, Woody held court, his raspy voice rising and falling, and Nolan enjoying his tale as much as everybody else.

But the scene suddenly blurred. He could feel a hand on his shoulder. It was still dark as he opened his eyes.

"Nolan, we're being mortared. You need to get up."

Nolan was struck by how gentle Sgt. Harris's voice was. Harris, his E-5 roommate, clearly didn't want the newcomer to panic. As Nolan stood up, his head slowly cleared. In his undershorts and barefoot, he moved quickly through the dim hallway, toting his M-16 and a cloth bandolier holding several clips of shells. He didn't know where Harris had gone. He could hear a voice from the radio room, someone reporting the attack. Crouching as he moved, he followed the light from the building's doorway, stopping briefly to slam an ammo clip into the rifle stock. He had no idea if the VC were attempting to penetrate the compound, but he watched and listened for movement, his heart racing. He had heard only two, possibly three, shells land outside the building, none that close. From the doorway over to the other side of the courtyard, he noticed a few wafts of smoke, but no visible damage. Excited Vietnamese voices rose in the distance, along with a smattering of gunfire.

After a few moments, he heard steps behind him. Lt. Hardy appeared at his side. "See anything?" Nolan's mind flashed back to a moment in Song Mao and Walker's question in the bunker.

"No, sir. Just a little smoke."

No additional incoming rounds hit the compound. Hardy and Nolan remained quiet, letting their eyes and ears focus on the courtyard. Nolan's senses strained for clarity. Crouching in the dark, Nolan became aware that he had shaken off all of his initial sleepiness. Now embarrassment distracted him. He realized that he might have slept through the entire episode had Harris not awakened him. After a few more minutes, the

Major came up behind them, his voice reedier than at the table the previous morning.

"Hit and run, most likely. I'll check with Major Thieu about any casualties."

Nolan and Hardy watched as the Major, in his combat helmet and armored vest, warily traversed the courtyard in a pronounced crouch. Hardy glanced back at Nolan from the doorway, his stocky figure in silhouette.

"I assume this disturbance passes for hospitality in Duc Pho. The folks back home in South Carolina would surely be appalled."

"Better not tell them, sir. We want to keep this beautiful spot all to ourselves and discourage rampant tourism."

Hardy laughed. His first night in Duc Pho and Nolan's second had turned out to be much more anxiety-ridden than either expected. Nolan hoped whatever the morning brought would be decidedly more peaceful. Sleep would come hard. This new brush with death had unnerved him. Yet he knew the full-moon activity would soon pass, and in a day or two he could probably count on more rest, that is, unless the VC were beginning a new offensive like Tet. Not out of the question, he thought, even with the large US presence. Slowly, with the air bearing more light, he realized he wouldn't be returning to bed again this time as he did yesterday morning after guard duty. It was already tomorrow, arriving just a little prematurely. Time to get back to work.

Within a quarter hour, Major Stewart returned from his impromptu briefing with Major Thieu. He reported that no one on the compound had incurred injury and that damage was minor, which seemed to relax the men enough so that they could resume normal conversation. No one, of course, admitted openly to any fear. Nolan was aware that the others were vetting him, making sure that they could rely on the new guy.

Hardy, of course, shared the initiation, and he weathered the incident calmly. Nolan hoped that augured well for their work together. They needed not only to get along but to pick up each other's spirits from time to time, as well. Nolan wanted so much to believe that they would work well together.

An hour or two later, Nolan could see in greater light that a shed's roof had collapsed under the shelling, and a few shallow craters marked the courtyard. Otherwise, the compound seemed the same as the day before. The sappers, probably no more than a half-dozen, may have realized that the proximity of the artillery base made sticking around foolhardy. This attack served more likely as primarily a message, something to annoy the compound residents, as if to say, "We're capable of going anywhere. Fear us."

Chapter 9: Counterparts

Following the well-trodden path between the village and the paved roadway, Nolan had walked back to the jeep to get the small black notebook he used to jot down assorted items during his daily forays. It was not yet hot, actually a very pleasant morning, and his boots seemed lighter than they had felt the previous afternoon in a nearby refugee camp. On his return leg, he caught sight of Lt. Hardy and Mr. Nguyen standing next to each other by a recently completed well, attempting to converse in broken English and Vietnamese, with a little sign language thrown in, too. What struck him more than their earnest conversation, though, was the physical contrast. The stocky, young American in US Army fatigues weighed in at just under two hundred pounds or so, and the thin, almost fragile-looking Viet couldn't weigh more than two-thirds that much. The straggly mustache above the latter's lip attempted, perhaps, to lend some social stature to a thirty-two-year-old man who might otherwise be confused with a teenager.

These men were counterparts: the American Civil Affairs officer and the Duc Pho district welfare officer. Nolan acted as their go-between, decidedly more informal with the two of them in private than they were with each other. His language ability facilitated their communication, but from what Nolan could see, each of them certainly respected and liked his counterpart, and in time might need a go-between less. It was Lt. Hardy's idea to address his opposite as "Mr. Nguyen," using the family name instead of a given name, which ran counter to the Vietnamese tradition. Hardy, of course, Nolan referred to as "Lt. Hardy" or "Trung úy" (First Lieutenant) when the three of them were together. Hardy felt these choices struck a good balance between formality and friendliness. On every occasion, it seemed, Mr. Nguyen appeared to appreciate the slight lean toward formality, greeting the Americans with a nod and a shy, slightly lopsided smile, though never compromising his dignity.

As team members, Nolan and Hardy, naturally, got to know one another very quickly. Riding side by side in Maybe Tomorrow, and later during most evenings in their building, they conversed about work as well as their backgrounds. They didn't use first names, but after a few days Nolan felt comfortable asking the Lieutenant about his.

"Sir, is Reginald a Southern name?"

"No, when I was in school, it stood out. I made sure to play football and wrestle in high school to deal with all the teasing. My friends called me "Reg" or "Reggie," though the teachers preferred calling me "Reginald." It must be a British name. My granddaddy, still a young bachelor then, hustled right over from England to claim the family property when his older brother died suddenly."

"Your mother and your father were American born, then? She probably had roots in South Carolina, right?"

"That she did. A descendant of plantation owners, which my father's side didn't particularly appreciate since they abhorred the concept of slavery. My mother wasn't racist, though, if that's what you're thinking."

"Not at all. "

Nolan didn't want to admit that the thought had crossed his mind.

"So, your dad was a farmer, then?"

"No, he was a lawyer, more a gentleman farmer. He made clear that he wanted his children to achieve in school and not just be a good ol' boy or a Southern belle. That's how I and my sister might have ended up. I liked math and science, so I went on to get a business degree at South Carolina while taking quite a few engineering courses, too. I think that's why I got assigned to Civil Affairs."

"Makes sense to me. I took a whole bunch of foreign languages in both high school and college, and here I am."

104

"I guess the Army gets some things right now and then."

Nolan didn't mention his doubts about his eventual Vietnam assignment when he had first arrived and his great relief at not being assigned a combat role. He also felt gratified that his job served a beneficial purpose. Helping refugees and needy villagers left him little time or interest in dwelling on the reasons he possessed for opposing the war or his resentment at being drafted. He liked his job. He was getting better at it, to boot.

Befitting his gentlemanly demeanor, the Lieutenant reciprocated by asking Nolan a few questions about his background. He expressed particular interest in Nolan's siblings.

"Three brothers and a sister, and all five of you college educated. That's quite an achievement, for your parents especially. They must have set some goals for you, same as mine. I didn't show interest in the law, which disappointed my father somewhat. He didn't begrudge me my interests, though. I think he likes the fact that I am a problem solver, even if I can't claim the problems are of any magnitude."

"Well, sir, I'm glad you have some practical skills. Wish I had more. Civil Affairs has its challenges."

"I must say, Nolan, I didn't expect to see so many refugees. It makes me appreciate how fortunate we both were to grow up in middle-class America, between wars, and without any invading forces."

"Not the Indian perspective, though, right?" Momaday's novel was still fresh in Nolan's mind.

"No, definitely not. Let's just say that most of us growing up had it good, at least in our generation."

It was too soon to talk about their love lives. Nolan knew that Hardy was single from earlier conversation around the compound. To Nolan, marriage appeared distant on the horizon because, in his mind, being married meant having first a solid economic base. He lacked that, for sure. He remembered his mother's comment that rural Irish men often marry late because they must first inherit land to make a match. Maybe the custom carried over to America. So far neither of his older brothers had married. He did try to earn enough in summer jobs to take pressure off his father paying tuition. Loans and a small scholarship at Holy Cross helped, but he was always scrambling to stay afloat. Even after having been a grad student for only one full year and working a part-time job much of that time, he had wiped out his savings. He had become aware that his local draft board in Maine placed single men at the top of its induction list, but he never wanted to rush into marriage just to fend off the draft. That seemed imprudent, and prudence was a virtue his father especially esteemed.

He knew from a brother's experience with one year of Air Force ROTC that ROTC wasn't for him. All that marching around and standing for inspections struck him as silly. Still, he was not surprised to hear that Hardy had finished Army officer training in college. Not only did financial benefits attract many young men, but also the University of South Carolina probably possessed a campus environment that harbored few objections about the military presence. South Carolina itself was a conservative state, and the state university experienced little political protest in the 60s over the growing US involvement in Southeast Asia, certainly compared to other large public universities in the Midwest and on the West Coast.

Despite these differences, Nolan and Hardy shared a background of middle-class stability, each raised in two-parent households. They fully expected to follow their parents' lead. After the Army, they would probably remain bachelors a short while, though they could see marriage and family not that far down the road. America was undergoing major changes politically, but despite the new emphasis on "free love," basic family structure remained more or less constant.

Finding out Mr. Nguyen's background took Nolan much more time. The first day they had met Nolan had asked the affable welfare officer if he was married, one of the first questions the locals often put to him. Mr. Nguyen had said 'yes,' and that he had two children, a boy and a girl. After hearing their names and ages, Nolan asked how long he had been in this current position.

"Two years," he responded in Vietnamese, adding that before landing this position in Duc Pho he had worked as an assistant to the welfare officer in Quang Ngai city. He smiled but said nothing more. Nolan quashed the impulse to ask him if he enjoyed what he did. He suspected that the job did not pay well, but it was steady work with all the recent American aid made available to the district. A father of two children needed to be practical, not dreamy.

It was another week or so before Nolan asked about Mr. Nguyen's early years, and then only because the two of them had a few moments to themselves one morning in the courtyard while waiting for Hardy to join them. The young man had grown up in Quang Ngai City, his father a shopkeeper, his mother a seamstress before marriage. She later gave birth to three children. She continued to take in some work to supplement the shop's income. Life was hard growing up. He had been too young to be drawn into the efforts to break with French rule, not that his family were political. His father tried to get along with everyone. Running a shop, he knew affability was better for business. He encouraged his children to be friendly, too. That much Nolan learned at a snail's pace from some new vocabulary that Mr. Nguyen had written down in Nolan's notebook, recorded in the careful script that the Civil Affairs team became accustomed to seeing on the various inventories Mr. Nguyen prepared for visits to camps and villages.

What about Mr. Nguyen's military service? Nolan wondered. It appeared that he hadn't been in the army recently. Picturing the gentle young man as a soldier beggared the imagination, yet Nolan had seen many Vietnamese soldiers of similar slight physique. He saw them struggling with the weight of their packs as they prepared for a military operation, never being quite able to stand erect with the heavy load on their backs.

Mr. Nguyen didn't volunteer any information about the intervening years between childhood and marriage other than to say he had learned bookkeeping while in school. His teachers praised him for his diligence. He said that with quiet pride in his voice, not so much to tout his skills, as to suggest he had found his niche as a civil servant. Unlike for Nolan and Hardy, higher education at a university never arose as an option for him. Growing up at a distance from cities with universities, he dutifully focused more on how he might help his father with the shop. Somehow early on he understood that an eye toward detail and hard work were his best chance to earn a steady income.

Shortly after the new team's arrival in Duc Pho, Mr. Nguyen, in a welcoming gesture, had invited both men to dinner at his makeshift house behind the compound. They sat on mats placed on the small main room's floor, together with Mrs. Nguyen and the two small children. Nolan could draw on his experience eating Vietnamese food during meals with teachers in El Paso and later in Song Mao cafés, so he could tell the Nguyens applied spices much less liberally for the sake of their American guests. He took the initiative and praised the rice and chicken, small slices of the latter Mrs. Nguyen mixed with the rice and steamed vegetables. He could see Hardy was doing his best to show appreciation with smiles and simple Vietnamese phrases, though this was a new experience for him. The Lieutenant had presented their hosts with flowers and cigarettes purchased on the main street earlier in the day. Nolan had found some paper toys in the marketplace for the children. Both men knew that the Nguyens could not afford to have guests frequently, and while Major Stewart didn't appear ready to host Vietnamese visitors at the compound, the

108

Americans could reciprocate by treating Mr. Nguyen to afternoon beverages at roadside cafés or up in the compound lounge.

Gaining each other's trust was proceeding well, Nolan thought, after just a few weeks of cooperation. An incident, however, at the compound one Saturday raised some doubts for the team. Unannounced, a heavyset, middle-aged man, dressed in a clean but worn white shirt, arrived at the entrance asking to speak to the Civil Affairs officer. Nolan introduced Hardy and himself, and the man identified himself as Si (pronounced "She") from the village of An Ke. He knew Hobson, he said, because of his stops at the village. Looking around warily, he asked to talk in private. No one was in the upstairs lounge, so the three men climbed the stairs for their talk.

Si wasted little time getting to his reason for the visit. He said his village was supposed to receive a shipment of building materials through Mr. Nguyen and Civil Affairs weeks ago, but so far nothing had been delivered. Hardy looked surprised when Nolan translated.

"I'm not aware of anything being scheduled for An Ke. Let me check our records right now. Excuse me. I'll be back in a few minutes."

Hardy got up and went downstairs as Nolan translated for Si. While waiting, Nolan and Si made small talk, asking about each other's families and such. Nolan detected nervousness and some reticence from the guest, who sat somewhat stiffly, his eyes wandering about the room. Hardy returned after ten minutes.

"I couldn't find anything about a shipment being scheduled. I'm positive that I didn't hear anything about it during my orientation in Da Nang either. Maybe, Mr. Nguyen has a record of the schedule."

With Nolan translating, Si replied that would certainly be so.

"I don't want to cause trouble," he added. "Perhaps, this is because Major Thieu wishes it."

"Why do you say that, Mr. Si?" Nolan asked in Vietnamese.

Si shook him off. "I don't want to cause trouble," he repeated.

Nolan translated for Hardy when Si said nothing further.

The Lieutenant squinted. "What has this got to do with Major Thieu's wishes?"

When Nolan put the question into Vietnamese, Si raised a single finger to his lips. Nolan detected a slight smile, he thought, but then Si looked away.

"We will take it from here," Hardy assured Si. "You will hear from us in a few days, after I have asked Mr. Nguyen about the shipment."

Si asked that his name not be mentioned, which seemed odd to Nolan, but the Lieutenant agreed. After handshakes, they descended to the ground floor, and Si left immediately, not pausing for any further talk. Nolan wasted no time in expressing his puzzlement.

"That was strange, sir. While we haven't known Mr. Nguyen a long time, I can't see him overlooking a shipment. He's very meticulous with his paperwork."

"I'm thinking the same. The mention of Major Thieu intrigues me. Why wouldn't he want An Ke to get this shipment? I may have to get Major Stewart's insights here without making a big deal of it."

"Could it relate to money, do you think? Expectations about some kind of payment?"

"I don't want to go there yet, Nolan. This is going to require some careful handling. For now, don't say anything to anybody, especially to Mr. Nguyen, until I'm ready to move on it. That man acted very uneasy with us. I got the feeling that he saw danger in what he was doing."

"I had the same feeling. I just don't see Mr. Nguyen taking any money under the table, not from the modest life he's living. I'd hate to find out differently."

110

"Me, either. Maybe he's just trying to hold onto his job, doing what he's told to do. Look, we can be patient and look into the matter on our own, quietly. I don't want to make a fuss without having more information. Again, keep it on the QT for now."

Nolan knew the silence mattered more around Mr. Nguyen than anyone else. He felt uncomfortable having suspicions and keeping the An Ke matter out of their conversations, but he figured the Lieutenant was right. Better to take the slow, cautious approach.

He found out that Hardy made getting answers a top priority. On Monday morning, Hardy told him at breakfast that they would make an impromptu visit to An Ke to assess needs. The Lieutenant would leave a message for Mr. Nguyen that they had other Army business to attend to and would touch base with him later in the day. Once they were alone in Maybe Tomorrow, he opened up about a conversation he had had Sunday with Major Stewart.

"The Major said he tries to stick to military advice unless Major Thieu asks specifically about something. Sure, there might be some money exchanged in the civil administration of the district. He hears that buying favors is endemic in Vietnam. As long as the military mission is not negatively affected, he isn't going to pry into civilian matters. He recommends that we do the same."

Nolan didn't want to press the matter. How much change could the team bring about to the local system without alienating all the officials they worked with? It made sense, too, to see first if Si had spoken accurately about the village's situation.

To neither man's surprise, Si was not around to greet them, nor did any official greet them as they walked through the village. A few curious onlookers watched them from a distance. From what the Americans could see, An Ke's needs fell somewhere in the middle on a prioritized list of camps and villages. Nothing seemed particularly extraordinary. Some huts needed roofing repairs, either new tin sheets or scraps for mending problem areas. The wells had been there for decades, it appeared, so bags of cement for new ones made sense. The small, aging school showed cracks here or there in the foundation and in the walls, and definitely could use some paint. Compared to the refugee camps, no crisis existed concerning living conditions. Like so many villages and hamlets, An Ke could benefit from some sprucing up.

"Well, at least it's not a disaster area," Hardy remarked. "It would really bother me if I thought Mr. Nguyen was hiding something like that."

Nolan nodded. "We still haven't heard his side of this. Maybe he has a reasonable explanation for the omission in the schedule."

"Yeah, let's ask him this afternoon. I'll try to bring it up without raising too much suspicion. I also want to contact HQ to see if Hobson has any information worth hearing. I don't know if he's left the Army or is being reassigned somewhere stateside. It may take a while to track him down."

"Talking with Mr. Nguyen, sir, could we suggest it was a coincidence that we stopped at An Ke, having the time on our way back and realizing that it was a village we had not yet visited?"

"A half-truth of sorts? True, we haven't seen the village before. OK, I can live with that, but I hope that we don't get some song and dance from him. I like the guy."

Nolan didn't feel comfortable either. He wasn't eager to see Mr. Nguyen tested this way. So far, he had enjoyed their partnership, too.

Around three in the afternoon, Mr. Nguyen arrived at the entrance to the Americans' building, his demeanor both genial and diffident, as usual. The three men quickly went up to the lounge to talk. Hardy started off by inquiring about his counterpart's family, expressing the hope that everyone was well. Then he got straight to the point, talking about the team's stop at An Ke earlier in the day and his curiosity about any shipment of materials there might be in the works. Translating, Nolan noted Mr. Nguyen's look of surprise at the question. After a short pause, the welfare officer said indeed a shipment was planned, but some paperwork remained to be completed. He smiled tentatively while Nolan translated for Hardy.

"Paperwork?" the Lieutenant asked, being careful not to smile back. "Is that something we could expedite somehow? There appear to be some significant needs in An Ke."

Hearing Nolan's translation, Mr. Nguyen looked directly at Hardy and then spoke in Nolan's direction, the gist being that he would need to consult his records for details. More tight-lipped than usual, Nolan noted.

"Fine," said Hardy. "Could we talk about it again tomorrow?"

Mr. Nguyen said, "OK." An awkward pause followed. No more to do now. Nolan seized the opening to offer Mr. Nguyen a beer and he got a nod in response. Smiles emerged all around as Nolan handed out the cans. Hardy offered a toast: "To partners."

After a half hour of good-natured talk with everyone pretending nothing was amiss, Mr. Nguyen left. Nolan immediately turned to Hardy.

"A lot of truth in his statement, sir, considering that cash is paper, too. Maybe he topped our half-truth."

Quickly, Hardy put the beer can to his lips for one last swallow.

"Excuse me, Nolan. I need to contact HQ by radio and make some inquiries before business ends there for the day."

Nolan knew Hardy wanted to send out a message that would eventually get to Lt. Hobson without any further delay, so the abrupt good-bye didn't surprise him. Nolan could get some reading done with the extra time, always a pleasure. He felt glad to have the awkward meeting over so quickly.

An hour or so later in the dining room Hardy appeared to be in a good mood, cheerfully chatting with the other officers at their table. Nolan took a seat with the other enlisted men, but he caught a glance from Hardy along with a raised eyebrow. The gesture puzzled him, but he saw that the Lieutenant's mood remained jovial.

The next morning the Civil Affairs team did not rush off in the jeep. They spoke casually in the courtyard while waiting for Mr. Nguyen, who appeared a few minutes later than his usual time, eager to talk. Hardy suggested they talk inside, out of the sun. The three men climbed the stairs again to the lounge and sat down in a semicircle of chairs, Nolan in the middle. With a gentle smile, Mr. Nguyen said that he had checked his records and talked with Major Thieu, who indicated that the delay in shipment to An Ke might not last that much longer. Nolan translated.

Hardy smiled broadly and leaned forward. "Excellent news. And the timing couldn't be better. I've just heard from HQ in Da Nang that An Ke has been chosen to be the village in Duc Pho that will receive a special award in the new 'A Better Tomorrow' program. American and Vietnamese officials are interested in documenting positive changes in rural locales— press releases and photographs to be made available. I told HQ that An Ke would be a perfect choice in Duc Pho district."

Nolan was hearing this for the first time, not sure he was getting a clear picture, but he cobbled together a translation as best he could.

His eyes widening just a tad, Mr. Nguyen took the news without any clear sign of alarm, saying that Major Thieu would be pleased to hear that. In fact, he would tell him that morning, and a minute or two later, after a hasty good-bye, he scurried off.

"How come, sir, we haven't heard about this program before?" Nolan asked, leaning forward in his seat. "You would think we would get a heads-up to be thinking about the worthiest locations."

"Let's just say, Nolan, that HQ can take a suggestion now and then."

"You mean this program is your own idea?"

"Well, I thought the shipment could be sped up a little. And Mr. Nguyen doesn't need to play the patsy any longer. He might eventually figure things out on his own regarding this award, but public recognition such as this has to help his job security, wouldn't you think? I suspect Major Thieu will be grateful as well for the positive publicity and won't begrudge his lost payments. They couldn't have been a large amount, but large enough for the villagers to balk."

"Pretty smooth, sir. I don't think I would be your match in a chess game. But 'A Better Tomorrow' has a familiar ring. Isn't that some corporate slogan?"

"You might be right, Nolan. I should have consulted you before talking with Mr. Nguyen. My apologies."

"No need, but thanks. You did some quick thinking"

He mused a few seconds more on Hardy's ingenuity. Was everything so easily settled, he wondered.

"Hmm, won't Major Thieu be suspicious if he doesn't hear anything to confirm An Ke's selection?"

"HQ will cover for us there, though I will probably need your help with some paperwork to make it all look good. Sound OK?"

"I assume you don't mean cash, sir."

"Definitely not, Nolan. Just some official-looking announcement."

Nolan nodded emphatically. He liked Hardy's style. The man got things done.

"Count me in."

Chapter 10: Scrounging

Like the Americans at Mo Duc, those in the Duc Pho compound lived largely by their wits. This proved true not only outside the compound where danger was the greatest, but also inside. Without a mess hall on the compound, the men received a compensatory stipend in their pay statements for "separate rations." Ostensibly, they relied on the local Vietnamese marketplaces, and they hired their own cook. Nolan liked Vietnamese food, having been introduced to it through his teachers' social invitations back in El Paso and later through Mr. Nguyen's hospitality. While not a particularly adventurous eater, he enjoyed delicately cooked chicken with steamed vegetables, and rice with nuóc mắm, a spicy fish sauce fermented in outdoor pits tended by villagers. Nolan acknowledged it as an acquired taste. Few of his fellow team members would hazard even a sample of the fish sauce, once hearing that the locals aged it in pits. They wanted good, reliable American chow. Exotic was out. Nolan discovered that Major Stewart encouraged a particular bartering system to keep expenditures as low as possible in acquiring this food as well as other essentials. The men called it scrounging.

NCOs stood out as the most reliable food scroungers. It made sense. Seniority ruled the mess halls, typically overseen by E-7s who had served at least ten years in the Army. If advisers of that rank didn't actually know someone running a mess hall at a local base, they could probably at least find sympathetic ears among those overseers of similar backgrounds. So, a Latino NCO like Sgt. Hernandez could seek out a mess hall with a Latino NCO in charge; Sgt. Childress could seek out a fellow black NCO, and so forth. They garnered food, especially meats, not only of excellent quality, but just as importantly, free. This reduced the need to shop the local marketplace, though Nolan enjoyed that activity and often wandered about the stalls in the early mornings talking with the vendors. The others preferred to indulge in their American favorites.

As far as Nolan knew, no money ever changed hands during scrounging. The providers got special favors, though. If a targeted NCO wanted a night in town off base, maybe in the company of a prostitute if he wished, the Duc Pho MACV compound, sitting quite centrally in the town, provided a convenient starting point and often a bed later for the returning reveler. It was not unusual to find an extra soldier or two around for breakfast, particularly on weekends. From what Nolan saw, no one questioned the system's legitimacy. That was just the way the MACV compounds operated.

Typically, Major Stewart would ask an insinuating comment at breakfast, such as: "Sgt. Hernandez, do you think your friend at LZ Bronco, Sgt. Martinez, might be able to part with a portion of pork today? I haven't had a good pork roast in a long time."

"I'll see what I can do, sir."

Nolan never joined the quest for food, but he did need a motor pool. Since the assigned motor pool for the Civil Affairs jeep operated many miles away in Da Nang, he had a problem getting parts and repairs. Nolan soon realized he needed to think locally. He never thought he would have the same advantage that the NCOs had, a military and ethnic brotherhood, so to speak. Nor did he think he would find many fellow graduate students of literature either. Though he lacked experience scrounging, he couldn't put off a trial run indefinitely.

One morning he set off to a local artillery base with more than a little hesitance. Though Hardy had said nothing, Nolan couldn't help but notice that the jeep's tires were wearing. Because his rank was Specialist 4th Class, equivalent to only a corporal, he decided against approaching an NCO of higher rank at the motor pool. He would certainly skirt any officer, too. Instead, he buttonholed a young, slouching guy of the same rank.

"Hey, man, I got a problem. My jeep's tires are shot, and our motor pool is up in Da Nang. Can you help me out?"

No guile involved, he just laid out his need. He expected that he might have to extol the benefits of a short R&R in Duc Pho as a bartering chip, but that proved unnecessary.

"Not a problem, my friend. Pull the jeep into that bay and we'll get you fixed up in a jiff."

With name tags ironed onto their shirts, the two young men skipped introductions. They chewed the fat, commiserating on their slow-moving tours, and cracked a joke or two while another young GI helped with the task.

A little over a half hour later Nolan drove away with four new tires mounted on Maybe Tomorrow and an invitation to come back if he needed any other parts. He felt proud of himself. His new friend might have done the same for anyone who asked, especially if the one asking didn't assume that the help should be automatic. Yet the bond seemed so immediate: one GI weary of strict military protocol and the attendant paperwork helping another GI out. If ever he needed a favor in return, the fellow would ask for it, and Nolan was sure to give him another chance to ask. No telling what would go next on the jeep.

The following evening Nolan was parking the jeep in the makeshift carport under the basketball backboard as Major Stewart walked by on his way back from a confab with Major Thieu. When Stewart saw the jeep, he did a double take.

"Are those new tires, Nolan?"

"Good evening, sir. Yes, they are."

"Nice. My jeep could use tires, too."

He cast a downward look at Nolan to indicate he had finished speaking.

"Uh-huh. I'll look into that, sir. I can't go to the well so soon again, but later, I could try."

118

As it turned out, Major Stewart could not wait that long. Seeing the Civil Affairs jeep look so much less shabby than his own was just too much to bear. Within a week, he ordered the radio operator, Grabowski, to trek over to the motor pool. Grabowski got the same result, likely because Nolan tipped him off to look for someone of the same rank. Nolan felt he was doing Grabowski, a likable, hardworking guy, as much of a favor as he was the Major. He didn't want Grabowski to take flak if he failed to make a connection. He was passing along some good karma.

Nolan's biggest coup, though, came about two weeks later. A chopper dropped some pallets of bulgur near the compound. However, Hardy and Nolan didn't have a truck to transport the heavy burlap bags to their destination, a small fishing village at the southern end of the province. Nolan returned to the base motor pool hoping to find his new friend, but he wasn't working that day. Another Spec 4 came through, and Nolan drove back to the compound in a borrowed two-and-a-half-ton truck, familiarly known as a "deuce and a half." Up to then, he had never driven anything larger than the 3/4-ton in Song Mao.

The next morning, with Nolan at the wheel and Mr. Nguyen and Hardy as passengers in the cab, the truck rolled down Highway One. To load and unload the truck, Mr. Nguyen found two middle-aged men, who rode sitting atop the bulky bags in the covered back. The team delivered the bulgur to the happy fishermen, short on rice that season. In return, they gave Nolan several squid for that night's dinner at the compound, not that something of comparable value was expected. The squid were a gift.

On the way down and back, the truck passed a US Army tank perched on an outcropping. The tank guarded the road at a point where the mountains converged on the coastline, merely a small stretch of sand lying below the road. A few GIs gamboled in the water, carefree with their security provided up on the road. Nolan remembered how warm the ocean water had been at the beach in Nha Trang a few months back. It was such a contrast to the near frigid waters of the Atlantic on the coast of Maine, cold even in August. Lobsters love cold water. Bathers in Maine often took several minutes wading up to their waists to allow their bodies some time to adjust to the cold. Here one could just dive forward into the waves and remain submerged for many seconds without jarring any nerve endings. Driving by on the return trip, Nolan longed to join the GIs in the water, to float a few minutes on the gentle undulations of the azure sea. But the team needed to get the truck back to the artillery base.

His mind wandered. He imagined glossy travel brochures in succeeding years touting the unspoiled beaches of Vietnam. Maybe venture capitalists would spur the government to build an international airport nearby with luxury hotels dotting the coastline, offering cocktails all around for the pampered guests in their cabanas. He sniggered at the thought, since he knew the beauty of such unspoiled places was fleeting.

As the truck rounded a curve just beyond the tank's position, the cab's passengers caught a wide view of the placid, sun-kissed sea. Such beauty, Nolan thought. At that exact moment, automatic gunfire broke out from the rear of the truck. What was happening? Nolan didn't have his rifle in the cab because there was no room for it. Nolan exchanged startled looks with Hardy and Mr. Nguyen, but the shooting stopped abruptly after the initial burst.

They quickly realized no one was attacking them when they heard some laughter from the rear.

"Outgoing, sir. I guess someone got bored back there," Nolan surmised. "They saw my M-16 on the floor and decided it was a great place to fire off a few rounds."

"They might have told us they were going to do that," the Lieutenant said.

"And ruin the fun?" Nolan asked. "Look at the bright side, sir. Now we know my M-16 works."

Their blood pressure slowly returned to normal long before arriving back in Duc Pho. Another successful day of scrounging buoyed their spirits. Nolan hoped that the cook, Bà Hoa, would know how to prepare the squid. She did. The men acted surprised at how tasty it was in its breaded batter, the tentacles resembling onion rings.

Nolan assumed that officers did favors for each other from time to time, but they surely felt that scrounging for tires and for vehicles to borrow lay beneath them. He found it curious that enlisted men, even draftees, could arrange matters in the daily operations of a unit more quickly and less embarrassingly than an officer could. The power of a company clerk was legendary, even of a stoner like D'Amico. Nolan knew from academic life, too, how department secretaries, so full of valuable know-how and yet sympathetic to the powerless, could speed up a process for students if so inclined. He still didn't feel that the role of virtuoso scrounger or fixer fit him that well. Finding such shortcuts was just not his forte, though he knew bonhomie—a wisecrack or two-- could go a long way in the Army.

He had to admit to himself that he would never be as stinting with Lt. Hardy as he would with Major Stewart. In fact, Hardy didn't even have to ask for him to get new tires or find a truck. Over weeks working together they had bonded as teammates in a way the Major never could. They had been riding side by side through the sniper-alley rice paddies for weeks now, ready at any moment to dodge rifle fire. They depended on each other. In addition, they shared stoically the frequent blunting of purpose in their mission. How often they heard that a village official was not there-- "Maybe tomorrow." True, Hardy expected Nolan to keep their aptly named jeep running. They couldn't do without it. Otherwise, they took equal turns driving and riding shotgun, though in Nam an Army cousin, the M-16, lay across the passenger's lap.

From the very start, Hardy made Nolan feel he had a significant role to play in their mission. The Lieutenant relied on Nolan, of course, because of the language difference, but it appeared to go beyond that. Since they were both about the same age and college-educated, their world views overlapped somewhat, even given Hardy's more conservative background growing up in South Carolina. They could chat easily during time in the jeep about sports, popular culture, and other things back in the world, especially when their surroundings didn't demand special vigilance.

After hours, Nolan sometimes spent time talking with Hardy and the other officers in their wing. When Hardy and he finished planning visits for the next day, Nolan felt no need to rush off. He stayed instead and conversed openly about the war or other subjects that came up. Generally, the conversation flowed easily and informally. Hardy set the example for Nolan's inclusion, just by continuing their relaxed style of communication during the day's work. Differences in opinions arose. On one occasion, the youngest officer, Lt. O'Hare, the tall, baby-faced and earnest graduate of Officer Candidate School (OCS), took issue with Nolan's objections to the war.

"So, what do we do, Nolan, if we withdraw without victory? Do we just desert these people who have risked their lives for democracy?"

"No, sir. Definitely not. We have a moral responsibility to take in as many refugees as we can. That's an understood consequence of war."

O'Hare didn't push back, but he shook his head at what he likely saw as a hopelessly liberal knee jerk. Nolan remained ever conscious that O'Hare served as the adviser to the Phoenix program, which Hardy had quietly informed Nolan was an unofficial killing machine to do away with suspected Viet Cong sympathizers. Nolan never challenged O'Hare for the likely errors made in such vigilante Phoenix operations. He also made sure to stay clear of Long, the head assassin, whenever he dropped by the compound.

Hardy neither touted nor openly questioned the war. As for Major Stewart, Nolan deferred to him, never debating with him as he did with O'Hare. Yet he didn't try to hide his disapproval of the war. None of the other enlisted men had those conversations with the officers.

Nolan's habits did not go unnoticed. Sgt. Colson, an E-7 who had long ago determined to make the Army his career, stood squarely "old school" when it came to military discipline. While he, too, was expected to scrounge, he wasn't as effective as either Sgt. Hernandez or Sgt. Childress. Part of this may have been because he lacked a similar Caucasian brotherhood, but Nolan thought it related more to Colson's unwillingness to bend the rules. Hernandez and Childress focused almost entirely on their advising roles with the notable exception of scrounging. Colson took it upon himself to supervise the younger enlisted men and would occasionally criticize them. He appeared to see a need the other NCOs didn't, as if wary of the insidious effects that the large influx of draftees was having on the Army—his Army. These young men appeared too prone to ask questions or to be lax in their habits. A war zone was not a place to relax discipline. One day Nolan overheard Colson reprimand PFC Elston, the most laidback individual on the compound.

"Straighten up, soldier," he barked. "It's high time to get your uniform washed and pressed. Just because you're a draftee doesn't mean you have to dress like a slob."

Elston usually worked alone, his handyman skills allowing him to establish some distance from Army protocol. He didn't put much stock in appearances. He slouched whenever he stood still, and when he moved, he shuffled his feet. In contrast, Nolan tried to look presentable. He worked in the public eye. Following Hardy's example, he had his uniforms pants taken in to attain a more tailored look and his uniforms laundered and pressed. That didn't mean he escaped Colson's censure. The sergeant saw Nolan, like Elston, as another draftee subverting the system. Colson eyed him suspiciously when he conversed with Hardy inside the compound. While Colson wasn't privy to the informal chats in the officers' wing, he noted Nolan's comings and goings like a hawk.

"What are you working on, Nolan, that takes so much evening time to work out?"

"We're just planning tomorrow's routes, Sarge. A truck shipment is expected in the afternoon."

Nolan sensed there was something behind the out-of-the-blue question. Didn't Colson have enough on his plate? Hardy and Nolan stayed busy with their work monitoring the distribution of aid. They certainly weren't slacking off.

From what Nolan saw, the Lieutenant and he worked at least as conscientiously as anyone else, and in one specific case they went the extra mile. It became apparent in their visits to villages and camps that some common birth defects often went uncorrected in the countryside. They saw a number of people with extra digits on a hand, and others with cleft lips and palates. Those affected sometimes lived a much lonelier life, cut off from the likelihood of romance and marriage. It seemed such an unnecessary stigma to Nolan and Hardy. Modern medicine in the West eliminated those defects. They found out that a Quaker hospital outside Quang Ngai city, staffed primarily by doctors from the US and Canada, was starting a program to repair afflicted children surgically. One afternoon they drove to the hospital to offer their help.

They got a chilly reception. Their uniforms drew disdainful looks as they requested to speak with the director. Here they clearly stood out as warmongers among pacifists. One staff member put it bluntly when they suggested helping, "It's your war that makes this hospital necessary." Nolan understood that reaction and felt shame again, the first time in some months. These people were doing something truly unselfish and brave, coming to a war zone where death played no favorites. He didn't have a ready response, an inclination to attempt defending his presence in Nam. He often couldn't explain that to himself let alone to others. He feared hearing a false note in what he would say to these admirable volunteers. He was gratified now when Hardy took the lead and spoke out softly yet firmly, with more than a trace of the Southern gentleman.

"We understand how you feel. We're not here today to try persuading you differently. This is a practical matter. There are children that need help. You have the skills to help them, and we can go where you cannot go to find those who need the help."

A few frowns followed, but resistance melted away in face of the challenge. It was agreed that the Civil Affairs team would help locate these children and transport them and their parents, too, in some cases, to the hospital. This would mean more road trips and overall work time for the team, but they embraced the task. Within a few weeks, Hardy and Nolan had found several children, and in each case, successful surgery followed, allowing the children to look forward to ordinary lives back in their familiar surroundings. Word soon spread among the villages that medical transports were available to people. Almost immediately, trust in the camps and the villages appeared to rise. At the Quaker Hospital, too, change was in the air. After a first and then a second transport of patients, Nolan felt the chill turning to warmth by way of friendly greetings or looks from hospital staff.

"What are you shaking your head about, Nolan?" Hardy asked one afternoon. They were walking back to their jeep after dropping off a young girl and her mother.

"The young nurse, the dark-haired one—she smiled at me just now."

"Your Irish charm, no doubt. But then again, wasn't I standing next to you?"

"That must have been it, sir. You dazzled her with your shiny bars."

Hardy acted pleased to help. He didn't need extra motivation, but Nolan wondered if the Lieutenant felt that he had just earned his scrounging badge. He had found a way to get something done that didn't involve the usual channels and the prolonged wait. He was improvising and seemed much happier about the overall mission after these transports. Nolan knew how good it felt to be contributing something extra. He took pleasure with every new case.

"Wouldn't you like to be a fly on the wall and see how these hospital kids get along with other kids now? "

"It has to be amazing I would think, Nolan. That reminds me, though. We need to document more of the work at the camps. Some photos might help, like with the An Ke project. I have to remember to take my camera with us. Maybe take some photos of the kids, too."

The photo documentation made sense to Nolan. Mr. Nguyen, after being initially blindsided by the An Ke project, appeared to appreciate the care the Americans were taking on projects, asking to see photos for visits he missed. Maybe Hardy had been right that Mr. Nguyen's job security would benefit from the added publicity.

The very next day, in a good mood, Hardy drove the jeep northward along Highway One, with Nolan riding shotgun. Hardy's expensive camera in its pouch lay on the back seat. They hoped to take photographs to document some of the progress made at a camp where bags of cement and sheets of tin had been distributed weeks earlier. The road detoured onto gravel and dirt to the right because of damage to the main road, maybe from an explosion. As the jeep barely inched forward along the perimeter of a village, a dozen or more children flanked it on both sides of the rutted and uneven bypass. Nolan realized instantly their game: Seize and run. They had seen the camera lying on the open seat. This might be the biggest prize of the day. With as much gusto as he could muster, Nolan shouted, "Cút di!" ("Beat it!") and threw out his free arm at the children. Some of the smaller kids stopped in their tracks, taken aback by the suddenly animated American. Two of the older kids pressed closer, one on each side, hands ready to grab the camera. Nolan raised the M-16 without pointing it and pulled back the slide with a dramatic flourish, chambering a round from the clip. That did it. The kids scattered. The jeep returned to the main road and resumed speed.

"Thanks, Nolan." Hardy quickly resettled himself in the driver's seat.

"I wasn't going to shoot. If they grabbed the camera, it was a goner."

"I know that. Still— thanks."

They dropped the subject, but on the way back to Duc Pho they made sure to hide the camera from view. When they reached the detour, the jeep passed through without incident even though the progress was slow. Fewer children greeted them this time. Nolan couldn't be sure if any were among the group that had surrounded the jeep earlier. No one seemed to recognize them either. Later that night, quaffing a cold beer in the officers' wing, Hardy related the incident.

"The little bastards," O'Hare growled.

"Yes, they are," Hardy replied. "But *they* have to live, too. I shouldn't have left the camera out to tempt them."

"I suspect much of their loot ends up on the black market undermining the war," O'Hare added. Everything stood out in stark relief for him. No gray areas existed.

Nolan and Hardy both shared O'Hare's view of the black market. But they particularly resented that many GIs traded and sold items on that market, which seemed especially hypocritical if they also claimed the war was just. Hardy told Nolan recently that the body of a GI had been found in a Da Nang alley, a soldier thought to be dealing in the black market who ran afoul of his business associates. In the rising death toll for GIs in Nam, more than a quarter, Hardy claimed, related to categories outside "Killed in Action." Hardy thought it not unreasonable to believe that, at least, dozens of deaths related to the black market. Of course, no reliable figures existed on how many weapons sold on the market were used to kill

American GIs or their Vietnamese allies. Some of the hidden cost of war.

Nolan or Hardy could have pointed out to O'Hare how American money was driving this deadly market. Nolan wondered if Hardy had privately shared his thoughts about the market with O'Hare. For now, Nolan decided to take another tack rather than confront O'Hare directly.

"Maybe," Nolan suggested, "they wouldn't sell the camera on the black market. They could come up with a Pulitzer-winning photo shoot instead."

The Major laughed. "Nolan, when you get back to the States, you'll probably write up a big expose' in *Look* magazine. Everything bad about the war."

Nolan had never thought about *Look* in that way before. Hardly a radical mag. He struggled to suppress a smile.

"I don't think so, sir."

"Why not?"

"A couple of reasons, sir. I don't think America needs another expose'. From what I've read, public opinion is now against the war. Secondly, though, I just want to go back to school and get my life back to normal."

"And do you think you're going to be able to do that?"

Nolan was surprised by that question coming from the Major. He, too, had obviously been thinking about the cost of the war, both in material and in lives. He might not be as gung-ho as he appeared in front of the enlisted men. Who knew how much of his thoughts ran to doubts about the war? Maybe he saw My Lai and similar incidents as signs of inevitable defeat of an armed force purporting to "win hearts and minds." In the evening he often made himself a martini or two to spice up his conversations. Maybe, too, he drank to take his mind off the folly of the war. Now he stood waiting for Nolan's reply.

"I don't know, sir. That life seems so far off right now. But I suppose we can all dream."

Chapter 11: Outcast

The sweltering heat prompted Nolan to think of the hottest weather he had ever experienced, which was not hard to pinpoint. It had been the summer he spent in graduate school in Bloomington, Indiana, just two years earlier when he was completing course work for his master's. The heat and humidity were so oppressive that classes, whenever possible, were scheduled in the basements of buildings, the earlier in the day the better. When Nolan typed papers in his unairconditioned, second-floor dorm room, the finished sheets, pulled from the typewriter, would roll up like parchment scrolls within seconds. Any breeze arrived as a godsend. Fortunately, in Quang Ngai province summer breezes frequently accompanied the heat. Yes, a Quang Ngai was hot, but no doubt about it—Bloomington's climate was worse.

In late spring he had visited the university golf course one hot, humid morning, hearing that it was a fine course, but even with a loan of clubs and a free day in hand, he had decided not to play. Maybe he had been spoiled by the more temperate Maine summers when closing windows on many summer nights was necessary to ward off chill. Now, when Hardy and he walked on scorching days through the villages and camps in their bush hats and rolled-up sleeves, he didn't complain about the heat.

One morning in a village not far from Duc Pho, the two Americans, accompanied by Mr. Nguyen, came across a small, skinny boy with a cleft lip, following a few straggly chickens with a stick along a dirt path. Barefoot, and dressed in a ragged shirt and faded shorts, the boy warily reacted to Mr. Nguyen's friendly greeting, quickly looking away. When Hardy saw the boy's face, he spoke out.

"Hey, Mr. Nguyen, ask him his name, please."

Mr. Nguyen did so and got a shy reply: "Hieu."

Nolan said hello in Vietnamese, using *em* as the form to address a young person. He gently explained to Hieu that the Lieutenant and he were Civil Affairs and wanted to speak to his parents. Hieu didn't look directly at them or say anything, but led them right away down another path, to where a slight, middle-aged woman was working at the far end of the village. Wearing the conical straw hat of a peasant, she squatted over the damp ground, sifting rice outside the door of a small bamboo hut. Mr. Nguyen, in a soft, friendly voice, introduced himself and the others. She appeared startled by the attention of the three strangers, especially the American soldiers. Next to her, Hieu stood silently listening as Mr. Nguyen explained to his mother the program at the Quaker hospital to repair cleft lips and palates. He pointed out that it was a free program and that the Civil Affairs team would coordinate everything including transportation for Hieu and a parent to and from the hospital.

The mother appeared initially confused, but Hardy showed her a pamphlet with photographs from the hospital. Her eyes widened. She said nothing for a few seconds. Then she looked at Hieu standing a few feet away from her and taking care to avert his eyes from the strangers. She began sobbing as she asked Hieu if he understood. He nodded his head but said nothing. Finally, she said she would need to talk with her husband when he returned from working in the paddies. The three men exchanged shrugs, and after a quick parley, Mr. Nguyen said they would return in two days to see what the family had decided. As the men were leaving, Nolan added in a combination of Vietnamese and hand signals that five children from neighboring villages and camps had been helped so far. He smiled his gentlest smile at Hieu as he carefully wrote down in his notebook the family name and Hieu's age, 12.

Hardy and Nolan didn't think there would be much hesitation about this offer from Hieu's family. In past instances, families jumped at the opportunity, so when they returned to the village as promised, they were surprised to find that Hieu's father opposed an operation. Inside the family's modest hut, his thick black hair swept back like a movie star's, he stood stolidly alongside his wife, answering questions with an air of impatience. His abrupt manner made it clear that he wasn't inclined to listen to any pitch from the three men.

Hieu's father insisted that he needed the boy's help in the paddies every day. Hieu had an older brother, he said, who was absent from the village. He didn't say if the war caused the absence. But Nolan knew that most young men of service age had departed the paddies, leaving the hard work to older men, women, and children. Mr. Nguyen stressed that Hieu would be gone for only a day or two, that he would get good care. Still, the father wouldn't budge. No surgery for his son.

The father's excuses fell short of making sense to the three men. Didn't he want his son to have the opportunity to live a normal life? Most likely, the villagers treated Hieu as an oddity, especially the other children. He wouldn't have much of a chance for marriage and children without the surgery. Could a few days of idleness really outweigh a lifetime of normal social activity?

"Maybe," Hardy speculated in an impromptu huddle outside the hut, "Hieu's father thinks his son has bad karma, and there's nothing that can be done to change his fortune. That's what a Buddhist might think, right? What I understand of Buddhism, anyway."

"Bad karma, Mr. Nguyen?" Nolan asked in Vietnamese. "Does the father think nothing can be changed then?"

Mr. Nguyen dismissed the idea with a wave of his hand and answered in English. "Not Buddhism. The father, he afraid, I think."

"That could be it, yes. I keep forgetting what parents might feel about their child having an operation," Hardy said. "We have to allay his father's fears. I've got an idea. There is that boy in the village just south of here who had this same operation a month ago. Phong, right? He's doing fine, last we knew. Perhaps we could arrange an opportunity for Hieu and his parents to see how this boy is doing now. It's worth a try."

Nolan translated for Mr. Nguyen, who, in turn, helped Nolan to convey the Lieutenant's suggestion to Hieu's parents. The father appeared unmoved and said nothing. But the mother, her eyes widening like they had at first hearing about the opportunity, seemed more receptive to the idea. She suggested the men come back later, in a few days. Clearly, the parents were not finished discussing the matter.

"I think this is going to happen," Hardy said as the men walked back to the jeep. "In fact, I'm so confident this is going to happen, I want to stop at Phong's village on the way back so that we can make sure his parents are OK with having the boys meet. It shouldn't take us very long."

Wiping perspiration from his brow, Nolan said, "After that I'd like to buy Mr. Nguyen and you some roadside beer to celebrate—that's how right I think you are, sir."

"It's a deal. Let Mr. Nguyen know our plan. I'm sure he won't object."

The plan went forward without a hitch, first at Phong's dwelling and later at a humble café nearby, a simple hut just a few feet off the road, where the owner poured beer from warm bottles into three separate glasses. Not having refrigeration, he poured over ice chipped off a large block covered with sawdust, watering down what was already mostly water. Flies buzzed around them, but they were glad to be out of the sun's reach.

Hardy raised his glass in a toast. "To happy kids."

They sipped the beer leisurely, the two Americans trying their best to hide their squeamishness. Mr. Nguyen didn't appear to notice any uneasiness.

That night Nolan developed some diarrhea he attributed to the ice or drinking from an unsanitary glass. The flies in the hutch didn't help matters, he thought. Still, the day remained a success. If Hieu's parents could agree, the two boys could probably meet in a few days. If all went well then, Hardy could immediately contact the hospital about having another patient to transport. One more kid would get a chance at a normal life, knock on wood. That is, Nolan realized, if the war didn't interfere.

Hieu's mother must have argued persuasively because, just a few days later, she and Hieu rode in the jeep with the Civil Affairs team to meet Phong in his village. Hieu squirmed in the back seat, mostly silent except for a few low words he murmured to his mother next to him. Nolan caught a glimpse of the boy's darting eyes in the rear-view mirror. The kid couldn't hide the mix of excitement and apprehension that he was feeling. Nolan didn't say much himself, focusing on his driving and acting as nonchalant as he could about the occasion. He had seen similar nerves before when the team previously took children to the hospital. He also remembered having his tonsils removed as a kid and waking up with nausea from the ether. No operation was routine. He wanted to reassure mother and son the best he could.

The village was sleepy at midday, most of the men and women busily working in the rice paddies. When the two boys first spied each other, Hieu said nothing in response to Phong's "cháo." He seemed confused by Phong's appearance. Except for a faint scar on his lip and nostrum, Phong appeared to be just another wiry kid, roughly Hieu's age. Phong was much bolder. After his greeting, he rattled off a few excited words at Hieu that surprised Nolan. Had he heard them right? Laughing, he quickly translated for Hardy: "You will be like me soon." The perfect thing to say, Nolan thought, shaking his head in amazement.

Hieu's mother clapped her hands repeatedly. Soon she and Phong's mother engaged in their own spirited conversation, much too fast for Nolan to follow. It was a very happy conversation, though, the women bonded by their similar situations. Hieu and Phong mostly just looked at each other. If the adults, particularly two American soldiers, hadn't been around, they probably would have acted more comfortable with each other and maybe even become fast friends. That was still possible, of course, with time.

On the way back to Hieu's village, Nolan sat in the front passenger seat and slowly explained to mother and son the arrangements Hardy was making. The operation could take place soon, with only a short stay in the Quaker hospital, in the company of a parent if they wished. They were animated, but not particularly vocal; their fluttering hands said more. Both mother and son were ready for him to undergo what would be a life-changing operation.

The next day, Hardy made the arrangements with the hospital staff by radio, setting the date for surgery for the following week. Hardy promised written confirmation would follow, and then passed on the news to Nolan. Now that the initial delay was over, Nolan giddily expressed his feelings at the positive turn of events.

"Man, I thought we were going to get our first rejection. That was so frustrating. Now the streak goes on!"

"That it does," Hardy calmly replied, though Nolan knew he was pleased, too. "We can keep looking for different opportunities. Some birth defects aren't as easy to spot as cleft lips and palates. We need to check with Mr. Nguyen about those possibilities. No reason to slow down now."

Mr. Nguyen considered it unlikely there were many others in the Duc Pho district who were good candidates for the same surgery unless the doctors would consider adults. Hardy and Nolan couldn't say for sure if the doctors would, but they thought that the refugee camps likely contained similarly afflicted children. "Many of these refugees," Hardy said, "come from places so far from towns or cities that they'd never been in a hospital or even seen a doctor. A few medical clinics might help us discover some more candidates."

Two days later Nolan and Hardy were sitting in Hardy's quarters going over some plans when O'Hare suddenly appeared at the open door, clearly a man on a mission. He had a hard look in his eyes and remained standing close to the door.

"I hear you have another kid lined up for a harelip operation. There's a problem. You need to scrap your plans."

"Why—what's up?" Hardy asked.

"Long tells me that the family are Viet Cong sympathizers. Their older son, Danh, is thought to have run off and joined the VC after being called to military duty by the South."

"OK. The older brother. How does this relate to a 12-year-old kid? He's not VC."

"Not yet maybe, but you can imagine how this would go down with the other villagers if the kid gets this operation. Why should we be helping the VC? Think about it."

"Ah, now I think I see why Hieu's father was so reluctant at first," Nolan mused aloud. "The parents must be getting flak from some of their neighbors, or at least the cold shoulder, about their older son. The father knew the villagers would find out about the Americans helping them."

"Yeah, and it didn't take Long any time at all to get a report," Hardy added, his face reddening as he realized how the intelligence reached O'Hare. "Has the older brother—this Danh—been spotted with the VC?"

"Maybe he just didn't want to kill anyone—had moral reservations," Nolan interjected. "That could be why he disappeared from the village."

O'Hare gave him a withering look. "Conscientious objection doesn't exist in Vietnam, Nolan. 'You're either with us or against us.' That's the attitude. I don't know what confirmation Long has regarding this guy's actions, but I know Long, and I trust him."

Hardy set his jaw for a few seconds before speaking again. "This doesn't seem right, though, to deny Hieu his chance just because of some lousy, god damn suspicions about his brother."

O'Hare wisely picked up on the rise in tension. Spreading his palms open, he continued in a milder tone. "Well, Long has passed on the information to Major Thieu, and both he and Major Stewart won't want this operation. Sorry, guys, that's just the way it is."

"Damn it all," muttered Hardy, who grimaced but said nothing more. Nolan had never seen him angry and sensed he wanted to argue the issue, but with O'Hare that would be a dead end. Hardy probably didn't want to say anything else, especially in anger, until he had had a chance to talk with Major Stewart. Nolan wouldn't be part of that conversation, but he could find out what came of it soon enough.

The next morning in the jeep, Hardy told Nolan that O'Hare had been right about the majors. Major Thieu had nixed the plan, and Major Stewart wasn't inclined to persuade him otherwise. VC sympathizers needed to be discouraged, and Civil Affairs couldn't make an exception for Hieu. Nolan took the news hard. This was going backward, not forward.

"How do we tell Hieu and his mother that the operation is off? If they didn't trust Americans before, they'll surely hate us now."

He could have voiced a more cynical idea, that a little money put into the right pockets in district headquarters might change the situation. He didn't want to suggest that option yet. Corruption irked him—bribes, graft, the black market, all of it. Everyone looking out only for themselves. Couldn't helping a kid be exempt?

Hardy didn't say anything at first, but Nolan could see he, too, was thinking. After a long pause and a deep breath, he spoke as he often did when making a decision—deliberately.

"You know, the Quaker doctors don't care whether or not Hieu's family is VC—they're here to help anybody. Theirs is a humanitarian mission. The trick is that Hieu has to get to the hospital by other means. We can't take him. Someone else can do it, though. Everything is set with the hospital. We don't have to give up on the operation. We just have to make our hand invisible."

Nolan became animated, impressed once again by his boss. "Yes, why not? We can step to the side and still see this matter through. Clearly, though, someone is watching the family, so getting Hieu to the hospital will be tricky."

"Yes, no mistake, it's going to take some careful planning. We need to play dumb for the next week or so. Maybe this plan will require a ride to the hospital just before dusk when people are winding down for the day and not so likely to be observant. It can be done, I'm sure."

"But that doesn't leave the family much time to work this out. And how much money will it take to hire someone to provide the transportation discreetly? "

"I don't know. It couldn't be all that much. Maybe the hospital knows of some possibilities. Many of their patients probably require help with transportation. I hate to do any of this behind Major Stewart's back, but passing along some information about transportation seems OK to me. We won't be bucking orders exactly."

Nolan mulled that over, wondering if they were splitting hairs about orders. A look of concern spread over his face. "Major Thieu and the others will find out about the surgery after the fact, and they'll naturally suspect us, won't they? We'll have to have an alibi."

"If we can arrange this on a weekend when we will be, as usual, hanging around the compound, that should cover it."

Nolan nodded. "Today's not a bad day for a drive to the hospital, wouldn't you say, sir? We could make some other stops, too, to get a full day in. We've got enough gas in the jeep."

Hardy grinned, pleased at the suggestion. "Drive on, Nolan. I hope the nurses are ready for us. We can stop on the way back to let Hieu and his mother know about the change in plans. They may need some reassuring."

They wasted no time getting on the road. The drive to the hospital seemed longer than usual as though a physical roadblock slowed them down, not just an officious one. Fortunately, the staff at the hospital went along with the change, and even had a likely driver on their list, someone who didn't mind late in the day runs to the hospital for the right incentive—some cash. Unfortunately, they said, the hospital depended on donations to keep afloat, and money was tight right now. Hardy and Nolan got the idea.

"I'll cover the cost," said Hardy.

"Let me, at least, chip in, sir."

"No need, Nolan." He smiled wryly. "You got the beers the other day, remember?"

"That's not all I got. But, really, this will cost more, maybe a lot more."

"It's OK—I'd say the difference in our pay grades speaks more loudly here."

"Fine, Lt. Rockefeller, have it your way."

The conversation with Hieu's parents proved to be more difficult. Hardy told Nolan to let them know that a concern about Danh's political affiliation necessitated the new plan, but to say nothing about how the report reached them. The parents probably had a good idea of who provided intel to the authorities. Everyone knew that this particular Civil Affairs visit would be reported, too. To counter that report, Hardy needed to let Major Stewart know later that evening that the team had stopped by the village to deliver the bad news to the family.

After listening to Nolan's translation of Hardy's new plan, Danh and Hieu's mother jumped to the defense of her older son, claiming that he hadn't joined the VC. She insisted that he hated the idea of fighting and chose to go into hiding rather than report for duty. Nolan assured her that none of this would matter to the hospital staff. They didn't pick sides. They would take good care of Hieu and treat him as if he were their son. As far as he could tell, that placated the mother, but the father only grunted, saying nothing about the matter. Nolan hoped that he wouldn't object later and spoil the plan. Before

138

they left, Hardy re-emphasized that no one else in the village could know. The plan had to be secret.

Nolan felt uneasy after the conversation. After they departed the hamlet, he looked over at Hardy in the adjacent seat. "What are the chances, sir?"

"I am confident this will go well. Maybe less confident than I was originally, but we have to realize that the Vietnamese population have been making these kinds of decisions for themselves all along, regardless of war or any other obstacle. We have facilitated here, but they are perfectly capable of running their lives."

"I agree with that. Let's just hope, for Hieu's sake, all goes well this time."

Nolan found it impossible not to think about the family on the eve of the operation. He imagined in the twilight a tiny Lambretta ferrying Hieu and his mother out of sight from prying eyes. Both Hardy and he made sure to say nothing about what was going on around others on the Duc Pho compound, keeping even Mr. Nguyen out of the loop since he couldn't afford to irritate Major Thieu. Better that the compassionate welfare officer knew nothing about the new plan in case the Vietnamese major inquired later if he knew.

The team realized that they would need to wait a few days to check on how Hieu had fared. It wouldn't be wise to stop at the village to see for themselves. They would be watched, for sure. Instead, they decided to wait several days to make another quick trip to the hospital. They had put quite a few miles on Maybe Tomorrow in recent weeks, the new tires coming in handy. While maybe helping one 12-year-old boy might not look so significant in a list of their accomplishments in the past month, to them it sure felt that way.

At the hospital Hardy immediately went off to find a physician, so Nolan was free to wander and look around for the friendly, dark-haired nurse. The hospital wasn't that large. He wandered down a narrow corridor smelling faintly of antiseptic, past a patient ward, and through an open door spied her stacking some supplies in a storeroom. Looking up, she smiled, seemingly both surprised and happy to see him.

"Hi," said Nolan, "just a quick visit from your lovable, gun-toting Civil Affairs team, the pride of Duc Pho."

"I'm always glad to see you, Nolan—glad to know you're safe. And Lt. Hardy, too, of course."

She had a sweet smile, Nolan thought.

"Of course," he replied. "But this isn't just a social call. What can you tell us of our young patient Hieu? We've been anxious for news."

"Hieu is doing great. We discharged him a few days ago. He should be a good-looking little guy once the healing is done. Perhaps, he'll be as good-looking as his older brother."

"That's great news about Hieu." He hesitated, feeling just a nip of jealousy about her last comment. "His mother, then, must have shown you a photo of Danh."

"Oh, she didn't have to. He was here the day of the operation, riding up on a motorcycle. I got a definite Marlon Brando vibe."

She caught a startled expression on Nolan's face. "You look surprised."

"Yeah, Danh's a hard man to find these days. Did he stay very long?"

"No, he left an hour or so later, saying he had to get back to his work, whatever that is."

"Back to work, huh?" He paused, deciding not to explain the situation. "Well, I guess I do, too."

He hadn't meant to sound so disappointed.

"Just another cowboy riding off into the sunset, huh?"

"You have a job for me?"

He was happy for the crumb she threw him.

"Yes, Nolan, we always could use someone to clean out the bed pans."

"And, on that note, I will take my leave, fair lady."

"No fair lady, just Mary Ann, a girl from the outback." She stopped smiling. "Nolan, all of us here are grateful for what you two fellas are doing, even if we don't say it very often."

He sensed he was blushing.

"We think the same about you, Mary Ann. You've got a big heart doing this work, and you're here in Nam with a much clearer conscience than mine. I couldn't place your accent before. All the way from Australia, huh? That's impressive. I admire your courage."

"Don't be too hard on yourself, soldier."

Nolan grinned. He couldn't resist flirting a little. "See ya, Mary Ann. Next time I may be able to round up a motorcycle with a sidecar."

"I don't think Lt. Hardy would like that," she said, and winked a lovely, green eye before walking away.

Chapter 12: Long Range

Several months of his tour passed before Nolan finally discovered what the war smelled like up close, a fetid odor both vegetative and animal. One afternoon, the new Civil Affairs team returned to the Duc Pho compound to find that a half-dozen muddy and tired Army Rangers had commandeered the upstairs lounge. They were LRRPs—pronounced Lurps—members of a long-range reconnaissance patrol. Over a period of two months, they would repeat these sudden arrivals and equally sudden departures, their destinations and schedule kept secret from the rank and file.

Elite soldiers, they shared the unenviable mission of being dropped by helicopter into remote areas of the thick highland forests for a week or two at a time in order to locate Viet Cong and NVA patrols and camps, avoiding contact if possible, especially if the size of the enemy unit necessitated artillery bombardment instead. That often wasn't possible. They dressed in dark jungle camouflage and carried AK-47s, grenade launchers, claymore mines, long knives, flares, and many pounds of ammunition in addition to food, underwear, socks, rain ponchos, and medical supplies. They bore heavy packs. The humping over dozens of kilometers in rough terrain must have been exhausting. One man carried the radio, their only contact with friendly forces, and another team member, the sole Viet, served as both an interpreter and a scout.

His name was Ca, and he was the most Americanized of the Vietnamese Nolan had thus far met. Dark skinned and lithe, the feisty 21-year-old demonstrated an uncanny skill with his flagrant use of American slang and expletives. Ca acted very much at home chatting and swearing away with his platoon members and the Duc Pho compound residents, both American and Vietnamese. He swaggered when he walked and rarely smiled. Everyone liked him.

The LRRP team leader, Captain Barnes, stood six foot-three and weighed 220 pounds, a strapping graduate of West Point, where he had played rugby. Starting with that initial meeting in the lounge, Nolan saw the special qualities of the captain at work in even the most trivial of circumstances.

"Ca, don't hog all those chips. Toss the bag over here," Barnes boomed from a sprawled position in a chair that seemed much too small to support him. His captain's bars discreetly revealed themselves stitched atop the shoulders of his camouflage uniform, the sleeves rolled up to uncover beefy arms.

He snagged the bag from the air with the swipe of an outsized paw, while calling over to a burly NCO with a shaved head: "Want some, Curly?"

Handsome, with chiseled features, the Captain commanded attention with his boyish charisma. He showed a remarkable ability to shift from a casual one-on-one chat to a fill-the-room presence. No one remained immune to his charm. Almost twenty years older, Major Stewart, treated him like a proud father would, putting his arm around him and attempting to draw him aside for private conversations whenever he could. Nolan never heard any specifics, but he imagined Stewart was debriefing the younger man on the latest encounters of the team in the bush. Major Stewart had led troops before, but being a few steps removed from that activity now, he appeared to relish vicariously these combat reports from the rugged captain.

It was odd, Nolan thought. He liked Ca, often joking with him in the quieter moments around the compound. He also liked Captain Barnes, but he never tried to elicit tales from either of them about the team patrols. He wasn't sure if it was out of respect for the trauma they endured or his repulsion at the ruthlessness required of the team. They carried the long knives to cut the throats of sentries. That much became clear.

Late one afternoon in the enlisted men's quarters Curly let Sgt. Harris examine the AK-47 he carried on missions. Nolan stood a few feet away as Harris held the captured weapon on his lap and admired its efficient, functional design. It looked like a cross between an M-14 and an M-16. Neither Harris nor Nolan had seen one up close before. The Automatic Kalashnikov, developed in the late 1940s by the Russians, possessed a cachet among many GIs, the standard-issue M-16 being prone to jamming. The AK's curved magazine that could hold up to thirty rounds or more, one of its most distinctive features, was empty now. While the AK-47 weighed two more pounds than the M-16, it was easier to maintain and repair, making it a durable rifle.

"Is this your preferred weapon now, Curly?" Harris asked, almost lovingly stroking the wooden stock.

"For now, yeah. It's a bit beat up, probably an older rifle. I might sell it. Funny, we find some VC carry M-16s. Plenty around, I reckon."

"I know someone who'd be interested in buying your AK," Harris said.

"Yeah, maybe. I'll think about it. I can always get another one, you know."

As if to explain how, the bald, tattooed LRRP reached up to remove something around his neck. From a distance it looked like dried apricots on a string. Up close, Nolan saw a necklace of human ears.

Harris acted awed, "Man, that's cool."

Curly smiled in silent pride. Nolan only glanced at the necklace and said nothing.

Later, when alone, Nolan tried to come to terms with this aspect of human behavior, to understand how fear and aggression could combine to create such sordidness. He sensed he did not share this violent trait with these gritty, seasoned warriors. Yet he did share the primal elements that produced the mix. What would he do in combat if he patrolled with these men? What would keep him from acting similarly under what must have been a state of pure fear, augmented by peer pressure? Decency seemed too weak a word. Would he have the courage to be his own man?

He thought back to the oral exam he took for his master's at Indiana University a year and a half earlier. One professor had asked him to identify the main theme of *King Lear*. Nolan had answered "love—and the absence of love." He was asked to expound, which he did, somewhat haltingly. Several kinds of love appeared in the play—filial love, lust, and *agape,* the highest form of love—but now in Vietnam he could only think of the unspeakable cruelty, Cornwall plucking out the eyes of Gloucester. The seeming indifference of God (or gods) in the play made that cruelty even more unnerving.

While Nolan did not seek to know more about the patrols, it stood also true that no one from the LRRP team ever asked Nolan and Hardy about the work they did. The two teams clearly followed parallel tracks, one inherently more dangerous than the other, but both strategically important to the US military. With the Civil Affairs team busy all day conducting their village visits, Nolan's mostly flippant interactions with Ca tended to be in the mornings at breakfast. His encounters with Captain Barnes more often took place in the evening during confabs in the officers' wing. In that way, the real war sandwiched the placid days of his own existence.

Nolan learned from Pho that Ca came originally from a village outside Hanoi. He was a Chieu Hoi, an enemy soldier who had been captured and "turned." The elders of his village had pushed him into the war before he was eighteen, urging him to do his duty to his fatherland. Wounded and then captured, with a tell-tale scar from an M-16 round running down his neck, he had seized the chance to fight alongside the Americans and had not seen his family in several years. Most likely, his family presumed he was dead. He acted as if his conversion was no big deal. He appeared completely at home, telling Nolan, "Man, I'm where I wanna be. No lie. We LRRPs are fuckin' tight!"

Around Pho and Nolan, Ca could also show another side, a more sentimental one, when the other LRRPs occupied themselves in rowdy activities. He might sing a Vietnamese love song, particularly a melancholic one from the repertoire of the songstress Thanh Ly. He had learned to play a guitar from an earlier team member, an American who gave the guitar to him upon completing his own tour. Strumming it softly in these "stand down" moments, Ca would turn much more wistful. Often, he would ask Pho about one of his sisters on whom he had a serious crush. Nolan wondered if the attraction was reciprocal, but he felt that he didn't know Pho or Ca well enough yet to ask. The three young men would switch back and forth between Vietnamese and English to keep each other sharp. Nolan learned some useful slang. Maybe not as tight as the LRRPs in the field, they nonetheless found a bond in the playfulness of language. When Ca went away on patrol, the guitar sat in a corner of the lounge. No one else ever picked it up.

Nolan found out that Captain Barnes had a wife and young daughter back in Pennsylvania. He had committed himself to this dangerous mission despite his wife's feeling that he should transfer out to a safer job. His father had fought in the Battle of the Bulge during WWII. A career officer, his father only recently had shared some of the horrors. Nolan thought that maybe the older Barnes expected his son to do the same. Nolan had heard that LRRP members were volunteers. One night he asked the Captain if that was the case for him.

"Sure thing. I don't want a desk job, Nolan. For one, that's not the kind of job that gets career advancement, and I'd be bored to death for another. I just don't tell my wife much about what I'm doing. In fact, I don't tell anyone back in the States. My dad understands, but the rest—they wouldn't understand, man. Plenty of time for that later, in any case."

That's about as far as Nolan got in knowing the Captain's mindset. He thought it likely the Army would be a career for

146

Barnes as it had been for his father. Normally, Nolan didn't ask questions of the officers regarding the war. Even with Lt. Hardy he retained some reticence. Nolan knew better than to push the envelope. An officer expressing doubts about the war to enlisted men would be more problematic than enlisted men grousing among themselves. Major Stewart had come close to voicing his doubts openly that one evening after the near theft of Hardy's camera. Nolan didn't press the matter. He had sensed that it wouldn't do either one of them any good to discuss the matter further.

The little socializing Nolan did with the officers still seemed harmless enough to him. Yet, after Sgt. Colson asked him about what he was doing in the officers' wing in the evenings, Nolan's antennae stayed up. Colson appeared to be resentful that a draftee so casually crossed the line between officers and enlisted men. Nolan being just another college boy like most of the officers wouldn't excuse his behavior.

While Nolan sensed that Colson was keeping an eye on him, he found it just too comfortable after his Song Mao dorm-like experience to consider changing his social patterns. He continued to fraternize in the evenings. He thought to himself, what was the big deal? Conforming to Colson's world view was not his own priority. He certainly didn't think of himself as subverting any system. That was Colson's problem, and probably reflected a flaw in his personality as much as anything else. Colson had little to do with the other NCOs, Hernandez and Childress in particular, which may have resulted from a racial bias, but nothing obvious indicated that. He didn't joke around with them as they did with each other. More likely, he was just a loner, but one who had set ideas about how an army should run. Any laxity in US Army protocol would not be excused because of the distance from headquarters or the location in a war zone.

One evening Nolan left the officers' wing and headed to his room. As he turned the last corner, Colson approached him from a tangent, quite warily, Nolan thought.

"Nolan, I'm going to require your assistance Saturday on a project I've got going on with the generator. You're available, right?"

"Sure, Sarge, I think so, though you'd better ask Lt. Hardy about that day, just in case. He might have something scheduled."

Nolan figured he could count on Hardy for support in regard to this extracurricular detail. Working with Colson did not relate to his assigned job description. He certainly didn't want to spend any more time around him than he did now. The MACV and Civil Affairs chains of command were disparate, as Nolan answered to Lt. Hardy, who in turn answered directly to Civil Affairs in Da Nang. For defensive purposes on the compound, everyone chipped in, of course, but now Colson was stretching things. Nolan sensed that Colson had not chosen him for the detail because of his mechanical skills. Grabowski and Elston, the other low-ranking guys on the compound, possessed much more competence than he did in such matters. No, this was a message, Nolan decided, a reaction to his chummy behavior with the officers.

As Nolan hoped, Hardy came through for him. He told Colson that he needed Nolan on Saturday and invented a village visit for the team that day. Colson may have smelled something fishy, but he didn't say anything to Nolan about it. Instead, a week or so later he approached him with another detail in mind, a painting project in the kitchen. He looked Nolan in the eye to read his reaction, hoping to ferret out a shirker, Nolan thought, but he kept a straight face and sounded almost as sanguine as before.

"I don't know, Sarge. It's probably OK, but we may have something going then. I'll ask the Lieutenant."

He didn't want to overplay the act. Colson had an animal cleverness about him. He may have been "old school" about fraternizing between officers and enlisted men, but he was no fool. As before, Lt. Hardy came through with another excuse, sparing Nolan from hours of menial work on a day he normally

148

could relax. Nolan suspected these refusals by Hardy would not deter Colson for long, and that soon he would likely ask the Major to step in.

In the end, though, fate or chance intervened.

As Nolan read him, Sgt. Colson envied some of the "men at war" aspects of the LRRPs even if Captain Barnes came across as too familiar with his men. Colson certainly was not a lazy or timid man. One day he decided to accompany a maneuver by the provincial forces in the foothills. While riding in a helicopter overseeing the action, he took a sniper round in the upper leg. The helicopter was not damaged seriously in the shooting, so the crew was able to get Colson to a field hospital for initial treatment. Later he was transferred to an Army hospital in Da Nang. A few days after the incident Major Stewart informed the team that Colson had passed out of danger and would eventually recover. But he never returned to Duc Pho. It looked like his war was over.

Nolan couldn't be sure if anyone else shared his relief that Colson was gone. No one said that. He suspected that PFC Elston likely did, since he had drawn much of Colson's criticism. Nolan hadn't wished anything like this to happen to Colson, but he didn't feel any regret either. It was simply easier to think that Colson was an angry, unhappy man, someone who didn't like to see others enjoying themselves when he couldn't.

Perhaps, not coincidentally, more of the men began to gather around the basketball hoop out in the courtyard in the wake of Colson's departure. Up until then, Nolan would shoot baskets by himself in the early evenings. Soon Pho became curious about the game and watched Nolan shoot one evening. After a few minutes, Nolan beckoned Pho onto the court to try his own hand. He gave Pho some pointers, showing him how to hold the ball to shoot and how to dribble. After that, most evenings they would shoot baskets for fun. Nolan was not a great all-around player, but he had a good shooting eye and a knack for hitting shots from the outside. With his long arms, he also could block shots or deflect an opponent's dribble. He didn't do that with Pho, nor with Grabowski and Hardy when they participated some evenings. They contented themselves with taking turns tossing the ball up at the hoop. No one suggested a game. That changed with the presence of the LRRPs and Colson's absence.

As Ca had claimed, the LRRPs were a tight group, despite their squabbles now and then. One night, a very brief fist fight broke out between two NCOs who had drunk numerous beers up in the lounge. A quick jab and then a sore jaw the next morning didn't cause any lasting grudge. Most of the time, they hung together—men whose every action in the bush could determine the survival of their comrades.

Eventually, someone suggested a game between the LRRPs and the Duc Pho guys. One game led to more. Captain Barnes loved the physical contact of the game under the basket. He was like a big puppy, Nolan thought, strong but not meaning any harm. He laughed when the less athletic Lt. O'Hare, who was about the same height, fouled him under the basket. Tempers rarely flared. It seemed natural for the LRRPs to make up one team, and the MACV/CA guys to form the other. Major Stewart, along with Sgts. Hernandez and Childress, watched from the sidelines, howling at plays good and bad.

For the most part, officers guarded officers, enlisted men guarded enlisted men, and Pho and Ca guarded each other. Ca was more athletic, but Pho was taller, creating a standoff between them. Neither one dribbled or shot very well. The Americans overlooked traveling and double dribbles, except for now and then making light-hearted reminders about rules. The two Viets appeared to enjoy the exercise and the camaraderie as much as the others. Nolan usually carried the load for the home team, sinking a high percentage of one-hand set shots and jump shots when Curly, his most frequent LRRP defender, eased off in coverage. He passed up a lot of opportunities, too, shuttling the ball off to Pho, Hardy, or

O'Hare when there didn't appear to be a pressing need for a score.

Most of the time, humidity weighed heavily on the evening air. Sweating off several pounds in an hour or so became a nightly occurrence. The players didn't carry many extra pounds to begin with except for the water weight they may have regained the previous night drinking cold beer up in the lounge. The game was simple—an occasional screen, a rare pick and roll, and a lot of gunning from the outside. Rebounding was tough. Captain Barnes owned the inside, but his teammates didn't pass the ball that much and often ignored him under the basket. He would good-naturedly holler, "I'm open, Ca," or the like. He never showed any pique at being ignored. When he missed a shot, often being hacked on the arm by O'Hare, he just grabbed the rebound and put the ball back up with a laugh. He was in his element. It could have been a rugby scrum.

Occasional pauses in the action took place for players to catch a breath or wipe off some perspiration. Few players bothered with hydration. With the beer waiting inside, that would come later. Games went to 15 points, with no foul shots. Out of bounds didn't really exist. A wall, post, or vehicle established the confines. The courtyard could be dusty if not swept before play, so Nolan or Pho took it upon themselves to sweep the yard now and then if it hadn't rained. That proved perfunctory at best, and dust mingled with sweat.

They played each night until the light failed. Graceful basketball, it was not, the combat boots preventing sharp cuts and the desired elevation on jumps. Usually the games stayed close. Often the outcome came down to Nolan nailing a long shot or Captain Barnes muscling up a short shot with O'Hare hanging all over him.

Post game up in the lounge, the beer flowed unabated for an hour or so. Nolan would drink several cans in a matter of minutes before he slaked his thirst and restored his body water. The physical exhaustion felt good. Since they were all young men, aches and pains never hampered them the next day, even with turned ankles and after elbows in the ribs.

If a film had been delivered that day by helicopter, Nolan would thread the first reel in the projector once he saw everyone was settled in. When that reel was finished, he replaced it with the second, putting the first aside for a Vietnamese soldier to pick up and carry over to his side of the compound for a separate viewing. Grabowski could also run the projector, but Nolan was quick to take charge and let Grabowski relax a bit after his long, solitary shifts of radio duty. "Grabo" liked everything about being in the army as if it were just an extension of being a Boy Scout. He had enlisted without any thought about the draft. He liked hanging out with the LRRPs. In the evening he relished being one of the gang again.

The basketball nights usually tumbled by free of complications. If there wasn't a full moon, no one needed to stay sober for guard duty, though Nolan never approached the drunken state several of the LRRPs fell into almost nightly. The combination of muscle fatigue and alcohol did its job, however. Bedtime was not a time for wakefulness. Nolan slept well, and he suspected the others did, too.

Evenings followed this convivial pattern when the LRRPs were standing down, resting up for the next sortie. During these days and nights, Nolan had little time for writing letters home or thinking about the future. Consults with Mr. Nguyen and visits to villages and camps filled the days. Basketball, beer, and films took care of the nights. The men consumed their evening meals quickly. No one lounged at the table. Competition brought the teams out to the courtyard once again until dark, the air as usual no less humid than during the day. They took only short breaks between games, eager to get in as much basketball as they could. Someone would usually claim, "There's time for another game" even if they could barely see their teammates in the gloaming.

Over the passing weeks, the LRRPs came and went with startling suddenness. They left quietly as if practicing the stealth on which their lives would depend in just an hour or so. They were also readying themselves for the shock that Nolan had tried to imagine some weeks earlier while drinking beer in the air-conditioned comfort of the Quang Ngai base bar.

Several days after another departure of the LRRPs, Major Stewart entered the dining room for breakfast and sat down heavily at the officers' table. He usually chatted with the men then to demonstrate both his position and his sense of rapport. This morning he didn't greet anyone. After a few moments, he glanced up at the others with a grim expression no one had seen before. His red eyes startled Nolan. His voice rose barely above a whisper.

"Captain Barnes was killed yesterday. He stepped on a mine. It may be hard to gather all the pieces."

The room fell silent. No one wanted to make eye contact. Looking down at the table, Nolan realized that he had not known anyone killed in the war, except for a college classmate who had died several years earlier after flunking out his freshman year. Captain Barnes had not been a friend per se as the officers in Song Mao had been. Protocol here in Duc Pho, though relaxed to some degree, didn't allow for that kind of friendship. Still, he felt a sharp pain in his chest. Did the LRRPs ever talk about this danger? he wondered. He hadn't asked. This was their realm.

"There will be a service over at the artillery base tomorrow morning. Who else is going?" the Major asked, his eyes and voice resuming a sense of purpose.

Looking first at Hardy and seeing a nod, Nolan said, "We'll go, sir."

Several others murmured their consent.

"We're all in, sir," Hardy added after making a quick survey of the room.

Then, the men sat alone in their silence.

After what seemed a minute, Nolan bit his lip, got up abruptly from the table, and as if on auto pilot went out the courtyard door to get Maybe Tomorrow ready for the day. For just a moment he stood still on the outside steps. The morning had already grown hot, with no sign of a breeze. At the bottom of the steps lay the basketball, dust covered, unused for days, discarded like a child's toy. He picked up the ball, poised it up on the fingertips of his right hand, and with barely a glance, heaved it high toward the rim. Rotating in flight, the ball reached its apex and rapidly descended. It passed cleanly through the hoop, slicing the net, which exploded into a thousand shards of light.

Chapter 13: Rest & Recuperation

Some changes in the daily life on the Duc Pho compound dampened spirits, making the men both lethargic and moody. For one thing, the LRRPs moved their "stand down" quarters to LZ Bronco, though less than a mile away. Ca occasionally came back to the compound for visits on stand-downs, but he and Nolan didn't play the language games as they did before.

His first time back, Ca reported that the new Ranger captain was an OK guy, but then he blurted out, "Fucking-ay, man, life is shitty." He seemed somehow older, wearier, but the compound residents lacked enthusiasm for almost everything, as well. The basketball games had ceased. Nolan and Pho tried shooting around one evening, but after only a few minutes, Nolan stopped and said, "I've had enough." Pho nodded silently. They stayed inside most evenings now or just sat on the steps talking.

Hardy and Nolan tried to get back into their daytime routine as quickly as they could. They visited two or three villages or refugee camps daily, most often accompanied by the even-tempered and ultra-efficient Mr. Nguyen. They could see that the demand in the camps for better housing and new wells had only increased in recent weeks. Fortunately, Mr. Nguyen was very organized in his approach, with his carefully scripted lists of villages and residents. He also spoke a little more English, which made Nolan's job easier. Occasionally, Nolan would talk with camp or village officials while the other two men carried on basic conversations on their own.

Nolan wasn't visiting the officers' quarters much anymore. He had found a fascinating, but improbable, book in a recent USO shipment, a guide to Japanese characters, kanji. That book took up a good part of his down time. He was eager to see how much he could learn in just a few weeks. Every GI was entitled to R&R after the halfway point in his tour. His six-day opportunity was coming up, and he had chosen to visit Tokyo. He hadn't made an effort to coordinate with any of his classmates or Song Mao teammates, so he wouldn't know anyone to hang around with on the trip. That was okay. He imagined himself as a flaneur of sorts, a solitary observer of life in the city. He liked to walk in big cities, to take in as many sights as he could. While he worked on learning some essential conversational phrases for communicating his needs in Japan, he also wanted to be able to read Japanese signs for getting his bearings more easily.

He found fascinating how the stylized characters in Japanese could often be traced back to pictographs. In this manner, the character for "mountain" resembled a mountain in shape, and those for people consisted of boxy figures with arms and legs. Whereas the French colonials insinuated the Roman alphabet into Vietnamese early in the 20th century, Nolan was aware that the Japanese held onto their alphabet more tightly. He welcomed the challenge, though, of learning at least the basics of a new language to get more out of his visit. In preparation, he tested his knowledge by trying to reproduce common kanji on index cards. It was slow going, but he enjoyed it.

PFC Elston, one of his roommates, registered surprise at Nolan's choice of Tokyo.

"Man, why are you going there? You could shack up with a hot Thai honey in Bangkok for less than $100 a week. Sex all week."

"Yeah, so I hear, but . . . ."

"Is it the slant-eye thing? Well, Sydney can give you all the round-eyed girls you want."

"No, it isn't that. I find Asian women of various nationalities attractive. I just have more interest in Japan as a place to visit. Culturally, there's so much to see and do in Tokyo alone."

"Whatever floats your boat, man. I'm just saying . . . ."

Elston stopped there, no doubt thinking that Nolan was a hapless loser, a prude. Nolan could have mentioned "the clap" Elston had caught on a recent foray into the town, necessitating a special trip over to the field hospital on the artillery base for an antibiotic. Most GIs acted carelessly by having sex with Vietnamese women without using condoms. Instead of reminding Elston about the medical troubles he had encountered because of his behavior, he just smiled and made an offer.

"I'll see if I can find you some erotic postcards, Elston, to brighten your day."

Japanese culture had its allure, but Nolan harbored other reasons for his choice. One of these he had no intention of sharing with Elston. Recently, Nolan had been thinking of his off-and-on girlfriend, Karen, more often, their letters increasing with frequency as he planned his return. She had offered to find him an efficiency apartment in Madison not far from where she shared a house with another woman. They weren't ready to attempt living together so soon after his return. Without really talking about it, they knew neither set of parents would be OK with that. More importantly, they were still exploring their feelings. He thought of her honey-colored hair, her blue eyes, and the way she drew from him an interest in understanding more of life. He didn't know how much of his longing was missing Karen herself, and how much was missing young female companionship, generally. From time to time, he wondered how the ten months of separation would affect their relationship's rekindling. He felt that his Vietnam experience was shaping him in ways still not clear. He had seen so much in the camps and villages. And he had seen death and experienced grief. No doubt Karen had changed, as well, since they last spent time together. Was he expecting too much from their reunion? He had no clear idea of what the future held for them. In the last two years, they hadn't spent but a few hours together. Still, sex with underage Thai prostitutes didn't appeal to him.

He also needed to save for graduate school. In Tokyo, he could stay in the barracks on the local Army base for free and put aside at least some money for tuition and living costs. GI Bill or not, non-resident tuition would be high at Wisconsin. He had taken out student loans at Holy Cross and Indiana that he would need to repay once his schooling ended. All that hung over his head.

Not that he wouldn't spend money in Japan. Back in the barracks at HQ, D'Amico had told him about a huge PX in Tokyo where GI's could get incredible bargains on stereo equipment such as TEAC tape decks, Sansui tuners, and various makes of speakers. Nolan's ears pricked up since he could easily imagine how all a complete, top-quality system would look and sound in his Madison apartment. Apparently, he could also find Nikon cameras and Seiko watches at very low prices. He planned to surprise his parents and Karen with some gifts on his return home. The Tokyo PX offered a great opportunity to do this without busting his budget.

The PX would also ship everything he bought directly to the States. He appreciated that convenience, but he also was aware that military regulations limited what he could take back to Nam. The black market already flourished with buying and selling of such goods. He heard that anything was available for the right price. He wanted no part of it.

In addition to D'Amico's tips, another GI in Da Nang had mentioned that the US military maintained a fine golf course in Tokyo. With decent weather, he might be able to play the course on one of his free days. Outside of a single round on Cape Breton, Canada, he had never played golf in a foreign country. The golf could provide him with both relaxing and somewhat exotic exercise. He missed the game that filled so much of his summer days the past ten years when he played rounds with friends or worked on the course crew.

So, Tokyo it would be. Rest and Recuperation there sounded just fine.

As his departure neared, Nolan sat up in the lounge one weekend morning reading from the Japanese language manual. Major Stewart told everyone that a US general was planning to pay a visit that morning. In preparation the residents had scurried around the day before to make the environs presentable. But Nolan felt no need to make himself scarce. Hardy had not scheduled any visits that day; he was free to relax. Just before lunch, the Major led the general up the stairs to the lounge. Nolan jumped to his feet and saluted. The general immediately said, "At ease, soldier," and proceeded to ask Nolan what kind of work he did and where he was from— friendly questions, a chance for the general to show his common touch. Later that evening, his inspection anxiety still running high, the Major recounted the general's visit to the others in the dining room.

"And there was Nolan up in the lounge reading some porn book."

At his table Nolan snapped alert. "No, sir, it was a Japanese language book. The general was quite friendly and said he considered me a neighbor since I'm from Maine and he's from New Hampshire."

This may have appeased Major Stewart a little, but he had seemed edgier in the past few weeks. Nolan didn't take his caustic comments to heart as everyone was still feeling down about the loss of the captain. Mealtime seldom passed lightheartedly anymore. The major would fret over how long a pork roast had been cooked, or if there were the right condiments on his table. No one could say anything, but Nolan knew that in civilian life a friend would have said, "We miss him, too."

Getting away from the compound for almost a week would be a welcome respite. Hardy would fare just fine without him for a few days, Nolan thought. Over the recent weeks, Hardy had forged a solid connection of his own with Mr. Nguyen. When the day came for leaving, Hardy gave Nolan a ride as far as Quang Ngai city in Maybe Tomorrow. From there Nolan hitched a ride in a small convoy up to the headquarters in Da Nang.

When Nolan entered the modular building that served as the HQ, he half expected to see his old pal D'Amico sitting at the desk nearest the door. The pale face before him was unfamiliar. The name tag read "SANDERS." Nolan introduced himself.

"Ah, yes, Nolan, from Duc Pho. I've got you a seat on a plane early tomorrow, direct to Japan."

Nolan wondered if it was all business with this guy. "Good, I thought I might have to swim there."

Sanders chuckled. "Oh, don't worry. We make sure our guys from the boonies get first-class treatment for their R&Rs. And just wait until you dine Chez Da Nang tonight, the greasy spoon that passes for our mess hall. After a meal there, you'll know for sure how much we care."

"I can see that D'Amico broke you in well. He was quite hospitable on my last stay here. I hope he flew the coop on schedule."

"Oh, you haven't heard about D'Amico. Sad story."

Nolan started. Not another man down. "Don't tell me. He didn't get smoked in his last week here, did he?"

"Well, 'smoked' is the operative word, but not the way you think. He got out of Nam in one piece, but before he could muster out at Fort Lewis, he was busted for smoking reefer in the barracks. It's not like here. He may be court martialed."

"Cripes. That must be a first—getting busted for dope as you're going out the door. Why can't they let it go and just be rid of him? There's a war going on if they haven't noticed."

"Got to set an example, I guess. Anyways, after getting the news about D'Amico, the brass here decided to keep a closer watch on our barracks. Not so relaxed anymore. I hope you weren't expecting a puff-fest tonight."

"I can manage without it. I don't get an opportunity to smoke down in Duc Pho. Enlisted men and officers live in the

160

same building. But I'll need to pop a can to toast D'Amico. That's still legal, right?"

"Yep, beer's no problem. Back to business. Here's your pass and flight info. Have a great time. But, Nolan," he smiled, "be sure to come back."

Nolan stifled a joke about flying to Canada.

While the chow in the mess hall was sufficiently edible, Nolan appreciated more the good night's rest. He slept the larger part of the flight to Tokyo, as well, which surprised him. While riding on buses and trains, he slept easily; planes were another matter. He must have had a sleep deficit to fill without realizing it. Once back on the ground in Japan, he felt energized again. Outside of New York, Tokyo was the biggest city he had ever visited. The city sights fascinated him. On the bus ride into the heart of the city, he was amused by seeing a taxi driver standing beside his cab swinging a golf club while awaiting a fare. A minute or so later, he saw a triple-deck driving range, the largest he had ever seen. He surely would play golf during his visit. The neon lights and noisy traffic, mostly small cars, disconcerted him somewhat after the quiet of recent months. As planned, he tried to read as many signs as he could, with mixed results. Some places revealed the nature of their business though quick peeks in the windows, restaurants in particular. He imagined his walks would stimulate him even more. So many people on the move. Walking among them was definitely the best way to see the city.

The military base occupied a big chunk of acreage surprisingly close to the city center, a reminder of the devastating war with Japan and the following occupation. He had traveled in uniform but immediately changed to civvies to see the sights. Not that people wouldn't know he was a soldier, his short hair a dead giveaway. The first full day he walked all about the central city, speeding up on occasion to match the efficient walking patterns of the locals. No one seemed to be in a great hurry, but no one loitered either to gawk at the sights as he might have otherwise in the busiest spots. Men and women dressed in conservative business attire as in any bustling city, with a few miniskirts among the young women and colorful school uniforms for the kids. He ate lunch alone in a small café, delicious miso, getting by by pointing to the menu and a few stock phrases. Mostly, he browsed shop windows, taking particular delight at one narrow bookshop where nearly every visitor stood in isolation thoroughly engrossed in a comic book or other colorfully illustrated paperback, all the while standing stock still facing the high shelves during these precious moments of privacy. While he felt an urge to join them, he kept walking. He could stop in later once he had the lay of the land. It felt so liberating to be wandering about without any fear for safety. No snipers or sappers to occupy his thoughts today.

He crossed the busy avenue at a traffic light and found a souvenir shop at the opposite corner where he purchased a few inexpensive items for his mates in Duc Pho. He bought a geisha figurine for Elston that would have to suffice for the handyman's prurient interests. He thought he would get something for Pho, too, to let him know that their friendship wasn't just about shooting baskets. By the end of the afternoon, he calculated he had walked several miles in his Army dress shoes, the farthest he had walked in months. The pavement made his feet sore. He willed himself to ignore the discomfort. He wouldn't get blisters. The Army toughened your feet. And he would probably never get to visit Tokyo again. He wanted to keep busy, to take in as much as he could.

The next morning he decided to play some golf even though it was just as foggy as the previous morning had been. He knew he couldn't wait for a sunny day, and at least it wasn't raining yet. The temperature trended lower than in Vietnam, so it would be comfortable playing. As the fog lifted, the impeccably conditioned Army course gradually revealed its beauty. He played alone with a set of clubs and a pair of worn spiked shoes borrowed from the pro shop. On one fairway,

Nolan saw a phalanx of Japanese women kneeling in what looked like woolen kimonos and large sun hats, weeding the grass by hand. No wonder the course looked so good. Playing again after so many months seemed odd at first, but he eased into it, occasionally hitting the slowly rising shots that he had learned to carve on the base course in windy El Paso. It fleetingly crossed his mind that tracers would be useful in the misty air, but otherwise the war remained a world away. His short game was the rustiest. Still, at the end of the nine holes, he felt satisfied. Golf was golf, no matter how far away from home he was.

That afternoon he visited the spacious base PX and made the purchases he had considered before arrival: four Seiko watches, one for each of his parents, one for Karen, and one for himself, along with a complete hi-fidelity sound system. The PX offered a dizzying assortment of items, including row after row of electronic components, deeply discounted from retail prices. He had to keep reminding himself that all this was temporary. In just a few days, he would be returning to the simple life in Nam.

He started out on foot the next day, but then opted to share a cab with another GI because he wanted to see the Imperial Palace Gardens. The gray skies loomed low that day, too. Nolan was beginning to think that smog created a persistent condition in Tokyo, a sign of too much internal combustion from a thriving economy. In the East Garden, though, the combination of slow-moving streams, placid ponds, and exquisitely shaped trees and shrubs made for a feeling of serenity he hadn't experienced in months. He had never seen gingko trees before, or fields of small white stones raked into soothing patterns. The world could be an orderly place, the garden seemed to say.

On his last full day, dawn brought clearer skies, and on a recommendation of another GI, Nolan decided on a day trip by train to Mount Fuji less than sixty miles away. He boarded the sleek train without any special provisions except for some fruit he had purchased at a stand. He wouldn't have time for a long hike, but he heard that a shuttle bus operated between the nearest station and the mountain's base. The countryside introduced a Japan Nolan otherwise would not have seen, hundreds of small farms carefully tended. Every inch of land in the intricate patchwork appeared vital. The train moved more swiftly than any other he had been on in the States. In barely an hour he was standing on the arrival platform, looking for directions to the shuttle. The sun shone brightly, without much humidity, a great day for sightseeing. The sacred mountain posed magnificently on the near horizon. Not, he noted, that much different from the paintings that he had seen, which he had always assumed to be idealized—a peak floating in the sky.

Fuji shone forth in beauty, the summit still bearing snow despite the early summer warmth. Deciduous vegetation, primarily beech, grew around the base. Higher up, fir and hemlock dominated, providing a wondrous green canopy over the steepening slopes. Nolan walked an hour or two in the invigorating air along the well-groomed mountain trails, stopping to sample his lunch where a commanding view of the countryside drew him to pause near a small Shinto shrine. He stopped at the torii gate, its vermilion pillars and crossbeam overhead marking the approach to the shrine. This traditional "bird's nest" suggested a meld of the natural and spiritual worlds. While he ate an apple he had brought, he remembered traversing the low, forested mountains of Maine. He recalled their granite outcroppings emerging from the pines and spruces, all stretching northeast toward Mt. Katahdin, the terminus of the Appalachian Trail. But he felt too much at peace to allow any homesickness to cloud his thoughts. He realized, too, the wooded walk here appeared free of annoyances such as the mosquitoes and black flies that plagued Maine woods in summer. A hit of D'Amico's dope couldn't have relaxed him more.

Eventually, a group of gamboling school children with their teachers joined him around the shrine, a cue to start back. He strode quickly down to the mountain floor enjoying the adrenaline rush, his long legs making the descent almost twice as fast as his ascent. On reaching the trailhead, he figured that the bus would be arriving in a few minutes. The exercise left him thirsty and still hungry. He drank copious amounts of water from a fountain, and then purchased two ears of grilled corn from a vendor, a treat glazed with soy sauce. He sat on a bench munching on the ears while reflecting on the recent days spent both in the crowded city and by himself. Just as at the gardens the day before, he felt completely at peace.

His trip to Japan had relaxed him completely. Oddly, he didn't feel apprehensive about returning to a war zone. In a way, he thought of the next few months as the last quarter of a football game, time rushing toward a conclusion. Nolan boarded the train returning to Tokyo in an expansive mood. More crowded than on the morning run, the train appeared to have picked up a full complement of sightseers. He found a seat opposite an older Japanese man dressed in a traditional robe and a boy of about fifteen, more casually dressed and engrossed in a pulp publication like the ones Nolan had seen in the Tokyo bookshop. The man did not appear to see Nolan, but he was alert and spoke to the boy briefly when Nolan sat down, and the boy looked up, then over to Nolan, before muttering something to his companion. Apparently, the man was blind. Nolan guessed the boy, possibly a grandson, acted as the old man's guide. Nolan smiled briefly and bowed his head a little toward the boy as a way of greeting. The boy reciprocated, but Nolan didn't know enough Japanese to start a conversation.

Nolan looked out at the passing countryside. The speed of the train made for only the briefest of glimpses. Turning back, he noticed the boy was looking at a pictorial article on baseball, a sport Nolan loved. He knew that some Japanese baseball terms were direct phonetic versions of American terms. A hit was *hitto* and a double play was *getto-tsuu*, or as a manager might say, "Get two." He recalled listening to a friend's tape of a game broadcast in Japanese. An announcer was rattling away matter-of-factly, only suddenly to raise his voice and shout unmistakably in English, "Squeeze play! Squeeze play!" The broadcaster continued on amid a crowd's roar, the rest totally unintelligible.

Nolan hadn't spoken since breakfast in any language. When the boy looked up, Nolan tapped his heart twice and said, "Baseball." The boy's eyes lit up. "Yes. Me, too." He knew some English. He held up the magazine for Nolan to see. It was a photo of Sadaharu Oh, the Japanese slugger.

"*Supaa sutra!*" he said proudly.

"Yes, a superstar!" Impulsively, from his seat, Nolan mimicked a left-handed swing with his upper torso and arms.

The boy smiled and asked, "Do you live in Japan?"

Nolan said "no." He wanted to say he was a soldier, but all he could think of was "samurai." That would sound so stupid. He didn't measure up to that warrior image. Finally, he said, "GI," and the boy nodded.

The old man seemed to ask the boy for an explanation. The boy fired off some Japanese. With a blank expression, the man grunted.

Nolan asked the boy, "Do you live in Tokyo?"

"Yes, my grandfather lives with us now. He lived in Hiroshima."

Nolan noted the reference but didn't acknowledge it. "You speak good English."

"Not too good," the boy laughed. He spoke a few Japanese words again to his grandfather.

Nolan let the boy get back to his magazine. He didn't want to complicate things by asking too many questions. Perhaps he had been too forward in speaking. Nonetheless, the boy looked happy, while he old man stared straight ahead, apparently content to be silent.

When the train came to a stop in Tokyo, Nolan rose from his seat and bowed again to the man and the boy. "Sayonara," he said.

"Sayonara," the boy replied. Then, his grandfather turned his head slowly toward Nolan, uttering a few Japanese words. No trace of a smile.

Nolan waited for a translation if there was to be one.

"My grandfather says, 'Be well.'" The boy hesitated. "He also says, 'Do not harm.'"

Chapter 14: Monsoon

In-country air travel was definitely improving, Nolan mused, reclining his cushioned seat on a spanking new Lear jet operated by Air Vietnam, a CIA enterprise. So, this is how Thayer, the Song Mao CORDS man, got around, he thought— very comfy. Nolan was hitching a ride from Than Son Nhut, where his flight from Japan had landed, up to Da Nang and the 29th Civil Affairs HQ. He remained surprisingly unperturbed about returning to an active war zone. No doubt the smooth ride helped to relax him even more. Glancing around, he didn't see any other enlisted men aboard, just a single Army captain and several civilians, to judge from dress. Though back in uniform, he resolved that his R&R wouldn't end until he checked himself into HQ. He stretched his legs languidly, closed his eyes, and without another conscious thought, fell soundly asleep.

In Da Nang, Sanders, D'Amico's replacement at HQ, acknowledged his return with a studied indifference.

"You again, Nolan? Weren't you just here?"

"Maybe I never left. If I said I had second thoughts about an R&R and decided to see the DMZ instead, would you believe me? You know, by going there I might've ended the war on the spot. The NVA would cower at the sight of GI Joe in the flesh."

"I guess they didn't see you, then. No change in the war as far as I can see, which admittedly isn't any further than the walls of this room."

He reached across his desk to a pile of paper on a low file cabinet.

"OK, let me look on my magic clipboard to see if there's anyone headed down to Quang Ngai soon. You wouldn't mind riding a water buffalo, would you?"

"No, I'm used to slow travel. I own a car like that."

He was not exaggerating that much. His '65 Chevy II, with the Hi-Thrift engine so dependable in all kinds of weather, was sadly no sports car. Now sitting mostly unused on the family property in Maine, the Chevy II would again become his wheels, ready for a new chapter, he hoped—his life after Nam.

As it turned out, a two-and-a-half-ton truck loaded with supplies was headed down to Quang Ngai city the next morning, a decided drop in the comfort department from the day before, though he rode in the cab. The husky driver chatted amiably a bit with Nolan to break up the tedium of the miles.

"They say the monsoon season will be here soon. Not what we're used to seeing in summer months, hey?" the driver said, turning his pasty face toward Nolan, eyes momentarily off the road.

"Roger that" Nolan replied. "If you're going to grow rice, though, you need plenty of rain. Probably, the farmers—what's left of them anyway—will be happy."

"It sounds like you know some of these farmers."

"Actually, I spend more time with farmers who wish they could be growing rice again. They were cleared off their land."

"No offense, pal, but they're all just gooks to me," the driver said, "clogging up the road with their Lambrettas and bicycles."

So much for a friendly chat, Nolan thought. He realized there wasn't much chance of a meeting of the minds here. So many GIs showed a similar disposition, a racially charged impatience with the locals, though Nolan never heard such crap from Civil Affairs or MACV personnel. He yawned. "Wake me up if you hit anything."

His companion laughed half-heartedly.

At a checkpoint in Quang Ngai city, Hardy sat alone in Maybe Tomorrow waiting to meet the truck. Nolan appreciated the Lieutenant's solo trip up from Duc Pho without some backup. As Hardy steered the jeep down Highway One south, Nolan described his relaxing week in Japan. The last part of the ride took place in a light but steady rain. Monsoon season so soon, Nolan wondered.   At least, the truck driver got one thing right.

Nolan resumed the conversation with Hardy. "All in all, sir, R&R filled the bill. I guess I needed it. How did you and Mr. Nguyen get along in my absence?"

"Just fine, though apparently my Southern accent carries over into Vietnamese, too, I'm afraid. We had some misunderstandings early on. After a while, I let him try his English more. So, I suppose we did miss you a little."

"Glad to hear it. I can't say that I missed Duc Pho a whole lot, but for sure there are worse places to be. I'm ready to get back to work. That's a good sign, I think."

"It probably means you're not cut out to be an idle tourist. anyhow. Still, I don't expect you will want to re-up and skip going back to school."

"No, sir. Not a chance of that happening. Just two months now. I'll try not to get too squirrely if I can help it."

Rain fell hard the next two days in Duc Pho, which made travel in the door-less jeep a soaking experience. The compound's courtyard filled up with puddles, but the main building stayed dry. Along the highway, the rice paddies began to crest with the excess water. Not surprisingly, few village officials surfaced for consultation. Nolan and Hardy heard "Maybe tomorrow" quite a few times. On the third day, though, only a gentle mist descended in the morning, which lifted spirits considerably. Mr. Nguyen wanted to show Hardy and Nolan a hamlet that had put to use a recent shipment of tin sheets to re-roof some old huts. In low visibility, they drove north a few miles, and then followed a dike road as far as they could across some partially flooded rice paddies until it was clear that the rest of the journey, a few hundred yards, needed to be on foot.

"Nolan, maybe you had better stay with the jeep in case anyone needs to get by." Hardy pointed to the courtyard of an adjacent house, a solid structure, immediately adjacent. "You could probably pull over there if you need to. It looks like firm ground for now."

Nolan thought the Lieutenant was just being diplomatic in front of Mr. Nguyen and didn't want to mention his concern about someone stealing the jeep. This place, a virtual pastoral scene, seemed unlikely for such theft, but losing their vehicle that way would be damn embarrassing.

While Hardy and Mr. Nguyen followed a dike path to the hamlet, Nolan settled behind the wheel, removing his bush hat in the humid air. He brushed his short, auburn hair with a bare hand. His hair had grown out enough, at least, to make the stateside military cuts with the bare "sidewalls" a distant memory. He stretched his arms as a few drops of rain began to fall onto the windshield. Then, he glanced at the house a few yards to his left and saw through an open window a young woman, probably about twenty, sitting at a small loom. She was busily working the loom or patching something—he couldn't be sure exactly--but after a while she started to sing in Vietnamese what appeared to be a love song. So many of the songs Nolan had heard in Vietnam were melancholic and romantic. This one was no exception. Ca had sung more than a few of them back in the compound. Nolan made out some of the words, the singer imagining her lover off to war, "a soldier standing alone in the rain." He smiled at the near coincidence. She had a sweet voice, and her diction was clear. Nolan had pointed out to the Lieutenant how so many older rural people had bad teeth. The red stain about their mouths resulted from the daily habit of chewing betel nuts to alleviate tooth pain. Few older people had many teeth at all. Understanding their speech could be a challenge, nothing like the carefully enunciated language he heard from his young, educated teachers back at Fort Bliss.

At first, he didn't know if the young woman had taken note of his presence. Then, at one point she slowly raised her eyes in his direction as she intoned the words, "Em yêu anh ("I love you"). Nolan laughed to himself, but he kept a straight face.

She appeared to be playing a private game, making him part of her romantic reverie, while retaining the social distance expected between a young woman of a respectable family and an American GI. She sang another verse: more rain and the soldier sad to be so long away from his home village and his sweetheart. Again, she lifted her eyes from her work, looking soulfully toward the jeep and singing the refrain, "Em yêu anh." Nolan suppressed a laugh, even more certain that she was having some fun. He also knew that she would be incredibly embarrassed if he somehow let her know that he understood what she was singing. So, he sat there silently, content to be the butt in her game. He also decided to keep this serenade to himself, a light yet touching few minutes in the middle of a war zone. Hardy would probably just say he was imagining things.

As he had hoped it would when he first arrived in country, his translating ability had evolved into a practical fluency, although he still had trouble with slang and understanding some speakers. He also knew he wouldn't be able to converse very well about abstract topics. He didn't need to. He just needed to speak well enough to do his job.

Pho had been very helpful in Nolan's learning process over the past few months, filling in the missing words when he was at a loss. Pho also provided tidbits from Vietnamese folklore from time to time. Regarding the monsoon, he said the people believed that it was actually the god of the sea attempting to flood the land out of jealousy because the god of the mountains had won the hand of a beautiful princess. The water always stopped short of the mountain slopes.

Nolan was grateful for this enlightenment and other acts of friendship. Their brief conversations pleased him, gradually becoming longer sessions of storytelling. He remembered a story Pho told him some weeks ago about having a pet chicken when he was young.

"My mother, she saw I liked the chicken, so she didn't kill it. She called it 'Lucky.' Lucky lived a long time."

"How long?" Nolan asked.

"Three years, I think. I don't remember."

"I guess that's good," Nolan said, suddenly thinking of his canine pal Tasty in Song Mao. He hadn't thought of him in many weeks.

Remembering Pho's story in the Tokyo souvenir shop, Nolan had selected a small, plastic chicken from some traditional lucky charms called *engimono*. It wasn't very expensive, and he knew Pho would like it. Wrapping it would be unnecessary.

He had presented it to Pho the same day he had returned to Duc Pho.

"Here you are, my friend. May luck stay with you."

It was just a trifle, but Pho acted excited to get it.

"Thank you, No-LANN." For Pho, he was always No-LANN.

They no longer shot baskets in the courtyard during the early evening hours, but now they frequently sat at the steps and conversed, content to be idle. Nolan learned that Pho was an only son who had two younger sisters. He told Pho about his own family, and they shared more and more stories about growing up.

One morning, as they talked, Long, the Phoenix assassin, appeared, looking as wary as usual. Not bothering to greet Nolan, he brusquely asked Pho where he could find Lt. O'Hare. Pho pointed to the dining area. When Long passed through the entrance, Nolan thought he saw a troubled look on Pho's face.

"A strange man," ventured Nolan.

Pho didn't say anything. He just shook his head, his eyes downcast. Nolan knew they shared a similar dislike of Long, but he didn't want to put Pho on the spot. He let it go.

Rain had fallen steadily almost every day since his return, but when the sun came out, the heat became strong. On a particularly hot afternoon when their canteens had run dry, Hardy, who was driving the jeep, offered to buy Nolan a bottle of Coke at one of the make-shift cafés by the side of the highway.

"I'll wait here, and we can drink as we go," he said, handing Nolan a few Vietnamese bills. "I don't want to hazard any ice in a glass."

"Thanks for the reminder, sir."

In such places, the server would chip some slivers from an ice block covered with sawdust, place them in a fly-surrounded glass, and then pour the soda or beer from a warm bottle over the ice before handing it to a customer. Nolan and Hardy had tried to hide their squeamishness previously when treating Mr. Nguyen to afternoon refreshment. Nolan had already endured one case of diarrhea that he attributed to this practice. A soft drink, even lukewarm straight from the bottle, appealed to him more today.

Nolan covered the short distance from jeep to hut in a few long strides to avoid the rain. He parted the plastic curtain strips in the doorway and ducked into the interior darkness. Two men were standing in the rear of the room, their backs to him, unaware of his presence. One man was speaking rapidly in an excited voice and Nolan caught just a few words, "bắn Thieu," or so he thought. He was startled. "Shoot Thieu"? Were they talking about shooting someone named Thieu? Major Thieu? Stewart's counterpart? Nolan realized he had to play dumb. This was not the time to speak any Vietnamese. The speaker now turned toward him and greeted him with an awkward "hello" and a brief nod. Was he uneasy about Nolan overhearing? The man's face appeared flushed.

"Coca Cola," Nolan said, holding up two fingers and tilting his head toward the entrance to suggest the order was to go. He glanced at the man but didn't hold his gaze. He had a rough idea of what the cost would be, so he handed over a few single bills and got back two coins. He smiled and nodded his thanks, exiting with the two lukewarm bottles.

Getting back into the jeep, he didn't say anything to Hardy about the incident. He had to process it first. Did he actually overhear part of a plan to shoot the Vietnamese major? He wished he could rewind the moment. It wasn't as if he could

174

ask for a clarification. The man had acted somewhat uneasy with him, but then he probably didn't get many American GIs stopping there. Nolan's pantomime could have factored into the uneasiness, too. It was an awkward exchange. Nolan felt torn. Had he really stumbled across something sinister? Should he say something to Hardy about it, or just let it go as something he must have misheard?

He kept quiet about it the rest of the day, wondering if his distraction showed. What would Hardy do with the information? If he thought it warranted some action, he would no doubt want to pass it on to Major Stewart and O'Hare. Nolan would have to describe exactly what he had heard and witnessed, and then identify the men—in essence, be certain about the incident. But he wasn't certain. He didn't get a good look at the other man. More to the point, he hadn't heard enough to get a good sense of the context. Maybe he had overheard a joke. He was a decent interpreter, but hardly infallible.

Lt. O'Hare's involvement with the Phoenix program was troublesome, too. What if the situation was turned over to the cutthroat Long and Major Thieu? Would they vet the men in question fairly, provide a due process, or would they deem the men as too potentially dangerous and kill them? That was not farfetched. Suspicions of guilt could be all that mattered.

On the other hand, if there actually was a plan underway to shoot Thieu, shouldn't Nolan make sure the Major took precautions? It dawned on him that a small roadside business like this could be a convenient cover for the Viet Cong. It would be easy for the men to obtain and pass along intelligence while seemingly just trying to make a living. He stewed for a few hours, trying to decide if he should confide in Hardy. They had a good relationship built on mutual respect, but would Hardy have a solution that didn't lead to Long and O'Hare getting involved?

He couldn't risk it. He realized that he would be putting his lieutenant in an impossible position, expecting him to keep something so inflammatory under wraps. As an officer, Hardy was expected to keep his superiors informed of intelligence. He might even overestimate Nolan's skill as an interpreter, largely out of a misplaced sense of loyalty. He was a good man, that's for sure, and Nolan could not leave him in the middle. He felt a personal responsibility to get answers without putting any innocent lives in danger. It was not much different from pulling solitary guard duty on the roof during the full moon. Vigilance came with a heavy responsibility. His senses had to remain keen.

He tried to think of some similar sounding phrasing that might actually have been spoken in the café, but nothing likely came to mind. He kept going over the same possibilities, feeling more powerless as each minute passed.

He noticed his hands were shaking. He forced himself to calm down and to approach the problem methodically. He needed to find something plausible enough to explain his confusion, but he couldn't rush to judgment either. Major Thieu might very well be in imminent danger.

Back at the compound, Nolan headed to the enlisted men's quarters for a quiet place to think things out. He found Harris, Grabowski, and Elston boisterously playing hands of poker, with several open beer cans on an upended crate in front of them. No chance to think there. He collected his dictionary from a shelf by his bed along with paper and a pencil and left the room to find a better place to think. The lounge upstairs stood empty—no film that night.

Sitting down at a table, he decided he would start with the letter B. What words were close to the verb meaning "to shoot"? Then, he looked through T. He was writing possibilities down as he read so that he could suss out the best bets when he was done. He sensed someone standing behind him.

"Whatcha doin', Nolan? Writing a love letter to your Vietnamese sweetie?"

Elston had walked up the stairs without Nolan hearing any footsteps.

"Just working on my skills, man." He paused. "I guess it's like sharpening your tools, right? You're a carpenter."

He didn't want any interruption right now, but he needed to maintain a sense of normalcy.

"My tool is always ready to go, Nolan."

Nolan just shook his head. He knew that Elston liked being thought of as totally incorrigible. He would likely see Nolan's nonverbal reaction as totally normal.

"Don't overdo the lovey-dovey stuff, Nolan. See ya." Freshly retrieved beer in hand, Elston headed back down the stairs.

Glad to be alone again, Nolan got back to work. He wrote down several possibilities among near homonyms in his "B' list, and then he moved onto "T." Nothing clicked. He pored over both lists for a half-hour. Still, none of the other possibilities seemed likely. He had reached a dead-end. He didn't want to admit defeat, but he saw that he needed help from a native Vietnamese. He thought immediately of Pho. Nolan would be putting their friendship to a test. To be safe, he would have to limit what he told him. It was not a perfect solution, but time loomed crucial if there was a plot against Major Thieu.

His new watch showed it was already after nine thirty. On the other side of the compound, Pho would be resting up for another day of work with Major Stewart. Pho took his job seriously, maybe out of a sincere belief in the democratic process that the Americans ballyhooed. Maybe to not shame his family. Nolan didn't know what motivated him. He did see a sense of decency, though, when Pho intervened on behalf of local people who occasionally made requests to Major Stewart. Nolan decided to trust his instincts. It might be desperation taking over, but he would risk asking Pho to help.

Shining a flashlight before him, Nolan crossed the courtyard to the barracks of the Vietnamese enlisted men, something he had never done before. At the doorway, he encountered a soldier smoking a cigarette. He asked for Pho in Vietnamese. It took a few minutes before Pho appeared, stripped to shorts and a sleeveless t-shirt. His face registered surprise at Nolan's presence.

"No-LANN, what's happening, my friend?"

"Nothing much," he feigned, "but I need a small favor."

He proceeded to tell Pho about stopping at the café that afternoon, leaving out the part about the words that he thought he had overheard. He just said that something about the place bothered him, and he needed Pho's observations to put his mind to rest.

"Would you go with me tomorrow morning back to that place? I don't know who runs it. Maybe you could pretend to be a customer, ask some questions, get an impression. I may be imagining things."

Maybe only a few seconds elapsed, but Nolan wondered if Pho had understood him. Finally, he spoke,

"I will do it. I will ask Major Stewart for a free hour. Nine o'clock?"

Nolan thanked him and said he would drive. Perhaps, Hardy would believe an alibi about meeting Pho's family. Both Hardy and Nolan had dined at Mr. Nguyen's home and met his family. A visit to another family would not seem out of character.

Sleep evaded Nolan much of the night. At first, his mind raced with anticipation of what the next day would reveal. Then, seemingly right after falling asleep, Harris woke him for radio duty. Despite eating breakfast, he was still somewhat groggy when he met Pho in the courtyard at nine. Hardy accepted the story about a family introduction without hesitation. Nolan felt bad about the deception, but he had made his choice.

Once on the road, the two men didn't talk much. Nolan felt relieved that Pho wasn't asking him questions. He himself was having second thoughts about asking Pho to help. Was he putting him in danger? It took only ten minutes to get to the rustic café, but when they arrived, Pho didn't appear to recognize it.

"It must be a new place. Not very safe at night without soldiers nearby."

Nolan shuddered. How dangerous was this place?

"I would go in with you, Pho, but it's better that I stay here in the jeep."

"Don't worry. I'm cool."

It had started to rain again, so Pho jumped out of the jeep and quickly entered the hut. Nolan tried to sit patiently, but he couldn't help throwing looks at the doorway every few seconds. Five minutes passed, maybe ten. Nolan wondered if he should take a closer look. Maybe the occupants *were* spies and had smelled a rat. He would wait just a few more minutes. The M-16 remained within easy reach.

Then, from the dark opening, Pho emerged, a paper bag in hand. He jogged to the jeep, head down in the light rain. When he sat down, his face beamed.

"No problem, my friend. Nothing unusual about the place, but I'm glad you took me here. The owner had a big secret."

"How so?"

Reaching into the bag, Pho handed Nolan a small, puffed pastry, deep fried and covered with seeds. It was warm and surprisingly light. "His wife—she just began making bánh tiêu for sale yesterday. He says they are the best."

Nolan stared at the doughnut. The raindrops began to fall more insistently on the windshield.

"Bánh tiêu," he said softly to himself. Then again, "bánh tiêu."

He felt his body almost melt back into the seat. How could he have been so stupid? He shook his head slowly. He tried to sound upbeat.

"After you, Pho. What is your expert opinion? Are they the best?"

Pho took one from the bag and held it out for consideration.

"Still warm—that's good," he opined before biting into it with gusto. A fully enunciated comment followed a few seconds later. "WON-DER-FUL. Your turn now."

Nolan took a bite from his pastry. Nothing ever tasted better—so delicate, with a hint of sugar. He took a final bite and immediately reached for his wallet.

"Let me repay you, Pho. You did me a big favor."

"No can do, No-LANN."

Nolan smiled with mock exasperation at his friend. He was about to object, but paused, remembering what he had told Hardy. One more thing to do. He still had time to extricate himself from his phony excuse. And he owed Pho an explanation, but that would have to wait.

"I can see, Pho, that these aren't going to last long, so how about if I buy some more to take to your family? They're not far from here, and maybe we can stop by and see them before returning to Duc Pho."

His companion slowly raised an eyebrow in a sidewise glance.

"You want to meet my sisters, No-LANN. Yes?"

"Oh. Sure. If you say so, Pho."

Chapter 15: Road Trips

As the summer progressed, the persistent rain that permeated every inch of Duc Pho subsided to occasional showers with increasingly more sunshine. Nolan saw more light on his personal horizon, as well. Only a perfunctory physical for admission to the University of Wisconsin remained in his plan for early release from duty. Pending a good report on the physical, he had been accepted by the graduate English program there. As luck would have it, Ben Ames, a former medical-school buddy of his brother-in-law, currently served as a trauma surgeon at the EVAC Hospital in Chu Lai, north of Quang Ngai city. Nolan's sister had heard that Ben had been called to duty after a residency in Boston and forwarded his address to Nolan. Ben wasted no time responding to Nolan's own written request, saying that he would be glad to examine him. The two had seen each other occasionally in the four years since the wedding of Nolan's sister and got along well. Nolan scheduled his trip to Chu Lai for a Saturday afternoon, Ben having told him which weekend seemed best in regard to his schedule, with no guarantee that the physical could be performed on the spot. So, he suggested staying over one night. Nolan wouldn't be able to return in the dark on Saturday, in any case.

This was to be his first solo trip north of Quang Ngai. For company part way, he offered Pho a chance to ride along in Maybe Tomorrow as far as his family's home. After Nolan had told Pho about Karen in Madison, he stopped kidding Nolan about a possible interest in his sisters. Nolan needed to conceal what he had felt when he first saw Pho's sisters, though. They were as beautiful as advertised. Thi, the older of the two, radiated a power of attraction greater than he had ever felt since discovering girls. As slender as Pho, she featured large, dark eyes highlighted by even darker lashes, set off by a beautiful, clear, ivory complexion. When Pho first introduced him to the family, Nolan couldn't help but glance repeatedly at Thi. He forced himself to look away toward the others more than once. Pho explained that Nolan had purchased the bánh tiêu as a gift. Both girls were delighted, the younger one, Thanh, nearly beside herself with joy, her long black hair secured by a red ribbon, bobbing behind her and falling nearly to her waist. Both girls dressed simply in plain white tunics and black pants, not expecting that Pho was bringing a guest home, let alone a young male foreigner.

Pho's father, Bao, appeared to frown at the sight of the American soldier, but when Pho mentioned that his father spoke French well, Nolan ventured a few phrases, and Bao loosened up considerably. They sat inside the small, well-kept home and ate the pastries with some tea brewed by Pho's mother, Mai. Nolan didn't have much chance to engage the girls in conversation. Bao directed the talk, asking him questions about his education and his reading interests. Nolan gave some of his answers in Vietnamese so that the girls could understand him, too. Taught to be reserved in the presence of strangers, the girls sat quietly and listened as Nolan strove to focus on the conversation and suppress his glances at Thi. His relief at finding out there was no serious plot against Major Thieu made him more garrulous than usual, but Pho's family did not seem to mind at all.

The two young men couldn't stay long that first visit because the Lieutenant was expecting Nolan back with the jeep. Naturally, Nolan had looked forward to this second visit, brief though it, too, would be. He wouldn't be able to spend more than a few minutes there if he wanted to reach the hospital in the relative safety of daylight. He wanted to ask Pho more about Thi, specifically what she planned to do now that she was home from art school in Saigon. He decided to wait until the subject came up in polite conversation with the family. He didn't want to show too much interest. He found it easier to talk about work as they rode along, and Nolan appreciated that Pho felt comfortable enough with him to open up a little about Major Stewart.

"He is a good man. Major Thieu thinks he is funny, maybe not a tough leader, but I like him. He has treated me well."

"I respect him, too. There is more to him, as we Americans say, than meets the eye."

"A good saying. I will remember that."

"He may not have told you, but the other night he let me take a wounded Viet guy and his friend to the base hospital. The two of them showed up around ten o'clock at our doorway, one guy clutching his stomach in pain. I didn't see any blood, but the friend kept saying 'hospital.' I checked with the Major, and he gave me the go ahead. I hadn't driven the jeep at night before, so it was scary without any lights on the road. LZ Bronco is close, though."

"They knew they needed an American as liaison to get help. Otherwise, they would be refused."

"Yeah, I knew that, too. I was glad to do it. Anyhow, the American doctor and nurse took him right away. They saw that he had been shot, but it was a small hole from a pistol, not a rifle."

"I can tell you, a friend shot him. They were arguing about a woman. I was the one who told them you would take him to the American doctors."

"Well, you can thank Major Stewart for giving me the OK. He probably suspected that the shooting wasn't duty related. I heard the guy will survive."

"If he leaves other men's wives alone, maybe."

They chuckled about that. Nolan decided not to tell Pho all he saw at the hospital that night. Not the time. A few minutes later, Nolan stopped the jeep in front of the family home. He knew he could only spare a few minutes, but the opportunity to see the girls would make his day.

"Pho, I can only say 'hello' if I want to keep on schedule. I hope your family doesn't find that rude."

"It's OK. Everyone will understand. Come in and have some tea, at least."

As it turned out, the girls were not at home. They were visiting a friend nearby. Nolan's face must have fallen with the news, as Bao added in somewhat formal French that his daughters would be sorry to have missed him. It was a friendly exchange, however. Bao invited Nolan to return some other time when he could stay longer.

"Merci, Monsieur Bao."

They exchanged good-byes, and Nolan started Maybe Tomorrow very slowly down the dusty road toward the main highway just in case he spotted the girls returning. He rolled the jeep slowly past the row of equally small neighboring houses, but no sign of the girls. It wasn't going to be his day.

After clearing the checkpoint at Quang Ngai city, he drove directly to Chu Lai, making excellent time, the road mostly clear of traffic. He fantasized briefly about not stopping at Chu Lai and driving on in the remaining daylight, maybe as far as the city of Da Lat, the place lauded for its beauty in the language manuals at Fort Bliss—the fantasy he shared with Murph months ago on the road to Cam Ranh. Sited in the pine forests at almost a mile-high elevation, the city he heard remained temperate year around, a perennial Parisian spring in lieu of tropical heat. The French had developed the city as a colonial resort earlier in the century. Maybe an eternal truce presided there befitting the city's beauty.

His memory would not allow him to bask in that illusion for very long. He remembered hearing that the city took heavy damage during the Tet offensive. And, to top it off, he realized that he was actually driving in the opposite direction from Da Lat, which lay far to the south. He wasn't going to see any beauty today, he finally acknowledged to himself—the missed opportunity to see Pho's sisters still gnawing at him. He settled for Chu Lai.

Once on the drab base, a mishmash of tents and low modular structures, he found the hospital building easily, figuring that it would be near a helipad. At that very moment a chopper was unloading some badly wounded GIs. Nolan felt squeamish about getting any closer after his last hospital visit. He parked the jeep down the road and skirted the trauma unit, sensing that the doctors billeted nearby.

Ben had been expecting him, so he had come out from one of the modular buildings, waving to Nolan and inviting him in. He had just gotten off his shift, and when they shook hands, Nolan noted his eyes looked weary.

"Good to see you. I'll be OK, just give me a minute. A beer sound good?"

He led Nolan in and introduced him to a colleague, a fellow New Englander. The three young men took seats around a low table, beers in hand. Nolan said he appreciated Ben's willingness to help him out with the physical.

"Not a problem. Glad to do it."

"Well, thanks, I know you're busy here."

Ben asked Nolan how his sister and husband were doing in Boston. They had a two-year-old son and were expecting another child. After a few minutes of family reports, the conversation turned to work.

"So what's it like being an interpreter?" Ben asked.

"Not bad. It's a challenge every day, but I seem to be getting business done all right. Most people can understand me, and I understand most of them. As I told you in my letter, we work monitoring aid to refugees, and there seems to be no end to them. The camps are full."

Ben glanced first at his colleague, and then back at Nolan, his earlier smile more a grimace now.

"Full of vermin, right? The bastards!"

Nolan was taken aback. This was not how he remembered Ben. He stammered to reply.

"Not really. I mean, they're people in pain. They've lost their homes, their livelihood—really all they had except for some clothes."

The other doctor quickly weighed in. "How do you know they aren't VC and haven't been setting booby traps to blow up GIs on patrol?"

"I can't vouch for all of them. Most refugees, though, are peasants, rice farmers, and from what I have found out don't have political leanings. They just want to be left alone."

"Someone is doing a number on our guys," Ben interjected. "We're busy day and night here trying to save limbs and lives. How can you trust these people?"

"I get the feeling you mean any Vietnamese."

"Yeah, I do. Who's a friend? Who's an enemy? We get wounded ARVN and wounded VC, too. I can't see any real difference. And the Vietnamese who work on the base—they just want favors all the time. Why don't they do more to help themselves?"

Nolan thought he could see what lay behind the doctors' reactions, saddled as they were with the responsibility of triage, trying to determine if they could keep breathing the mangled body of a young man perfectly healthy an hour ago. Often, they were treating multiple patients at the same time. They could expect only a brief respite until more badly wounded GIs arrived on stretchers. It was the same every day. Here they made decisions of life and death. The pressure on them must have been enormous.

He sensed this wasn't the ideal time to make a case for the Vietnamese. Let Ben and his roommate get a bite to eat, a chance to unwind first. He thought of the East Indian story of the blind men and the elephant. Each felt a different part of the elephant and came to different conclusions about the nature of what they were sensing. Who were the Vietnamese? The doctors had their view, and he had his. Damn it, though—his experience with the people went further. He knew the language and some of the culture, not that he was any great expert. He respected nearly all the people he had met. He couldn't let these negative attitudes go unchallenged. The doctors had no time for exploring culture, too busy with more urgent matters, saving lives. Still, Ben was a decent, smart guy, who should know better. When the time was right, Nolan was determined to say something in defense of his friends and acquaintances.

For now, he decided to show more interest in what the two doctors were hearing from family and friends back home and about their plans after they finished their tours. They even talked about the Red Sox, who had not been able to extend the magic of the '67 season. Making small talk proved easy enough through an evening meal in the small mess hall next door. The chow was actually pretty good, Nolan thought. At least, the Vietnamese cooks were taking good care of the medical staff.

After dinner, they returned to quarters and sat down to another round of beer. Ben said he was off until Sunday afternoon unless there was a sudden overflow of patients. Nolan could tell Ben was exhausted even though he tried hard to keep up his end of conversation.

"So, have you had any close calls with the VC. I imagine it's not all peace and quiet for you."

"I've been very lucky, really. We got mortared one night in Duc Pho, and there are times on the open road when we hear rifle fire and wonder if somebody is sniping at us. We worry about hitting mines on roads to hamlets, but we don't take big chances."

"Glad to hear that."

Nolan brought up the friendly fire incident back in Song Mao, treating the incident much more humorously than he tended to see it back then, talking more about his fears than about what he did. He mentioned a few of his American colleagues, what amused him about them, skipping the sad story of Captain Barnes.

After Ben's roommate excused himself for the night, saying he needed to get some beauty sleep, Ben's voice took on a more confidential tone.

"Sorry about earlier. We didn't mean to imply your work was of questionable value. The job gets us down at times."

"Hey, Ben, I understand. I don't know how you guys can do it. I rode over to the small hospital at LZ Bronco not long ago, having brought in a wounded ARVN for care, a guy who got shot during a domestic dispute. While I was there, a chopper came in with wounded GIs. I was glad to get out of there. But I got a quick look at what you're dealing with on a daily basis. It freaked me out."

"Yeah, we keep busy. I think I'll be ready for any trauma by the time I get back to the States. So, tell me more about your job. You seem to like it."

"Like I said, I've been lucky. My boss, Lieutenant Hardy, is a good egg. We get along well. He's not a career soldier and puts up with my gripes about the war. By the same token, he likes helping people, maybe more than I do. I can't wait to go home. He's more dedicated to the mission."

"So, what keeps your spirits up besides the fact your tour is ending soon?"

Ben's eyes seemed almost closed now.

"I'll keep it brief, Ben. You're beat, I know." He took a breath. "I've been able to use my Vietnamese to make some friendships. These friends are people I work with and their families. It's hard to go very far off the beaten path, as you can imagine, but I do feel I've learned something valuable from these friendships. I know that my view of the war has changed somewhat. It's still a mistake. We shouldn't be here. But my short stay in Nam—like yours—has an end point, a calendar date, and then we're free. My Viet friends have only a troubling uncertainty. They don't know what's ahead for themselves or for their loved ones. War and strife have dominated their lives for decades. We can't blame them for living in the present much of the time, for not being enthusiastic about the cause of democracy. They won't be able to shut the door behind their experience as we all think we can. Or maybe hope we can."

Ben's eyelids started to close again. "Sorry, man. I'm listening."

"I won't go on. You're exhausted. I'm very grateful that you could work me in for a physical. Let me just finish by saying that I wish you could meet my friends Pho, Mr. Nguyen, and their families. They are generous people, Ben. You would like them if you had the chance to know them."

Nolan stopped. Ben didn't say anything, so Nolan couldn't tell if he had made even a slight dent in his attitude. He just looked spent.

"OK, Ben, I know you've heard enough. Where do I bunk?"

Ben pointed out a cot in the corner and excused himself for the night. Lights went out earlier than Nolan was used to, yet he fell asleep quickly, waking only once in the night from the sound of a chopper landing. He suspected that Ben may not have heard the one chopper that landed that night, a routine backdrop for him.

Visibly refreshed in the morning, Ben wasted little time filling out the medical form, taking Nolan's pulse and blood pressure, checking his heart rate and lung capacity, asking a few questions about medical conditions, to all of which Nolan said no. Ben signed at the bottom of the second page. It wasn't as thorough as his draft physical, but Nolan enjoyed it more. Wisconsin probably was mostly concerned about malaria. This removed the last impediment in his way. He felt very thankful for Ben's help and said so.

After some upbeat good-byes, he stayed in a good mood on the jeep ride back to Duc Pho. He may not have convinced Ben that his negative view of the Vietnamese was based on an understandably limited perspective. The work of saving lives had to come first. But Nolan thought it would have been cowardly if he didn't say something to defend his friends. The Vietnamese have their scoundrels as any ethnic group does. Yet taking part in casual dialogue often revealed how much people from different parts of the world actually shared—the desire to love and be loved, to live long, healthy lives with their family around them. Earning public respect might not seem as important, but without such respect the other goals might be unattainable.

He had been back in Duc Pho only a few days when an incident one morning disrupted the usual quiet. A distraught Vietnamese woman wearing a conical straw hat appeared at the steps to the MACV building, crying uncontrollably. Pho hastened down to help her, thinking like Nolan and Hardy that she had been injured or wounded. She was in her late 30s, maybe 40, dressed in a gray tunic and the black pajama-like pants so common in Nam. Pho was holding her by the shoulders, trying to calm her, but he wasn't having much luck. Nolan couldn't make out what she was saying through her tears.

"What's wrong, Pho?"

"She's looking for her husband. She says he was shot."

Major Stewart emerged from the building to find out the cause of the din. The woman immediately fell at his feet, grasping his knees. She apparently recognized the oak leaf on his lapel.

"What does she want, Pho?" Stewart asked. He braced himself with the doorjamb, looking worried that the woman might knock him down.

"She is looking for her husband. She says some men shot him last night and took him away in the back of a truck."

"I don't know anything about this. Tell her to see Major Thieu. He might know something."

Pho passed along the Major's message, but the woman was having none of it. She shouted in despair.

"Sir, she says she asked Major Thieu. He wouldn't listen."

Major Stewart looked perplexed. "Well, I can't help her, not unless Major Thieu asks me to help. Tell her I will talk with him, but she has to leave."

Pho and another Vietnamese soldier each took an arm and led the woman toward the compound gate, Pho trying hard to reassure her. Hardy and Nolan just looked on dumbfounded.

They were often asked for small favors in the camps and villages, but no one had sounded as desperate as this woman. Major Stewart went inside to finish his breakfast. Nolan didn't doubt that Stewart would check with Major Thieu later. He appeared, though, to be in no rush. A few minutes later, Pho returned from the gate, shaking his head.

"Pho, who were the men last night she's talking about?" Hardy asked. "VC?"

"She doesn't know, sir. There were three, but not in uniform. If they took him to a hospital, it would be in Quang Ngai. That's the closest for Vietnamese."

Nolan's mind was racing. "But if they shot him, maybe they weren't trying to save him. Could it have been a feud?"

"I don't know. His name is Truc Vinh. Maybe I have seen him. He has a store in town. I'll go with Major Stewart to see Major Thieu. He may know the man."

The Lieutenant and Nolan had an appointment with Mr. Nguyen that morning, so they couldn't wait around for answers. When Mr. Nguyen arrived a few minutes later, they drove off to a refugee camp to the north. They filled Mr. Nguyen in with what they knew, and in turn he said he knew Truc Vinh because Vinh had a fish store on the main street. Mr. Nguyen knew a few other details, as well, which Nolan passed on to the Lieutenant.

"Mr. Nguyen says Vinh was an ARVN soldier but was wounded two years ago. He was discharged from the army. His fish business did well."

Hardy began thinking out loud. "Men with a truck, a shooting here in town? That doesn't sound like VC to me." He paused. "Well, we can't spend the whole morning speculating. We have a schedule to keep."

The men dropped the subject and got on the road without further delay. Work in the camp had progressed well in the last month. Several new small houses with tin roofs stood at the far end. Mr. Nguyen checked his paperwork and pointed to a new well along the way, which they inspected close up.

Happily, they found no cracks or flaking. Sometimes, the builders skimped on the cement so that they could use the remainder for private projects. Mr. Nguyen smiled in satisfaction. "Good work," he said, which had become his go-to phrase of late.

The three men talked casually with a camp leader, who offered them tea in his modest hut. They complied out of courtesy, but Nolan found his attention drifting after some minutes of small talk. After saying their good-byes to the camp official, they strolled back to the jeep.

"What are you daydreaming about, Nolan?" Hardy asked. "You're not really here, are you?"

"I'm just thinking, sir. We wrapped up business in under two hours, and we aren't that many miles from Quang Ngai city. Maybe we could do a quick run and get some supplies?"

"And isn't the hospital in Quang Ngai, too? Do you suppose we might check it out for new patients?"

"You know me too well, sir. My love for hospitals and all."

They exchanged smiles. Nolan realized, though, that going back to Duc Pho to drop off Mr. Nguyen first would put a wrench in their plan.

"Mr. Nguyen, do you wish to go to Quang Ngai today?" Nolan asked in Vietnamese.

The answer was affirmative, so Hardy hopped behind the wheel and Maybe Tomorrow coasted up Highway One, passing the scattered hamlets along the way, in addition to more than a few tiny buses overloaded with passengers. Nearing the city, they overtook an impromptu caravan of bicycles, some of them pulling carts with vegetables, intended for the marketplace no doubt.

Hardy didn't make any pretense about stopping at the market. Because Mr. Nguyen knew the city so well, they didn't have to ask where the hospital was. They found it just off the main road, away from the hectic marketplace. Hardy parked the jeep, and they entered the two-storey building, a plaster structure whose arched entrance reminded Nolan of the Civil Affairs building in Song Mao.

"Let's ask that nurse over there about a wounded man brought in last night," Hardy said. As they moved toward the desk, they heard a voice call out.

"No-LANN, why are you here?"

They turned to see Pho and Sgt. Childress sitting on a bench off to the side.

"And, you, Pho? Same reason, I suspect," Nolan retorted.

They smiled in unison. Childress smiled as well, somewhat sheepishly, Nolan thought. The hospital visit was, no doubt, Pho's idea. Childress spoke first, though.

"We're waiting for the chief doctor. So far we know nothing, but we're hoping he can tell us about Vinh."

They waited some more, Pho filling in the others about the morning talk with Major Thieu, who had told Major Stewart that this was not a military matter. The local police would handle it as a domestic disturbance. Other than that, he said nothing. Major Stewart appeared ready to drop the matter, so after the brief parley, Pho had a brainstorm not unlike Nolan's own.

"Sir, it's market day in Quang Ngai. Maybe Sgt. Childress could get some vegetables and chicken very cheap at the market. I could go with him."

The stratagem worked, and here they all were, acting on their separate impulses, taking time off from their usual work. An older doctor approached them quizzically, asking what they wanted. Pho took over, but he translated directly for Hardy. It seems that no one had brought Vinh to the hospital the previous night. However, a body of a man was found along the roadside that morning. The man had been brought to the hospital too late for help. The body might ordinarily have been left there by the road, but the man was not dressed like a VC. Mr. Nguyen was the only one who would know if it was Vinh, so he agreed to look at the body. He went off to another room with the doctor and returned in five minutes with the sad news. It was Vinh.

Hardy, Mr. Nguyen, and Nolan somberly rode back to Duc Pho. Someone would need to tell Vinh's wife. Most likely, Pho would have to do it, but he would be another hour or more in returning since he and Sgt. Childress needed to stop at the marketplace first, having indicated such was their mission to Major Stewart. As Nolan feared, when Maybe Tomorrow approached the compound gate, they saw the widow out front squatting on her haunches, awaiting news. Neither Hardy nor Nolan could make eye contact with her. Nolan knew he lacked the words to tell her in a sensitive way that her husband was dead. But he also knew how insufficient any words would be. He felt both relief and shame looking straight ahead as the jeep passed into the courtyard.

Major Stewart apparently never found out about the convergence of Duc Pho team members at the hospital in Quang Ngai. Nolan wasn't sure how he would have reacted to the improvised trips, but he hoped that he would have approved after the fact.

A few days later, though, while riding in their jeep on the way to another village, Hardy decided to share some information with Nolan.

"I think it best that you don't mention this to Pho or Mr. Nguyen, but Major Stewart took me aside last night. Lt. O'Hare confirmed what Major Stewart said he had wondered himself. Long and his team killed Vinh. They suspected him of spying. That's the way Phoenix works."

Nolan let the words sink in. He should have known.

"Do you think Vinh's wife knew all along what the shooting was about?"

"I don't know, Nolan. And I don't know if Vinh was actually a spy either. Gray areas abound in this war, and unfortunately, people die regardless of the truth."

Nolan had no reply for that. He thought about Vinh's wife, how she was probably under suspicion, too. Were there children? If a spy, would she risk their well-being for a cause and continue her husband's work? Nolan realized that he couldn't truly counter the doctors' skepticism about knowing the Vietnamese. Maybe he was being overconfident again.

Nolan wanted to believe that the woman's pleading had been genuine. If he saw her again, though, would he talk to her, ask how she was doing, and about any children? That would be the humane thing to do. More likely, he admitted to himself, he would pretend he didn't see her and look away.

Chapter 16: In the Know

"Damn it, Pho, tell the cook again how I want my eggs. We told her about this just yesterday."

A week had passed since the Vinh assassination, and Major Stewart was irritable.

"Yes, sir, I will tell her again. She's worried about her son. She hasn't heard from him in three weeks."

Stewart shifted his weight in his seat at the head of the table and gritted his teeth but said nothing more. With a calm voice, Pho usually could appease him. This time the mention of Bà Hoa's son, a young ARVN infantryman, about whom his mother fretted, did the trick. The Major's recently increased moodiness made everyone else cautious about inadvertently crossing him. Some days they knew it was wiser, even if downright cowardly, to stay out of his way as much as possible.

Barely ten minutes after breakfast, the Civil Affairs team pulled out of the compound and headed south, this morning without Mr. Nguyen, who planned on meeting with other district officials. The night before Nolan had passed along to Hardy a magazine clipping a friend in the States had included with a recent letter. Nolan broached the subject somewhat nonchalantly as he drove.

"Did you get a chance to read that *Newsweek* article about My Lai?"

"I did," the Lieutenant replied, shaking his head. "It's getting worse for the Army all the time. How far up the ladder the blame goes has become the big issue now."

"So, what do you think of the Army's claim that Lieutenant Calley acted on his own in ordering all those executions of civilians?"

"That seems really unlikely to me, Nolan. Captain Medina, at least, would have known what was going on, I would think. There was a lot of pressure to get results."

"Hundreds of civilians gunned down. It goes against what we want to believe Americans would ever be capable of."

"I know. It's shameful." Hardy paused. "By the way, avoid this topic with Lieutenant O'Hare. He's in full-denial mode."

"Oh, I will. But surely he must have some idea about Army secrecy."

"You would think so. But he essentially bleeds red, white, and blue. He can't start to doubt."

Nolan shook his head. "Pho told me something alarming the other day about incidents that happened in Duc Pho three years ago. Did you ever hear that our artillery mistakenly shelled a refugee camp here and killed dozens of civilians?"

"No, I wasn't briefed on that. Did he give you any details?"

"He said it occurred in June '67. Apparently, a sudden influx led to refugees being placed in temporary shelter, some huts and tents just outside of town. During a VC attack, US artillery requested and received permission to fire on coordinates that turned out to be the camp."

"Cripes, I never heard anything about this. I did, though, hear about some atrocities that South Korean forces perpetrated in the province—Binh Hoa and another village. They killed over 400 civilians along with all their animals. It was total annihilation."

"I didn't know South Koreans ever fought here. All this, though, explains to me why there would be so much resentment and resistance in Quang Ngai."

"It's a vicious circle. Resistance to foreigners has been strong here for years. And violence has a way of escalating when revenge figures in. But we have to trust that things are looking up, Nolan. We're doing a lot better by these people now. We just need to make sure we avoid big blunders."

Nolan knew Hardy believed what he said. He was a good man. Still, Nolan could not shut out dark thoughts about the war. The arrival of August and the approaching end to his tour of duty did not provide him with the lift of spirits he expected. He couldn't complain about the work getting done in the refugee camps. Both Hardy and he concurred with Mr. Nguyen that living conditions had vastly improved in recent months. Better housing was being erected, new wells were being built, and the bulgur, though not as popular as the traditional staple rice, was at least plentiful. He should be pleased with so much getting done.

Nolan, though, did not feel comfortable withholding secrets from Pho. On one hand, Nolan appreciated the trust Hardy had shown by revealing to him the reason behind Vinh's death. He definitely understood why secrecy was important. Pho, and Mr. Nguyen, as well, trustworthy though they might be in most matters, would possibly react negatively to finding out the role of the Phoenix program and of Long, in particular. For all they knew, Long might actually be targeting some of their relatives and friends. Nolan would have to keep silent on the matter. He also worried that Pho's tendency to act as an advocate for others might compromise him if Viet Cong sympathizers decided to take advantage of him. Vinh had, after all, left behind two children, Nolan heard. He felt protective of Pho, a good man, like Lt. Hardy. People expected him to do them favors because of his job, his liaison between the two majors. As for Mr. Nguyen, the Lieutenant could decide how much he should know about the Vinh case. In any case, the discreet welfare official was less likely than Pho to push for answers.

Pho's demeanor hadn't shown any change recently. How much he knew about Vinh's death Nolan couldn't tell. Neither of them brought up the incident. The fact that Pho didn't mention it struck Nolan as unusual, but it dawned on him that Pho might already know. On the plus side, they continued to share details about personal matters. Pho chatted about his dream of one day attending college, to move on from the war. Nolan felt a lot of empathy in that regard, thinking of his early release. He still felt uneasy about misunderstanding the situation at the roadside café. He had jumped to conclusions, allowing his imagination to take hold when his supposedly trained ear failed him. Keeping the matter secret from Pho

198

only weighed him down more. He owed his friend an explanation. He had almost said something a few times, but the situation never seemed right. He was waiting for an idle moment when no one else was around, which turned out to be a quiet evening when the two were sitting on the courtyard steps after the evening meal. After listening to Nolan's tale with a cocked ear, Pho calmly took in its significance.

"Did you worry, my friend, that maybe I was a spy?"

"That was one crazy thought, yes. But then I asked you for help."

"Maybe you were more worried that I would laugh at you for making a foolish mistake?"

"I'm still worried about that. But, looking back, it is funny, I admit. How dumb could I be?"

Pho laughed. "Yes, it is funny, No-LANN. Sorry." He laughed again, shaking his head slowly. "But I won't tell anyone—for now. I can't promise about the future."

"Maybe you can leave out my name or wait a few weeks until I'm gone. OK?"

"No worry. You're my friend." He paused and then suppressed another smile. "I knew it was very important or you would not ask for help."

"Thanks, Pho. Now you know ...." Nolan trailed off before he might say "everything."

Having divulged that much felt good, but Nolan still couldn't stop thinking about what had happened more recently, what appeared to be feeding Major Stewart's moodiness. He sensed that Stewart felt frustrated by how matters were working out in the district. Though he said nothing within Nolan's hearing, his relationship with Major Thieu showed serious signs of fraying. From his very first day in Duc Pho, Nolan was aware that people frequently hung around the compound in civilian clothes, with no seeming official duties there. No doubt some were just visitors making bureaucratic requests. For those, Major Thieu decided case by case. However, a few would also hang about the steps of the

Americans' building, both men and women. Some, most likely, were spies for Major Thieu, keeping an eye on the Americans. Again, Major Stewart never said anything Nolan remembered, but he must have noticed.

Now Nolan wondered how Major Stewart saw Major Thieu's prevarication about Vinh to cover up Long's involvement. Was Thieu circumventing his American counterpart? Nolan considered the possibility that Thieu and Stewart communicated well enough in English and that the original conversation with Pho as the intermediary was followed up by a one-to-one talk later in private. They may not have wanted Pho to know any more about the incident.

Something Hardy had said recently had got Nolan thinking about Major Thieu's tactics. Both of them had seen the two majors standing in conversation alone. No interpreter present. Hardy remarked on it.

"I don't think Major Thieu needs an interpreter all that much. He and Major Stewart appear to do just fine on occasions when Pho's not around."

"I think you're right, sir. It may have to do more with status, Major Thieu believing he deserves an interpreter. He's aware that speaking broken English around Americans can create the impression that he isn't that intelligent. With an official go-between, he can carry on business on an even plane with Major Stewart in public. With dignity intact. It's crafty on his part."

"He's a proud man, that's for sure."

And yet, Nolan couldn't tell how much Thieu shared with his American counterpart about the Vinh case. As Hardy reported, Major Stewart had told O'Hare that he suspected what had happened to Vinh, not indicating he had heard anything directly. Unless he was covering for Thieu and possibly his own complicity, he was sincere in his comment to O'Hare. If so, he would certainly be less than pleased about Thieu's end run.

Being thus played by Major Thieu would be bad enough, but Stewart also was hearing complaints from the artillery units about the accuracy of reported locations for nighttime patrols Thieu oversaw from the Duc Pho compound. Did Thieu know something wasn't right? Over a period of several weeks, US artillery personnel insisted on the secure line that the positions provincial forces supposedly manned in the countryside at night were often not authentic. No friendly forces actually occupied these positions, the men choosing to stay back in safer locales such as nearby hamlets. From the artillery command's perspective, any movement in the countryside would then be the enemy's.

Major Thieu provided the coordinates of the patrol positions on a daily basis to the American advisers. These coordinates determined whether or not US artillery received political clearance to fire 155 mm. shells when forward observers detected movement. Before giving clearance for the artillery rounds, a radio operator on duty at the MACV compound would need to check the radio room map to assure a minimum safe distance of 500 meters from a designated "friendly" position. Over the secure telephone line, Nolan had first-hand experience with the frustrated artillerymen denied clearance. The most recent caller had been adamant: "I'm telling you, Nolan, there are no friendlies there. That has to be VC movement."

Nolan could only repeat what he knew. "The map is what we go by. I'll pass on your concerns to our commanding officer. That's all I can do."

Nolan did pass on the complaints, as did the others who received similar complaints when they took turns on the radio. Eventually, Major Stewart would have no choice but to intervene. While Nolan never heard that the two majors had broached the subject, Pho let a hint drop one morning while they sat on the courtyard's steps.

"Major Stewart is not a happy man. He's been complaining a lot to Major Thieu."

"Yes, I've noticed his moodiness. What's the problem between them?"

"I don't know the details, No-LANN. Sorry. I think he is hearing rumors, though. Maybe something is wrong at home, too?

"I haven't heard him say that. But something is bothering him, that's for sure. We all have bad days. He's had more of them recently. I never know what mood he'll be in."

A few days later, Major Stewart let Pho and Grabowski know that the three of them would be accompanying a patrol of provincial forces the following night with Major Thieu. That meant spending the night at a strategic position about five miles south of Duc Pho, well off Highway One. As far as Nolan knew, this would be the first such venture Major Stewart had made in months. The Major preferred the comforts of the compound at night. Who could blame him? Pho didn't say anything about how he felt going out on patrol, and Nolan didn't ask.

Grabowski, however, actually seemed energized by the mission and was more voluble than usual at the breakfast table. He would be the one packing the heaviest load that evening, with almost fifty pounds of gear. "I gotta get the extra battery charged for the field radio. I hope the generator doesn't conk out today."

The last outage occurred only a week earlier. Not able to read, Nolan stood after dark on the roof of the compound casually looking around as he waited for a restart. When the compound lights went back on, so did those in a few nearby buildings outside the walls. Someone must have run lines out to nearby buildings. He thought, no wonder the generator gave out to demand now and then. Elston must have known about the extra feed as he was the principal mechanic on the generator, though supposedly overseen by Sgt. Harris. Nolan hadn't recently thought about the absence of the hyper-vigilant Sgt. Colson, but he had to admit that matters would be more shipshape were Colson around. Still, he preferred the present circumstances.

When Hardy and Nolan returned to the compound late the afternoon of the planned night patrol, they found the Major busily preparing for departure. No martinis for him that night. He checked one final time for his maps and flares. Entering from the radio room, Grabowski dropped to his knees, adjusting straps on his fully laden pack in the entranceway, while Pho stood to the side looking very much a genuine soldier, having gathered a helmet, M-16, and a small pack that he slung over his shoulder. Nolan doubted, however, if Pho had received any more training for combat than he had in basic training. Grabowski mumbled to himself as he double-checked his pack while Pho quietly paced the floor, clearly wanting to be ready before Major Stewart signaled departure.

As Grabowski stood up, swinging the overloaded pack onto one shoulder, the Major spoke in a higher register to Hardy and Nolan. "I marked our position on the radio map. Our call name is Papa Dog, but don't call us—we'll call you if necessary. Radio silence, otherwise. Here we go."

"Good luck, sir," Hardy said, while Nolan patted Pho on the shoulder. Grabowski had already exited the building, ready to dump his pack with the extra battery and all into the back of the jeep before taking the driver's seat. Nolan reflected on his own good fortune not to be joining them. He thought fleetingly of the LRRPs' departures, particularly of Ca and Captain Barnes. They had never shown any emotion or hesitation heading out the building, striding off to some remote location only God knew where. The Major's mission would last just a single night, not weeks, and take place only a few miles from the compound. Contact with the enemy was not likely that night. The situations were not really the same, yet Nolan knew that danger was never a distant possibility in Nam.

At supper that evening Hardy took a glance at the empty officers' table before sitting down at the enlisted men's table, beckoning O'Hare to join him when he entered the room. The mood was quieter than usual. Having arrived earlier, Sgt. Harris had almost cleaned his plate.

"Well," he said, addressing the obvious, "at least the Major chose a dry night."

"Charley likes dry nights, too," O'Hare answered. "He likes all kinds of weather."

"Roger that, sir," Harris added while getting up from the table and pointing toward the radio room. "I'll go see how active he is. Nolan, you'll relieve me in four hours, right?" Radio duty lay ahead for them both.

"Will do, Sarge."

Nolan wrote two letters in the interim and read a bit, somewhat morbidly, the names of recent KIA in the *Stars and Stripes*. So many PFCs, E-4s, E-5s, and lieutenants, younger men more likely to be in fire fights. Nolan was spending more time thinking about how short he was, both the letters and casualty lists sparking his ruminations tonight. He didn't often think of his nearing departure during the day. Unless Pho or Elston mentioned it, he pretty much ignored the subject. He also didn't rag Elston, who surely would have done so to him had the tables been reversed. With Pho, it would have been insensitive to talk much about the end of his tour. Pho had no similar horizon. The damn war could go on for years. Nolan did mention that he looked forward to seeing his family in Maine, a yearning to which Pho could definitely relate.

Nolan went up to the roof where, if anywhere, he might feel a breeze. The stars shone bright overhead. He looked out to the east, toward the modest buildings shrouded in darkness. He heard a few distant voices, nothing distinct. Someone worked a pump handle, but he couldn't see the exact location. He was glad for the overall quiet, the howitzers at LZ Bronco silent for the time being. He wondered how his friends from Song Mao were faring, if all were well. With luck, some may have left Nam intact by now. One language school classmate, Whitley, had written recently. He had just returned from a reunion with his wife—R&R in Hawaii—and wouldn't see her again until November, his departure date. Up to now, he had used very little of what he learned at Fort Bliss. His Civil Affairs unit decided his typing and filing were more important than an interpreter's skills. He had not visited a single refugee camp or village. Another D'Amico by occupation, and just as cynical.

Nolan arrived at the radio room a few minutes early. He didn't mind that duty if he felt rested enough. Harris sat leaning forward at the desk talking emphatically on the secure line.

"Our CO is in the vicinity tonight. Too close to those coordinates." He looked at Nolan, a quick flash of exasperation showing before responding, "OK, call back in ten."

"They want to hit those coordinates I take it?"

"Yeah, and between you and me, Nolan, the presence they picked up could be the Major and them. This isn't something the Major has a lot of experience with. Did he set up where he intended? I wonder."

"On the other hand, if it's Charley and Major Stewart doesn't know he's near, that's bad." For a few seconds, Nolan mulled over the situation. "Damn, we can't warn him by radio without maybe alerting Charley, too."

"Right you are. Better get Lt. Hardy or O'Hare here to call this one."

Nolan found Hardy in his room, boots off, ready to retire for the night. "We have a situation, sir. The Major could be in a heap of danger."

He filled Hardy in as they hustled around the corner. The tinny sound of the secure phone ringing greeted them.

"We're checking the coordinates again," Harris said after answering, "and we have our next-in-command here. Hold a second. What do you think, sir?"

Hardy looked at the map. Exactly 500 meters stood between the artillery target and the Major's designated position. Normally, permission to fire would be in order. Nolan could see the furrows rise in Hardy's high forehead.

"Gentlemen, I sure hope the Major got it right. Tell them to go ahead and fire."

Nolan was used to hearing the 155 mm. rounds resound as they began flight—a concussive force producing a sudden whoosh—, and it was always less than thirty seconds after permission had been granted. The interval seemed even shorter this time. Harris squirmed nervously in his seat while Hardy and Nolan stood behind him. No one said anything. Then, the radio crackled.

"Cease fire! Cease fire!" Grabowski was yelling full bore, though it sounded more like a squawk.

Harris hurriedly relayed the message to the artillery center. At least, two more rounds passed overhead, presumably in the same direction. A few seconds later, they heard Grabowski again.

"This is Papa Dog! Cease fire! Cease fire!"

Nolan didn't know how many rounds were fired in all, but the air finally cleared. Nothing. Harris grabbed the transmitter.

"Papa Dog, this is Romeo Foxtrot. All clear. Confirm status, over."

No voices, just some static audible. The seconds ticked by. Straining to stay positive, Nolan pictured Grabowski getting up from the ground, gathering his wits and checking on things with the Major. That was the best case. He didn't want to consider another.

More seconds dragged on. Harris was about to speak again into the mike, but this time they heard the Major's voice.

"Romeo Foxtrot, this is Papa Dog. Zero casualties. I say again, zero casualties. Over."

"Roger, Papa Dog. Good news. Out."

Harris looked at the others with a stunned expression. "Fuckin' A. That was close. We're going to hear about this shit tomorrow."

"That we will," Hardy said. "Sgt. Harris, go ahead and get some shuteye. Nolan can take it from here. Right, Nolan?"

206

"Yes, sir." He took Harris's seat at the desk after the sergeant stood up. "I sure hope that all the commotion for tonight," Nolan added, as much to himself as to the others.

He got his wish. The rest of the night proved quiet, except for the artillery CO calling on the secure line to check on casualties. Nolan said little other than all was fine, though he doubted that was actually the case.

Restless in bed for an hour or so, Nolan finally dozed off. He overslept a little the next morning, but Hardy didn't seem to mind. The Lieutenant decided to wait until the Major returned for what was likely to be a spirited rehash of the night before. And so it was. Both the Major and Grabowski were still agitated when they barged into the building. Behind them trailed Pho. He said very little in greeting, wearily plunking down on a bench, making a single aside to Nolan.

"You know, my friend, I don't believe there is a bullet with my name on it. I worry about one that says 'To whom it may concern.'"

Not a new sentiment, Nolan thought, but true enough remembering his own close encounter with the friendly fire in Song Mao. Major Stewart was not in the mood for quiet reflection, however. Even after Hardy explained that everyone had followed proper protocol the night before, he was still livid.

"Damn artillery. Those guns need to be calibrated. I'm heading over to Bronco this morning. They screwed up!"

After they hastily showered and changed uniforms, Grabowski chauffeured the irate Major out the gate. Pho used this rare free time to get some breakfast. Though he had already eaten, Nolan decided to sit with his friend. He wasn't sure what Hardy thought was the cause of the snafu, but he decided to feel out Pho.

"Pho, do you think you camped in the correct place last night? Did you see the map?"

"I think we did, but only the Major looked at the map. Maybe Grabowski, too. I don't know. They didn't tell me anything."

"Major Thieu would have been more certain, perhaps? He knows the area."

"Yes, but he didn't go. He had a stomach ache. He sent his assistant, Lt. Tran. He's new. He speaks some English, too."

"I see."

Nolan did not bother to ask Grabowski for his opinion when he returned with the Major. They had not gotten satisfaction from the artillery CO, who insisted the 155s were accurate and no one from his unit had messed up. He was adamant about that. The investigation would likely go no further. Major Stewart unhappily had to accept that he wasn't going to get any admission of error from the artillery.

But the complaints about empty night positions ceased coming from Bronco artillery. When clearance was denied over the radio, no further communication took place. The secure phone sat on the desk in silence.

A few days later, Major Thieu invited Major Stewart to dinner, just the two of them. Stewart told Pho he didn't need his services. Nolan would have liked to have known what transpired that evening. Hearing nothing at breakfast about the parley, he was left to observe how Major Stewart acted as the day went on. He didn't appear edgy or irritable, just a little tired.

When the work day ended, everything appeared more or less normal. The Major was back to two very dry martinis.

Chapter 17: Malady

Lieutenant Hardy didn't feel well. He awoke one morning to chills, unusual in such a warm climate. He slowly got up, dressed, and arrived in the dining room looking noticeably ill. The others all sat at their designated tables.

"Are you OK, sir?" Nolan asked, the first to look up.

"Not really, but I'm going to try to drink some coffee," Hardy gamely replied. "No breakfast," he said to a concerned Bà Hoa, accompanied by a wave of his hand, palm turned down.

"Go back to bed, Lieutenant," the Major ordered. "You look like crap. It may be nothing, but I'm sure an hour or two more rest won't hurt."

Hardy tried to smile but could manage only a grimace. "I'll do that, sir. Thank you." He carefully poured his coffee "Nolan, check with me in two hours. The jeep could probably use an oil change this morning."

Coffee mug in hand, Hardy left the room on unsteady feet.

"Nolan," the Major asked when Hardy was out of sight, "did you two eat or drink at a roadside café yesterday?"

"No, sir. Not yesterday."

"Well, I sure hope it wasn't something he ate here. Anyone else feeling queasy this morning?"

Looking around at one another, the men just shook their heads.

"Probably nothing to worry about, then. Finish up eating, and let's get on with our day. Lots to do."

Nolan didn't think Hardy's illness was anything serious. The Lieutenant's constitution appeared to match up well with his surname. After breakfast, Nolan busied himself tending to Maybe Tomorrow, driving over to the motor pool at the artillery base to see if someone would change the oil on a lift. Luckily, it was a slow day at the pool. He received immediate help, with enough time left over for an idle chat. Mission accomplished, he returned to the compound on schedule and immediately went down the corridor to the officers' quarters. He found Hardy in bed, his face somewhat flushed.

"Feeling any better, sir?"

Hardy quietly groaned. "No, I have a fever now. I just took some aspirin. I don't know what I've got, but I need more time. Come back in an hour, OK?"

"Will do," Nolan replied. He turned and headed back to his room. Had Hardy caught a bug? Probably. Nothing to worry about, Nolan thought. His boss and friend would be back on his feet later in the day. In the meantime, Nolan could catch up on some reading.

Nothing urgent stood out on their schedule, no shipments expected anyhow. Monitoring them constituted the most pressing aspect of their work. They couldn't count on simply rescheduling deliveries of material for just a day or two later. Too much rigmarole, Hardy said. Whenever they were told a shipment was on its way, they made sure to be on hand. Nolan supposed they had done this often enough that he could handle a shipment on his own if it ever came down to it. It did help, though, having two sets of eyes watching the distribution to make sure that no one siphoned off something for their personal use. While still based in Mo Duc, Nolan had learned that the drivers often expected a few bags of cement or sheets of tin to be left on the truck. Village or camp officials might practice some light-fingeredness of their own, as well, but the Americans wouldn't likely hearing anything later about that if an official surreptitiously added to the distribution list a ghost name or two. Mr. Nguyen could act as a deterrent, though. The delay of an entire shipment, as in the case of the one meant for An Ke a few months earlier, was a different matter.

Nolan read for a while in his room, feeling only a little guilty for the bonus opportunity Hardy's illness afforded. He lost track of time until he happened to glance at his watch and saw that more than an hour had expired. He hustled out into the

210

hallway and was about to turn for the officers' quarters when he encountered Major Stewart coming full steam from that direction.

"Nolan, I want you to drive over to the artillery base and pick up a Captain Fleming at the MASH unit. I'm getting more concerned about Lt. Hardy. While it could be something minor, we're in malaria country, and I want to play it safe. Fleming's a doctor. He can rule out malaria or something really serious."

"Yes, sir. I'm sure the Lieutenant has been taking his anti-malaria pills. We talked about that recently."

"That's good to hear, but it doesn't rule out anything. Better get a move on. Capt. Fleming is expecting you."

Nolan made his second trip of the day over to the base to fetch the doctor. Upon their arrival back at the compound, Fleming, a ruddy-faced, no-nonsense man, took over immediately, tending to Hardy after sending everyone else away. Fifteen minutes later, he emerged from the room and met the Major and Nolan waiting impatiently back in the main hallway.

"I think it's the flu," he announced. "Nolan tells me no one else appears to have symptoms. That's what I hoped, but you'll need to take precautions. Limit your contact with him and be sure to wash your hands frequently. He should be OK in a few days. I'll prescribe an antiviral medication."

Major Stewart thanked him, and Nolan immediately offered his services as a chauffeur back to the base. On the ride over, Fleming asked him if Hardy and he may have visited anyone ill the past few days.

"We did visit the Quaker hospital the other day, dropping off a patient, but we weren't in any of the wards."

"That's a possibility, though."

"We're scheduled to go back there tomorrow to pick up the patient. I could ask about the flu, maybe see if anyone has any symptoms."

"Do that and let me know what you hear. We don't want this thing to spread."

Nolan said he would. After driving the doctor back and picking up the medicine from him, Nolan immediately returned to the compound and checked in with Major Stewart. He reported mentioning the Quaker hospital and the doctor's reply.

"Tomorrow, "the Major said, "you should have someone else go along with you. Too far to go alone. Take Pho. I can get along without him for a few hours."

"Thank you, sir. That would be great."

He left the medicine and itsinstructions with Hardy, who lacked the energy to talk much. Lying in his bed, Hardy wished Nolan well for the following day, adding he was confident he would be back on the job soon. Nolan asked if the Lieutenant wanted any supper brought.

"Not tonight, thanks. I'll take some of this medicine and call it a night."

"Right, sir. See you tomorrow."

Knowing that Hardy didn't seem to face any serious danger perked Nolan up. He liked having Pho ride along with him as his wingman, too. He knew that he always learned more about the countryside when they rode together. Pho dispelled the monotony of the miles of rice paddies, providing information about tree varieties and other diverse flora. It was like having a tour guide on a nature trip. He also told Nolan about local customs and the people who lived in the area. The next morning, only a klick from the hospital, Nolan caught glimpse of a pond on the other side of the road and slowed the jeep to a halt. Hardy and he had made this trip more than a dozen times, he calculated. What was so different now? Previously, he remembered seeing the small pond covered with what resembled green lily pads. Now, though, a sea of red blooms spread across the pond's surface. The sight dazzled him.

"Wow, look at that, Pho. What beautiful flowers."

"That is lotus, my friend. The lotus is very important to the Vietnamese. A symbol of the country's endurance."

"Really? Tell me more."

"The growth of the plant means everything. The roots in the mud, the stalk in the water, and the flower reaching for the air. Buddhists believe that this symbolizes the path to enlightenment."

"Are the flowers always red?"

"No, they can be white, pink, yellow, or as my father says, blue. I have never seen blue. Supposedly, that color symbolizes wisdom. White means purity, red means love or compassion, and pink often suggests the Buddhist way. Yellow is thought to mean enlightenment, but all the colors can mean that."

"Isn't the plant edible? I remember reading something about Lotus-Eaters."

He thought it was in Homer's *Odyssey*, but he didn't remember the context.

"Yes, the leaves can make tea. Also, some people believe the leaves and stalks can be used as medicine to calm the stomach."

"Well, the blossoms sure are beautiful, just floating there on the surface of the water."

"The blossoms rise up above the water a little. They close up at night and then reappear in the light. It is like magic."

"Do people sell them in the market?"

"Yes, now that it is summer. You can see them for yourself."

"I never knew this. Thanks. But I guess we better move on."

Reaching the hospital a few minutes later, Nolan sought out Mary Ann right away and, on finding her coming out of a ward, introduced Pho.

"Pleased to meet you, Pho," she said. "But where is Lt. Hardy? Too busy to come with you?"

"No, he's flat on his back," Nolan answered. "I'm sure he would prefer being here. He has the flu, we think."

"Oh, no," she said, her face flushing. She appeared to be searching for words. "I'm afraid I may have passed it on to him. I didn't think I was contagious anymore. We talked only a few minutes when you dropped off Hai and her mother. They are ready to go home, by the way. But I feel terrible about the Lieutenant."

Nolan recalled that Hardy and Mary Ann were not present when he interpreted for the doctor who would repair Hai's lip. That brief amount of time must have been enough to do the trick.

Mary Ann continued, "Fortunately, no one else caught the flu here. I picked it up from a new arrival on our staff. It appeared to stop with me. As far as we know, we're clear here now. Please, though, let Lt. Hardy know that I'm sorry. I've kept him from his work, too."

"Yes, but I don't think he feels too bad about that. Pho and I are on the job. Right, Pho?"

"Everyone needs a rest," Pho answered, moving past Nolan's levity.

"Still, I feel so bad about it," the nurse said. "Anyway, I suppose you'll be wanting to get Hai and her mother home. The paperwork is all done. They'll be happy to see our backs, I'm sure."

"A pretty woman," Pho observed as the two men parted from Mary Ann. "She sounds different from you."

"She's from Australia, a volunteer. She didn't always like us because we're soldiers. Now we're pals."

"Friendship takes time. Not always possible to find time, is it?"

Nolan didn't say anything. Pho knew the two of them were friends. On the return, they stopped along the roadside again to admire the lotus. Nolan wanted to get blossoms for their passengers, but Pho said that wasn't possible without a boat. Local women used small boats to gather the plants for themselves and for the market. The flowers would make nice gifts, Nolan thought, but he realized, too, that the locals wouldn't welcome Americans gathering blooms and cutting into their profits.

Back at the compound, Nolan checked on Hardy. He found him awake but still feeling below par. Nolan told him that all went well with Hai and that she was now home with her parents. He decided not to tell him about the likely source of his illness. He would tell him later. Then, he hastily excused himself to let Hardy rest.

When he saw the Major in the hallway, Nolan reported about the likely source and that the danger appeared to be past at the hospital. The Major said he would personally apprise Captain Fleming. He had some other questions to ask him. Free for what remained of the day, Nolan decided to go up to the marketplace before the vendors left. At the very least, he would enjoy stretching his legs after so much time in the jeep.

When he arrived, many vendors were beginning to close up shop. Still, Nolan browsed among the rickety stands, taking his time. Some people recognized him and said hello, inviting him to take a closer look at their wares. He didn't really have anything specific in mind to buy, but near the end of the row his browsing came to a halt. Partially shaded, a small table displayed lovely flowers in earthen vases while some lay in beds of green leaves spread out on the nearby ground. Pho was right. This vendor had lotus to sell, red and pink ones. Nolan impulsively made a decision. The coincidence pleased him. He would buy some of each color. He would give half to Bà Hoa and half to Mr. Nguyen to pass on to his wife. He decided that the steeper than normal price for cut flowers wouldn't deter him. He wanted to do it. It just felt right after the discovery along the road.

On the way back through the compound, he stopped in at the administrative building where he thought he might find Mr. Nguyen still working. A young woman exiting the building passed by in a red aó dài that exactly matched half of the blossoms Nolan carried. She appeared to give the flowers a longing look as she went by. Too bad, he didn't have extras,

Nolan thought. He entered the main room and saw Mr. Nguyen sitting at a small desk in the corner, smoking a cigarette as he pored over some paperwork. Looking up, Mr. Nguyen saw Nolan approaching with flowers in both hands. His face lit up.

"Those for me?" he asked in Vietnamese, gesturing with his free hand toward himself.

"No," Nolan replied. "For your wife. Which color do you think she would prefer?"

"She would love those," pointing to the pink ones. "Her favorite color."

"Pink, it is. Do you have a way to keep them fresh for now?"

"I am planning to go home in a few minutes. Not a problem. I hear Trung-úy Hardy is ill. Will he be OK tomorrow, do you think?"

"I can't say. But you and I can probably handle business tomorrow without him, don't you think?"

"Yes, we can. Wait a moment, please. I'll walk out with you now. This work can wait."

He extinguished his cigarette in a small ash tray and lined up the sheaf of paper neatly at an upper corner of the desk. The two men, each now with a bouquet of flowers, departed the building, a bit self-conscious about what they carried. They said their good nights in the courtyard and then went their separate ways.

Nolan entered the advisers' building and sauntered into the dining room to find Bà Hoa. He glimpsed her busily scurrying about in the kitchen. An enticing aroma rose from the stove. The diminutive cook exclaimed with delight when she saw the flowers.

"So beautiful," she said in Vietnamese. "For a girlfriend?" she added.

"For you, Bà," Nolan replied, offering her the bouquet of red flowers. "For taking good care of me all these months. Thank you."

He bowed toward her as she took the flowers. Bà Hoa giggled and touched Nolan gently on the arm. "Thank you.

216

Now you can help me take care of Trung-úy Hardy. He must eat some phở I made. It contains good medicine. You can use that tray on the table."

"What medicine?" he asked, as she ladled a heaping portion from a steaming pot into a large bowl. Nolan knew he would have to look up in his dictionary what she rattled off now. Some kind of root, he gathered.

Until the Major said otherwise, Hardy would be eating in his room to reduce the chances of anyone else catching what he had. After Bà Hoa placed the bowl on the tray with a spoon, Nolan carried the contents off to the officers' wing. There he found Hardy awake and sitting up on a chair. He looked only a little better, his face wan.

"I have dinner for you, sir," Nolan announced at the open door. "A special soup, compliments of Bà Hoa. Where should I put it?"

"On the bed should be fine, Nolan. It's stable enough if you leave the tray, too. Thanks."

Hardy still looked uncomfortable, but he said his fever had subsided a little. Nolan didn't leave right away.

"Mary Ann at the Quaker hospital sends her apologies. It seems she may have given you the bug she had. She thought she was well past contagion. She feels very bad about it."

Hardy's eyes widened at the news, but he shrugged. "Some things can't be helped." He attempted a smile. "I don't feel great right now, but I think I'll live."

Nolan took that as a signal to leave. "I'll check back with you in a little bit, after our supper. You OK for now? Need anything else?"

"I think I have all I can handle, thanks. Yes, check back later."

An hour later, Nolan returned to Hardy's room and through the half-closed door saw the tray on the floor, the bowl empty. Hardy appeared to be sleeping, so Nolan quietly picked up the tray and left. The empty bowl was a good sign, he thought.

The next morning, though, Hardy didn't show for breakfast. Major Stewart said that he had just talked with Hardy and decided it was too soon for him to get back to work. Nolan should plan on carrying out the day's schedule with Mr. Nguyen. Bà Hoa would check on Hardy during the day. That seemed reasonable to Nolan. Maybe they could venture a short distance without armed protection. He didn't think that any problems would come up that Mr. Nguyen and he couldn't handle between them.

Nolan found Mr. Nguyen waiting patiently for him in the courtyard. "My wife says 'thank you,'" the welfare officer said in his native tongue. "She loved the flowers."

"You could have said that they were from you. "

"She knows better than that. No such luxuries with children."

"I'm glad she liked them. OK, where to today?"

As it turned out, their destination that morning lay just a short distance from town, a refugee camp. That made Nolan feel somewhat less uneasy about their security. No need to worry about traveling through the wide-open spaces of the rice paddies where snipers might be lurking.

Mr. Nguyen wanted to check on the construction of a well that would supplement those already in the camp. He and Nolan found a camp leader they had met during earlier visits. The heavyset man squatted on the ground in front of his shelter playing a dice game quite noisily with several other men. One, after joyfully clapping his hands, swept his winnings off a cloth lying on the ground. Nolan noticed that the dice didn't have the usual pips, but rather a colorful figure on each face that he couldn't identify from a distance. The leader didn't greet them as enthusiastically as he usually did, especially on days that a truck arrived with supplies. Nolan guessed that he was losing. Reluctantly, the camp leader abandoned the game and guided his visitors through the camp to a far corner. The well sat unfinished, a few empty bags of cement strewn on the ground by it.

218

"No one working today?" Mr. Nguyen asked, clearly enough so Nolan could follow.

"We have no more cement," he man calmly replied.

"But you received many bags of cement in the last shipment," Mr. Nguyen said, holding the relevant paperwork up for his evidence. "You had more than enough to finish the job."

"This well was deeper."

Mr. Nguyen didn't say anything right away. Nolan guessed what he was thinking. Why would the water table be so different here from that of the wells only yards away on the same level of ground? Could it be that some of the cement had been diverted to other purposes? Maybe even sold on the black market?

Mr. Nguyen didn't make any promises that the camp would get any more bags soon. He said he would have to consult with his counterpart, meaning Lt. Hardy. The camp leader didn't plead. He must have sensed that he was up against someone who demanded accountability.

Back in the jeep, Mr. Nguyen expressed his doubts about the man's explanation. Maybe, he said, the man needed some quick money. He liked to gamble, that was clear.

"What was that game the men played?" Nolan asked.

"Bầu Cua. A favorite game in our country. Children sometimes play, too. It doesn't always involve much money."

Nolan sensed that his companion seemed to be musing on that thought.

"A few bags of cement is not much," Mr. Nguyen acknowledged. "But we must discourage any pattern. Soon, more material will disappear. I suggest that we wait before providing any more cement. I would like to return and ask some other people here about what they know. We must show that we are keeping track of how the material is used."

Nolan agreed, thinking to himself about how Hardy and he had tested Mr. Nguyen when they first began their work together. No worries now. The welfare officer went by the book.

When the two men returned to the compound, they parted, the camp visit a mild disappointment. Nolan dropped by Hardy's room to see how he was doing. Hardy was sitting up again, reading a magazine. Bà Hoa apparently had brought him another bowl of phở, the empty bowl on the tray attesting to his continuing recovery.

"You look a lot better, sir," Nolan observed, though standing at the doorway to minimize the chances of catching the Lieutenant's flu.

"I'm feeling much better. The soup may have helped, but I needed the bed rest, for sure. I think I'll be good to go tomorrow. How did things go this morning?"

Nolan recounted the visit to the camp, highlighting Mr. Nguyen's resolve to keep a close eye on how the camp residents used distributed material.

"Makes you wonder," Nolan concluded, "how much is going on behind our backs in the camps and villages."

"I'm sure, Nolan, more's going on than what we see. The most important thing, of course, is making sure there's enough to provide for the essentials of life. While I'm not happy that some people might be profiting personally, I don't want to stop the supply line completely either. My father told me that many of the larger charities in the States spend a lot of money on high executive salaries, fancy digs, and lavish parties. They justify it by the belief that the donors and suppliers need to see a structure that mirrors their own work environment. But that means less money for those who need it the most. It seems impossible to develop a perfect system."

"I guess you're right. We Yanks can't be high and mighty about corruption. It does irk me that even GIs gung-ho about the war undermine the efforts by using the black market here."

"Unquestionably, Nolan, it's like organized crime. I hate it, too, how our own troops get involved in that. An ROTC instructor at South Carolina told us stories about all the trouble GIs could get into within a war zone that wasn't related to combat. Now I hear that especially in the bigger cities in Nam how to keep GIs safe when they're off duty is a major concern. Guys get drunk in bars, get reckless looking for sex, and make bad decisions, some involving deals in the market involving weapons. We've talked about this before, right? You know about the GI they found dead in the Da Nang alley, right?"

"Yeah, I haven't forgotten about him. Any death in war is horrible, but I can't imagine families getting informed that their son died under those circumstances."

"Accidents, suicides, and homicides make up a significant portion of military deaths here. But I'm guessing the parents don't get all the lurid details about their son's violent death. The deception may be more comforting for parents to hear, but it also protects the military and supports the illusion of a noble war."

Hardy, Nolan noted, was grimacing.

"Sorry, not a pleasant topic, sir, I know, especially when you're not feeling well. Is there anything else you want me to do this afternoon?"

"Not really. I feel I'm getting my strength back slowly. We're not behind in paperwork. I can get a half day in tomorrow at the very least. Maybe I can consult with Mr. Nguyen in open air where I'll be less likely to pass on a virus. I plan to take it easy tonight. The rest helps."

"That's good, sir." Nolan was about to leave when he caught sight of two red blossoms floating in a shallow bowl on top of the low file cabinet Hardy used for storing paperwork. The blossoms looked identical to the ones Nolan had given to Bà Hoa. "Those are very pretty flowers. How did you happen to come by them?"

"A secret admirer," Hardy responded, lifting his eyebrows. "They were delivered by a third party while you were gone."

Sure, Nolan thought, a secret admirer. He decided to let it pass. The Lieutenant could have his fantasy. Maybe it would help him recover faster. A little fantasy, like a little rest, never hurts.

Chapter 18: Enterprise

On a warm Saturday afternoon in August, Nolan and Hardy returned to the compound after checking on another well project recently completed in a nearby village. Grabo must have been in the radio room as usual, but no one else appeared to be around. The sergeants may have been off on scrounging missions or just checking in with their contacts on other bases. The Major, O'Hare, and Pho had planned on attending some official function that afternoon with Major Thieu. Hardy went off to the officers' wing while Nolan headed for his room to stow his M-16.

As he entered the room, he could hear what sounded like panting noises in the far corner, someone trying to catch his breath. When he glanced over, he saw that he was only partially mistaken. It was her breath. On a bed, Elston's, crouched a young, naked woman, on all fours, straddling the lower half of a recumbent figure, and facing Nolan as he entered the room. Her lithe, brown body shone with perspiration. She made no effort to change her position or cover herself when they made eye contact, the friction that she created between her thighs as she thrust her pelvis back and forth evidently too intense to interrupt. Nolan didn't go a foot further. He turned on his heel and left the room.

The sight flabbergasted him. Unbelievable how he kept stumbling across naked women. At least, he didn't linger this time as he did when he saw the woman bathing in the river. Apparently, Elston thought the quiet surroundings created a perfect opportunity for some furtive lovemaking. But that was crazy. Too many residents shared the building for him to assume any prolonged privacy. Plus, Elston knew the Major would not be happy to have this activity going on within quarters. Even when scrounging partners from the local bases paid their weekend visits to the compound, Major Stewart made it clear that any womanizing must take place outside the compound. He reserved the beds for solo occupants, usually NCOs crashing at the compound after forays in town. Nolan shook his head at Elston's recklessness. His roommate consistently chose to do his Army time on his own terms. Nolan decided to go up to the lounge and read for a while. As he mounted the steps, he wondered if he would be able to concentrate at all with that vivid image still in his head.

He didn't think he had seen the woman before, but he didn't really get a good look. A local prostitute maybe? Most of the guys knew that early on in his tour Elston ventured some evenings outside the compound for an hour or two, slinking back quietly to avoid questions. But after Elston's unfortunate episode with "the clap," those trips had dwindled in recent weeks. Nolan felt somewhat envious of this new companion, whoever she was. He missed the company of women, too. He thought of Karen often. Still, what was Elston thinking, bringing a woman here? He laughed sardonically to himself. Of course, Elston didn't consider the consequences at all. He was just randy as hell, like most GIs were.

After ten minutes or so, Nolan had managed to read only a few pages before Elston came heavily up the stairs. Back in uniform and looking somewhat flushed, he lumbered past Nolan's chair to get to the refrigerator. He pulled open the door, bent down to reach the bottom shelf, and removed a can of beer. Nolan didn't doubt that Elston saw him sitting there. Since it didn't appear Elston was going to say anything, Nolan spoke up.

"Sorry about that, man. I didn't know you had a visitor."

Elston squinted in Nolan's direction. "What do you mean 'sorry'?"

"I walked in on you and your friend. I guess she didn't say anything. She must've been having too good a time."

"Ha, ha, you're funny, Nolan. I hope I can count on you keeping your mouth shut."

"Well, I promise to be quieter than she was. You, on the other hand—I thought you might be asleep. Or, for that matter, dead."

Elston twitched his lips as if ready to retort, but he caught himself, paused, and smiled weakly.

"OK, I guess I could tell you how this came about. We didn't plan on this happening. Ngoc, my friend, came to the compound on a business errand, something about renewing a business license. I bumped into her in the courtyard. I knew our building was practically deserted, so I invited her in. After that, things developed fast. This wasn't the first time we fucked. But it's the only time here. She has a place just behind our back wall, a hair salon."

Nolan thought of saying how becoming Elston's hair looked these days, but he decided to show mercy instead. Elston was making an effort to be straightforward with him, not his usual way of communicating.

"I understand, man. I must admit I envy you, but you're going need to be more discreet. The Major would have a conniption if he knew."

"Yeah, I know. I appreciate you trying to help me out. Keep it low, though. OK?"

"Don't worry about me. My lips are sealed."

Nolan meant it. He certainly didn't plan to get Elston in trouble. After all, this was private stuff. Also, his relationship with Elston proved edgy enough as it was. He thought back to college days when dorm residents, following a time-honored code, made themselves scarce when roommates brought girls back to the room. He would give the guy a break.

When he thought about what Elston had said, though, some recent events began to add up. He recalled hanging out on the compound roof not long ago one evening when the generator restarted after being briefly down. He had seen several lights suddenly go on *outside* the compound. He would bet that an exterior feed ran out to Ngoc's hair salon. Since Elston maintained the generator, he had to know all about the feed even if he hadn't been the guy who initially set it up. Considering Elston's laidback demeanor, Nolan thought it much more likely that Ngoc had approached him rather than the other way around. She needed electrical power to run her styling equipment, so they made a deal. They both benefited from the mutually satisfying arrangement—electrical power for sex—only Ngoc got both. While Elston and she probably didn't have intense feelings for one another, they clearly enjoyed the sex.

The more Nolan thought about it, though, the more he wondered. Did Sgt. Harris know about the deal? What part did he play in this? When he replaced Sgt. Colson as Elston's supervisor on maintaining the generator, he became privy to anything Elston did with the equipment. Extending the electrical cord though the wall of the compound required some time and stealthy labor. Besides drilling a hole for the cord, someone needed to set up a conduit for it, something to protect it from rain and other elements as well as to hide it from view. That likely called for a trench covered over, extending the few feet across to the salon and to any other building that was being supplied. When did that work take place? Was it after Colson left, or did he know about the filched power all along? Did he want Nolan on the job in order to lessen the influence of Elston and anyone else involved?

This latter possibility gave Nolan greater appreciation of Colson's canniness. Maybe the loner sergeant wasn't just a straight-arrow lifer who did everything by the book. Clearly, he liked control. If he just wanted to blow the whistle, he could tell Major Stewart right away. He had an angle, too, perhaps. Well, Nolan admitted to himself, it wasn't the first time he had underestimated somebody if, indeed, that was the case here.

It irked him that he had not seen some of this going on under his nose, but then again, he had spent a lot of time in the officers' quarters. Maybe, too, he just chose to ignore some signs. Harris and Elston spent a lot of time in mumbled conversation. In any case, he didn't possess any thoughts of

226

blowing the whistle on his roommates. He admired these shenanigans to some degree. In the Army, these functioned as survival techniques, much as he and his fellow students in El Paso had used humor to combat the tedium of repetition.

As the sultry afternoon turned into evening, he found himself still fixating on the secret activities going on around him. He couldn't help but think that there might be something more here than just a couple's transaction for sex. Since Nolan had agreed to keep silent about Ngoc and their arrangement, Elston wouldn't worry anymore about hiding from him what was going on. Nolan entertained no illusion, though, about what Elston would do if he knew about the bánh tiêu confusion. In no time everyone would hear about it.

The following Monday morning after breakfast Nolan walked outside to prepare Maybe Tomorrow for the day's use, checking the radiator and hoses, in addition to oil and gas. As he looked up from the engine block, he saw, heading his way, a petite young woman wearing a yellow aó dài and carrying a fashionable matching parasol to block out the sun. Though he wasn't used to seeing such finery often in Duc Pho, he realized that he had seen this woman previously inside the compound, dressed in a red aó dài on that occasion. He assumed then that she had some business to attend to in the administrative building. Gentle curls framed the woman's face, one carefully made up—not beautiful—the eyes having an intensity that seemed somehow unfeminine. Still, she could turn heads. It took him a few more seconds for him to recognize Ngoc, Elston's sex partner, so much more composed now than when he had seen her in ecstasy.

"Nolan?" she inquired, with no sign of stress in her voice. Elston must have provided her with his name. "I am Ngoc."

She said that much in English, but Nolan switched to Vietnamese. "Yes, I know. How do you do?"

He used the formal "Cô" to address a young, single woman. She arched an eyebrow. "We haven't met, have we?"

She stood close enough so that he caught a strong scent of a floral perfume.

"No. I may have seen you, though."

She didn't say anything immediately, looking quizzically at Nolan. Then, after a coquettish blink of her eyelashes, she laughed.

"Are you married, Nolan?"

"No, I'm not."

"That surprises me." She hesitated as if mulling something over. "I have a friend that you might like to meet. Very pretty. She likes tall men."

"Thank you. I'll remember that. We all need friends."

"You're a smart young man." She smiled almost sweetly.

He felt tempted to say that if he were smart, he wouldn't be here in Vietnam, at least not in war time. He gently bit his lip instead.

She smiled once more, said good-bye briskly, and walked away with short, mincing steps, peeking back over her shoulder just once to see if he watched her. It had been a brief performance, but his intuition told him that this would not be the last time they would talk.

Despite his best intentions, he thought of Ngoc at various times during the day. She came across as confident and direct, yet calculating, too. She knew how to use feminine wiles. But Elston's slovenliness and unguarded speech made them quite a contrast. Strange bedfellows, as the saying went. Although Hardy would probably enjoy hearing about the dynamics of their tryst, Nolan kept everything to himself as they worked that day in the camps. Still, he couldn't deny being intrigued. He wanted to find out what else might be going on around the compound that so far had eluded his attention.

His opportunity to talk alone with Sgt. Harris came quickly after the workday's close, with the two men both seeking some down time in their room before supper. With an air of nonchalance, he called over to Harris.

"I met a woman named Ngoc today. Do you know her, Sarge?"

"You just met, huh? I thought everyone knew Ngoc. She comes to the compound off and on. She's a friend of Major Thieu, I believe. I could've introduced her to you earlier if I knew you were interested."

"Interested in what? I suspect she's got many admirers."

"Yes, she does. I meant she's someone who can get you what you want, or give you cash for something she wants."

"Ah, a businesswoman. She deals in greenbacks, too, I suspect."

"Any currency you want. Most of the guys enjoy dealing with her. She's generous."

By "most," Nolan assumed that Harris meant Elston, and probably Childress and Hernandez. They likely didn't make any fine distinction between doing their routine scrounging and using the black market to make some extra money. Nolan doubted Grabo possessed much time for these dealings even if he was interested. He couldn't imagine that either Hardy or O'Hare used the market, let alone the Major. Hardy, especially, agreed with Nolan about the market's insidious nature.

"Yeah, she practically handed me a business card," Nolan said, "and I don't think she wanted to give me a haircut."

"Well, that's her official business. Give her a chance on other things. She'll surprise you."

Nolan momentarily considered saying that she already had, but he thought it best to leave the matter there for the time being. He wondered if Pho knew anything about her. On second thought, he realized that he probably knew a lot about activities around the compound. Nolan sensed that Pho wanted to protect him from knowing all that was going on. Of course, he realized he had chosen to do the same for Pho.

Later, while getting ready to retire for the night, Elston sidled up to him with a sheepish look. Nolan wanted to like the guy, but he didn't make it easy.

"Ngoc tells me she talked with you today. You made a good impression. She thinks she might be able to help you out."

"To enrich myself or to get a little nookie?"

"The second, but you never can tell about some cash. She's got just the right woman for you, she says."

"So she said." Nolan hesitated. Sure, sex was tempting, but something held him back. He smelled trouble. "Tell her, 'thanks, but no thanks.' I'm doing OK in that department."

He knew he was stretching the truth.

Elston smirked. "I told her that you had some hang-ups about sex, but she thought you could help her with some translation. You know, just some business stuff. It wouldn't take much of your time, she said."

The hang-up shit again. Nolan felt anger rising. Maybe he did have hang-ups, but he wasn't about to sell his soul. Still, getting angry with Elston didn't solve anything. He thought about the guys at the motor pool doing favors for him, a fellow GI, though a complete stranger. Plus, everyone on the compound here depended on one another in the pinch. He needed to stay cool. Not take the bait.

He looked Elston directly in the eyes. "Hey, man, let's bury the hatchet. I don't want to make this into a big deal. I'll keep my word. I'm not ratting on you. This stuff just isn't for me."

Another smirk from Elston. "Well, you're not so smart, Nolan, for all your degrees. Why not get something out of this fucking mess? Why should we be total schmucks? The Army didn't have a problem drafting our asses whatever we thought about the war. Now let'em pay the consequences."

Nolan wanted to hold back, but he couldn't. Elston needed to hear the facts, and no one else appeared likely to inform him. Nolan silently cursed his luck.

"I know what you're saying. Yeah, neither of us wants to be here. Look, we're not buddies, Elston. But I wouldn't like to see you get hurt. Letting someone hook into the generator is one thing. The black market, that's another. You know very well that the market deals with arms and ammo, as well as the

230

usual things, and the traders don't worry about whose hands they end up in. Just be careful, man. You may end up in the middle of some very nasty stuff like that GI did in Da Nang a while back."

Elston's face quickly flushed. Nolan could see that Elston had heard about the dead GI found in the alley. That guy's pals had come forward to say that they suspected people their friend did business with. He sold to the market all the time, often military equipment, including weapons. Maybe he thought he had been cheated in a deal and put up a fuss. Did Elston consider what could go wrong?

"I don't need another mother, Nolan. I already have one."

"Yeah, that's me, your mom. Look, I'm sorry about laying this heavy stuff on you. It's just the way I feel, what I fear. How can you be sure that something won't backfire on you? Who can you really trust to have your back? "

Elston scrunched his face in apparent disdain. "I wouldn't be doing this if I didn't think Thieu was overseeing things. He's got everything under control."

So, Thieu was involved. Not too surprising, Nolan thought.

"Maybe for now, he does, but a bigger fish may decide he's expendable, too. It's all about power. All I'm saying is that you can't trust your business partners. You have to decide where to draw the line. You may be at that point already. Be careful. These people are dangerous."

At that exact moment, Sgt. Harris walked into the room. After a quick glance over his shoulder, Elston decided to let the conversation drop. This could be a good sign, Nolan thought. He might actually think about the situation.

No one said any more that evening. Nolan figured he had to give his roommate some space. He decided to take a quick shower and read some before the others settled in for the night. He didn't read for long. Lights in the room went out within minutes. Looking up at the ceiling, Nolan succeeded in entertaining a comforting scenario about his new life after

Nam, driving westward toward Madison, alone in his Chevy II, the war far behind him. He had no trouble falling asleep.

The next morning the mood in the dining room resembled a celebration. Bà Hoa, her tiny figure virtually dancing among the tables, greeted everyone effusively, face beaming. After so many weeks, she had heard from her son. He was fine. His commanders had ordered strict silence about the recent military operation undertaken—no correspondence allowed. With luck, she would be seeing him soon.

Nolan told her in Vietnamese how glad he was to hear her news, saying that her son must miss her wonderful cooking. Hoa patted him gently on the shoulder and teasingly suggested that Nolan was trying to get a larger breakfast.

"No, Bà, just some strawberries."

Fat chance on getting that delicacy, he thought. Fresh fruit rarely showed up on the dining room tables, though the sergeants occasionally scrounged up canned fruit from the mess halls they frequented.

The good mood carried over into the day as the Civil Affairs team went about their work. Nolan tried to put aside his concerns about Elston. He didn't feel overly optimistic about getting through to his feckless roommate, but he had tried. He doubted that his own motive to put Elston straight stemmed from jealousy even if he did feel physical attraction to Ngoc. On the other hand, soon his life would return to normal in the States, which meant Karen's company and the chance for developing a healthier romantic connection. He could wait just a bit longer for sex. Elston obviously couldn't. And another thing. In helping others, Nolan found purpose in what he was doing in Nam. Elston hadn't.

Then, too, maybe Elston didn't get the support Nolan got from home. Karen's letters always stayed buoyant, and so did those from his parents and others. He couldn't complain about his own support system during his tour. While he had felt fear and loneliness at times over the past nine months, he never felt that he had been forgotten at any time. Of course, it helped to put out of his mind what his loved ones might be doing at any given moment. On birthdays and holidays, this proved harder to do. But he found reading helped a lot to distract him from self-pity, just as the basketball had, and volleyball back in Song Mao.

A few more days passed and once again his path crossed with Ngoc's. After breakfast, he walked up to the compound gate with the intention of checking that day's market activity on the main street where he could sometimes find fresh fruit. From the other direction, Ngoc approached on foot, not yet aware of his presence. She carried no parasol this time, but her orange áo dài was quite becoming, he had to admit, set off by her bronze skin, the little that showed. He flashed back to her naked pose and hoped she couldn't read his mind.

This time Nolan caught her eye and opened the conversation in Vietnamese.

"Hello, Ngoc, you look nice today." He used the informal word "chi" for a sister or a female friend.

"Thank you, Nolan. I didn't think you cared. You like men, not women, perhaps."

"So, Elston told you I didn't need anything from you, yes?"

"Yes. No problem, GI. Maybe I don't want you anymore. I want to know what else you said to him."

"About what?"

"About me."

She fixed her eyes on him.

"I'm sure I said he was a lucky man."

"Ha, I don't think so. He has been acting strangely with me."

"I know he likes your company."

"Maybe. He doesn't seem as happy. He usually likes to talk. Did you give him advice?"

"You know, Ngoc, Elston and I are not really friends. We need to get along with each other, but we don't talk a lot."

"You Americans think you know best about everything. Do this. Do that. Maybe you think small, yellow people can't take care of themselves. Too weak. You tall people must control their lives."

Nolan was taken aback, but quickly scrambled to recover. He strained to find the right words in her language.

"I understand why you might think that," he said carefully, looking her in the eye. "This war has turned good intentions into bad. I think my job is important, but I try to keep quiet about how the Vietnamese should live."

"Maybe not quiet enough."

"Maybe not." Feeling cornered, he eagerly leaped to change the conversation. "So, you are here to see Elston?"

"No, today I have lunch with Major Thieu. We have business to discuss."

She narrowed her eyes. Did he detect menace there?

"I see," he said. "I won't delay you any longer then. Stay well."

"Good-bye, Nolan."

Nolan watched her pass by—no seductive walk this time. On reflection, she struck him to be a tough-minded person, probably naturally suspicious about everyone. He guessed that Elston had not said anything directly to her about the argument the two of them had about the black market. But coming, most likely, from a background of hard knocks, she tended to look at small changes in behavior from different angles. She sized up people so that she could put them to use or not. He suspected she could be dangerous if angered.

Later, after finishing the work day, Nolan decided to use the empty lounge upstairs to write a letter home. In the hallway Major Stewart stood in a relaxed pose, martini in hand, chatting with Lt. O'Hare. He stopped Nolan as he approached the stairs and signaled him aside, speaking softly so O'Hare would not overhear.

"Major Thieu asked about you today, Nolan. He wondered how much longer you'd be here. His interest surprised me."

"It surprises me, too, sir. We haven't had a lot of contact. I can't say we know each other that well."

234

The Major paused. "Sometimes, Nolan, I wonder how well I know him. That's between you and me, though."

"I understand, sir. If you will excuse me, I want to write a letter or two before dinner."

Excused, Nolan mounted the stairs. He realized now that Ngoc had told Major Thieu about her suspicions regarding him. Maybe he was lucky to be leaving soon. He didn't want Thieu as an enemy.

The dinner tasted especially good that night, a wonderful pork roast with browned potatoes, reminding him of a dish that his mother might cook on a weekend to feed a crowd at their house. Bà Hoa was really on her game now. Nolan continued to note how infectious her newfound joy was. Everyone seemed happy about how their day had gone. He didn't see Elston at the meal, though, and he found out why a few hours later.

Nolan showed up a few minutes early for radio duty later that evening, and he found Elston at the desk, sitting in the silence with a *Popular Mechanics* magazine open before him. That appeared to be his only other reading material besides the precious copies of *Playboy* someone in the States sent him. Nolan decided on the spot to be as friendly as he could, to not push the envelope. He had said all he could reasonably say to Elston the previous night. Yes, the black market was as nefarious as he said, and he didn't regret speaking out as he did. He did regret, though, not doing it more tactfully. He would try to do better.

"I'm guessing it's been quiet, man. Am I right?"

"Very quiet, Nolan. That means your shift will probably be wilder than hell."

No sign of lingering resentment, Nolan thought—good.

"Yeah, it happens that way some nights. Just the luck of the draw, right? Got a poker game tonight?"

"Most likely. Sgt. Harris is on a winning streak, so I suspect he'll be eager to play. He loves to take my money."

"I'm sure he does."

Elston closed the magazine and slowly rose from the chair. He stretched and started for the door before stopping short.

"By the way, I probably won't be seeing Ngoc so often now. She's pretty busy, and she might be traveling more in upcoming months. That's what she told me this afternoon."

"I bet you'll miss her."

"Yeah, the sex is great. She seems OK with things, though, and she even says that she has a cute friend who can gift me some putang while she's gone."

Nolan noted the crudity but stayed focused. "That's quite understanding of her. It's good that she's not the possessive type."

"Well, she likes attention. That I know."

"She's used to getting what she wants, too."

"Yep, roger that. But I'm no pushover either. I'm confident she knows that."

"You're probably right, man. She doesn't miss much."

Chapter 19: Convergence

In the upstairs lounge, the white-shirted CORDS man picked up from the table a .38-caliber pistol, balanced it in his palm as if to admire its lean profile, aimed with an extended right arm, and pulled the trigger. The retort echoed loudly. Glass from the ceiling light bulb scattered across the room. Nolan and the others in the room jumped.

"Damn!" the shooter yelped. "I didn't think it was loaded."

"It's better to check first, don't you think," snapped the usually cordial Hardy, angrily shaking his head.

What is it with these CORDS guys, Nolan wondered to himself, that they are always so eager to show the military how it's done? Too many John Wayne movies, maybe. This guy, Wilson, friendly and unassuming, came across as OK to work with. He didn't flaunt his importance like Thayer had in Song Mao, but Nolan didn't feel inclined to laugh off this incident. Now, with less than a month to go in his tour, he had more reason to feel a little jumpy.

Just a few days earlier, while Nolan and a few others ate their supper, an M-16 rifle had gone off in an adjoining room. Nobody knew where the bullet went. Everyone froze.

"Don't worry, it's OK," a voice rang out, Sgt. Hernandez's, Nolan recognized after a few seconds. "I was cleaning my rifle. Sorry. I'm a dumb shit."

Nervous laughter followed, but no one could sit still after that. Suddenly, everyone needed to be somewhere else. Back then, Nolan saw it as an isolated incident, nothing to dwell on, but now he could not help but wonder if there was a message from the heavens in these close calls. Two in less than a week, as if to say, "Your days are numbered, Nolan."

Hardy told Nolan that if he wanted to sit out some of the camp and village visits in light of how short he was, that would be fine with him. He and Mr. Nguyen could get by OK on their own.

"No reason to test fate," Hardy added.

But to his own surprise Nolan found himself refusing the offer. "I'm not that superstitious, sir. I appreciate the offer, but what would I do around here? The next few weeks aren't really any different than all those that have gone before. Besides, I want to get some last looks at the work getting done. Something to remember this place by, I guess."

It wasn't so much bravery talking, he knew, as experience. Like it or not, he had become a more hardened soldier. He could have added that he didn't hold much confidence in Mr. Nguyen's prowess with the M-16, Hardy's sole support if Nolan didn't ride shotgun. While VC activity along Highway One during the day didn't loom so likely now, the danger remained. Nolan sensed it more keenly than before, that's all, being so close to the finish line.

Over the past few weeks, the refugee flow slowed to barely a trickle, a welcome development. Once the infrastructure of new houses and wells was in place, a new stage would begin. Would new schools be needed? What occupations availed people in the uncertain interim while they waited for the time when they could return home? Nolan didn't envy Hardy's new challenges in upcoming months or those of both their replacements in upcoming years. Camp officials already had their hands full trying to keep kids away from various forms of mischief, including petty theft. Social problems that go with a crowded, bored population always seemed to rise as the next obstacles to overcome.

Nolan's own social life picked up in any case. Mr. Nguyen insisted that the Civil Affairs team come for dinner at his house in honor of Nolan and his pending departure. Nolan appreciated this parting gesture and knew the expense it entailed for Mr. Nguyen, whose small salary made it a challenge to support his wife and their two young children. When Mr. Nguyen hosted him on an earlier occasion, Nolan brought a paper kite and other trinkets for the kids. After that, he asked his mother to send him animal stickers and other paper items that she thought they might like, things easy to mail. Kiddingly, he added, "Not my baseball cards, though." For Mrs. Nguyen, he would buy some flowers at a shop, and for Mr. Nguyen, some of his favorite cigarettes.

Nolan's visit with the Nguyens reminded him of the time Pho brought him home as a new guest. He thought back to his gift of bánh tiêu to Pho's family and how the pastry made a big hit. After the brief second visit when the girls had been absent, Pho's parents invited him to return again anytime. Pho told them that he had been their first American guest. Bao, Pho's father, a schoolteacher well-respected in his community, did not possess a high opinion of Americans, generally. Pho explained why.

"You must understand, No-LANN, what happened at My Lai was not so unusual a year or two ago. Before ARVNs took over most of the patrols, many innocent people died in villages all around us. American soldiers killed them without knowing who they were. My father calls these killings 'crimes.' No one gets punished."

"Sorry, Pho, I didn't know about Americans in Duc Pho. I've been reading about My Lai, though. I thought our soldiers couldn't do that. To think that it's a pattern, damn. That's awful. I'm surprised your father would even want me around."

"Or think it's OK I work for the Americans? He is—what do you say?— practical. He thinks I will be safer in this job, being with the Americans and not in their line of fire."

"We both know how common friendly fire is, though. No safety there. Anyhow, I like your father. He is an honorable man. And, your mother is so charming."

"And my sisters?" Pho said teasingly, shifting his mood.

Nolan picked up the shift.

"Wow. No wonder Ca likes Thi so much. She is a beautiful young woman. And Thanh is much like her. We Americans would call her cute with her combination of good looks and innocence."

"Not so innocent, my friend, but we all love Thanh—maybe too much."

"No way, Pho. She deserves all that love. And I like Thi, too. She has a quiet elegance about her—lovely inside and out."

"They both like you, Nolan. They think you speaking Vietnamese are amusing."

"Yeah, I know I still make mistakes. I'm getting a little better, I think."

"It's OK. They want me to invite you again soon. You must be 'charming,' too."

"Hard to believe, right?"

"How about Saturday? We can go together for dinner."

"Thanks. Sure, that would be great. I bet the Lieutenant will let us take the jeep. 'Home before dark,' he'll say, like a parent, only with a smile. As if I wanted to be on Highway One in the dark."

Nolan thought it would please Pho's family if he again brought bánh tiêu. He found it ironic that his one silly mistake, so embarrassing on one hand, could, on the other, bring him so close to this delightful family. He would miss them along with Mr. Nguyen and his family.

Saturday started off warm, but the afternoon did not turn steamy, so often the case, Pho said, after the monsoon season. The two young men pulled up in front of the modest family home with its whitewashed plaster to find Bao working in the courtyard, tending to his special trees. Pho told Nolan that many years ago his father had planted a lychee tree from seed on one side and transplanted a plantain tree on the other side. Both produced wonderful fruit now. These trees took up much of Bao's time when he wasn't teaching or reading. He nurtured them carefully. When the young men suddenly appeared by his side, Bao greeted them in both Vietnamese and French. During Nolan's first visit, he and Nolan discovered that they had read some of the same French authors. They talked with admiration about Voltaire and Moliere. Though Bao spoke French much better than Nolan, they managed quite well, Nolan searching for the right word only once or twice.

While they conversed, Pho's mother, Mai, and his two sisters came out from the house dressed in an array of stunning áo dàis. Thi, in emerald green, carried a small red bowl containing what seemed to be small, round pieces of white fruit. She smiled shyly and offered the bowl to Nolan. In turn, Nolan presented to Thi the paper bag of bánh tiêu with an exaggerated bow. He was tempted to go to one knee, her appearance in the verdant áo dài so dazzling in the summer light, but he thought better of it. Everyone laughed at the formality of the exchange. Suddenly self-conscious, Nolan wondered if he blushed as well.

"Càm on, No-LANN," Thi said in gratitude, mimicking the intonation of her older brother, whose tall, slender frame she also shared.

"Càm on, Thi," Nolan replied, bowing again.

Wearing a robin's egg blue áo dài as striking as her sister's, Thanh pointed to the bowl and said, "lychee," gesturing that Nolan should use his thumb and forefinger to transport the fruit to his mouth. So instructed, he immediately plucked a piece of firm fruit from the bowl and gently placed it on his tongue, knowing the others were watching for his reaction.

"Giỏi lắm," he exclaimed after a slow, savoring chew. The sweetness came through strong, a citrus taste, but not cloying. He smiled back appreciatively at the beaming family.

"These come from my father's tree," Pho explained, pointing to the tree with its pinkish fruit. "You don't eat the skin. The large seed inside must be removed, too."

"Je suis honore'," Nolan said, nodding to Bao. "Merci beaucoup, monsieur."

"Beaucoup, beaucoup," Thank said impishly, smacking her lips, peering into the bag of bánh tiêu that her older sister held. Everyone laughed, but Thi pulled the bag away to suggest she might not share the bounty. She smiled at Nolan to let him know she meant it to be a joke. She need not have bothered. He had admired her act from start to finish, watching the sudden change in her eyes from an even gaze to a wide-eyed, startled look, her face as beautiful in motion as in repose.

Poor Ca, Nolan thought. Her beauty would floor a monk, no matter his vows. Nolan glanced at Pho, hoping that his gawking at Thi didn't show that much. But he knew Pho had probably read his thoughts, nothing new for the older brother seeing this reaction to his lovely sisters.

The meal itself passed delightfully. It wasn't so much the food, which was fine in itself. Mai served a rice wine to accompany a heaping bowl of squid and shellfish, paired well with perfectly steamed rice flavored by piquant sauces that Nolan had never experienced before. Most of all, he enjoyed the two young women flanking him, doting on him with offerings from both sides. They chose to treat him as if he were a new pet, making sure he was eating more than he thought was his fair share. Stately in her dark red aó dài, Mai seemed a little embarrassed by her daughters' behavior, but Bao and Pho remained unfazed.

Conversation playfully took place in three languages. Bao spoke French to Nolan, who answered in the same. Pho was the only one in the family who spoke English well. Both Thi and Thanh knew a little and sometimes asked Nolan a question that he tried to answer in Vietnamese. In turn, he asked questions in Vietnamese that they tried to answer in English. It took a little longer to communicate clearly than if Pho had chosen to jump in and correct mistakes right away, but they all seemed to enjoy the game.

After the dessert of bánh tiêu, Nolan and Bao stepped outside to converse in French while Pho stayed behind to help his mother and sisters clear the table and store remnants of the meal. Literature proved again the topic, this time poetry predominating. Bao's knowledge ranged widely from French poetry to Chinese lyrics and even including some classical

Western epics. Nolan found himself thoroughly impressed by this cultivated man living here in rural Quang Ngai. The two conversed patiently and thoughtfully, which shouldn't surprise him, Nolan realized. After all, this was Pho's father.

The sun dropped closer to the horizon. Pho signaled to Nolan that the time had come to start back. No safety in darkness. Nolan bowed slightly in saying good-bye and thank you to Pho's parents. When he tried to do the same with their daughters, first to Thanh, she playfully held out her hand for him to grasp, which he did with a smile. Not to be outdone, Thi gestured him forward with an open palm and walked alongside him to Maybe Tomorrow, her brother a few steps behind.

"Will you write to Pho?" she asked hesitantly. Her voice was soft, but clear.

"Yes, I will." He paused. "And to you, if you wish."

She smiled, but this time she quickly lowered her eyes. Maybe, he had been too bold, Nolan thought. He had spoken what he did out of nervousness more than anything else.

"I can tell my father likes you," Pho said on the ride home.

"I like him as well, Pho. I feel that I finally know something in detail about the Vietnamese people because of knowing you and your family. Outside influences have been so strong here. First, the Chinese. Then, the French. And now the Americans. Yet, still a distinct pride in being Viet."

"Yes, I don't know if I could live anyplace else."

"Let's hope that you never leave unless you want to. It should be one's choice. I always wonder about my mother. She left her home—Ireland—because she felt she had no opportunity. She missed the family she left behind, but she is quick to say she is happy in her second country."

They rode on another half mile in silence before Nolan spoke again. "How old is Thi? Is she 20?"

"Soon. She is two years younger than me."

"I suppose she will marry soon. What are Ca's chances?"

"Not good. He is Chieu Hoi, as you know. My father has questions. But my father also prefers an educated man for her."

"Poor Ca. Is there someone else Thi likes?"

"Maybe. She asked if you had a girlfriend in America."

"Really, she did? What did you say?"

"I said 'I think so.'"

"That's a good answer. I would say the same if I were honest. I think I do."

"Her name is Karen, yes?"

"Yeah, Karen. We write to each other, but they are not love letters. Yet I think she would tell me if she was seeing someone else. At least, if it was serious. And she has found me a place to live, a small apartment close to the university. Not far from where she lives. I think that was her plan. Maybe I suggested it."

"You will have time to know her well. My father wants me to go to university after the war. Not a good time for marriage, so I am 'single' as you Americans say."

"Yes. We also call it 'playing the field' as if we can't choose a horse in a race."

Pho laughed. "That is me, for sure. A man without a horse."

Nolan caught a fleeting image in his mind's eye of a Vietnamese warrior flashing a sword above his head as he rode a powerful horse up into the sky.

They arrived back at the compound about twenty minutes before dusk. By coincidence, the helicopter drop of mail and supplies that afternoon included a letter from Karen. It wasn't a love letter as Nolan could have predicted, but it was warm, like the letter from a good friend. She acknowledged receipt of the check for the apartment's deposit and first month rent and reported on a still tense atmosphere around the Madison campus. The anti-war protests, begun early in the year and exacerbated by the Kent State killings in May, never went away despite the heat of summer. Nolan knew that Karen, given more to quiet discussion, wouldn't participate in these. She

244

remained calm about political issues, almost implacable. Her classes and labs in the biological sciences were not centers of the storm, though Dow Chemical recruiters had gotten a rough reception on campus. She said she looked forward to his arrival and expressed doubt that another letter would reach him before he left.

He decided to write a quick letter back to say he would call her at first opportunity once on American soil again, and that he looked forward to seeing her, too. The time spent around the two attractive young women that afternoon had put him in the mood to feel increased longing for Karen's company. Hers was a more full-bodied beauty than that of these Vietnamese sisters, accentuated by blue eyes, honey-colored hair, and a ready smile. Though she was a full year younger than he was, she showed admirable poise, Nolan thought—a strong woman owning a track record of accomplishing tasks with a combination of diligence and grace.

In the week that followed, he remained remarkably upbeat, popular song lyrics running through his brain at odd times, snatches of melodies from Armed Forces Radio. He pictured family members in their late summer rituals, a wonderful time in Maine, enjoying the fresh vegetables from the garden, the blueberry pies, maybe even some lobsters, and kidding each other about golf games. He knew they would be anticipating his return home, even if they all knew it would be for only a few days, just enough time for him to sort through some clothes—no uniforms anymore-- and to get his car ready for the distant drive to Madison.

Early on that week, he found a few brief moments to talk with Pho, who possessed more than the usual free time because Major Thieu had developed a bad case of gout. Pho referred to it at first as "goot," but Nolan congenially set him straight as Pho did for him many times in Vietnamese. Then, in mid-week, Pho had a chance to visit his home overnight. When he returned, he motioned Nolan aside and handed him an envelope.

Seeing Nolan start with surprise, Pho said, "My friend, I want you to know this was not my idea. My father asked me to give you this letter."

Puzzled but also intrigued, Nolan unfolded creamy stationery from the envelope. There in elegant black handwriting ran several paragraphs, all in French. Nolan jumped in, translating to himself, Pho standing silently beside him, not attempting to read the script.

Monsieur Nolan,

I hope my letter finds you well. Please excuse the means I have employed to communicate these thoughts, but we are both busy men and time is short. I know you will be leaving Vietnam in a few weeks, and your thoughts are turning to resuming your studies. I envy you in that regard. As a teacher and a father, I consider education to be both a necessity and a wonderful gift for young people. I have hopes that my children will be able to pursue university educations, though the war is a large obstacle. I will try everything in my power to assist them in improving themselves, but first I must try to guarantee their safety. Desperate times call for bold moves, and, often, sacrifice of one's own personal happiness.

I must be blunt, forgive me. I have observed that there is a spark of mutual interest between you and my daughter Thi. My son tells me that you do not have a serious romantic interest currently in America. You are a free man, and Thi is free, as well, but her life here is not safe. I know that both she and Thanh would be safer outside our country, and I judge you to be someone who would honor marriage and a responsibility to protect and support a wife. It is with that thought that I make you aware that my wife and I would welcome having you as a husband to Thi if you are so inclined. Of course, Thi must agree, as well, but I think I know my daughter.

Haste is never desirable, but given the circumstances, this matter requires urgency. If you are interested in the

possibility of a marriage, I request that you return to our
home this Saturday to discuss what can be accomplished
before you leave Vietnam.

I hope that my offer does not place me or my family in
a bad light. While it may seem desperate to propose
such a union after only two occasions, I can assure you
that I have thought of little else the past three days, and I
have confidence in the propriety of my offer.
Respectfully yours.
Le Van Bao

Nolan felt his pulse racing. Marriage? How had things gotten to this point? He thought back to his last words with Thi. What he thought had been more of a tease, something offhanded, she obviously took to heart. Or maybe it was more what her father thought he had observed between them, colored by the concern he had for his children's future. This development presented too much to digest.

Pho scanned Nolan's face, noting the look of astonishment.

"This is my father's worry, No-LANN. He wants to protect Thi. The war is wearing him down. So many years it has lasted. He is losing faith in peace."

Nolan nodded as he searched for words. The delicacy now required lay beyond his reach, he realized. He couldn't form coherent thoughts. What could he say to his friend? After what seemed an eternity, he tried again.

"Pho, you cannot believe how flattered I am that Thi, so lovely and graceful, would even consider me. Or that your father would judge me to be worthy of his daughter. I'm overwhelmed."

"You need time to think, perhaps? I will go away, my friend. We can talk later."

"Yeah, I need to think. Sorry, I can't say what I need to say right now. Can we talk tomorrow, Pho? That OK?"

His friend didn't hesitate. "Yes, of course. I understand. I will see you tomorrow."

When Pho had gone, Nolan went up to the lounge to be alone, but all three of his roommates were gathered there chattering away with opened beers, so he continued up to the roof. Leaning against the concrete wall, he reread the letter, more slowly this time, shaking his head at the amazing suggestion. For months he had looked forward to his eventual departure from the war, to freedom, and to a new life with all its possibilities back home in America. Karen had evolved into a major part of what sustained him, especially more recently. They shared a history, and just maybe, he thought, a future. Was it possible that he could reverse course so close to his departure and the resumption of his familiar life? Could he so impulsively take on a new adventure with a virtual stranger? An image of Thi appeared in his mind, the beautiful girl in the green aó dài, with its close-fitting bodice, yet so modest in its coverage from her neck down to the top of her slippers, like the plumage of a tropical bird. At that moment, he could imagine that her feet never actually touched the ground, that she had descended to earth to stand by him, on this rarest of occasions, under the spreading lychee tree.

This was a dream world, not real, he told himself. He saw that the decision pressing upon him so urgently matched in importance the one he had made almost two years ago, to allow himself to be drafted. That decision now seemed closer to a submission, perhaps, than to a real choice. He had considered his draft situation from different angles, never seriously considering a run to Canada that he and others at the language school joked about. He knew that much of his decision entailed what his parents tacitly expected from him, to be, above all, responsible. They accepted his willingness to teach high school as a way for service to be deferred at least another year. But he realized that option presented only a temporary solution. The Selective Service wouldn't forget him. Had he made the right choice then to report for induction? He still didn't know more than a year and a half later, though his astronomically high number in the subsequent draft lottery provided perfect hindsight. The delay would have spared him.

Now a beautiful young girl and her future depended on his decision. He looked out over the town to the distant hills. He vowed that this time he would be more certain about what he wanted.

Chapter 20: Last Rites

Nolan waited on the roof until he could be sure his roommates had retired for the night. Quietly, he crawled into bed with the lights out, having spent several hours weighing his options. He thought he had made up his mind, but when he tried to fall asleep, he didn't have any luck. He would think of Thi, her elegant beauty in the green aó dài and her sweet demeanor. Then, he would envision Karen, with her more familiar girl-next-door attractiveness and the alluring promise of a resumed relationship. In the end he fell asleep only because he completely stopped picturing the young women. He turned instead to a habit he had formed some years ago, playing the hometown golf course of his youth from the first tee on. In his mind, he skimmed, as if a few feet above, the freshly mown fairways with their challenging undulations, he comfortably alone in the brightness of a summer day. After visualizing a few holes, he would fall asleep, at least most times. It worked again that night, allowing for a few hours of sleep before Elston, probably just being his clumsy self, awoke him. Still half asleep, the handyman stumbled out of the room on his way to radio duty. After that, Nolan slept fitfully, but stayed put until it was light. As he placed his feet on the floor, he muttered to himself, "I need to find Pho."

He took only a few minutes for a hasty shower and dressed quickly. When he approached the dining room, he found Hardy standing in the hallway, hurriedly drinking a mug of coffee.

"I was about to come looking for you. We don't have time for breakfast right now. The Major and O'Hare left a few minutes ago on foot. There's apparently something going on just outside the gate."

"Do I need my rifle?"

"Bring it along, just in case. Whatever happened, though, appears to be over."

After retrieving his rifle, Nolan followed Hardy down the steps in a trot. They traversed the courtyard to the gate, past two guards out into the street. Across the street and down a few buildings, they saw three provincial soldiers guarding the entrance to the fish shop. A few curious onlookers stood around talking.

"That's where they must be," Hardy said.

"Vinh's place? I wouldn't think it would be open this early."

The guards parted to let them duck into the small shop. Inside it was dingy and smelled of the sea. They heard voices in the adjoining room separated by a beaded curtain. Peering inside, they found the room crowded. Lt. Tran, Major Thieu's assistant, stood just inside the doorway talking with Pho, while Major Stewart and O'Hare stood behind them, partially blocking the view of someone lying on a small bed. Nolan made out a face. It was Long and he wasn't moving.

"Heart attack," the Major said. "A few hours ago. He apparently was in the act of screwing the woman of the house."

The "woman of the house," Nolan realized, would be Vinh's widow, who was not in the room now. How could this be? Long and the widow? And Long was probably only in his 40s, too young for a heart attack in Nolan's experience.

"A lesson to us all," the Major added, as if reading Nolan's thoughts. "Stick to home cooking and live longer."

O'Hare stood by silently with a grim expression. Pho turned to the Major and reported: "Lt. Tran talked to neighbors who say Long maybe came here often. Certainly after Vinh died. Maybe before. People saw him arrive some evenings and leave an hour or two later."

"Someone needs to tell Long's wife," Major Stewart replied. "No sense in hiding what happened. She'll find out anyhow. Take the woman over to Major Thieu for questioning."

Pho relayed the message to Lt. Tran, whose English was still somewhat rough. Because of Thieu's ongoing problems with gout, the young officer filled in for his commanding officer much of the time for any business outside the compound. He exited the room by a back door, presumably to wherever the widow was being kept under guard.

Nolan glanced at the corpse on the bed. Someone had covered the lower part of the body, but the face still wore a frozen expression of pain. No sign of repose. Nolan hadn't seen a corpse close up since the dead VC along the road to Mo Duc that first day in the province. He turned away now, determined not to look again. He realized he felt queasy, the small room suddenly seeming to lack enough air.

"Makes you wonder now, doesn't it?" the Major asked. "Was Vinh actually VC or was Long just trying to get the husband out of the way."

"Long had good intelligence, sir," O'Hare said, some sharpness in his voice. "He wouldn't frame someone."

"Maybe so," the Major replied. "Or maybe he thought he had too good a situation, shagging this widow whenever he wanted. Not that she's any great beauty. She's not that young."

Nolan wondered where her kids were. Could this have been a regular arrangement as the neighbors suggested? He decided not to ask any questions right then.

"Nolan, let's go back to the compound," Hardy said quietly. "We should get some breakfast and then get on the road."

Nolan nodded, though he didn't feel hungry. He was glad to get out of the room. At the door, he muttered to Pho, "We need to talk later. "

O'Hare interjected, "Keep this matter on the Q.T. We don't want Phoenix compromised."

"Yes, sir," Nolan said, not bothering to explain. For now, he didn't want anyone else to know about the letter from Bao. Once outside the shop, Nolan asked Hardy, "What happened here? These two people don't make sense. Do you think this was just an unfortunate accident?"

"That's what Major Thieu will try to find out. It did cross my mind that this wasn't just a case of death by sexual passion. If Vinh's widow knew the role that Long played in her

252

husband's death, she might actually have been seeking revenge."

They could see the lean, gray and black clad figure walking ahead of them, her conical straw hat surrounded by the dark green helmets of Lt. Tran and two soldiers. Nolan didn't see an avenger. Or maybe he didn't want to.

"So, Long's heart attack was not just the case of a bad ticker? What would have killed him?"

"That's out of my league. I could only speculate from murder mysteries I've read."

"But do you think Major Thieu knows more about these matters?"

Hardy hesitated. "Maybe not, but his interrogation won't be gentle. That I'm sure about."

Nolan thought back to his earlier doubts about the woman's innocence immediately following the death of her husband. He feared then that if involved in the same clandestine work as her husband, she might easily prey on Pho's good intentions to help her. He didn't think Pho would consciously pass on information to her about the assassins even if he heard anything confirming Long's involvement. Maybe, though, Nolan considered, she was as wily as his darker thoughts suggested.

Back inside the compound, Hardy and Nolan knew better than to talk openly about the matter. Bà Hoa and the other women who helped with domestic duties for the team members shouldn't hear any of this even if their English was limited. Plus, the other enlisted men might not be so discreet given the way Long was found.

Later, riding in Maybe Tomorrow, though, Nolan pressed the matter with Hardy. "I've been thinking about Long. Don't they need to do an autopsy?"

Hardy tilted his head as in doubt. "Under normal circumstances, yes. But Major Thieu runs the show in Duc Pho. He might not take the time and just figure 'why take a chance?'"

"Do you mean kill her like Long killed her husband?"

Hardy didn't answer immediately. He kept his gaze fixed over the steering wheel. "It's war, Nolan. I don't like it either. All this collateral damage."

After that, they rode in silence as Nolan scanned the rice paddies. He couldn't let his mind drift far from looking out for enemy presence, yet the events of the morning kept returning. He realized that he had overlooked something.

"Did you notice, sir, how Major Stewart spoke openly about Long and Phoenix in front of Pho? I guess there really isn't much secret between the Major and Pho, after all."

"Makes sense, doesn't it? If you can't trust your interpreter with intelligence, maybe you need a new interpreter, someone you *can* trust. The Major is past doubt with Pho, I would think."

"So am I. He's become a good friend over the last few months. I wonder how he sees all this shaking down."

"More tragedy, I suspect."

Nolan stayed silent as Hardy pulled the jeep off the road for the first village visit of the day. Nolan would need to put aside everything roiling in his head. In just twenty-four hours leaving Vietnam had become much more complicated than he ever thought possible. He should be happy that in only a few more days he would be home with family. So why did he feel he was running away, leaving so much unresolved?

They returned to the compound for a quick lunch and afterward picked up Mr. Nguyen for a visit to a village south of Duc Pho that was expecting a delivery of cement. Major Stewart and Pho were not around for lunch, possibly a good sign, Nolan thought. Maybe the Major would get involved in the interrogation and try to ensure some form of due process, not always available in a war zone. He had it in him, Nolan wanted to believe. War could tear people down morally, but it could also bring forward some positive qualities that lay hidden. Compassion, for one.

It was almost supper time when Nolan and Pho found a chance to talk alone. Pho appeared tired, slumped back in a dining room chair. Nolan sat down next to him and spoke softly: "I know you can't tell me everything, Pho. Do you think this woman killed Long?"

"No, No-LANN. I do not. Thuy—her name—came to the compound this morning to tell people what happened. She was crying, but not afraid. She did not run away."

"But what did she know about Long?"

"You mean that he killed her husband? She says she did not know, but she knew that it was possible. Long was a powerful man, and she was a poor widow. He gave her money and presents for her children. Without those things, she could not stay in Duc Pho. The shop has little business now."

"So, you think the sex with Long began after Vinh died?"

"Yes, I believe that."

"Does Major Thieu believe her?"

"He has not made up his mind. He wants Thuy to fear him, and she does fear him. Major Stewart is polite with her."

"I am glad Major Stewart was there. Maybe he can keep Major Thieu from making too hasty a decision."

"Major Stewart is a good man, yes. How much can he do? I do not know. Thuy will stay under guard tonight. Who knows after that?"

"I can tell this has been hard for you. Interpreting is one thing, interrogating is another."

"Major Thieu asked the questions mostly. Major Stewart occasionally had questions, and I asked those."

Pho stopped talking. After a moment, he looked directly at Nolan, smiling almost shyly. "Shall we talk about a different woman?"

Nolan returned the smile. "I wanted to talk with you this morning. I looked for you. I didn't sleep well last night."

"I think I know what you decided but go ahead and tell me."

"My mind and my heart were both divided. They still are. I just see a clearer future with Karen. We know each other. Thi and I might regret this arrangement after we knew each other better. It's too soon, that's all. I believe she should have more time to choose whom she wants. That's what I want, too."

"It seems too strange, yes?"

"Like a fantasy, a dream. Thi is so lovely. I won't forget her. Ever."

He was determined not to cry. Pho looked at him.

"Don't be sad, No-LANN. Thi doesn't know what my father wrote. We probably will not tell her. My father, he will be sad. I think, though, he will understand. I will tell him you care more for another girl. He can understand that."

"I will write him, too. Now, *you* look a little sad," Nolan said, touching Pho's nearer shoulder.

"I am sad because a friend is leaving, and now I know he won't be returning."

Nolan thought that over a second. "You can never tell. At least, we will write each other. Agreed?"

"Agreed, my friend."

The others began arriving for the meal, so Nolan got up and went off to wash off some of the roadside dust. He felt some relief from speaking with Pho, but he knew his torn feelings, his regret, would not go away so easily.

He had a middle shift for radio duty, which meant he wouldn't be getting to bed until around two-thirty in the morning. It also meant he would struggle to stay alert after his previous, restless night. He didn't mind the routine now as much as when before the artillery unit called so often on the secure line for explanations after he had to withhold political clearance. He had become accustomed to the percussions of the 155's that followed within seconds of his giving approval. Most of the time, the requests seems to lack urgency. Interdiction fire—keeping 'em honest—punctuated the night air.

He had time now to think of a reply to Bao, something kept short but respectful. He would thank him, say he was honored to be considered worthy of being his son-in-law, but that he felt a greater pull. He thought, too, of the last line from Voltaire's

256

Candide, a reference that he knew Bao would recognize: "il faut cultiver notre jardin." He immediately felt shame. While the ending in that book seemed wise enough, to focus on what one could nurture locally—one's garden as a metaphor—instead of trying to change human nature, it sounded so insensitive in this new context. Certainly, he was looking forward to putting the war behind him, to repairing his life. But he was writing to a father who was trying to secure the lives of his daughters in a war zone. They couldn't just pick up and leave like he could, and soon would. Their future was so circumscribed compared to his. Yes, he had doubts about how his return to school and to Karen would go, but real change was possible too—a better tomorrow. Not just a hollow phrase.

Nolan wasn't sure if he dozed off, but he became suddenly aware of someone standing behind him.

"Quiet night?"

It was Sgt. Childress, his relief.

"Well, not completely, Sarge. I was just about to go and wake you."

"No need tonight. I'm sleeping light most nights now."

Childress was almost as short as Nolan, just a month to go, and he had gone through this process before.

"I know what you mean. It won't be long until you're leaving Nam, too, but you might be coming back, I hear."

"I've done two tours now. The money is good, but I don't know what situation I might find next time. Maybe I'll be sent to the damn DMZ." He chuckled in an unconvincing way. "You'll be back in school. That right?"

"That's the plan. I hear the university is becoming like the DMZ in some ways. A lot of angry people. The good thing is that these people aren't armed. At least, not yet."

"I guess I prefer the Army."

"It's good we have a choice, Sarge." Nolan stood up. "Hope the rest of the morning is quiet for you."

Once back in his room, he fell asleep promptly, almost as if knocked out. He dreamed, but strangely. He wandered lost in a big city that resembled Tokyo, but after descending a flight of outdoor stairs, he entered a less populated area, a beach with tropical trees. He stood looking out at the ocean, maybe the South China Sea. He found alongside him a girl in a white tunic and black pants. It was Thi as she looked when he first saw her, her long, lustrous hair and ivory complexion stunningly set off by her beautiful dark eyes.

The two stood comfortably side by side, not talking. She gently took the sleeve of his arm, pulling him closer as if she had something to whisper in his ear. He bent down toward her lips and appeared to catch a sweet, fruit-like scent from her breath. He was giddy with excitement as he neared her face. Then, looking closer, he saw that her skin had taken on a leathery appearance as if toughened from years of sun. Her hair no longer hung down her slender frame but was constricted in a bun. He backed off a few inches and saw that the white tunic had changed to gray, and the woman was not as tall as Thi. The woman looked familiar but was not Thi. He searched along the shore for Thi, thinking he had just misplaced her, but he couldn't find her among the suddenly growing crowd of fishermen and their families.

The dream segued into what appeared to be a refugee camp with young children running alongside Hardy and him, Mr. Nguyen leading the way through a maze of small huts. Nolan didn't see Thi again. He awoke with his roommates already dressed and moving about. He slowly sat up, feeling only partially refreshed. He knew he would feel sluggish much of the day, but nothing he could do about that now except drink some strong coffee.

In the dining room Major Stewart acted very business-like, eating quickly and saying little to anyone. When Pho appeared at the door, the Major got up right away and left the room with him, the two men silent as they exited the front entrance. Nolan knew that Thuy's interrogation dominated both majors' agendas, but he tried to focus on assisting Hardy with their immediate Civil Affairs business. Nothing he could do about his lack of sleep or this interrogation, he realized.

Mr. Nguyen's gentle smile of greeting in the courtyard picked up Nolan's spirits a little. The morning passed without any hitches, the three men chatting amiably as they went about their business of assessing material needs for the two villages they visited.

When they returned to the compound around two in the afternoon, they saw a Vietnamese woman, hair in a bun, hands manacled in front of her, being guided by Lt. Tran into the back seat of a jeep. He joined her as a soldier with an M-16 swung into the front passenger seat. The jeep lurched forward, exiting the gate to the north. Pho stood at the bottom of the steps to the MACV building, watching silently.

"Was that Thuy?" Hardy asked.

"Yes, sir," Pho answered glumly. "They are taking her to police HQ in Quang Ngai."

"Did she say anything new?"

"No, sir. Same story. Major Thieu believes HQ will know better what to do."

Nolan said nothing but walked around the jeep to stand by his friend. He exchanged a look with Hardy. No one wanted to say how this looked for Thuy.

"Who will look after her children, Pho?" Nolan asked after the awkward pause.

"They are in high school and can look after themselves. Neighbors will help, too."

"Keep me informed, Pho, "Hardy said. "I'll ask Mr. Nguyen if his office can help them for the time being."

Nolan glanced at Pho, both grateful to hear Hardy's suggestion. Nolan felt so powerless himself. He could only imagine how another disappointment of this magnitude made Pho feel. On the outside, at least, Pho remained stoic. Other than to give him a note for Bao, Nolan didn't have a chance to speak with him again that afternoon. Nolan had finally written a more thoughtful one that he hoped would not offend anyone.

"Please give my regards to all your family, Pho, when you see them this weekend. I won't have time for another visit."

Pho took the note but said nothing other than "good night." His mind seemed miles away. At the beginning of his final week in Duc Pho, Nolan did not see his friend much. The full moon meant guard duty on the roof for a couple of nights. It seemed Nolan was always trying to catch up on sleep. The strange dreams had stopped. He dreamed mostly of Karen and his family, settings familiar to him in the States. With each trip to a village or camp, he said good-bye to officials he had worked with. While none of them were as close as he was to Mr. Nguyen, they appeared sincere in their good wishes and offered tea or coffee to create a parting ceremony. Nolan appreciated the generosity.

Saying good-bye to Mr. Nguyen proved more difficult. His wispy mustache and gentle smile had become as familiar to Nolan as his own reflection. Amazingly, he had never seen Mr. Nguyen angry or frustrated despite the challenges of his job. Nolan knew he wouldn't have much need for Vietnamese currency now in his remaining hours in country, so he placed small amounts into separate envelopes for each of the Nguyen children. In farewell, he put his arm around Mr. Nguyen's shoulder as Hardy snapped a photo.

The night before departure, Major Stewart toasted Nolan at the supper table, joking about what condiments the table needed to remind Nolan of his limited Vietnamese vocabulary.

"Kidding aside, Nolan, you did good work. We'll miss you around here."

The others said, "Hear, hear," raising their glasses. Even Elston and O'Hare chimed in. In the last weeks, the animosity that had arisen between Nolan and Elston subsided considerably. O'Hare remained somewhat in shock about Long's death, so Nolan had given him a wider berth in the past few days. He did not want to bring up the politics of the war so close to his departure. The men seemed genuine in their good wishes, but also envious, too. Nolan knew that most of them

260

longed to be in his shoes, aware he had shaved a few months off the usual tour of duty. He had another half day to say good-bye to the Lieutenant, who would drive him up to Quang Ngai the next morning. From there Nolan would then hitch a ride with a convoy to Da Nang.

One more night in the compound to survive. Fortunately, he was sufficiently tired to drop off into sleep without nagging thoughts.

He looked for Pho that morning and found him standing outside his quarters across the compound. What could he say to his gentle friend, his closest friend in Vietnam?

"I was afraid I had missed you, Pho. I want to wish you well. Chin up, as the old-timers say."

"Sorry, I couldn't stick around last night, No-LANN. I was in the dump."

"In the dumps, plural, Pho. Don't ask me why. Come to think of it, I can't explain much at all about this American we speak."

"You have helped me greatly, my friend."

"Not as much as you have helped me. And thanks again for keeping the bánh tiêu story to yourself."

"If you don't write me within two weeks, I'll tell everyone I know."

"I hear you loud and clear. I promise."

They looked at each other, Nolan wanting to say more. But sensing that he might only embarrass himself by talking too much, he didn't. Pho probably felt the same way, he thought. Nolan looked down briefly. When he lifted his gaze, he saw Pho had done the same. Silently, they shook hands. Nolan turned and walked away, not looking back.

Within a half hour, Hardy and Nolan were riding in Maybe Tomorrow on the road north, Nolan scanning the paddies for possible snipers one last time. He turned his shoulders to catch some of the breeze in the open doorway. He said nothing as they passed the refugee camps and villages that had constituted much of his daily life for six months. Once in Quang Ngai and quite early for Nolan's ride to Da Nang, Hardy suggested they stop in the base bar for some cool refreshment. It seemed like only yesterday, on his first day in the province, that he had done the same with Lt. Collins, the Marlboro Man.

When the Lieutenant and Hardy sat down at a table with their cans of beer, Hardy asked, "Was it hard saying good-bye to Pho?"

"Very hard. He did his best to perk up at the end. I think he feels that Major Stewart washed his hands of the Thuy affair. Let him down, as it were."

"Is that what you think?"

"Yeah, that's the way it looks. Nearly a week and still no word about her."

"Yes, but I doubt she would have lasted a week with Major Thieu. Major Stewart knew that Thuy wouldn't get a fair shake in Duc Pho. He was the one who pushed for sending her here. If there isn't hard evidence against her, I think the provincial officials will release her before long. You and I can't say what part she played in all of this, but today, at this moment, she's better off than she was last week."

Nolan bobbed his head a few times. It wasn't the first time, but it was likely the last that his superior—a term Nolan seldom used—had enlightened him about something.

"You have a knack for getting me to see things differently. I will miss that unless graduate school in Madison is more exciting than the last time I took courses."

"Nolan, grad school sounds pretty good to even little old me right now, especially all those co-eds. That can't be too hard to take."

"What about you? You have R&R coming up. Have you decided where to go?"

"Yes, I think I'll go to Sydney."

"Australia, huh. Why there? Do you know someone to visit?"

"It so happens I do, and so do you, though she will be a visitor in Sydney, too. Her family lives off in the country somewhere."

A light suddenly went on in Nolan's mind. "I'm guessing that your Southern charm plays well in Australia, at least with dark-haired nurses."

"I can't explain it. It's just natural, I guess."

They laughed. Nolan realized he was happy for his team leader. After musing on what he could say in the few minutes remaining, he broke the silence. "I do think I learned something important while in Nam, and you had a lot to do with it. I learned to rely on my instincts more, particularly about people, like when to trust someone and when not to. That's big."

"That it is, Nolan, and we also occasionally have to stick our necks out to get something done. Despite the risks."

"You've done that, for sure."

"I've had a good partner."

"It wasn't always fun, but it was never dull. Take good care of the jeep. It did well by us, ol' Maybe Tomorrow."

"One more pearl of wisdom while we're assessing everything." Hardy froze momentarily and looked Nolan in the eye. "I feel as if I should throw some salt over my shoulder. If I had to name another necessary ingredient for success, that would be easy. Good, old-fashioned luck. You can't beat it."

Nolan hoisted his can in Hardy's direction. "I'll drink to that, sir. And the best of luck to you."

"Thanks, right back at you, Nolan."

It was their final toast together.

Chapter 21: Ascent

Nolan drank only the single can of beer with Hardy, but it rendered him drowsy enough to nod off in the warm, covered bed of a ¾-ton truck in the small convoy north. When he slowly grew more alert, he and his fellow passenger, a GI headed out for R&R in Bangkok, talked about their destinations. Neither had all that much to say. His companion dropped off to sleep before long, leaving Nolan on his own.

Besides the truck behind them and the receding pavement, he could see little scenery, though he occasionally glimpsed the distant mountains in the background. He had served nearly all his time in Vietnam within camps and villages on flat land, among rice paddies, but the mountains continued to fascinate him, sometimes dark and foreboding, and other times an ethereal blue, mist shrouded in the lower regions, promising something he couldn't quite identify, something hopeful and fulfilling. He knew that the NVA and Viet Cong established their camps in the highlands, sometimes in tunnels. Sadly, U.S. Army and Marine forces who deployed there had suffered terribly in the ongoing confrontations with the enemy, being sorely outnumbered. Yet the mountains promised as well as intimidated. From a distance they appeared beautiful. They suggested that more possibilities existed than what lay nearby. It was a land of dreams.

When Nolan eventually turned his eyes back to the canvas-covered interior, the ride provided him an opportunity to reflect on those he had met over the past ten months. Of these, his Vietnamese friends clearly touched his heart more: Pho and his family—Thi especially—, Mr. Nguyen and his family, Ca, and Bà Hoa. He would miss all of these, along with the kids in the villages and camps, especially those second-chance kids he had driven to the Quaker hospital. Silently, he wished Bui and Nap well, the two men almost forgotten amid the welter of recent happenings in Duc Pho.

Others would remain mysteries to him, as much as the forested mountains he looked at every day but never visited. He admired the cleverness of Major Thieu and the businesswoman Ngoc, even if he didn't trust them. They were survivors, and Thuy was, too, he suspected. He also wondered what became of Hieu's brother, Danh, whether he embraced peace or the Viet Cong. So many people remained enigmas to Nolan. Maybe it was just as well that he knew so little. Back in Song Mao, he longed to get to know the Vietnamese better, to get beyond the walls of the American enclave. He did that in Quang Ngai province. Yet once again, uncertainty prevailed. Given his initial reluctance to participate in the war and his ongoing doubts about its ends, he hoped that one way or another he would somehow find solace from his service here. He tried to do good work, but did he, in reality, cause more harm just by being here? The elderly Japanese man's words still resonated.

Nolan considered his options for talking about the war once home. What would he tell friends and family about his experience? Would he become politically active? Discharged from the Army, he would be free to join the efforts of those against the war to stop it or argue that a stalemate might be a necessary step to serious peace talks. He hoped that what his Vietnamese friends said they wanted, a real democracy, remained possible.

He wondered how much the lives of the rice farmers and poor villagers would vary under either a free-market economy or a communist one. In either case, he thought, their lives, so elemental and earthbound, so focused on ancestral ties, would remain dominated by physical labor. System builders, who cared little about others save for their own families and closest friends, would continue to manipulate the economy. Graft ran rampant in Vietnam, in step with long-bred hostility.

He intended to write Pho soon, knowing that encouraging words could lessen the burden for his friend on the long, seemingly endless road that lay ahead. Would Pho ever realize his dream of attaining a university education in his homeland? Nolan didn't see that happening soon. He remembered saying to O'Hare that the US might need to get ready for a flood of refugees. He hadn't changed his mind. While peace talks could lead somewhere, they could also fail.

After having worked so closely together, maybe he would stay in touch with Hardy. He didn't know if a new guy would take the job of assistant as seriously as he had. Maybe, though, his replacement would outpace him. That would be great. He smiled to himself, glad that Hardy would get to spend some time in a more peaceful setting with Mary Ann, the Aussie nurse. Secret admirers, indeed. Who knew how that might turn out?

While Nolan doubted that he would have any future contact with the other Americans in Duc Pho, he wished them well, too. He knew that dealing with those of such different backgrounds and attitudes in the Army removed him from the cocoon that family and academic life had so long provided. He now knew what it was like to deal with difficult personalities, and with those holding very different political views. He had encountered some racists and scoundrels, too, who opened his eyes to challenges ahead. He might now be able to spend much of his down time with those he admired, but moving about in the world would require him to be patient and willing to compromise at times. Still, he needed to have backbone, too.

He intended, over the last few months, to stay in contact with some of his friends from Song Mao, but that didn't happen. His small, black notebook contained a smattering of addresses for them, some here in Nam, some back in hometowns. Most of them probably ended their tours in recent months. His classmates from language school in El Paso stood to serve two more months in Nam unless any had found an early release option as he had. Then, too, only if they had bucked the odds and all escaped harm. In his recent letter Whitley reported that the most voluble and high-strung member of their class, a guy from the Bronx, Mickey Levin, survived an attack when the VC overran his compound near the DMZ. Nolan shook his head, imagining Mickey's terror. Luck spared his classmate's life even more dramatically than it did in Nolan's narrow escapes. His daily fears slowly gave way to the reality that he was actually on the road home, at last. So close now. He was just a day from departure.

At Da Nang HQ, Sanders greeted him at the front desk. Judging from the clerk's curtness, Nolan surmised that he was not having a good day. Maybe processing men out of the company gave Sanders less joy. Maybe the tedium of paperwork was wearing him down. So their conversation ran more matter of fact than their banter a few months earlier. Nolan tried to pique Sanders' interest.

"What news of our friend D'Amico? Has he avoided court-martial?"

"Yeah, he did. Some Congressman went to bat for him. So, he got an honorable discharge after all, the lucky bastard."

"And a job, too?"

"I don't know about that. Last I heard, he was living on a commune in Humboldt County."

Nolan laughed. "Thrown into the briar patch, huh? I hope he's mellow."

After turning in his M-16, helmet, and other combat gear, Nolan felt significantly less burdened. His lighter self led him to believe that he was nearing freedom. The next morning he would be flying down to Long Binh, and then boarding the big bird home. He remembered the long ride over, almost twenty-four hours. The return flight wouldn't be much shorter in actual time even with tail winds, but it looked to be a lot more enjoyable.

As usual, time in transit weighed heavily on him, but once in Long Binh again, Nolan relaxed considerably, not allowing himself to get emotional. To his relief, he found diversion in reading. In the morning he didn't want to load himself down with extra baggage, so he left most of the paperbacks from his duffel bag in the barracks, something for the next man through. A bus carried him to final processing in a building near the airfield. A cursory medical check with advice about taking his anti-malaria pills for a short time after discharge eventually led him from one line of GIs to another. Then he realized it must have been one continuous line.

Finally, he found himself walking down the right side of a long corridor, following the man ahead in single file, a glass partition between the two halves of the hallway. On the other side moving toward him appeared the faces of the soldiers arriving in country. His mind flashed back ten months to his arrival and looking at the faces of the men leaving Vietnam, some smiling, some glum, and some staring straight ahead. He instantly realized that the arriving men scanned his face now. He decided to look away. None of them really knew what lay ahead. Some would fare OK, some would be wounded, maybe maimed, and some would die. Nolan wanted no more part of that.

He wanted this moment to be anticipatory, about his future, to be free of any misgivings. He found that he wasn't getting off so easily. He thought of Thi, her beauty and sweet temperament, and of his decision. Was he abandoning her? He thought that he made the right choice. They hardly knew each other. He was keeping open for both of them the chance to choose life partners on the basis of love, to not have their lives arranged or, more accurately, controlled by circumstances outside their hearts' desire. He knew Karen so much better. Wasn't that the right decision?

He had passed on the more heroic option, to help an innocent person out of the dangers and uncertainties of war. Some would say that action took precedence over everything else. Once safely in the States, if they found it impossible to create a happy life together, they could separate then. In that scenario, though, Nolan still would want to return the trust Bao

268

extended to him. He would want to make sure that Thi was doing well in her new life. They could stay friends.

He wasn't a hero, though. He lacked that impulse. Once again outside in the sultry air, the sad realization hit him. His head throbbed. He tried to focus on the back of the soldier inches ahead, one last line leading across the tarmac toward the long staircase on wheels that abutted the body of the waiting jetliner. He did not look back. The men's pace increased ever so slightly as they neared the plane, the roar of the turbines as strong as the heat of the noonday sun.

The line stopped abruptly at the stairway. Nolan looked up over the shoulder of the man he followed toward the open doorway of the jet. The GI at the very top wasn't moving. Nolan felt a moment of panic. He hoped they were not running out of seats. The smell of jet fuel intensified. His first scent and his last scent of Vietnam.

The line started to move again. Nolan climbed the metal stairway, grasping the railing with one hand to keep his balance. He reached the doorway at last and entered. Flight attendants, coiffed and perfumed American women, greeted the men with smiles. Nolan entered an empty row and buckled himself into a window seat, momentarily closing his eyes. A young, lean black GI swung into the seat beside him, Armored Cavalry, as indicated by his arm patch. He looked somehow familiar. Nolan wondered if he had seen him in Quang Ngai province outside Mo Duc, atop an armored carrier. No rush. He had plenty of time to find out. The plane wouldn't land in the States for almost twenty-four hours. For now they nodded at each other, trying to remain cool, as if all this was routine.

The mood around them elevated with each passing second, energy now high. The flight attendants, in sing-song voices, gave instructions for take-off. Nolan closed his eyes again as if that could hurry the process along. He sat perspiring, the seat belt firmly across his lap. How much longer? He looked out the window at the heat waves rising from the tarmac. He couldn't tell for how long. Maybe a minute, maybe several minutes. Finally, the engines came to life, the jet shuddering into motion and steadily taxiing to its take-off position, and once there, slowly spinning into place. After the briefest of pauses, Nolan felt a lurch forward, then his body firm against the seatback. The jet started hurtling ahead, engines aroar, and after the longest seconds in Nolan's life, lifted off the runway. Above the engine noise, the cheer was deafening.

Acknowledgements

While my own experience as a civil affairs interpreter in Vietnam provided me with the basis for this novel, I am indebted to many online and print sources for additional information. Of particular help were *Cult, Culture, and Authority: Princess Lieu Hanh in Vietnamese History* (2007) by Olga Dror, and *Kill Anything That Moves: the Real American War in Vietnam* (2013) by Nick Turse.

I am also grateful to Megumi Kobayashi for patiently answering questions I posed about Japan, and to Jeff Hall, who read and commented on an early version of a chapter. I thank all the people who expressed interest in the book, thus keeping me on task.

Mike Shurgot read an almost entire draft of the novel and offered valuable suggestions for improvement, in addition to encouraging me along the way.

Dan Wallace, my principal editor and best friend, provided detailed comments and encouragement throughout every stage of the project, and then shepherded the book through production. I made great demands on his time and patience. Only he and I truly have any sense of what we owe each other, but we are not keeping score. At least, I'm not.

I thank Molly Wallace for the attractive cover design, and Ivey Wallace, her mother and Dan's wife, for her expert editorial advice.

Mary Wills, my beloved wife, so patient in regard to the time I put into this project, listened to my ideas and asked probing questions early on. She is, of course, my ideal reader in addition to making my life so much worth living.

As I wrote, I thought of many family members and friends, as well as former colleagues, some in America and some abroad, not all living. To fellow veterans and the people of Vietnam especially, I express my appreciation of the sacrifice you have made. We are so imperfect a species. I ask forgiveness for any offense my intensely personal perspective on the war may have caused.

About the Author

During ten months in 1969-70, Jim O'Donnell worked as an Army interpreter for Civil Affairs in Vietnam, after which he received a Bronze Star for Meritorious Service. A long-time college English instructor, he now enjoys retirement with his wife, Mary, in Portland, Oregon. *Maybe Tomorrow* is his first novel.

Jim O'Donnell and his friend Mr. Si in 1970

Made in the USA
Coppell, TX
25 November 2019

11867759R00162